BOOK ONE OF
THE ISLE OF STORMS

ANAHERA

VIANNE MAX

CRANTHORPE
—MILLNER—
P U B L I S H E R S

For my warrior-poet,

a virago who never gave up,

and loved the bees.

1. THRESHOLD

If Isabella had known she was going to be covered in a dying man's blood later that evening, she wouldn't have worn her favourite shirt.

Oblivious to the approaching carnage, she currently sits on the low stone wall in front of her cottage, sipping coffee and absently swinging her legs. The cottage is a recent acquisition, with whitewashed stone walls and a porch at the front.

Although it is approaching midnight, the pale blue sky still arches overhead in this far northern summer. Before her stretches the Sandsound voe, an inlet running from the sea between long fingers of low Shetland hills. The air is clear and fresh, the breeze lifting strands of her auburn hair and twisting them. Isabella takes in a breath then lets it out, revelling in the sense of freedom.

It was the right decision, coming here.

Her reverie is interrupted by her next-door neighbour, Mairi, grey hair ruffling in the breeze above clear blue eyes, which miss nothing.

"Evenin'!" Her face creases into a grin. "Is du comin' then?"

Isabella frowns. "Um, where?"

Mairi raises a large wicker picnic hamper and waggles it. "Calum's party. It's dee first Simmer Dim! Midsummer's Eve. Du has ta celebrate it." The crofter shakes her head in amusement. "Du's welcome to join us, *withoot* an invitation."

Isabella smiles, faintly embarrassed. How often in the months since her arrival on the island has she been gently scolded for loitering

1

on the doorstep, waiting to be invited in? The Shetlanders around her have been welcoming but Isabella is still a little shackled by an upbringing of cultural politeness.

They are interrupted by the thrum of a quad bike as Calum appears around the corner, slowing to a halt beside the two women. The fisherman taps a finger to his beanie in greeting and glances at the heavy picnic basket in Mairi's hands. He tips his head, indicating the back of the bike.

"Jump on, Ah'll take dee doon."

As the crofter wedges the basket into the metal frame attached to the back and climbs on behind him, Calum looks at Isabella again.

"Du's commin, isn du? Du canna sit aboot on dee own at Simmer Dim. It's da shortest night o da year, so du has ta celebrate!"

"Wi' whiskey." Mairi raises an eyebrow behind him.

He shrugs. "No better way, apart from da food, right?" He guns the bike for emphasis. "Wir aff!"

Mairi grips his fleece jacket tightly as they roar off along the road, giving Isabella a slightly desperate little wave.

Isabella pulls in a deep breath and makes her decision, swinging her legs back over the wall and striding up the path to the cottage. Once inside, she makes for the bedroom to riffle through the wardrobe for something to wear. It is a woefully small collection, illustrating how little she has needed over the last couple of years of travelling. She pulls out the two pieces she feels most comfortable in - a pair of loose black cargo pants and a white wrap shirt her friend Lianne had made for her as a leaving present.

Her dark, auburn hair tumbles down her back in a mad cascade of loose curls. She pulls it up into a high ponytail then into a thick bun behind her head, finally dropping it down again in defeat. Nothing seems quite right.

Her gaze catches on the display of photos to the right of the mirror, pinned around a map of Aotearoa, New Zealand, and she smiles.

Home.

It is covered with photos of family and friends, arms around one another, laughing or waving at the camera. Beside is a larger map of the world, dotted with coloured pins. A traveller at heart, her decision to rest a while in these northern islands still feels strange, but the allure of the Shetland archipelago is too powerful to resist.

She taps her phone and the display reminds her that sunset will fall just after one in the morning. Reaching up, she unhooks the greenstone pendant from the mirror, running her thumb over the twisting jade pikorua. Amidst the rush and tumble of her travels, it has remained the one constant connection with her home.

Bringing it to her lips, Isabella stills herself for a moment. It is a touchstone, a point to steady her and bring her luck and protection. She smiles and hooks it back over the edge of the mirror.

What need for protection could one have at a neighbourhood party on Midsummer's Eve?

From the road outside, she can hear a steady stream of laughter and conversation as members of the village trek their way around the hill and down to the secluded cove.

She picks up a small vial of perfume from the table and dabs it around her pulse points. The layered, woody scent of rose sandalwood rises up and invigorates her.

I can do this.

Despite all the travelling, she is still an introvert at heart, albeit one prone to bouts of sarcasm and a little light rebellion. She touches the pendant once more for luck then strides away, grabbing her fleece jacket and tying it around her waist as she goes.

She is just in time to join Calum's wife Joanna and their two small children as they stroll along the road. She takes one of the bags strung about the woman's shoulders and they fall to chatting as the children race ahead. Across the voe, the land dips and rises, and long shadows stretch across the golden landscape as the sun drops steadily towards the horizon.

3

Isabella hefts the bag, pausing for a moment to look down the hill towards the Sandsound Cove. A wide beach covered in polished stones curves away to the base of the steep hill, forming another long finger of land stretching into the sea. Nestled just above the tideline is the ruin of a two-story smokehouse, its solid stone walls once again protecting those within. Calum and his younger brother Magnus have already set up two barbecues and under Mairi's sharp-eyed direction, a series of trestle tables are now laden with salads, homemade bread, pies and bannocks.

Children race around the ruin, leaping over the churning stream running down from the heart of the narrow valley or crouching to make mini dolmens with the rocks on the shore. By the time Isabella and Joanna arrive, there are upwards of twenty people milling about, chatting and laughing. There are crofters, fishing folk, a collection of windsurfers staying in a holiday cottage, council workers and artists, and all the while the lilting Shetland dialect weaves in and out between them.

Mairi greets Isabella with a grin, hands her a crusty bannock roll filled with juicy roast lamb from her own croft, then shoos her out to sit on a rock on the far side of the ruin. Twilight is finally falling about them, as the shadows deepen in the valley and the tips of the hills glow in the last flare of light.

The young crofter, Magnus, drops down beside her, clutching a plate piled with sausages and a mound of potato salad. His broad face is ruddy from time on the windswept hills and his blue eyes regard her with amusement.

"Du's da new teacher at da school."

Isabella nods.

"Da one who slid doon da hill and…"

"Broke my leg? Yes." Isabella winces, the embarrassment still fresh after several months. "That would be me."

He shakes his head. "All dis way and du lets a bit o mud get to dee."

4

"What can I say," Isabella shrugs, "falling over is a talent." She decides to divert him away from her reputation for clumsiness. "Did you grow up here?"

Magnus finishes a mouthful of sausage before answering. "Vidlin originally, but ma uncle left me his croft."

She peers up at the hill behind him. "I imagine you know a bit about the history of the place."

"Aye. Why?"

"I counted twelve ruined croft houses on the hills around this valley. What happened to all the people?" She finishes the bannock and brushes her hands on her cargo pants.

He frowns. "No sure aboot dat. Better jobs in other places? Mebbe a fishin' boat went doon? Nearly all da young ones o da toonship woulda been on a boat in da old days and dat's a complete disaster for da place. Du could mebbe ask Mairi."

The woman in question appears beside Isabella and hands her a tumbler of whiskey from a tray. "I'm no sure aboot this valley, I would have'te check. One o da old folk said it's been empty for over a hundred year."

Magnus grins. "Well, du knows what dey say aboot Simmer Dim, it's da time when da barriers atween worlds are at dir weakest..."

"Och away with you!" Mairi laughs and swats playfully at the back of his head. She turns to Isabella. "Da sun sets, touches da horizon and then rises again. True, there's a strange feelin' in dat space atween da night and da dawn. Da very birds fall silent. But," she waves a finger, "dat's all there is to it."

She moves away, doling out whiskey to the adults and juice to the children. The twilight has deepened and beneath the chatter, the steady lap of waves on the shore adds a calming beat.

There comes a sudden whoosh and shriek of a firework, arcing through the air above and exploding into fragments of light. Isabella tips her head back and laughs, revelling in the scent of bonfire and barbecue, the warm burn of whiskey in her belly and the stars drifting

5

into the darkness above. The clear air of a Shetland evening is intoxicating and she takes a deep breath in as she gazes at the people around her, a mix of personalities and accents, each of whom has welcomed her in some way. It is as close to a feeling of a true soul-home as she could possibly get.

Magnus suddenly shifts in his seat. He frowns, staring intently up the valley.

"Yin's strange." The young crofter rises and points. "Look."

The deep blue of the Midsummer night sky is darkening further, as if the sun is continuing to set rather than touch the horizon and rise again as it should on the longest day of the year.

Isabella moves to join Magnus. Around them, others are rising too, confusion and concern shadowing each face. Over the steep hills that create the walls of the valley a thick fog falls, tumbling in silent, crashing waves. The leading tendrils are deep grey, questing over rocks and around the stone carcasses of ancient crofts. The hiss of the sea lapping the polished stones of the beach grows muffled as the fog boils swiftly towards them from all directions, including the sea.

"That's definitely strange," she murmurs, twisting her lips in disgust. The air tastes of hot tin.

The fog has reached them, wrapping around the old smokehouse ruins and dampening the bonfire to sullen embers. The laughter and gasps at the fireworks dilute, resolving themselves into shouts and screams. The fog deepens to a dark, stormcloud grey and tiny motes of glitter and ash shimmer through it, sticking to her exposed skin. Isabella raises her hand to examine it more closely when there is an abrupt jolt to the side, not just her body but the landscape as well, twisting violently around itself.

She staggers forward and falls to the ground, hands like claws clinging to the turf as everything tips and twists. All she can do is screw up her eyes and clench her teeth in agony. The land feels as if it is falling away either side of her and dropping into space, even though the turf still remains. Every cell in her body feels like it is

6

being twisted.

Panting desperately, Isabella manages to turn her head sideways, immensely dizzy and ill. She can see Magnus several meters away, curled into a ball with his head pressed against the earth as it warps and shivers.

Abruptly, everything is still.

Isabella pushes herself up on her hands and knees and her stomach contracts, forcing her to vomit onto the grass. Wiping her mouth with a shaky hand she crawls to the nearest lump of lichen-encrusted rock, clinging to it and pressing her hot cheek to its chill surface, trying to catch her breath.

Something fizzes and flares, spinning slowly past her head and Isabella looks up to see glowing orange embers drifting like tiny scraps of bright paper around her. Her nostrils sting with the reek of hot metal and smoke and her eyes water painfully. A terrible, crunching cold forms in her gut along with a sense of crashing grief and loss. She realizes with a pulse of shock that the Midsummer night has turned to day.

She turns her head to check if Magnus is okay, only to see the fog curling around him, obscuring his body until it is nothing but a dark mound. Another shape fades out of the ether, an enormous figure towering over him. It bends down and suddenly Magnus is shouting out in fear and pain. At the agony in his voice, something deeply primal grips Isabella and that fear propels her over the top of the rock, dropping onto the damp ground and rolling down the slope towards the stream.

The soft peaty ground cushions her body and she comes to a halt just before the water. For a moment she lies there, breathing hard from exertion and terror until she hears the bark of rough voices downstream. Hauling herself to her feet, she trips across the shallow stream, sliding over brown-slimed rocks and soaking her shoes, but the creek is far wider than she remembers and she slips and staggers for some time, disorientated by the change. With a gasp of relief, she

7

spots the far bank and clambers up the other side, grabbing handfuls of tussock grass to pull herself forwards.

Isabella can see little through the murk but remembers that there is a farm track up the slope from the stream. She moves forward, trying to distance herself from the shouts and hoots behind. Another vicious cramp twists in her abdomen and she pauses, hunching with her hands on her knees, riding the pain. As it subsides she looks up, finding herself face to face with a man.

He is clothed in dirty brown leather and a skullcap is jammed tightly over grubby blond hair. His narrow face is marred by scars but it is his eyes that send a wave of panic through Isabella; vicious amusement mixed with the promise of violence. For the first time in her life, she realizes that she is prey.

She tenses, ready to run, but from behind her rolls the stench of another unwashed male and the sound of a low chuckle which drives right to the primal pit of any woman, bringing with it the certainty of violation.

Shifting one foot and turning slightly, she keeps the first man in her sights but glances towards the second. He looms over her, his forehead creased with an enormous scar which slices down over an unseeing eye to end just above his fleshy lips. He wears a pock-marked breastplate over a grubby tunic, a spatter of fresh blood coating his right arm and sleeve.

How is this possible?

Isabella gulps down bitter terror but it quickly resolves itself into anger. She took basic self-defence training in high school but she has not used it since. Clearly, that was a mistake, but despite her terror, she refuses to let them have her without a fight and so steps back, hands curling lightly, trying to balance in preparation for the attack.

Skullcap dances forward, waggling his head and crowing at her. He reaches out, grabbing her by the shoulders. As he does so, she shoves her hands hard against his chest, arms straight, kicking out and connecting with his knee. He grunts and pitches sideways as she

8

wrenches away from him, but the big man is already upon her, punching her to the ground.

The blow is fierce and she lies there, stunned. Yet she has enough bloody-minded drive to push herself to her hands and knees and try to crawl away. The two men watch her with amusement, Skullcap rubbing his knee and muttering. Just as she is about to haul herself to her feet, they stroll forward and the big man places his muddy boot on her back and pushes her to the ground, laughing. Skullcap crows with delight.

With practiced ease they flip her over and secure her, nausea and exhaustion making her struggles pathetic. Skullcap drops behind her, his knees either side of her head, clamping it in place as his hands pin her arms roughly to the ground. The big man kneels between her legs and begins to unbutton his trews, an unholy stench rolling off him. All Isabella can manage is a choked snarl.

The fog swirls behind the beast in front of her and a shadow emerges. A rough gloved hand grabs the marauder's rank hair and yanks his head roughly backwards. In one swift movement, a blade flashes out and slices across the man's throat, a spray of bright blood flying from the gaping wound and across Isabella. The figure flips the dagger, catching it by the blade then flicking it through the air to embed itself deeply in the left eye of Skullcap behind her. Hot blood splatters over her hair, face and formerly white shirt.

The figure shoves the body of the first marauder aside and retrieves the dagger from the man crumpled behind Isabella as she struggles to sit up. He stands beside her and offers a hand. She glares up at the shadowed face under the hood and ignores his hand, pulling herself unsteadily to her feet. Her head spins as she almost falls again but he catches her, his fingers biting into the soft flesh of her arms. He is a head taller than her, his powerful upper body encased in tight, matte-grey armour.

He stands silently, head cocked, listening for the sounds of movement in the swirling fog. Shouts erupt to the left, coming closer.

9

He glares at Isabella, who is barely holding herself upright, points the blade at her and barks an order. Like the marauders before him, the sounds coming out of his mouth make no sense. He rolls his eyes and snarls, grabbing her upper arm, dragging her around and shoving her forward up the hill.

"Let go of me, you bastard!" She struggles but his grip is iron and he ignores her efforts, pushing her ahead of him. Out of the fog and smoke looms a copse of low scraggly trees, their branches curved protectively to the side by years of fierce winds, making an effective barrier. He shoves her between the branches and into the centre, the sharp twigs tearing at her skin and hair.

She rallies enough to turn and try to claw at him, fear once again rising through her chest, but he catches her wrist and spins behind her, twisting her arm up her back in a fresh explosion of agony. At the same time, he clamps a broad hand across her mouth to stop her from screaming. He pushes Isabella to her knees and crouches behind her, hissing a command. One finger of the hand across her mouth extends urgently to point out of the copse. She freezes. She too, can see the large group of marauders approaching and their stench reaches her just as their guttural words rip through the air.

They move closer and, peering through the branches, she can see several familiar faces from her village with them, including Magnus. His face is battered and bleeding and he stumbles along in a daze, his wrists roughly bound, the rope leading to the fist of a large, female marauder. They are clearly collecting stragglers.

Behind her, the warrior's grip tightens and his breathing slows. Isabella tries to slow her breath to match his. His body, pressed close to her back, is warm and solidly muscled and he smells of leather, fresh metallic sweat and the unexpectedly warm, spicy scent of cardamom.

As he feels her breath slow and her attempts to struggle free cease, he gradually releases her arm but does not entirely let go. He slides his hand from her mouth and as she twists to glare at him, he raises a

10

finger close to her face then presses it against his lips. The warrior's grey eyes are intense in their insistence, and in their warning.

They both freeze, staring at one another as a sword swipes the thick outer branches of the copse. Feeling her shaking as her muscles clench and cramp with exhaustion and her eyes widen, he gives a barely perceptible shake of his head.

Screams shiver out of the fog from nearby and the marauders move off quickly, hooting with delight. Magnus is swallowed up by the crowd and the curling fog.

When he is sure they have moved far enough away, the warrior motions for her to change position and sit back. She does so cautiously but flinches when he reaches out towards her legs. He pauses and holds up his hands, to reassure her that he means no harm. She eyes him suspiciously. The cramp growing in her legs forces her to bite her lip and the strange, cold nausea rises.

He places his hands either side of her left calf and begins to rub it, forcing the circulation back in and releasing the clenched muscles. Isabella clutches the rough undergrowth in pain, trying not to cry out. His hands are wide and strong and as the cramping begins to reduce, he moves to her right calf.

For a moment, she has a chance to look at him properly. The top section of his long, brown hair, slick with sweat and marauder blood, is tied in tight narrow braids from his temples. He has high cheekbones and a jawline covered in stubble. His sharply handsome features are marred by two vicious scars running parallel from his hairline, down over his eyebrow and cheek, biting into his throat and finally ending at his collarbone.

He finishes his ministrations, turns to peer out through the branches then crawls to the back of the copse, searching through the fog as it begins to dissipate in the developing breeze. The land behind rises in a low foothill, topped by a jumble of black and white rocks.

Turning, he motions to Isabella, speaking in low tones. His voice is deep and gravelly and she still has no idea what he is saying. He

11

pauses, glares at her in frustration, first pointing to her, then to himself, and finally up the hill. She shakes her head.

I'm not going anywhere with you, matey.

Shooting forward, he grabs her wrist and points his index finger sharply at her and back at himself. He snarls quietly, his finger making a circling motion around them.

We are surrounded.

He points at her again, makes a slicing motion across his own throat then flips his hand out, palm up, shrugging.

Do you want to die here?

Her eyes narrow and her shoulders slump.

I get it now, I give in.

She glares balefully at him but nods.

He helps her rise stiffly to her feet and they move to the back of the copse, the warrior listening carefully before leading her out onto the grassy hillside. Her ankles are white hot with pain and she can only hobble, so he is forced to pull her up behind him. Together they scramble up the steep slope, finally taking refuge amongst the pile of boulders at the top of the hill. Isabella slides down the back of the biggest one, breathing roughly whilst he crouches next to her, staring down through the gap.

He reaches behind to his belt and unhooks a device like a short, squat telescope wrapped in brown leather. He holds it up to his eyes and concentrates, scanning the valley below.

Once she has regained some semblance of free breath, he taps her sharply on the shoulder and holds out the device. She turns stiffly to lean towards the gap and holds it up to her eyes. Tiny red symbols glow at the edges of the screen but her attention is drawn to the view.

Small groups tussle on ground turned to mud and bodies lie scattered across the plain.

A plain?

Isabella's eyes widen. No longer does she see Sandsound Cove and its protective narrow valley, with the ruined crofts dotting the

12

hills, the little stream burling down the hill and the smokehouse by the shore. Instead, it is as if the Shetland landscape has been wildly stretched. The stream has become a wide, shallow river and the valley floor an alluvial plain, spreading towards far mountains. To the left, a road curves away towards the distant foothills. Several large wagons are drawn up in two ranks and she watches marauders haul their captives up into them, shackling each to bars inside. There appear to be far more captives than the number attending Calum's party at the smokehouse and Isabella wonders where they all came from.

She scans to the right, stopping as movement catches her eye – another skirmish, this time between marauders and a small group of soldiers in uniform. They wear grey cloaks and tight armour, the left shoulder piece of each stamped with a vivid red sigil. She glances at the man next to her, her gaze falling on the red sigil on the armoured plate covering his upper arm. The same uniform.

"You're with them?" She points to him and then to the skirmish.

He cranes his neck to see, then sits back, glaring at her and nodding.

"But you're not helping them?"

Despite the lack of common language, he understands her intent and anger flares in his eyes. He snarls at her, his voice deep and rough, then turns to stare down at the skirmish, his face falling into a strained expression of concern. Isabella feels her stomach drop when she realises what he means: he can't help them because of her.

She lifts the eyeglass again and scans the landscape until she sees two enormous, rough pillars rising near the shore where the smokehouse once stood. The sea behind is a dark green, with white caps over rough waves highlighting the fact that the pillars are still glowing.

"Is that where I came in?" She murmurs.

He glances in the direction she is looking, frowns, and scouts the ground around him, picking up a sharp rock and scratching two lines into the lichen-covered boulder. As he speaks, he points to her, then

13

between the two lines and opens and closes his palms.

"It's like a gate?" Isabella feels the pit of fear in her belly open wider as she points to the opening. "Can I get back through it?"

He stares at her then scratches the rock roughly across the lines. *No.*

He hauls her to her feet and pushes her uphill. It becomes apparent that this is merely a small foothill – behind is the tail end of a mountain range. He shoves her onwards and, breathing heavily and muttering to herself, she reluctantly complies. They continue to climb as night falls.

The temperature drops steadily and Isabella curses her choice of clothing. Her fleece was lost soon after she was pulled through the Gate and, although her clothes were fine for the Midsummer's evening, they are certainly not for this cold, windy night on a mountainside. Her black suede ballet pumps certainly aren't conducive to mountain hikes either. The increasingly icy wind tears at her, forcing her muscles to clamp into deep shivers.

Finally, as night falls the warrior sits Isabella down behind a clump of rocks and pulls off his grey cloak, wrapping it around her. It is surprisingly warm and smells faintly of nutmeg. Disappearing for a moment, he scales the dark hillside around the site, checking that a fire will not be seen. He returns, taking four smooth, bright red sticks from the slim bag attached to his back and placing them in a square, two underneath, two across the top. He rubs his palms together quickly and to her astonishment, sparks fall from the gap between his hands, drifting down onto the sticks which glow and then flare into flames.

He glances up to see her staring at him, her mouth slightly ajar. He frowns. Isabella leans forward, holding her freezing hands out over the glow, surprised at how far from the odd red sticks the heat emanates.

From his pack the man pulls a small, shallow pan and places it over the fire. He adds water from a canteen and a scattering of what

14

looks like purple oats. He stirs the mixture until it bubbles, hands her the spoon and she takes it, cautiously. Her reticence clearly irritates him as he flicks his hands, indicating that she should eat, so Isabella scoops a small mound of purple mush up and gingerly samples it. To her surprise, it tastes a little like rice seasoned with wild garlic. Her stomach muscles still ache from the cramping but the flavour spurs her on to take several more spoonfuls, the mush generating a welcome warmth inside her.

The man watches her then takes the proffered spoon and finishes the mix. He swirls a little water around the pan and dries it on the edge of the cloak, before sliding it back into his pack.

A wild cry floats up from the hillside below and he is instantly on guard, spinning in his crouch and peering around the boulder. Far below them, a string of torches flicker in the darkness. The warrior holds up a firm hand as Isabella moves to look. After several minutes he relaxes a little, as the search party curves away.

He pivots and motions for her to sit back. She is shivering again, even under the protection of the cloak and she curls against the rock, clinging to its semblance of protection. The man readies himself to sit sentry, and although that constant, nagging fear has solidified in her belly, as the night deepens, she drifts off into fitful sleep.

2. FREEDOM

[1]In the first cold, grey light of dawn, Isabella wakes. Every muscle aches with cold fire. She rubs her eyes and looks over at the grey-garbed warrior. He is asleep, breathing softly, his head bowed, chin resting heavily on his chest.

As silently as she can, she braces against the rock behind, using it to push herself upright. The cloak slips to the ground and she steps over it, wobbling slightly. The man behind snorts in his sleep and she freezes. Pressing her lips together, Isabella slides around the edge of the boulder, the grass muffling the sounds of her movement. Glancing up the slope and then down, she shrugs. One direction is much the same as the other, so she chooses down, moving off at a steady hobble and desperately suppressing the swirling nausea.

High on his perch, the warrior snorts again in his sleep, a familiar nightmare biting at him. This time, it is enough to tip him into consciousness and he opens his eyes, ready to chivvy the woman into moving on. He sits up abruptly when he sees nothing but the ashes of the fire and his fallen cloak in the hollow between the boulders. A snarl escapes his lips and he scrambles to his feet, glaring down the slope.

She is not difficult to spot, her clothes stark against the pale gold of the grasses as she slides and hops down the slope. He surges down the hillside and it is mere moments before he reaches her.

---

[1] Playlist: Anilah feat. Einar Selvik – *Warrior*.

Isabella hears him just before his rough fingers dig into her arm and spin her towards him. Immense rage punches up through her, fuelled by exhaustion, loss, fear and a burning desire not to have yet another man grappling her. It explodes out of her in a feral roar and her free hand grabs his shoulder, pulling him close as her knee comes up in a powerful jolt, right into his balls.

She shoves him sideways as he crumples to his knees and she turns to run, but she reckons without his own savage strength of character and even as he coughs and snarls into the dirt, his hand shoots out and grabs her ankle. She pitches forward and crashes to the ground, her ribs hammering into a rock sticking out of the turf, winding her.

The warrior pushes himself up onto his hands and knees, but this is as far as he can manage. The bitch certainly has an accurate knee and the pain is like a whirlpool, radiating out and pulling him back in. He spits his nausea into the grass bobbing in front of him and snarls out a series of curses. Strangely, this seems to help and he has enough strength to look up. The woman lies crumpled nearby, gasping and clutching her ribs, eyes locked on him.

With a supreme effort he crawls forward and before she can react he is upon her, shoving her back into the grass and shouting at her. He grabs her wrists and they grapple, but she can't push him off and with astonishing speed he binds her wrists with a black rope he pulls from his belt. One broad hand pushes her bound hands into her chest, while the other gesticulates as he barks at her, pointing back down the mountainside.

Isabella can't understand what he is saying – his language is harsh and guttural. In turn, hers sounds like a mad lilting song to him, although she is clearly swearing, judging by her snarling facial expressions.

In frustration, he reaches across to his belt, pulls a tiny vial of blue liquid from a pocket, clicks it into a small metal tube and jams it against her upper arm. She feels the scratch of a needle piercing her

17

flesh and a painful cold rushes through her veins. Isabella gasps as it spreads rapidly through her body and up into her brain, scattering like tiny pinpricks of unbearably cold light. Everything seems to stop for a moment, as her head tips back and her eyes close on the most astonishing fireworks light show behind the lids.

She screams, bucks and twists, caught in a dizzying sensation which feels as if she is falling through galaxies of tiny stars. Eventually, as the lightning sensations ease, she collapses.

There is just enough left in her to rasp up at him.

"Get *off* me, you arsehole."

He shoves her roughly once more but then lets go and rolls off her.

"Nice."

She freezes, stunned. "What?"

It is a blunt and idiotic response but it is all she can manage. She sits up, staring at him. He runs both hands over his braids, smoothing them down after the struggle.

"Your first proper words and you're already swearing. You'll make someone a bloody lovely wife." His voice is deep and coarse, layers usually developed through years of determined smoking.

This is too much for her to take in, so instead, she begins with something more simple.

"What the fuck did you just inject me with?" She goes to rub her aching arm but realises she is still shackled.

He shrugs. "*Nantines*. Tiny little buggers that'll swim through your veins and hang out in your head." With some amusement, he watches her eyes widen in horror. "Don't worry, they're harmless. They're translation bugs. I speak, you hear your own language and," he motions between them, "vice versa."

She raises her bound hands and tries to pat her own head.

"Yeah, that'll help." His sardonic tone causes her to stop and glare at him. Crouched, he is balanced easily on the balls of his feet, with his solidly muscled arms resting on his knees, the tanned skin marred

18

by old scars, scratches and nicks. He is clearly a man used to a fight.

On the back of each hand she notices a circular scar like a stamp, about the size of a twenty pence piece. He sees her gaze resting at that point, so he rubs one hand over the other in an old reflex.

"And there's no use fighting them – they'll self-replicate until you die." He smirks, then slaps his knees. "Come on, we're not safe here."

He rises to his feet, with less ease than normal, thanks to the deep ache in his groin from her well-aimed knee. He looks down at the culprit, only to see her tearing at the bindings on her wrists with her teeth.

Fuck's sake, she's unrelenting.

He leans over and slaps her hands down.

"Stop that." He glares at her. "You know you were running back towards the slave traders, right?" He feels a little dry satisfaction when her eyes widen at this. "You're a bloody danger to yourself and I'm not taking that off until I can trust you not to get yourself killed."

He offers his hand to help her up but she ignores it and struggles to her feet. The warrior shrugs and places his hands on his hips, looking her up and down. Her hair is dishevelled and dotted with bits of grass and mud from the tussle and her face is marred by splatters of dried marauder blood. She is not unpleasant to look at – passable breasts and an agreeably fertile curve to her hips, although her attitude is decidedly feral. Her shirt is smeared with dried blood and dirt and when he spots her feet, he frowns. Ridiculously delicate, black slippers, already torn and soaking after their climb up the peat-covered foothills.

What was she thinking, travelling through the Gate in such flimsy gear?

"Have you quite finished?" Isabella snaps, one scornful eyebrow arched. His gaze flicks back up to her face and he adjusts his stance slightly.

"Look, we've a long way to travel and this isn't getting us

19

anywhere. What's your name?" His voice drops to a soft growl.

She considers lying but then, what difference would that make in this mad place?

"Isabella." Her eyebrow resumes its normal place and her expression is more cautious. "Isabella Mackay, and you are?"

"Captain Eric Bannerman, King's Own Uhlan." He inclines his head in a semblance of a bow.

The eyebrow jerks skywards again. "You're a Captain?"

His expression resolves into a glare and suddenly, he is so close she can feel the heat radiating from his body. His hands slide around her wrists and she flinches but, in an instant, he has stepped away again and she realises that he is now holding a length of rope which is tethered to her bonds, and a triumphant smirk twists his lips.

"Oh, come on," she moans, her shoulders slumping.

The Captain shakes his head. "I'm not letting you off the leash until you can prove you can be trusted." He tugs at the rope. "Off we go."

She stumbles as she is yanked forwards. As they move off up the mountainside, the sound of her complaining soon reduces to ragged puffing as the incline increases.

They hike for several hours, although it begins to feel like an eternity to Isabella. At first she focuses on the view, which is astonishing. The folds of the hills wax green and gold as the light moves across the landscape. Elaborate bastions of clouds curl above them, pearlescent in the afternoon light. Up on the mountainside, the air is painfully fresh and the breeze causes the golden strands of grass to shiver and bounce, flowing around the humps of black rocks.

As the afternoon shifts towards evening, the wind begins to pick up and it holds a chill which promises a storm. The clouds smear across the sky and take on a distinctly vicious grey. Torn blisters gnaw at Isabella's feet, the grinding pain of each step competing for attention with the growing agony of the bindings chaffing around her wrists. Her muscles cramp and the pit of loss and fear sloshing within threatens to overwhelm her.

She focuses on the broad, grey cloaked back of the man in front of her. He is immersed in his thoughts, frowning to himself. The hike seems to be barely taxing him and he scarcely looks back until she stumbles, yet again. This time her foot catches the edge of a sharp rock and she falls, tumbling to the rough ground, the leash yanking Bannerman's arm downwards.

He turns to snap at her but then stops himself, for she kneels in a crumpled heap, her hair cascading across her back and down over her face, obscuring her expression.

Isabella's bound hands are raised above her, but her head sinks towards the earth and despite herself, she lets out an exhausted sob.

He curses and is instantly crouched beside her, dropping the rope. The Captain's bulk shields her a little from the biting wind, allowing the warm smell of cardamom and cigars to envelop her. He pushes back her hair to reveal her face, now pale with exhaustion, the dried blood streaked with tears.

"Damn." He mutters, lifting her hands, unwinding the bonds as gently as he can. The skin of each wrist is raw and torn and her hands are icy cold.

She looks up at him, her eyes dark with pain.

"I'm trying," she croaks, "but…"

Bannerman feels an unfamiliar twinge of guilt nip at him as he pulls his cloak from his shoulders and wraps it around her. He glances down at her feet and swears softly. Smears of fresh blood peep above the soaking black shoes. He swivels on his haunches to scan the mountainside. Not far away are two large boulders jammed beside one another and beneath is a flat rock, the right height for a seat.

"Let's move. We need to get out of this wind." He slides his arms underneath hers and lifts her upwards. Isabella bites her bottom lip, trying to suppress her cry of pain. She sags against him but he takes her weight.

21

"A few steps and we're there." He assures her.

They make their way slowly, crabwise, down the slope, reaching the lea of the boulders which are big enough to block out some of the increasingly vicious wind. He lowers her onto the flat rock and crouches in front of her. Every muscle in Isabella's body is fired with pain and exhaustion and the barren cold of the Gate shift anchoring itself deep within her, makes her constantly nauseous. She smells atrocious, too.

The Captain curls one hand around the back of her right foot, ready to lift it, but Isabella sits bolt upright and gasps.

"Whoah, whoah!"

He pauses and looks up at her. "I need to check." His expression softens a little. "Please."

Isabella grits her teeth and nods. He supports her foot with one hand and gently pulls the slipper off with the other.

She hisses as the pain bites. A muscle flexes in the Captain's cheek. The flesh of her foot is torn and bleeding.

"Why didn't you tell me sooner?" He growls, opening his pack and pulling out several items. He hands her a squat metal flask. "Drink."

Isabella unscrews the lid and sniffs it cautiously.

"It's water, woman. Just drink it." The Captain does not look up from his task as he mixes a tiny pouch of green powder into a pot of salve. She takes a small sip and then a deeper swig. The water is delicious, with a bright hint of lemon balm and it takes away a tiny edge of her exhaustion.

The Captain holds up two fingers, now covered in the salve. It is an odd pea-green colour and smells of early mornings, fresh and dewy. Isabella clutches the rough edge of the rock beneath her in readiness but when he smooths the salve onto the side of her foot, all she feels is cool relief. Her skin tingles slightly and she realises the salve has a pain killing effect. He works quickly, covering the ravaged flesh, pulls out a thin bandage and proceeds to wrap each foot carefully. Isabella watches him closely. His body is powerful and his movements deft. The twin scars running the length of his face lend him a vicious look, but he is being remarkably gentle with her.

He glances up briefly and she is surprised to see his flinty gaze soften for a moment, before he sits back, delves into his pack and hands her a small bar made from seeds and honey, unwrapping one for himself. They eat in silence and when she has finished, Isabella leans back against the rock and finally plucks up the courage to ask.

"Captain Bannerman."

He glances at her, his eyes narrowing.

"Why am I here? I mean," she continues in a rush, needing to get the words out, "one minute I'm at a party on a beach, the next I'm stumbling around and being dragged through some 'Gate'."

He watches her, his eyes now cautious.

"Then these mad bastards grab me and you appear and kill them, then you drag me up here." She flips a hand skyward. "And I don't even know where here is!"

He continues to regard her steadily but she appears to have run out of breath.

"Okay." His gravel voice is oddly reluctant. "A gate between worlds was opened. The last time it happened was over a hundred turns ago. We don't know how or who by, but people like you get pulled through." He begins to fit items back into his pack as he speaks. "Because you're so rare, you're considered very valuable. Everyone wants a piece, hence the slavers who were lying in wait."

His expression darkens. "We didn't expect them. How the hell did they know?" He murmurs this last thought to himself.

Isabella stares at him, the aching cold of the Gate shift widening as her understanding does. "If it's a surprise, how did you know the Gate would open?"

The Captain scowls. "One of the King's advisors tipped him off." He turns his head away from her and spits, contempt leaching into his voice. "Though how that white bastard knew it was going to open, I don't know. The Citadel's 7th Uhlan were tasked with collecting as many of you as possible."

"Why?"

He does not look at her, but zips the pack closed. "As I said, you people have value."

She thinks for a moment, the pit of understanding growing. "So, I'm valuable to the slave traders and to this…Citadel." He nods. "So, what makes you any different from them?" She stares at him, waiting for a reply but he does not look up, instead rising to his feet and shouldering the pack.

"We've a long way to go and night is falling. Let's get you up."

She clenches her fists as fear grips her again. "Why should I trust you?"

Bannerman stares at her for a moment. "Because without me, you're going to die on this mountain."

He holds out both hands and, after a moment of struggling with her fear, she gives in and grabs them, allowing him to help her. The Captain supports her for several steps until she finds she can walk without the biting agony, then they set off along the ridge.

The stunning view disappears as the clouds roll in and the light rapidly fades. Soon it begins to rain, the wind driving it in heavy sheets across the landscape. Bannerman slows down, his cloak draped around the plodding woman, his arm steadying her against the wind, but they cannot keep this up for long and as night falls heavily upon them, the howling wind competes with other wild cries in the distance.

Isabella merely stumbles on, her feet numb with cold, shoulders set against the vicious, tumbling squall. For her, the world has distilled down to one foot in front of the other, in a body heavy with pain. The Captain's words curl round and round in her head.

"You've got to keep going. If you stop, you die."

High on the exposed hillside, Bannerman spots a low shepherd's hut in the distance and ushers her towards it. They duck in through the opening and Isabella slides gratefully down into a corner. The floor is covered in old straw and sheep droppings, with several slates missing from the roof, allowing the rain to pour in.

Bannerman realises that, with the storm unabating, they aren't going to get very far and that Isabella's physical state is clearly deteriorating. Cursing himself for accepting this commission in the first place, he crouches near her and pulls out a brown leather pouch.

He flips the top open and peers down at the object protected inside. It resembles a large brass compass with a curved glass screen. He leans further over so that his hood will protect it from the scatterings of rain falling through the ragged holes in the roof and wipes his hands under his cloak to dry them. As he begins to tap on the screen, tiny red topographical lines stretch across the glass. The warrior grunts and taps a tiny blue dot near the top of the map. It expands to fill the screen, complete with a list of symbols embedded in the centre.

"Good, there's one nearby." Bannerman looks up and catches her staring at him. He sighs. "Look, we can't go much further with you like…this," waving a hand up and down, "and the rain is pissing me off so, we're going to have to catch a lift."

He taps a series of commands onto the screen and then closes the lid of the pouch with a snap. "I'm glad I'm not paying for this malarkey. Pyre flights don't come cheap."

She shakes her head. "What?"

Bannerman leans towards her and smiles, wickedly. "Don't worry, I think you might enjoy this." He tilts his head. "Hear that?" A speculative look crosses his face.

Isabella strains to separate the sounds of the storm and then frowns. From further up the slope comes the unmistakable sound of a sheep being loudly strangled. She stares at him, confused as to why he is grinning in a faintly piratical fashion, as he pats her knee.

"Don't move." He rises and ducks through the door, out into the burling night.

25

Several minutes later, a large bulk looms out of the sleet and halts near the doorway, the sound of strangled sheep echoing more loudly this time. Isabella stares at it in shock. The creature has a wide shaggy body, a pony's face, thick black horns curling backwards, and two thick legs ending in giant, black, clawed crow's feet. The Captain has fashioned a rope halter and is leading it. He leans down into the doorway, a triumphant grin slapped across his face.

"I've found a yarg. Time to stand up, girlie."

With the last of her strength, Isabella pushes herself up from the sodden floor and shuffles out of the hut, instantly buffeted by the squalling wind. Bannerman moves behind her, lifting the exhausted woman and shoving her up the side of the beast so she can pull herself over the top. It is like sinking into a large, shaggy carpet covering a sofa and she is suddenly wrapped in the rampant smell of wet wool and nutmeg. Bannerman makes sure that she is clinging on and then he leads them down the slope, his feet finding a specially carved track which snakes through the tussock.

As the clouds above curl and boil, gaps let through the stark moonlight, briefly illuminating the raw landscape. Exhausted and desperate for the tiniest shred of hope, Isabella raises her head and peers past the yargs' horns, catching a glimpse of an ornate platform jutting from a rocky outcrop. Bannerman trudges towards it, leading the soaking woman and steaming beast.

As they approach the platform, the yarg's feet click over a path made of large, flat paving stones. At the end, a bright green light attached to a pole flickers into life, growing stronger as they approach. Isabella clings to the beast's coat, her hands burning with the cold.

Bannerman shelters against the yarg's bulk as he listens, straining to hear the tell-tale hum. Eventually, he catches it and straightens, stepping forward to peer into the swirling clouds.

The hum grows, throbbing through the churning air. It even rouses Isabella, who lifts her head, heavy with exhaustion and the creeping threads of hypothermia. She pushes back the wet hair whipping against her face and squints into the clouds. One spot begins to roil, the clouds peeling back and curling away as the sharp prow of a ship slices through them. She screws up her eyes, rubs them with one freezing hand and opens them again. The ship is real.

Its sharp, rain-slicked hull is made from a deep, copper-coloured wood and it slices gracefully through the shuddering air. It has no masts, rather it reminds her of the sleek Vietnamese freighters from the Mekong Delta but with intricate carvings along its sides. She gapes as it begins to turn and come about, sliding smoothly alongside the platform despite the force of the squall. Isabella peers upwards and can just make out the name, painted in looping writing along the prow; the 'Selkie's Song'.

Docking clamps slide out and grip the metal bollards dotted alongside. A wide gangplank extends and as soon as it touches the slick wooden deck, Bannerman leads the yarg on to it, its clawed feet dealing with the slippery surface with far more ease than his boots.

As the yarg scrambles inside the hull, the gangplank closes silently behind them and the docking clamps release, sliding back into the ship.

Still clinging desperately to the beast's hide, Isabella feels large, warm hands take hold of her. A deep, masculine voice beside her head rumbles to reassure her.

"You can let go now."

As she unclenches her aching fingers, she feels the hands gently easing her down and into strong waiting arms. She is cradled against the huge chest of a man, his linen shirt smelling comfortingly of soft camphor. A woman's voice, quiet yet commanding, rises through the roar of the storm.

"The Camellia Room please, Kahu. That's the warmest."

The man holding Isabella nods and moves off, the gentle motion of his powerful body almost lulling her to sleep. They move down a corridor, wood-panelled walls glowing softly in the lamplight. Layers of sensation drift over her; the scent of lemon polish, the vague impression of being washed and plied with soup, warm clothes, blankets, the smell of cardamom and cigar smoke, before sleep finally claims her.

3. Clouds and Connections

When next she wakes, it is day and panels of light drift across the carved ceiling above her. She is covered in soft blankets and the bed beneath her is wonderfully comfortable.

Maybe the dash across a mountainside was just a mad, whiskey-laced dream?

Tilting her head sideways, her gaze falls upon a small child perched on the top of a high-backed wooden chair. The girl is staring at her intently, winding a pale brown lock of hair around a tanned finger. Isabella blinks at her.

"You smell funny." The little girl frowns.

Clearly not a whiskey dream.

"Thanks. You look funny." Isabella waggles her eyebrows and the little girl cackles in response.

"Do you want to hold my saur? His name's Belcher." She holds out a tiny wooden toy dragon, its wings creaking with the motion of her hand. Isabella smiles. She has always wanted a dragon.

She pushes herself up and takes the proffered toy.

"I've got new mittens," the little girl says thoughtfully, and Isabella is reminded that the attention span of a small child is approximately four seconds. "They're itchy."

"Islaria, stop bothering the Anahera. She's supposed to be sleeping." Another child stands in the doorway with a tray balanced carefully in her hands. Her long chestnut hair is braided at the top, the rest tumbling down her back. She is swathed in a knee-length calico

29

dress and black leggings, her feet in sturdy boots. She must be all of twelve years old, pretty, deeply tanned and apple-cheeked but currently frowning at her sister.

"Wasn't bothering her, Aroha," Islaria pouts. "Belcher wanted to meet her."

Her older sister rolls her eyes and moves forward, carefully placing the tray onto Isabella's lap – a poached egg on toast with a mug of strong tea.

"Mum says I'm not to leave until you've eaten it." She sits down in the chair, her small sister balanced above her. "She made it herself and she hates cooking. She'll be upset if you don't finish it."

Isabella has never required much encouragement to eat, so dives in. The orange yolk pops beneath her fork, the toast crunching underneath. It is delicious and the forkfuls disappear quickly. When finished, she lifts the steaming mug and leans back against the pillows.

"I don't think your mother has much to worry about – that is probably the best breakfast I've had in years."

Both girls grin.

"I have a question though. What was that word you called me? Ana…"

"Anahera. Well, Te Anahera is the proper term for a person who comes through the Gate." Aroha shrugs. "I've never met one before. You don't look much different from us." Her tone suggests considerable disappointment.

Te Anahera? That's a familiar term.

Isabella is sure it is a Maori phrase, from far back in her childhood. The word 'anahera' means angel, although she certainly does not feel in the least bit angelic after the last couple of days. Her feet have lost the bitter sting of agony but even lying down, the dull pain still nags at her.

Aroha pulls a leather-bound book from a large pocket, the cover etched with a silvery moon and two leaping hares.

30

"May I sketch you? I want to add you to my collection." She opens the book and flicks through the pages, finally halting at a blank one. Each page contains sketches and numerous notes. "I'm recording all the different sorts of passengers who travel on our waka." She looks up expectantly, her stylus poised.

Isabella has never had her portrait sketched and the girl clearly has talent. She takes a sip of tea, revelling in the added sweetness of honey swirling within.

"Of course, go ahead."

Aroha sketches quickly. When she finishes, she holds it out for Isabella to inspect. It is a fair likeness, down to the messy tumble of curls and the slightly battered expression.

"When you write your notes, can you please make it clear that the subject had just been dragged over a mountain and nearly died in a storm?" She asks wryly. Aroha grins in response.

Islaria's patience has reached its limit and she slides from her perch onto her sister's shoulders.

"Can we *go* now? Mummy's waiting!"

Isabella shifts her tray to the side. "Just tell me where the bathroom is and I'll be right with you." She has a pressing need to pee.

Aroha points to the end of the bunk where a door fits snugly into the cabin wall. "Mum left some clothes in there for you." She pats her sister's leg, the child gripping her like a spider monkey. "Islaria, you're pulling my hair."

Isabella eases herself up from the bed and places her bandaged feet on the ground, hissing at the sudden bite of pain. She hobbles to the door, slipping through and into a surprisingly spacious bathroom. It is panelled with pale wood and contains a shower stall, a toilet and a copper wash basin.

When she has finished her ablutions, Isabella turns to the dress hanging from a peg. It is cream in colour and made of soft wool. Once it is on, she smooths the material down over her hips and turns to the

31

full-length mirror. Reaching to the floor, the dress hugs her figure, the bodice pulled tight with lacings. The fabric is warm, the sleeves tapering to a lace band at each elbow then flaring outwards. There is even a hood which she tucks underneath her hair for the time being. Taking a deep breath, she opens the door and steps out.

Aroha is waiting by the doorway of the cabin, her sister still clinging to her back.

"You pee loudly." The little girl informs her solemnly.

"Islaria!" Her sister admonishes her. She points to the bed where a pair of extravagantly fluffy pink slippers now sit. "Mum sent those down for you."

It is not the slippers which hold Isabella's attention, rather it is the creature perched on the bed next to them, eyeing her expectantly. Its puffball fur is a brilliant white, contrasting with a black nose and hazel eyes. Neat fuzzy ears flick up expectantly. An arctic fox.

"Arsu brought them down. You might want to thank him or he gets a little huffy."

Isabella, having decided to give in to the madness for the moment, bows to him and speaks politely.

"Thank you, Mr Arsu. My feet are very grateful to you." To her surprise, the little white fox inclines his head in response then stretches luxuriously and jumps off the bed. He trots out the door and along the corridor, his claws clicking on the wood.

She slides the slippers onto her feet and gasps out a sigh in an ecstasy of relief. The slippers cushion her feet perfectly, so that she barely feels any pain.

As she is about to follow Aroha out of the cabin, Isabella notices Captain Bannerman's cloak and bag hanging above the bunk on the opposite side of the room, his armour neatly stacked on the trunk at the end.

Aroha spots her expression and laughs. "Your friend's funny! Mum keeps telling him off for swearing."

Islaria twists to look back at Isabella. "Mummy says he's a bad

32

'flute-ants on Daddy." She bounces as her sister trots up the stairs.

"He's a bad *influence* on Daddy, she said." Aroha corrects her. "I don't know what she means though, he makes Daddy laugh!"

Isabella raises a sceptical eyebrow. She can only imagine what sort of 'flute-ants' the Captain might be having.

She follows the girls, stepping carefully despite the exquisite cushioning of the fluffy slippers. Her body still holds onto the remnants of her ordeal, so when she reaches the top of the stairs and steps onto the quarterdeck, she has to pause for a moment, leaning against the doorframe to catch her breath. She looks down across the main deck to the bow and realizes that her chaotic memories from the night before held more truth than dream – the ship is indeed, floating in the air.

Isabella grips the doorframe tightly.

Ships don't fly.

Pulling in a sharp breath of chilly air through her nostrils helps her to keep from falling into a hysterical panic.

Did someone slip something into my drink at the Simmer Dim party? Have I gone mad? Does true madness have this kind of clarity?

Shoving the rising terror downwards, Isabella tries to pull herself together. She scans the lower deck which is alive with activity. Cargo is being ferried back and forth between the ship and a wide platform attached to a cliff-face. Metal struts hold it firmly in place and a wide stone staircase winds upwards to the top of the cliff. Far below, rough seas from the previous night's storm churn and slap against sharp rocks. Upon the platform, stacks of trunks, boxes and bags sit waiting to be stowed aboard. Isabella glances up to see clouds scudding across the pale blue sky and a jet-black guillemot swooping up towards a perch on the cliffs, the white flash of his wing feathers brilliant in the crisp air.

Islaria slides from her sister's back and runs across the quarterdeck, throwing herself into the arms of a woman who is sitting in an ornate black wooden chair large enough to be a throne. Her dark hair is pulled back into a bun at the top, the rest of her curls falling in an extravagant cascade past her shoulders, reaching her waist. Her skin is soft brown with a rosy glow over high cheekbones. Dark brows arch over eyes the colour of choppy seas.

Isabella blinks in surprise when she realizes the dark design curling from the edges of her bottom lip and down across her chin is in fact 'tā moko', a type of tattoo. If this woman's culture is anything like that of Aotearoa, then the moko is a sacred taonga[2], containing specific allusions to her family, tribe and social standing. Judging by her posture and imperious expression, that standing is somewhere near the top.

Islaria tugs at the fabric of her mother's dress.

"The Anahera's *finally* awake. Did you know, she snores!"

Her mother tips her head back and laughs, winking at Isabella.

The Anahera in question plants her hands on her hips and frowns, bending forwards to peer accusingly at the little girl.

"You're very critical for one so *short*."

" 'm not short..." Islaria begins, but is interrupted as her mother deposits her on the deck and stands, moving to greet the new arrival. She is wrapped in a long black woolen coat, her sumptuous curves cinched at the waist and topped with a collar of lush grey fur. She is not exactly tall herself, the top of her head coming up to Isabella's nose.

The woman slowly looks her up and down, assessing her. She appears to make a decision and inclines her head. The scent of orange blossoms rises from her before whisking away in the breeze.

"Emmeline Manaroa, the Ariki Tapairu[3] of the Selkie's Song."

"Isabella Mackay, Anahera apparently, and *yes*," she adds, as the little girl opens her mouth, "surprisingly loud snorer."

---

[2] Highly prized, valued and respected.

[3] *Ariki Tapairu* - paramount leader and guardian of the iwi (tribe), from a high-born family.

Emmeline grins and motions for Isabella to join her, noting her careful movements and the wince of pain. Leaning over the table, the Windpyre picks up a silver teapot and pours tea into three chunky mugs, each decorated with colourful spots. Aroha pulls up a wooden stool and perches between the two women, carefully pouring milk into each mug.

Picking up a silver stylus, Emmeline flips open a circular leatherbound device on the table.

"My apologies, I have to finish my calculations. We need to leave before midday. The wind is turning and we still have several passengers to process." She waves the stylus at Isabella. "Drink."

Isabella sits back in her chair and wraps her hands around the warm mug. The familiarity is comforting, yet the sense of crunching cold remains embedded deep within her. This is a new world, where even the air has an odd, disconcerting scent to it.

How on earth do I survive this?

She takes another deep breath and sips the tea to calm herself.

A fresh flurry of movement catches her eye and she leans against the railing to watch passengers being ushered onto the ship. She hears the gravelly bark of Captain Bannerman as he disappears beneath the quarterdeck with a container balanced on his shoulder. A young, flame-haired man and two young women step quickly up the gangplank. The taller of the two women has russet hair tamed into a plait and what looks like the skeleton of a fiddle strapped to her back. They wave up at Emmeline as she and her daughter wave back. The lad stares at Isabella a little too long, before turning quickly to scurry after his companions.

Aroha pulls out her notebook and begins a quick sketch of each.

A new passenger arrives with several trunks of gear. When the hood of their cloak slips down, Aroha gasps and is clearly very excited. The newcomer is tall, encased in geometric armour and most certainly not human. Their skin consists of iridescent green scales, tight lips stretch over sharp teeth and keen eyes glint from beneath a hooded brow. Their forehead stretches back and diverges into six thick horns curving back over their skull. The creature moves with incredible grace and as it turns, Isabella catches the flick of a long-forked tail beneath the sweep of the cloak. Her stomach twists in shock.

"Look, Mum, it's a Tuatara!" Aroha bounces in her seat but her mother cautions her not to annoy their passenger with questions.

Isabella peers at the newcomer. "Are they male or female? It's hard to tell."

Aroha snorts. "Neither, silly. They don't need to be one or the other. We call each one 'they' – definitely not 'it', that would be rude!"

Emmeline pauses from her work on her quire screen. "Apparently their goddess, Mother of Monsters, considers them her finest work."

Goddess?

Isabella murmurs, utterly bewildered. Aroha's enthusiasm, however, is delightful to watch.

"They're the first one I've seen in real life! They live far to the south, on the Isle of Ninian and they don't often leave." She grins. "I think this one is very brave, coming out into the open."

Emmeline nods. "We are honoured that their ambassador chose the Selkie as transport. And they pay well." She finishes her work, pokes the silver stylus into the top of her hair bun and closes the circular quire with a snap.

The Windpyre picks up the teapot and pats it, frowning. Raising a hand, she swirls her fingers in the air just above the pot, the heady scent of orange blossom whisking past Isabella again. In response, fresh steam rises from the spout. Clearly amused by Isabella's look of astonishment, she pours the freshly heated tea into Isabella and Aroha's mugs.

Isabella covers her shock at the woman's small act of magic by asking a question. "Why would they be brave to come out here?"

"They really hate the Drw, and with good reason." Emmeline

takes a sip of her tea and watches Isabella raise an eyebrow, confusion swilling in her face. The Windpyre takes pity on her. "Because Tuatara blood is so unusual, it's valuable to a race called the Drw-ad, so they're never really safe outside of their own lands. Would you leave the house if you were in danger of being enslaved and completely drained at any moment?"

The Tuatara has finished supervising the stowing of their luggage and pauses for a moment, gazing up at the three females on the quarterdeck. They place a leather-gloved hand on their chest and bow.

At that moment a tall, cinnamon-skinned man strides across the deck to welcome the Tuatara. He has the bearing a man used to command, yet is light on his feet and has an easy smile. His long, thick dreadlocks are tied back with a plaid bandana and his sleeveless linen shirt reveals muscled arms, patterned with tattoos. He speaks briefly with the Tuatara before clapping them on the back and ushering them below.

"Why is their blood so valuable to these…what are they called?" Isabella asks, wondering with faint horror if vampires actually exist in this strange world.

"Drw…" Emmeline begins, but her daughter interrupts.

"The Drw-ad, Mum. That's their proper title."

Emmeline smiles at her fondly and reaches out to stroke the top of her head.

"Muuuum. You'll mess up my hair!" Aroha ducks under her hand.

The Windpyre tips back her head and laughs. "Sorry love." Holding the back of her hand to the side of her mouth she says to Isabella in a mock whisper, "honestly, pre-teens."

"Muuuuuum." Her daughter glares at her.

Isabella smiles. She feels herself relax a little with this familiar family banter and she appreciates their attempts to explain things to her.

Emmeline sips her tea and peers down at the lower deck,

checking the progress of her team stowing the containers of supplies and merchandise. "The Drw-ad are a product of a goddess called First Mother. You'll be able to recognise them immediately…"

Her daughter interrupts again. "They're black and white! Or red and white. Or even white and white!" She riffles through the pages of her notebook until she finds a page with a lifelike sketch. As she searches, her mother explains.

"There are three types – the Black, the Red and the White. It's partially to do with their hair colour, but each type play different roles."

Aroha locates the section and hands the book to Isabella, tapping the page.

"That's a Black Drw-ad. It's only a rough sketch – I've never actually seen one close up."

"Beautiful." Isabella murmurs. The figure is humanoid, with bone-china white skin, in stark contrast to her long straight black hair, black eyes and deep blue lips. Aroha and Emmeline stare at her.

"Your sketch…I meant. She looks a bit like a Goth, actually. One of the very earnest ones." She peers more closely at the drawing. "Are those white tattoos on her flesh?"

Aroha shakes her head. "No, they're sigils. They're born with them as part of their skin. They help release the Drw-ad's power."

Emmeline grimaces. "And blood. Blood releases their power and they're not always fussy about whose blood they use either. I swear they see the rest of us as walking blood bags most of the time."

Isabella stares at her. "They drink blood?"

"Eeuuw, no!" Emmeline shivers. "They open a sigil in their own flesh with a blade and pour the blood into the wound."

Isabella gapes.

How is that any better?

She struggles to cope with this explanation, so takes refuge in another question. "What about…um, humans? Do they come in a variety of flavours?"

38

Emmeline grins.

"Flavours? That's a lovely description. Yes, we do. Our own goddess, Midnight Mother, doesn't like uniformity, so you'll find all sorts of colours and shapes. Even the Gentry in the Citadel are very mixed." She pauses for a moment, her expression souring a little. "Immensely stuck up and frequently psychotic, but certainly mixed."

She leans forward abruptly, glaring down at two figures loitering beside the railing of the lower deck.

"For the Goddess's sake!" She snaps, her voice carrying a surprisingly long way. "What part of, 'don't smoke on the waka' are you two having difficulty with? Kahu, *really?*"

The dreadlocked Windpyre opens his hands wide, grinning up at his wife as smoke drifts from his nostrils. "Not guilty, my love!" He calls to her, his voice deep and laced with amusement.

His fellow conspirator takes a final, rebellious drag on the small, offending cigar and nonchalantly flicks it over the side. Captain Bannerman, stripped to the waist, lifts his chin and stares up at the women, his face radiating insolence. He turns and continues his work, helping to stow the heavy boxes securely in the hold.

Isabella swallows. Grumpy bastard he may be, but he is certainly well built. His muscles are beautifully defined under tanned skin and watching him hoist a heavy box onto his shoulder is an education.

"It's hard not to look, isn't it?" Isabella hears the grin in Emmeline's voice as she speaks. The Anahera shakes her head and blinks to pull herself back from staring.

"I wasn't quite expecting that…" She manages.

Emmeline nods. "Some people really are a surprise." She is watching Isabella keenly. "Did you notice anything else unusual about him?"

Isabella takes another look, this time attempting to see past the powerful physique. His hair is pulled back in a half-ponytail, accentuating the twin scars marring his face. Squinting a little in the weak sunlight, she watches as he finishes stowing the last box and

39

moves towards the staircase leading to the quarterdeck. She realizes they aren't his only scars – his body is covered with evidence of countless battles. As he moves swiftly up the steps, her good mood evaporates. There is a strange uniformity to some of the scars. Long welts stretch over his chest and back, and his skin is peppered with odd, circular marks like the one on the back of each hand. They almost appear symmetrical. She wonders how much pain he endured in the making of them.

He strolls past, the scent of cardamom and fresh cigar following.

"Nice slippers." He winks at her and she pokes her tongue out in response.

He pauses in front of Emmeline who is watching him thoughtfully. He hooks his thumbs under his belt. "Kahu reckons we're almost set. Mind if I use your *scry* to contact the Citadel for an update before we leave?"

She nods. "The bridge is through the door behind you. Make it quick though, I'll be moving the Selkie as soon as Kahu gives me the signal."

As he turns, Bannerman catches sight of Aroha's notebook. He steps forward, wipes his hands carefully on his trews and holds his hand out.

"May I take a look?"

Isabella is surprised by how gentle his raspy voice has become. Aroha's expression is a little dubious but she hands the book up to him. He stares down at the picture of the Drw-ad.

"Impressive. You've a real talent, girl. That's a good likeness."

He hands the book back to her and turns back to Emmeline. "I didn't think Windpyre's carried those cun-"

"Language!" Emmeline heads him off.

"...kind of passengers." He finishes.

Aroha looks at Isabella and rolls her eyes. The Anahera fails to suppress her smile in response.

"We don't." Emmeline replies, her eyes flinty. "Aroha's only ever seen one and that was at a distance, through a spyglass."

"Believe me," he looks down at Aroha, "you don't want to get any closer." His gaze shifts to Isabella and his grey eyes darken.

"You pay attention. The Drw-ad may look impressive but they'll betray you in a heartbeat. Their only concern is themselves and how we might be useful to them." The scars on his face seem to deepen and his gravelly voice takes on a hard edge. One hand drifts to the circular scar on the palm of the other and massages it. "They can't be trusted, so don't go near them. They'd certainly love a piece of you."

Bannerman turns abruptly and strides through the open door towards the bridge, Isabella staring after him. She looks back at Emmeline and is surprised to see the Windpyre's face soften.

"Aroha, could you please go and ask Daddy to come up here?"

Her daughter opens her mouth to protest and then closes it with a snap when she sees her mother's suddenly stern expression.

"Yes, Mum." She slips from the stool, stuffs the notebook into her pocket and scurries off down the staircase. Emmeline waits until she is out of sight before she speaks.

"I've seen those scars before, but only on the bodies of the dead. I think your Captain was once a slave to the Drw-ad." She sighs. "When they want to punish a slave, they secure them to the wall using a 'hardbolt'…a sort of energy rod that goes straight through the flesh and into the stone." She motions lines with her fingers. "Those long scars are probably from an ergon whip. Needless to say, their slaves don't last very long. Your Captain must be pretty tough – I've never heard of one managing to escape before. Death is usually the only way out."

Isabella feels her stomach contract in horror. No wonder he seems in a permanently bad mood.

"I wonder how he ended up as a Captain in the King's Own Uhlan?" Emmeline murmurs. She shakes herself and sits up expectantly as Kahu appears at the top of the steps.

"We're all set." He leans down and kisses the top of his

41

diminutive wife's head then turns to Isabella. "How are you feeling?"

"Better, although still a little terrified." The Anahera smiles ruefully and waggles a fluffy-slippered foot. "I am grateful for your kindness. You're all definitely making this mad experience a little easier to deal with."

Emmeline eyes her speculatively. "You interest me, Anahera. You're not at all what I expected." She shrugs. "And you ate the food I made without complaining."

Kahu blinks. "You cooked?"

"Shockingly enough, yes. And nobody died." Emmeline slaps her knees and stands. "Time to move."

She walks to Isabella and places a hand on her shoulder. "You are welcome on my ship, Anahera."

Isabella smiles in response then watches the Ariki Tapairu trot down the steps and stride across the lower deck towards the bow, her coat swirling about dark-trousered legs and knee-high boots.

"You've never been on a Windpyre waka before, I take it?" Kahu's deep voice curls behind her and she turns back.

"No. Ships don't float in the air in my world."

He grins, white teeth against cinnamon skin. "Then this should be an education. My wee wifey's one of the best."

Isabella raises an eyebrow. "And how does she react when she hears you call her 'wee wifey'?"

Kahu laughs. "Hasn't caught me yet!" He nods towards the bow. "She's nearly ready."

Emmeline reaches the end of the deck and steps onto a small dais edged by a sturdy railing. She raises a hand and curls her fingers into a fist. The docking clamps release their grip on the platform and slide back into the hull. Panels begin to slide out of the wood, meeting in the middle to create a low roof and sealing the deck to make the vessel more streamlined. Emmeline uncurls her fingers and then raises both arms slowly. The waka rises smoothly up along the cliff face, the solid thrum of the engines in the stern growing louder with increased thrust.

42

The Ariki Tapairu's hair lifts from her shoulders to float around her and the scent of orange blossom billows across the deck. The waka moves forward through the air.

As they leave the shelter of the cliffs, the mountains to the east loom dark against the pale blue sky. Isabella pulls herself up and leans against the railing.

"So, she controls the waka?"

Kahu comes to stand beside her, his scent of camphor warm in the chilly air.

"She's our navigator. Her magic is required to spark the engines into life and to plot a course through the air currents. Windpyres can sense even minute changes in the air and since the waka is intimately connected to her, it adjusts itself at her simplest thought. She only needs to be this hands-on for certain manoeuvres though, depending on how the wind is behaving. It's a good day. She won't have much trouble."

Isabella shakes her head. "That's astonishing."

Kahu shrugs. "It's who we are." He lays a hand on her shoulder in an echo of his wife. "I've some paperwork to do on the bridge. Stay out as long as you like but keep to the quarterdeck. Emmeline will be back soon." He turns and slips through the door behind.

The chill breeze has freshened with the progress of the ship and Isabella reaches up and pulls the hood of the dress over her curls. As she does so, the sleeves which are split from the elbow down suddenly knit together, sealing in the warmth. She stares at them, fighting the desire to scream hysterically and rip them off. After a few moments she decides they are not trying to eat her, so forces herself to relax.

The waka tilts slightly and she grabs the railing in response, but it appears that Emmeline is merely adjusting their heading, the ship curving to follow the coastline. Stretching to the west is a long voe and more land rippling towards the horizon. Far below, little rectangles of walled farms dot the hillsides and in the voe, fishing boats leave glittering wakes.

43

Isabella shuffles to the far end of the quarterdeck and peers over the side. The Selkie's Song is tracking along the edge of a large bay and down in the white-tipped water a collection of shapes speed across the waves. She squints against the stiff breeze and realizes what they are; windsurfers. Bright triangular sails flick against the dark water. She wipes the tears from her eyes and searches for them again but the ship's course has shifted slightly, curving inland.

The scent of orange blossom heralds Emmeline's return and Isabella turns and shuffles back to the table.

"Here." The Windpyre dangles a pair of almond-shaped goggles in front of her. "If you're going to stay outside, you'll need these." She motions for Isabella to sit and hands her what looks like a leather-bound book. Isabella opens it to find a slender circular device with a domed screen similar to the one Captain Bannerman had used the night before. She strokes the glass screen and a map floats into view.

"This is a 'quire'," Emmeline explains. "I've loaded it with maps so you can track our progress." She points to one of the dots at the edge of the screen. "That's the town of Bixter. We've no passengers to pick up there so we're turning north and flying up over The Peats plateau. The next stop will be Aith."

She pats Isabella on the shoulder. "I need to catch up with our passengers so I'll leave you in peace. Don't stay out too long or you'll catch a chill."

The Anahera smiles ruefully. "Thanks, Mum." Emmeline snorts in response and moves off, leaving Isabella to scroll through the maps.

As the afternoon drifts into twilight the ship slows and Emmeline steps back on to her dais to guide the Selkie's Song into docking with the Aith platform which sits atop a low hill overlooking the city. The settlement stretches out for miles along the bay, under a broad sky gradually fading to layers of soft pink and amber. Far below, looping strings of lanterns flicker on over narrow, crowded streets. Each building is long and squat, with a sharply curved roof reminiscent of

44

an upturned hull and supported by whitewashed walls. The bay itself is crowded with hundreds of fishing boats, the piers prickling with cranes lifting boxes of catch.

At Emmeline's command, the roof of the Selkie's lower deck slides back, allowing the crew to emerge and begin the process of unloading cargo. Bannerman appears below, now more suitably attired in a blue woollen shirt. He and Kahu climb up onto the platform and disappear down towards the city, moving with purpose.

Aroha trots up the steps to the quarterdeck and waves to Isabella. "Mum says we're to freshen up ready for dinner." She motions for Isabella to follow her below.

When she reaches the cabin, Isabella closes the door and leans on it for a moment. Despite the conviviality of her hosts, a heavy cold has anchored itself in her core and her grief threatens to swamp her, a physical remnant of the trauma of shifting between worlds. She shivers and gasps, wrapping her arms tightly around her body as she struggles to suppress it.

When she eventually manages to control herself, her attention turns to the bathroom and she slides with considerable relief into the hot shower. As she dresses afterwards, Isabella finds she is suddenly tired again, her muscles heavy and her fingers fumbling for the lacings of the bodice. By the time she emerges onto the deck, the sky has deepened to burnished orange, edged with the royal blue of night.

The ship appears empty, but when she looks down, she sees the figures of Kahu and Captain Bannerman crossing the platform, each carrying a large wicker basket and looking very pleased with themselves. Bannerman spots Isabella and hands his basket to Kahu before moving towards her.

"What took you so long?" He rasps. "Come on." He offers his hand and leads her down the ramp, across the platform and down a set of steep steps. The fact that she is still wearing the fluffy pink slippers seems to provide him with bitter amusement.

[4]As she reaches the last step, Isabella pauses for a moment. The grassy brow of the hill has been turned into a carnival of light. At the centre sits a large, metal fire pit with streams of sparks drifting heavenwards. Lanterns in the shape of fat fish hang from long poles, bobbing gently in the night breeze. The ship's crew perch on low stools or wait in front of tall, cylindrical metal ovens, from which the most delicious aromas seep. Isabella recognizes the scent immediately and clutches the railing in delight. Each oven is a mobile 'hangi', gently smoking meat and vegetables for hours until they become succulent.

Kahu strides past, triumphantly raising the baskets aloft before plonking them down and hauling out two enormous scarlet crayfish from one. As the crew applaud, his daughters scurry up to help carry the baskets and their contents to waiting pots of boiling water. Emmeline appears at the base of the steps.

"Are you hungry?" She raises a hand as Bannerman opens his mouth. "No, Captain, I did not cook the meal. This is all Kahu's work." Her eyes narrow as she sees his shoulders sagging in mock relief.

As the Captain helps Isabella overcome the last step, Emmeline takes her other arm and, together they walk to a collection of squat wooden chairs near the fire pit. Once seated, and a 'karakia' prayer of thanks has been sung, Aroha and a kitchenhand deliver platters of prawns and chunks of crayfish barbecued with butter, a hint of chili, fresh lime and garlic. They are accompanied by wedges of freshly baked bread and bowls of wild rice mixed with basil, mint, tiny peppery nuts and plump sultanas.

Bannerman opts for a bowl of smoked spicy fish and is about to dive in with a spoon, when he catches Isabella's intense stare. He sighs and hands the laden spoon over for her to try. The Anahera takes a tentative nibble and her eyes widen. It is far spicier than she

---

[4] Playlist: Maisey Rika - Tangaroa Whakamautai.

anticipated. The Captain reaches out and firmly takes back his spoon, turning away and hunching slightly as he proceeds to wolf the mixture down.

Emmeline smiles at this. They barely seem like prisoner and captor, and the more she watches them the more intrigued she becomes. One by one, her daughters and various members of the crew stop to chat with the Anahera, asking her questions, sharing explanations and laughing with her.

The captor himself reasons that helping her hobble out to the bonfire for supper and sitting nearby, was merely to keep an eye on her. She has form for trying to escape, after all. But, in reality, he is fascinated by what she'll do next. He struggles to reconcile his first impression of Isabella as a feral, spitting cat with the woman laughing so easily with the Windpyres.

He finishes his meal and, relaxing a little, pulls a small cigar from his wrist vambrace and sparks it up. He is immediately huffed at by Emmeline.

"For the Goddess's sake, woman, we're outside!"

The Windpyre grins at him and he shakes his head, growling expletives, occasionally punctuated with the word 'women'. He takes another defiant drag on the offending cigar.

Leaning over the little table between them, Isabella pours spiced rum into diminutive glass tumblers and hands him one. He glances at her in surprise.

"What? I am capable of sharing too, y'know." She raises her tumbler and he clinks his against it.

Through the laughter and drifting smoke of the bonfire comes the steady pulse of drums and the distinct thread of a fiddle tune. The Windpyres surrounding them begin to clap and rise to dance. Islaria bounces up and tugs on Bannerman's sleeve, demanding that he come and, "dance with Belcher!" He grabs her up, throws her onto his shoulders and dances around the fire as she holds out the toy 'saur' to make it fly, giggling with delight. Eventually, he hands her over to her father, lifting her from his shoulders to Kahu's taller ones.

As he sits back down in the low chair, left ankle resting on right knee in a relaxed, arrogant posture, Isabella smiles.

"That was entertaining to watch."

"She's heavier than she looks." He grunts, but there is a real softness to his face and even his scars seem less livid.

"Do you have children, Captain?"

He shrugs. "Could have," catching her raised eyebrow, "but none who'll admit to it."

Before Isabella can respond, she notices a change in the formation of the dancers as the lithe figure of the Tuatara strolls out of the swirling smoke and stops in front of them, bowing politely. Their movements are light and smooth but there is real power rippling beneath their skin, glinting gold in the firelight. They are accompanied by the distinct smell of sulphur, making Isabella think of black rocks and bubbling mud pools.

"I am Subtle Sands Shifting. I am honoured to meet an Anahera!" The Tuatara's lids flicker over green eyes and their voice rasps with amusement.

"Isabella Mackay."

The Tuatara looks her up and down.

"You don't look tough, but you survived the slaverscum. Well done!"

"But you," the ambassador tips their head, throwing a shrewd look at Captain Bannerman, "you're the, 'One Who Survived'. We've heard much about you in the Ninian." They bow more deeply to him, as he shifts in uncomfortable surprise, narrowing his eyes.

"I've survived plenty of scraps, *lizard*. Were you referring to one in particular?"

Emmeline, sitting nearby, tenses. She'll not have trouble on her waka and the Captain's deliberate use of the insult puts her on edge.

The Tuatara crouches in front of Bannerman, staring at him sharply. They tip their head to one side then the other, looking him

48

over as if studying a specimen…or a potential meal. Bannerman does not move from his relaxed pose but his expression grows steadily more insolent. Even Isabella can sense this is a dangerous moment for both of them and that the Captain is ready, if not spoiling for a fight.

Suddenly, the Tuatara grins, displaying two rows of sharp white teeth.

"Funny human." They tip their chin upwards. "You know what I mean. You survived *them*. That makes you mighty. We would know how you managed it."

They lean over to the low table between Isabella and Bannerman and pour spiced rum into the soldier's empty tumbler, claws clicking on the glass. Subtle Sands Shifting lifts the tumbler and holds it out to the Captain who takes it slowly, his tanned fingers lifting it by the rim.

Before they let go, the Tuatara speaks quietly. "We know what you want, kaitoa[5], and this *lizard*," they smirk, "can help you with that." The Tuatara pats Bannerman's knee and stands. "Talk soon."

They turn and stroll back to their seat on the other side of the bonfire.

Bannerman is quiet, lighting another cigar and staring balefully into the night. He lets out a long, steady stream of smoke into the air through tightly pursed lips and dangles the brimming glass thoughtfully, before knocking the whole thing back.

Isabella tentatively places her hand on his arm. "Captain, are you alright?"

It is such an unexpectedly kind gesture that he stares at her. For a moment she sees utter desolation in his eyes. It mirrors the terrible cold she can feel camping within herself. It almost seems as if he is going to confide in her but then his lips press together firmly, his grey eyes becoming flinty again. He nods towards the Tuatara.

"That one's going to make a great ambassador, they're already a

---

[5] Brave warrior.

49

smug bastard."

He pours another tumbler of rum and throws it back, wiping his mouth roughly with the back of his hand. Isabella can see he is steadily drifting towards a pool of dark brooding and, not knowing where that will go, she decides to attempt a diversion.

"Would you mind helping me back to the cabin?"

Instead of his usual scorn, he merely nods and stands, helping her up and supporting her as they climb the steep steps back to the ship. Emmeline watches them and taps her lips with her fingertips. She feels Kahu's hand on her shoulder.

"He's in trouble, isn't he?" She looks up at her husband. The big man nods, ruefully.

By the time they reach the cabin, Isabella's feet have begun to ache again. Bannerman helps her to the bathroom where she washes and changes whilst he readies himself for bed. When she emerges, she finds him wearing soft, baggy black trews and bare skin. She frowns, taking in the livid scars across his powerfully muscled back.

He drops onto the bed, pulls a neatly wrapped bundle out of his pack and unwinds it. Inside is a book, which he opens.

He glances at her. "Yes, I can read."

"That isn't what I was thinking! I'm just impressed with the wrapping."

He shrugs. "I don't like getting blood on the pages – makes them stick together."

She blinks at him.

"You should get some sleep. You'll heal more quickly."

She snuggles down in the bunk opposite, her hand under her head and watches him. She has done nothing all day and yet she is exhausted.

Bannerman feels her gaze. He places a scrap of paper into the book as a marker and closes it, tilts his head and glares at her.

"What?"

"I'm sorry for hurting you, Captain." She watches his eyebrows

50

lift in surprise. "In my defence, I was terrified and nothing made any sense."

He nods, accepting her apology. "Sorry for tying you up."

But she hasn't quite finished and her tone is thoughtful as she speaks.

"I remember, years ago, sitting next to a homeless guy in Los Angeles and he said, "Life never takes you where you expect it to go." I've always accepted the truth of that, but I never thought it would take me quite as far as this."

The hard-bitten soldier does something that comes as much of a surprise to him as it does to the Anahera. He stretches out his arm towards her, palm up. Across the gap between the bunks, Isabella grasps his hand and squeezes it.

"Thank you for helping me." She sighs, takes back her hand and closes her eyes. Exhaustion pulls her down towards sleep, however, he catches her final murmur, not necessarily meant for him to hear. "And you smell nice."

He watches her breaths deepen as she falls into sleep, her dark auburn hair flung across the pillows behind her. He is loath to admit that he is almost beginning to enjoy her company. Life certainly isn't dull near her, but there is another, less pleasant feeling beginning to gnaw at him - guilt. He feels it squatting at the top of his chest and he rubs the spot slowly. She won't sleep so easily soon, when she finds herself in the Citadel's holding cells...and he will be significantly responsible for that.

Bannerman reaches down and carefully wraps the book back up. As he does so, he catches sight of the hardbolt scars on the back of his hands. He absently rubs the matching scars on each palm and thinks about what Subtle Sands Shifting said – what he survived and how the lizard might be useful. Running a hand roughly over his mouth and heavily stubbled chin, his fingers find the twin scars stretching over his cheek and down his throat. He paid a high price for survival, but he is determined that the Drw-ad will pay a high price

51

in return.

He reaches for the light pad behind him and taps it. The lights dim, then extinguish and he is left listening to the woman from another world breathing softly in the darkness. He settles into the routine he has used for years to lull himself to sleep – cataloguing each creative way to maim and kill the Drw-ad. On this night, he begins with a Red. He drifts off to sleep, his mind replete with blades slicing through vivid white flesh.

By the break of dawn, they are off again. Isabella spends the rest of the morning curled in a corner of the quarterdeck, studying the map quire and the corresponding landscape as they pass overhead. They leave behind the sprawling city of Aith, skimming over heather-covered moorland threaded with dark lines of rushing streams. Eventually the moorland gives way to low foothills as the Selkie climbs higher.

Emmeline stands at the prow, arms raised and eyes closed, navigating the waka through the air currents of the rearing mountain range. She would prefer to go the long way around, but her passengers and crew are eager to reach their destination. She wonders how discussions are going inside, where Kahu holds a meeting with the Tuatara in the stateroom. He is their Rangatira, a high-ranking chief and skilled negotiator, and she trusts that he will conduct business shrewdly. He is respected both inside the Windpyre community and out and is often in demand to assist with treaties. Revenue flows easily through his hands into the Selkie's Song coffers. Emmeline suspects that Subtle Sands Shifting, new to their post as ambassador, is eager to negotiate a trade deal with him.

On the quarterdeck, Eric Bannerman turns his gaze from the Windpyre at the bow to Isabella, perched against the side of the waka, scrolling through the quire and turning to lean over the rail and peer down at the landscape passing below as the first of the black mountain peaks slide beneath them. She appears fascinated by their progress but, as time goes on, he notices a change. She begins to nibble a fingernail in worry, repeatedly checking the map and peering over the side again to determine where they are.

As they sail steadily past the final peak, Emmeline allows the waka's automatic pilot to take over and moves to stand beside him, the fresh scent of orange blossom whisking past into the wind. She hands him a steaming mug of black chaoua, which he accepts with a grateful grunt. His head nips a little for the remnants of last night's rum and the buzz of the chaoua lifts him. She follows his gaze and leans her elbows on the railing, errant curls lifting in the breeze, her moko kauae dark against her skin.

"We'll be there before sunset. She's been tracking the route." Emmeline glances at him and recalls how often his eyes have strayed towards the Anahera since the pair first boarded the Selkie's Song. It is more than just checking up on a captive. "I'm surprised you're not more cheerful - you'll be free of her by tomorrow."

He grunts in agreement, but without much conviction, and he doesn't smile. He has increasingly conflicting feelings about the strange, stroppy woman, in particular a growing concern for what will happen to her once she reaches the Citadel. Although he still harbours resentment for the knee in the balls, it is rapidly diminishing, replaced by something approaching appreciation. He knows she will view his coming actions as a betrayal and finds that the prospect actually bothers him. He becomes aware that Emmeline is watching him with the last whispers of amusement, and something close to pity.

"Yeah," he murmurs, "can't come soon enough."

Emmeline shrugs a shoulder. "Honestly, I like her already. I'm tempted to keep flying and steal her away." Bannerman glances at her sharply and for a moment, she realises that he is actually considering it, but for a Citadel Uhlan, such an act would be considered treasonous and punished severely.

"Once she's in that nest of ratsnakes, I can't protect her." He rasps. "She's on her own." The prospect makes his chest feel strangely tight

53

again. "You know what the Gentry are like. She's feisty, but they're well practiced scum." Bannerman takes every opportunity he can to be posted out of the Citadel because he so loathes the Gentry and their arrogant politicking.

The Windpyre nods. Her kind are forbidden from entering the main city, considered by the Gentry to be too chaotic in their behaviour to be trusted, something that she is not terribly bothered about. She knows that, in truth, they are banned because so many of the Gentry owe them money. Not having to deal with the vicious politics and appalling arrogance of the citizens is an absolute blessing.

"You've done a good job of protecting her so far..."

"...even if she doesn't make it easy." He finishes her sentence and they grin ruefully at one another.

Emmeline shakes her head and narrows her eyes. "It's a shitty way to treat people from another world." She lifts her right hand, palm up. "Welcome to the Citadel; you can be a slave sold at market and end up the Goddess knows where, or..." she lifts her left hand, palm up, "you can be a slave with fancy clothes and live in a castle, where people will always treat you like inferior property and occasionally try to assassinate you, just because they're bored."

Bannerman snorts derisively.

She drops her hands to her hips. "And yet those numpties love to crow about how 'civilized' they are compared to the rest of us." Her voice takes on a mocking, sing-song tone.

"We're the guiding light in a dark world, blah blah, our way is the civilised way, yap yap..." Her tone becomes more serious as she turns back to the Captain. "*Do as we say or we'll wipe you off the map.* What makes you people any different from the slavers?"

Bannerman shrugs. "We give the Anahera a choice."

"And what choice do you think she'll make? Because she looks like the type to choose her own way, regardless."

He watches the Anahera pull her cloak tighter around her body and hunch back over the quire, scrolling thoughtfully through the maps.

"They won't know what's hit 'em." He drawls, a wicked glint crossing his narrowed eyes.

4. SANCTUARY

Isabella raises her arms above her head, clasping her hands together and stretching. She has been hunched over the quire for hours, her stomach twisting into nausea which threatens to choke her. It has certainly not been eased by the behaviour of Captain Bannerman. After their apparent moment of connection, the night before, his face has become steadily more sour as the day wears on. The heavy weight of desolation pulls her ever downward. She has no idea what she is heading into or how she might escape it, however she is determined to memorize as many of the maps in the quire as possible.

Despite the crunching fear within, Isabella has to admit that the landscape is stunning. After cresting the vast spine of mountains, the waka has turned southwards and now skims above a wide, alluvial valley. To the east, the vast forest of Kergord stretches to the far hills, ahead lie lush pastures and the twisting progress of the Bonhoga River. From her careful study of the maps, she realises that the hazy lump in the distance is the Citadel itself, and beyond that the glittering expanse of Weisdale voe. Try as she might to ignore it, her gaze is repeatedly pulled back to the dark shape, slowly resolving in the distance.

To her consternation, she feels the waka begin to slow and she looks up to see Emmeline back at the prow, her hair streaming behind her in the wind. Isabella bites her lip and checks the quire. There is a dog-leg curve in the path of the river where a small settlement sits.

She taps the screen and the symbol of a tree appears. There is no other explanation.

Suddenly, the door to the cabins flies open and Islaria rockets out, closely followed by her sister. The little girl trots past Isabella and proceeds to skip in a circle.

"We're off to see the Witch, the Witch, the Witch!" Her pigtails bounce in the air.

Aroha appears equally as excited, though less inclined to bounce. She is already clutching her notebook in anticipation.

"So, are we talking about a good witch or a bad witch?" Isabella asks.

Aroha blinks in surprise. "Witches aren't good or bad, they just *are*." She grins. "But Sister Alyss makes the best cakes!"

At the prow, Emmeline raises both arms, palms up. The waka tilts and Isabella stands, clutching the rail for a better view. Ahead of them lies a collection of buildings nestled against a wall of low, layered cliffs. The waka slows to a gentle drift, easing down into a gully barely wide enough to fit. At the head of the gully is an enormous tree, its branches arching out to shadow both the waka and the buildings beyond. At the base of its trunk, a docking platform just from the cliff and Emmeline skilfully slides the Selkie's Song alongside it. She makes a fist, then uncurls her fingers, allowing the docking clamps to attach.

Kahu and Subtle Sands Shifting emerge from the bridge and the Tuatara flashes her a toothy grin before shinning down the staircase to the main deck. Kahu catches Isabella's worried look and moves forward, lifting Islaria onto his shoulders and pulling Aroha in for a hug.

"Don't worry, you're not at your destination yet. We're docking here for the night." The Windpyre watches some of her tension ease but knows that it is a false hope he gives her. He wonders if it is a kindness or not.

"What is this place?" Isabella waves the quire. "This thing doesn't give it a name, just a symbol."

Kahu smiles. "The tree. It's our symbol for a Sisterhood Haven Holm. They're a pub, a sanctuary and a training centre all rolled into one. This one is run by a Witch called Alyss – one of the most powerful Sister Witches alive." He raises an eyebrow. "I certainly wouldn't want to piss her off."

"Dad," Aroha pipes up from under his arm, "is that word an example of Captain Bannerman's, 'bad influence'?"

Kahu winces and looks down at her. "Yes. Don't tell your mother." He receives a grin in reply.

Once the waka is securely docked, the crew set about unloading cargo and Emmeline joins them on the quarterdeck.

"I've had your original clothes laundered and packed, along with some of our spares." She lets out a sigh, her expression troubled. "I have enjoyed your company and I am loath to let you go…"

The scent of cardamom and cigars drifts upwards, heralding the appearance of Captain Bannerman. He stands at the base of the stairs, encased in armour once more and looking impatient.

Isabella feels the heavy weight in her chest sink further in.

"I thought you were taking me to the Citadel."

"This is as close as our ship is allowed." Emmeline glances at her husband, who shakes his head. She presses her lips together in frustration. "We don't want to let you go but we have no choice. We walk a slender line with the Citadel as it is." On the deck below, Bannerman has placed his hand on the pommel of his sword.

Isabella smiles tightly. "It's okay, I understand." She lifts her chin. "Thank you for all your kindness."

The Ariki Tapairu steps forward and pulls her into a fierce hug, her curls rising and drifting about them for a moment.

Kahu speaks quietly. "Eric doesn't want this either. He'll look after you for as long as he can." He reaches out and places his warm hand on her shoulder. His wife takes Isabella's arm and together they move to join the soldier on the deck.

Bannerman has been watching the interaction thoughtfully. Windpyres are fiercely tribal and rarely let anyone into their confidence, yet here one of the most prominent families has welcomed the strange Anahera with open arms. When she shuffles past him she glances up and her expression is soft, the hint of a sad smile on her lips. The sharp sensation in his chest twists again. He covers his reaction with a grunt, hefting the packs and striding past the family and up onto the platform.

As they cross the docking platform, under the shade of the enormous tree, Emmeline lets go of Isabella to turn and speak to her daughter Aroha. Isabella keeps walking, peering through the gaps in the branches at the complex below. In the distance, an extensive walled garden and an orchard stretches past a series of squat, circular white towers with pointed roofs, joined by enclosed walkways. She is so intent on the view, that she stumbles a little and grabs a branch for support. The tree, whose leaves have been drifting gently in the wind, stills itself completely. Every leaf freezes in place in the chilly air and the tree gives an unexpected creak.

Emmeline and Kahu look up and then glance at one another. They have never seen an Yggdrasil tree react like this, almost as if it is in shock. Isabella mutters "sorry" to the branch and lets go, not noticing that anything is amiss. As she moves off, the leaves resume their natural motion but the Windpyres have the distinct impression that the tree is watching her, and they are not the only ones to notice.

The wrought-iron steps of the platform lead to a wide limestone path which winds around to the front of the outermost building, the pub. Bannerman waits at the bottom of the steps for her and his mood seems to have lifted considerably.

"Come on, girlie, let's get you inside. The Witch is waiting for us."

Ensconced in visions of gingerbread houses and ovens, it takes a moment for Isabella to notice the building. It is three floors high and gently curved inwards in a half-circle, the whitewashed outer wall towards the road. The second floor is edged with a long veranda and the rooms below are busy with customers, some sitting at tables outside in the weak sunlight. When Isabella spots the sign above the large, arched doorway, she grins.

"The Mutinous Piglet? That's the name of the pub?"

Bannerman raises both eyebrows in assent, his grey eyes returning her amusement. "An ancient and venerable name, I'll have you know. This Haven Holm is one of the originals." He chivvies her towards the door.

He has been looking forward to this. In his absence, he knows that the Piglet will have moved onto their winter menu. It is his favourite time of the culinary year, for Alyss has broken out her store of explosively hot spices, ready to warm her patrons through the biting chill of winter. He drops Isabella's arm and steps through the doorway. The Sisterhood Witch is there to greet them, striding up to hug him.

"Eric! Welcome back!" She is a similar height to Emmeline, with lush curves and an ample bosom. Her honey-blonde hair falls in waves down her back and she almost seems to glow in the soft light of the day lamps.

"So, when are you going to leave that husband of yours and run off with me?" Bannerman grins.

Isabella is stunned.

Is this the same man? The eternally grumpy bastard who never seems happy with anyone?

Alyss laughs and pats his scarred cheek fondly.

A figure appears from behind the bar, wiping his hands on a rag. He is wearing goggles with lens extensions and his lithe body is wrapped in coveralls. He runs a hand through short, spiky salt-and-pepper hair.

"Quit trying to steal my wife, Eric. You won't win – I'm far prettier than you!" He grins and they slap wrists together. He leans forward in a mock-conspiratorial manner. "She's got some good stuff

60

this year – you're gonna love it."

"Neb, mate," Bannerman smirks, "I'm after her food, not her…"

"Eric!" Alyss interrupts him as she moves to greet Isabella. She halts in front of the Anahera, hands on hips, the heady scent of apples rising around her, then proceeds to walk slowly around Isabella, looking her up and down in a speculative fashion.

"Uhh…" Isabella doesn't quite know how to deal with such pointed scrutiny.

Alyss looks up at her and smiles. "Our first Anahera. You are welcome in this Haven Holm." Her voice is warm, although her words have an oddly formal tone as if the greeting were a time-honoured one. She looks down at Isabella's feet, still wrapped in fluffy pink slippers. The Witch's shoulders drop and she tilts her head. "Okay, why?"

"Silly mare trashed her feet hiking along the Sandsound Range in ridiculous shoes." Bannerman growls from behind her.

Annoyance burns through Isabella. "Because you dragged me!" She opens her hands and appeals to Alyss. "All I did was turn up to a party. I wasn't expecting to be sucked through a dimensional gate, tied up and hauled over a mountain!"

The Witch frowns. "Are your feet still troubling you?" Isabella winces and Alyss nods her head. "Right, let's get them sorted. Follow me." She moves towards a door beside the bar but as she strides past Bannerman, she glares at him.

"You dragged her? Eric." Her tone is distinctly unimpressed and he frowns in response. Behind the Witch, Isabella adds a little sashay to her walk and grins at him.

Alyss leads her through the doorway into a wide corridor, quite unlike the softly lit wooden interior of the inn. It stretches around the back of the building, the inner wall made of polished limestone, the outer a thick, curved glass wall framed with black steel. The floor is covered in pale flagstones and even through the slippers, Isabella can feel the warmth of under-floor heating. A sculpted garden lies beyond,

61

dotted with raised herb beds and delicate trees covered in leaves of autumnal red and gold.

Through the glass, Isabella can see Subtle Sands Shifting and the Windpyre family making their way through the garden, Islaria perched on her father's shoulders and pointing the way, Aroha skipping alongside her mother. A flash of white just ahead of them betrays the presence of the arctic fox, Arsu, before he disappears into the undergrowth with the flick of his tail.

"You were lucky to catch a lift with the Manaroa family. They're good people." Alyss smiles. "We've known them for years."

"Do they stay at the inn?"

Alyss shakes her head. "On their waka, although they are always welcome in the Sanctuary. In fact, they're heading for the plunge pool." She points through a gap in the trees, towards a large wooden gate set into the cliff. "It's geothermal – perfect for a dip after a cold flight."

Isabella pauses, looking longingly towards the gate then hobbles to catch up with the Witch. The corridor has taken them to the next building, smaller than the pub, squat and round. The scent of astringent herbs drifts from the doorway where Alyss waits for her. Inside is warm and bright, edged with wooden tables dotted with medical equipment. A large padded chair dominates the room and when Isabella sits in it, the chair tilts backwards and a footrest extends. It reminds her of a posh salon.

Alyss pulls up a stool and lifts the slippers from Isabella's feet, carefully unwinding the bandages. She frowns.

"You weren't kidding. Even with the salves they're a mess." She shakes her head and murmurs, "honestly, Eric." She gently prods the skin of each foot and Isabella wrinkles her nose at the resulting flicker of pain.

The Witch clicks her fingers and a trolley filled with little bottles and pots scoots across the floor to halt beside her. She selects a vibrant green bottle, shakes it and presses the top. A fine spray settles over

Isabella's feet and she feels them tingle. Alyss then picks up a small pot filled with a dark amber mixture and proceeds to smear it carefully along each tear in the skin with a slender spatula. Isabella frowns.

"Is that honey?"

Alyss nods. "The finest blend from a royal hive. Hjaltland bees have a number of unusual talents and making honey that can heal wounds and knit bone is just one of them."

Behind her, the door opens and three individuals enter. Isabella recognizes them as the group who boarded the Windpyre ship from the first platform. She gives a small wave. The tallest, fiddle still strapped to her back, tucks her long red hair over one shoulder and plants her hands on her hips.

"That looks painful."

Isabella shrugs. "Thanks to various people, they're healing." She sits back. "You were on the ship, weren't you?"

The young woman nods. "I'm Mara. This is Nari." She indicates towards the shorter girl, whose light brown hair is pulled up into a high ponytail above shaved sides tattooed with curling waves.

"And I'm Foddi – Fod for short." The flame-haired lad who had stared at her on the waka steps forward. He holds her gaze for a moment too long and Nari nudges his arm.

"Fod, you're being weird."

He blinks and steps back. "Uh…sorry."

Alyss stands. "We'll let your skin breathe for a while and give the honey time to work its magic. These three reprobates," she nods to the trio, "are my acolytes. I'm supposed to be training them." Beside her, Mara raises an eyebrow and flicks her gaze towards Foddi and back to Isabella, who smiles. "With varying success."

Foddi ignores the change in tone and lurches forwards. "We found out how they did it…" But he is interrupted by Alyss's suddenly raised hand. The Witch looks at Isabella.

"I need to debrief them. Do you mind waiting whilst we chat?"

Isabella shakes her head and with that, Alyss swipes her hand

63

through the air and a wall of ripples descends, stretching across the room, separating her from the Witches. Their figures become indistinct but their voices are as clear as ever. Isabella has a sudden craving for apples.

"Foddi," Alyss sighs, "haven't we discussed the need for discretion when we're near other people?"

The lad winces. "Sorry, Alyss. I just thought you'd want to know how bad it was."

The blonde Witch nods, her expression softening. "Well, she can't hear us now, so speak. Mara first."

Isabella listens intently. Assuming the rippling barrier is meant to affect both sight and sound, it appears to be defective. She stares down at her fingers, twisting the tasseled ends of the blanket covering her knees and tries to make sense of their words.

Mara crosses her arms and leans against a nearby table. "We arrived in time to see the Gate open, but there was so much smoke and cinder that we couldn't make out who opened it. It was like nothing I've seen before, as if our world and theirs were layered into one another." She looks thoughtful. "Perhaps your theory about there being ribbons of worlds which can occasionally touch, holds some truth."

"It was pretty disconcerting." Nari pats her chest. "Even from a distance I felt ill, like the world was twisting and everything that was 'right' suddenly wasn't. The Goddess knows how bad it must have been for the Anahera."

Alyss taps her lips. "How many of them came through?"

"We're not sure." Mara glances at her companions. "Maybe ninety, at most. They appeared in dribs and drabs and then staggered off into the mist. It was hard to judge."

"I'd say the slavers caught maybe forty or so." Nari's expression darkens. "They were waiting with cell wagons and they weren't gentle. We kept well back until they were gone." Her tone is laced with guilt. "You did say not to engage!"

64

Alyss nods. "I did. We need information, not hassle."

Isabella bristles.

They could have rescued Magnus and the others but chose not too?

She catches herself just in time, pulling in a breath to steady herself.

"When we had a chance, we checked the pillars." Mara pauses. The memory is not a pleasant one. "There was blood everywhere – halfway up each pillar and pooling in the trigger-sigils dug into the peat. Every step I took, blood seeped over my boots."

Alyss's expression tightens. "Drw-ad, then."

The acolytes look at one another.

"Maybe. We located the source of the blood. Three stacks of bodies, taller than me."

"I counted three hundred." Foddi's voice is quiet. "All slaves, judging by their scars."

Isabella forgets to breathe.

People died to pull us through the Gate?

Her stomach twists and she feels nauseous. She grips the blanket tightly.

The Witch frowns. "Why 'maybe'?"

It is Nari who answers. "We found Drw-ad bodies too – seven nailed with hardbolts to each stone pillar." Alyss stares at her as she continues. "Their hands and throats were slit and it looked like every skin-sigil had been opened. Each Drw-ad was surrounded by scorch marks. I think that's where all the ash and cinder in the air came from."

"Seven makes a brood." Alyss murmurs. "So, two whole broods?"

Mara nods and opens a pouch strapped under her arm. She pulls out a stack of vials wrapped carefully in leather.

"I took samples, but I'm pretty sure they're from the same broods. There was a mix of Black, White and Red. The Drw-ad don't go in for self-sacrifice. This is something new."

65

Alyss sighs. "Submit your data and we'll discuss this further. I want to know who'd go to such trouble to acquire the Anahera. If those cold, white bastards are behind it, we need to know why, but if someone's bumping off the Drw-ad, then we'll have to make sure they don't think it's us. I don't want another war."

The two young women make to move off, but Foddi remains. They glance at him.

"Something else?"

His eyes flick towards Isabella. "There's something odd about that one."

Nari snorts. "She's from another world ya eejit, of course she's odd."

"No," he frowns, "something else. Didn't you see it?"

Alyss sighs. "Fod, you're being obscure again – we've talked about this. Spit it out."

A look of chagrin crosses his freckled face. "Sorry, old habits." He steadies himself. "When we left the Windpyre waka, she tripped and grabbed the Tree. It reacted like it was in shock. It started paying attention to her. When has that ever happened before?"

The Witch crosses her arms.

"Never."

They turn and stare at the shadowy form of Isabella, who gazes resolutely down at her fingers, picking at the tassels of the blanket.

Alyss claps her hands. "I'll see what I can find out. You lot, shoo." As the acolytes leave the room, she waves a hand and the barrier dissipates.

"Right, let's have a look." She inspects Isabella's feet and seems satisfied. Snagging a pair of socks from the trolley, she edges them onto each foot. "These have healing properties too. Now," she holds up a finger, "don't move. I'll be back in a minute."

Isabella leans back and rubs her forehead, struggling to assimilate what she has just heard, however she is interrupted as Alyss reappears carrying a pair of sturdy tan leather boots.

66

"No woman should make her way through the world without a good pair of boots." She narrows her eyes. "You never know when you'll need to move fast and far. *Always* make sure you're prepared."

Isabella blinks, wondering if the Witch is suggesting what she thinks she is. Alyss slides the boots onto Isabella's feet and ties the laces. The boots are supple and comfortable. She stands back, hands on hips.

"I'll be honest, having you here is a potential boon. Among our other functions, Sisterhood Haven Holms act as research centres. We collect data on as many species as we can and act as Hjaltland's storehouse of knowledge. I've never met an Anahera before and I'm fascinated to know what sort of abilities you possess. May I have your permission to take some samples?"

Isabella's eyes widen. "You want to experiment on me?"

"Yes. Well, pieces of you at least. A few skin samples, a couple of vials of blood, a scan or two." Her tone is gentle but there is a practical depth to it, along with an expectation of assent.

Despite her misgivings, Isabella has never been good at saying 'no' to maternal pressure. "Fine. You might as well go ahead. Call it a fair exchange for rescuing me from my feet." She sighs. Alyss smiles in response and sets to work.

Sometime later, when Isabella's stomach has begun to remind her of the importance of food, Alyss helps her up.

"I take it you're hungry. There'll be a meal waiting for you in the pub."

The whiff of cigars intrudes and Captain Bannerman appears in the doorway, leaning against the frame.

"I've got something to show you, then we can eat." He looks down at her new boots and grunts, before turning away and flicking a hand for her to follow.

"Is that it? A grunt?" Isabella glances at Alyss. The Witch pats her on the arm.

"You can't expect much, he's a bit special." The two women grin

67

at each other.

Isabella's first few steps are tentative but the pain has finally gone. Bannerman waits beside an open door in the glass wall, motioning her through. The first glow of sunset has settled over the garden, adding a curious luminosity to the white-washed walls of the buildings. The Captain leads her along a path through the raised beds, the scent of rosemary, chive and basil rising to meet her as her hand brushes across their tips. At the far edge of the garden is a courtyard which backs on to the stables and pacing back and forth across it is an enormous beast.

It is feline, with thick grey fur and a sinuous twist to its powerful body as it turns, its long tail swishing in irritation. It resembles a lynx, though its shoulders rise to just above Isabella's head. When it catches sight of the approaching humans it sits on its haunches, waiting. The large head tilts slightly, furry ears topped with feathery tufts flicking speculatively.

Isabella stops in her tracks. It is not so much the sight of the beast which floors her, rather it is the sensation of images and feelings not her own suddenly washing over her. Strange, fractured annoyance gives way to a feeling of inquiry and images of the Gate, the Citadel and the Sandsound mountains crowd into her mind. She slaps her hands to her face and gasps. The Captain turns and catches her just before she falls.

"Whoah! I forgot you've never met a marron before." He lowers her to her knees, crouching beside her. "Proudleap, can you pull back a bit?"

The alien sensations recede and Isabella finds she can breathe again. She looks up at Bannerman. "What. The. Hell?"

"Just take a minute. First contact with a marron can be a little intense." His gravel voice holds a hint of amusement. After a short space to catch her breath, she waves her hand and he helps her to rise. She takes another look at the beast.

Proudleap holds its large, wide head steady, the only motion

68

coming from long whiskers drifting around its muzzle. It returns her stare, light green eyes seemingly unimpressed. Then it winks.

"He'll be carrying you to the Citadel tomorrow." Bannerman indicates that she should step forward. "Proudleap, this is your fare."

An image of scales, tipping back and forth with a heavy weight on one side flashes into Isabella's mind but although she winces, she finds the shock isn't quite so great. The inference however, is.

"Oi, I'm not *that* heavy!" She plants her hands on her hips. "There's no need to be rude."

Bannerman snorts and the tip of the marron's tail flicks.

"Wait, I'm going to ride him?" She turns to the Captain, suddenly worried.

He nods. "There's a special saddle. I'll show you tomorrow, but now," he claps his hands and rubs them, "time to eat." He steps up to Proudleap, who towers above him, and pats his shoulder. "Thanks mate, see you tomorrow."

The beast tips his head in assent and an image of a juicy steak flicks into Isabella's mind. He rises and strolls towards the entrance to the stables, powerful muscles sliding beneath the lush grey fur.

"Marrons can actually carry heavy weights," Bannerman smirks at her, "and their strength and agility makes them perfect for ferrying people around the city." He indicates towards a wooden door leading back into the pub and they move towards it. "They hire themselves out but they don't come cheap. They're the most comfortable and effective way to travel around here."

The early evening air holds a distinct chill and the warmth of the inn is a welcome relief. Alyss appears from behind the bar and shoos them to a table near the window. Several waitresses bring out a collection of little pots and platters, each containing a new delicacy. One plate holds a stack of small, round floury pancakes which resemble tortillas, another contains a corn sauce topped with scallops. Isabella lifts a lid on a clay dish to discover roasted asparagus with wild nettles, dark, juicy cubes of meat, dotted with melted cheese.

Bannerman dives into each dish, scooping up spoonfuls and depositing them on his plate.

Alyss sashays forth from the kitchen, dandling a little glass vial filled with tiny red seeds and Bannerman rubs his scarred hands together in aggressive delight. Isabella is already enjoying the layers of flavours and the gentle burn of some sort of chili spice, so she watches with interest as the Captain carefully separates one of the tiny seeds with a pair of slender tweezers, before mixing it in with his food. She asks him what it is and he grins.

"Like to try it?"

The barmaid bringing a top-up of cider looks horrified. "Don't say yes, that stuff's lethal!"

Bannerman sneers. "Don't mind Danala, she's a kill-joy. No sense of adventure."

Danala shakes her head and mouths, "nooo!"

Ignoring her, Bannerman spears a small piece of meat from the plate in which the single seed is mixed. He watches Isabella keenly as she sniffs it and then pops it into her mouth. At first, there is no heat, just the pleasant flavour of marinated lamb and something like coriander, but then it builds and builds and builds...as does the Captain's smug grin. As she gasps and chokes, the barmaid hurries back with a little painted glass filled with liquid.

"I knew it! You can't hold your spice!" The scarred man across from her laughs and slaps the table. Isabella decides she prefers him when he's being dour.

The sweet scent of fennel drifts briefly across the table as Danala murmurs a tiny spell over the mixture and it bubbles and clouds like dry ice. "I know it's hard, but sip it."

Isabella is grateful as the liquid rapidly begins to cool her down and when she has finally regained the ability to speak, she gasps.

"What the hell is wrong with you?"

He merely grins and asks if she wants the prawns in front of her, before skewering two of them and plonking them on his own plate.

His good mood is ruined however, by a sudden whirring noise, a flash of gold and a splash as something lands heavily in his mug of beer. Isabella's sleeve is drenched with yeasty bubbles.

"For fuck's sake!" He lowers his fork into his mug and pulls it back out. Clinging to the metal is a tiny saur, covered in sodden golden feathers, it's bat-like wings drippling beer all over the table. It burps.

"Danala!" Bannerman barks, outraged.

Isabella is stunned.

An actual dragon?

Her companion is not so enamoured. He is even less impressed when he sees her using her napkin to pat the little beast dry then scratch him behind a tiny, pointed ear.

He sighs. "We'll never get rid of the bugger now."

The saur croons happily as Isabella scratches his chest, wrapping his tail around her finger. Without warning, he twists, sharp teeth nipping her flesh and drawing pinpricks of blood.

"Ow! You little shit!" Isabella reacts instinctively and flicks him across the table. He rolls then steadies himself with sharply curved claws, digging into the wood. Bannerman prods him with his fork, eliciting a tiny snarl in response.

"They're like cats, Isabella." He explains. "Saurs love attention, until they don't. They'll use you for what they want then turn on you. This one," he prods harder, pushing the little beast to the edge of the table, "is a rampant alcoholic. Don't encourage him." With that, the saur slides off the table and flaps away, somewhat erratically.

"O…kay," is all she can manage as Danala appears with a small bandage, an amused expression and a fresh pint for Bannerman.

Isabella discovers that the Mutinous Piglet is just as busy in the evening as during the day. Tall flame heaters flicker near each outside table, lending the Piglet a welcoming glow. It has become a rallying point for many of the Uhlan and their captured Anahera as they drift in in small groups. Isabella is perched beside one of the outside tables, snuggled in a pale green yargswool cloak and watching Mara, Nari and Foddi check on the latest arrivals. There are a number of injuries which need attention, from both the Anahera and the Uhlan. Some captives are bound at the wrists and one man is chained by the ankle. He is battered, his dark hair falling over his eyes but still stands, proud and defiant.

Isabella inspects each new Anahera carefully, hoping to see Magnus, Mairi or one of the other Sandsound villagers, yet her eyes are drawn inexorably back to the glittering lump of the Citadel, shimmering against the last golden slivers of sunset in the distance. She shakes her head to distract herself, glances back towards the road and is stunned. Clopping tiredly into the light of the lamps is a large mare and perched upon her back is someone Isabella never thought to see again.

"Lianne!" Isabella gapes then rears up, scurrying across the courtyard as the blonde woman slides off the horse with a "whoop!" The two throw themselves into an embrace. She is being escorted by a dark-skinned female Captain whose hair is plaited into thick, glinting braids. She exudes a practical air and is clearly at ease with command. Hands planted on her hips, she stares in askance at the two women.

"This is Isabella. She and I grew up together." Lianne explains, once she has let go of her friend. "Captain Dae here kept me alive through all this madness."

Isabella holds out a hand and the woman slaps her calloused hand around her wrist, making the Anahera blink and fumble the greeting. The Captain grins.

"Call me Delilah. Good to meet you. I'll let you two catch up if you promise not to wander off." She looks at Lianne. "I think I deserve a beer, don't you?"

The blonde Anahera grins back and Delilah strides away to greet Alyss warmly. The Witch indicates towards the growing group of

Uhlan lounging around the far tables and the Captain moves off with renewed purpose. Alyss calls the two Anahera over and they sit at a table near the door, summoning Danala who appears with ceramic mugs, a carafe of cider and a plate of fried salt and pepper squid for them.

"How can you be here too? The Gate opened in Shetland!" Isabella is still struggling to process the sudden appearance of her oldest friend.

Lianne shakes her head. "I was at the Mountain Heart music festival near Palmy. I climbed the hill to get a better view of the site and take some pictures and all of a sudden these freaky clouds descended and everything went to hell." She takes a sip of cider and adds, "I'm glad I was wearing my walking boots – we hiked over a bloody mountain range!"

Alyss clears her throat and looks significantly at Isabella, who waves a hand and looks embarrassed.

"I know, I know."

The Witch pulls up a large high-backed chair and joins them. "So, you weren't in the same place when you came through the Gate?"

Lianne shakes her head. "Isabella was in the Northern Hemisphere, way up in the Shetland Islands. I was at the arse-end of the Southern Hemisphere, in the North Island of Aotearoa."

"More than one Gate opened on the other side?"

"Quite a few more, I'd say." Lianne nods and points towards a young woman sitting quietly under a tree, watching everyone very carefully. "She's from Japan." She motions to an older man, who sits at a nearby table cautiously sniffing the contents of the pint mug in front of him, then throwing it back. "He's Estonian." Finally, she nods towards the man with the shackle on his ankle, the chain running up to the belt of a sour-faced blonde soldier, her hair in tight braids. "I think he's from Chile. He fought back when he was taken."

A derisive snort sounds from behind them and Isabella twists to see Captain Bannerman leaning against the wooden post holding up the awning, arms folded across his broad chest and glaring at her with a sharply raised eyebrow.

Isabella holds up both hands. "I said I was sorry!" His other eyebrow arches and her shoulders slump. "You're never going to let this go, are you?"

He pushes himself from the post and leans over, plucking up her mug of bright cider and swigging it back. "Nope." He growls and walks away with the mug towards the other soldiers.

Alyss and Lianne stare at her.

"What was that about?" Her blonde friend gapes.

Isabella winces. "The Chilean dude isn't the only one who fought back."

"Izzy, what did you do?"

She sighs reluctantly and waves a hand. "I may have...kneed him in the balls."

Alyss chokes on her mouthful of cider and Lianne throws her head back and cackles.

"Ow!" The Witch coughs. "That went up my nose."

"Hey, we came to an understanding in the end!" Isabella shrugs.

"Yes, we can see that." Alyss nods towards Bannerman as she fills each mug.

The Anahera stares at his broad back and feels the good humour dissipate. She curls a hand around the cool clay mug and looks down.

"Actually," she admits, "he has been kind to me. Well, apart from pinning me to the ground, jabbing a needle in my arm..." Across the table, Lianne winces and reflectively rubs her arm, her own experience still fresh. "Shackling me and dragging me across a mountain..." She picks at the mug with her fingernail. "He killed two marauders to protect me."

She frowns as the image rears up again; the snarl and the reek of sweat, the knife ripping through flesh and the guttural bubbling of a man drowning in his own blood. "And he saved me from hypothermia."

74

"That's his job – to protect you." Alyss shrugs. "Anahera are valuable commodities."

Isabella flinches, once again feeling painfully cold and lost, even with one of her oldest friends sitting across from her. She has laughed with the man, struggled with him, made some kind of connection. He has become the one solid point in a drifting sea, but if Alyss's assessment is right, then there is nothing there to hold on to in this strange, terrifying world.

"Even with those scars on his face, he's still kinda hot." Lianne stares after him speculatively. "I mean, look at those arms…"

Suddenly, the bound Chilean standing near the soldiers, drops to one knee. Exhaustion is written all over him but as he bends, his jacket lifts and a flowering of dark blood can be seen through the shirt covering his lower back.

"Dammit." Alyss rises and makes her way swiftly to him, joined by Nari who has been working her way through the newcomers' ailments. The Witch makes a circling motion with her hands and the chains securing the man slip to the ground. She and Nari swiftly help him inside.

Lianne shakes her head and leans forward, lowering her voice. "Have you noticed something weird about these people?"

Isabella stares at her. "Lianne, look where we are! Everything is weird!"

The blonde woman waves a hand, dismissively.

"No, you twit, pay attention." She nods towards Delilah, telling an obscene joke in the corner. "They all seem to have a bit of…magic…power, whatever you want to call it, right?"

Isabella lifts her chin in assent.

"When Delilah created fire with her bare hands…" Lianne pauses for a moment and shakes her head, murmuring, "I can't believe I'm saying that out loud." She inhales, pulling herself together. "Whenever I saw her use 'magic', there was a definite scent, like a sudden burst of eucalyptus when you rub a leaf between your fingers,

75

and when Alyss undid that man's chains just then, there was a really strong whiff of apples."

Isabella frowns and looks towards Bannerman, lounging in the same corner and laughing at Delilah's joke.

"Aside from those pungent little cigars he insists on chain-smoking, my Captain smells…spicy. Kind of like cardamom."

Lianne smirks. "*Your* Captain?"

Isabella shrugs. "I'm his prisoner, aren't I?" She watches her friend's face suddenly pinch with tension.

"I'm trying not to think about that, Izzy. I'm afraid I'll have some sort of 'episode' if I do." Lianne flicks her ponytail over to the front and begins to comb through it with her fingers, an old sign of nerves. "What do you think they've got in store for us when we reach that city?"

Isabella finds she has been unconsciously gritting her teeth and now her jaw has begun to ache. She rubs her cheek to ease it. "No idea, but then again, I haven't got the most talkative of captors." She leans forward. "But we're not weaklings. We've carved lives and careers of our own and we know how to survive."

Lianne nods. "True, but we learned the rules early enough to know how to break them and get away with it and we've had immense freedom all our lives." She lifts her hands, palms up. "Nothing makes sense here." She thinks for a moment then sits straighter, a hint of steel behind her eyes.

"But you're right, we're more than capable of survival. We've just got to learn how to work whatever they throw at us to our advantage."

Isabella smiles grimly. She has always looked to Lianne's more steady influence and there is a real strength to the woman that her soft appearance belies. She is kind and generous, but ruthless when it comes to protecting herself and those she cares for. Isabella pours another mug of cider for them both, trying to grasp a little of her friend's pragmatism.

One by one, the Uhlan escort their captives to their rooms for the night, each taking care to lock the door before moving back down to the pub to celebrate. Delilah motions to Lianne who reluctantly follows her.

Bannerman lifts his chin, indicating the door. "Come on you, bed time." For once, his rough voice holds no hint of threat. Isabella sighs and rises, allowing herself to be herded inside.

The Captain pilots her through the crowd and up the curving wooden stairs to the guest level. The corridor is wide and pleasantly lit. One side contains guest chambers, the other is flanked by a long veranda. They walk to the end and Bannerman opens the final door. The room is warm, a fire flickering in the grate. Two single beds sit waiting, a large chest placed at the end of each. Bannerman's armour sits on one, a neat pile of new clothes for Isabella on the other. A window looks out over the starlit roofs of the complex.

"Make yourself comfortable." He waves a hand vaguely. "I'm sure you'll find what you need." He watches as Isabella stares around the room. She wraps her arms around herself and suddenly she seems smaller, a solitary figure in the glow of the fire. The heavy ball in his chest twists as he catches the expression on her face but he throws it off, slapping the doorframe with his hand to cover himself.

"I'll be downstairs." He turns and shuts the door firmly, striding down the corridor, his hand moving unconsciously to the pommel of his sword.

Isabella drops to the bed, rubbing her hands over her face. Despite the pleasant surroundings, she feels the room contract around her, the warmth from the fire almost suffocating.

I can't do this.

She tries to suppress the fear but it fizzes up into her throat, so she takes a deep breath and holds it, squeezing her eyes shut. It is just enough to pull some control back to the surface. Isabella opens her eyes and glances at the window.

Rising, she moves to it and peers out over the rooftops. Her fingertips drift to the window latch but when she twists it, she finds it locked. She cocks her head, glancing at the door as a sudden realization catches her.

He did not lock the door.

She riffles through the stack of clothing, selecting a dark blue woolen jacket and pulling it on. Moving to the door, she tries the handle and with painful slowness pushes it open, peering down the empty corridor. From the stairwell at the far end comes a glow of lamplight and the chatter of Uhlan, occasionally punctuated by the roar of laughter. Isabella steps carefully across the floor, her new boots making no sound on the wood. She reaches for the nearest veranda door, slipping through. The veranda shutters are open and the cold night air is a welcome shock. It serves to invigorate her, sharpening her senses. She steps to the railing and peers down. The building curves inwards at this point, with a narrow-shadowed instep before the walkway connects to the next circular building behind. Isabella smiles grimly when she sees a vine-covered trellis attached to the wall.

Throwing a leg over the railing, she has a horrible moment as her questing foot finds nothing but air. Finally, her boot connects with a strut of the trellis below and she uses the thick cords of the vines to aid her descent. There is a fair drop into the darkness at the bottom but once again her foot finds a purchase, this time on a covered water butt, before she finally drops to the ground. She takes a moment in the shadows to catch her breath, feeling wildly proud of herself. Climbing has never been one of her talents.

She peers around the corner of the building and scans the road. The night air has driven the remaining patrons inside and the area is empty. Isabella takes another deep breath and dives across the road, slipping through the low bushes on the other side then picks her way through clumps of pale tussock stretching down towards the river.

The gnarled branches of winter-stripped trees loom dark against the night sky and unfamiliar stars glitter far above. She focuses on the sound of the river, lifting her skirt above the drifting grasses and peering at the ground. She is concentrating so hard on not falling over that she does not notice the threat until it is too late. A deep huffing noise issues from the darkness in front of her and two puffs of breath rise into the night as a furred head appears and she is stopped in her tracks by the enormous grey marron.

A sickening sensation of failure floods her and she is overwhelmed. The alien feeling forces her to one knee with a grunt and she slides her fingers through her hair, gripping it tightly as she struggles to throw off the attack.

Far behind, Bannerman ambles out through the door of the Piglet, ready for a smoke and forbidden yet again from doing so inside. He leans against the awning post, shielding his spark from the breeze. Just as he is about to inhale, the marron's vision of Isabella, hair flaring with the motion of her escape, pulses into his mind.

"*Fuck*." He drops the cigar and breaks into a run, punching through the bushes and scooting through the tussock on the other side.

She's at it again!

However, his burn of anger fades when he spots her stricken form up ahead. He slows to a trot, knowing the power of a marron's censure, but to his surprise Isabella surges to her feet with a snarl.

Her rage punches through the gossamer veil of the marron's thoughts and she tenses, ready to dodge around it…or fight. The beast's eyes widen in surprise but before she can take a step, Bannerman's hand wraps around her wrist and he yanks her backwards, his grip like a steel band. His voice rasps in the icy night air.

"He won't let you pass – he's been contracted to take you to the Citadel tomorrow and he's not going to lose such a lucrative fare."

Her eyes narrow, rage still flooding her limbs. She flicks her arm, twisting out of the weak point in his grip then punches outwards, aiming for his throat. But he is ready for it and catches her fist, using the momentum to pull her round and push her arm up her back. He grabs the other flailing wrist and does the same, forcing her to her knees.

"Stop."

She is pinioned by the tearing pain and struggles not to fall face-first into the dirt. Yet what quenches her rage and desire to fight on is not the pain but the return of the marron's thoughts, washing over her. The feeling is imbued with layers of inevitability and acceptance, pushing her further down. Behind, Bannerman feels her resistance ebb and her head droop. He slowly releases her arms and steps back.

Hair hanging in curtains about her face, Isabella pushes herself to her feet. The marron's thoughts recede, replaced by her own despair.

Instead of his usual irritation, the Captain finds he is actually impressed by her determination and a little surprised by her sudden lack of resistance.

"Nice try, but you don't want me hunting you either, girlie."

She doesn't move, refusing to look at him. Instead, she rubs her aching arms. He takes a step forward. His voice is firm, but softer than usual.

"I don't want to do this to you, but if I have to shackle you and drag you into that city, I will. You and I have no choice in this."

When her voice comes, it is cracked. "You do, Eric. All you have to do is choose to step back and let me go."

"I can't defy my King."

No matter how much I may want to.

"Look, I promise you that what's waiting for you in the Citadel is far better than being owned by the slavers or starving to death out there." He motions into the darkness.

She glances back at the marron, who stares at her. His controlling influence has evaporated and in its place is the soft drift of sympathy. She grits her teeth. If she cannot thwart the Captain, then she will have to wait until he is no longer anywhere near before she tries another escape. Patience has never been one of her strengths, but she realizes it may be her only option.

80

"Fine. I'll go back with you."

He raises an eyebrow. "No more punching?"

Isabella rolls her eyes. "Can we just do this?" She moves back up the slope, stepping between the clumps of tussock whilst shaking out her aching wrists.

The marron comes to stand beside Bannerman and the two share a look. A shimmer of feline regret drifts over the man and he nods.

"I know. Thanks for your help anyway."

The beast blows a stream of breath into chill night air and turns, his form slipping smoothly into the darkness.

Back in the chamber, Isabella showers and prepares herself for bed. Eric leaves to have one last drink with his squad downstairs, taking care to lock the door firmly behind him. Dressed in a pale nightgown, Isabella stands at the window for some time, staring out over the roofs to the mountains beyond. Eventually, she sighs and returns to the bed, but sleep does not come and she sits up again, turning to perch on the edge of the bed.

After some time and several more pints the Captain returns, a little drunk now that he is so close to the end and feeling enormously cheered by the food and the fact that his captive appears to have given in. He clatters against the chest at the end of Isabella's bed and mumbles "*whoops*", grinning as he looks up. His good cheer fades when he sees her staring at him, arms clasped around her body. Her green eyes are dark with fear, something he had not expected from her.

"Hey," he holds up his hands, "it's okay." He realizes how weak that sounds so drops onto the bed opposite her, pulling off his boots, resting his wrists on his knees and leaning forward. He is a little thrown by how vulnerable she looks.

"I'm scared, Eric." She doesn't want to admit this out loud but a heavy wad of fear has lodged itself in her throat and she feels as if she might suffocate if she doesn't let it out.

Bannerman is surprised at her honesty, but he reaches over and

81

takes both her hands.

Isabella blinks. His skin is rough and calloused but warm. He smells of beer, soap and faintly of the small cigars he favours.

"You're a stroppy mare, but tougher than you think. I'll take you as far as I can, protect you when I can." He leans forward, holding her gaze. "Look how many people you've charmed since you fell through that Gate: A whole Windpyre crew, a lizard, the Sisterhood, a bunch of women notorious for being bloody difficult to please..."

And one bad-tempered bastard who's falling apart.

"Yeah, but..." She begins. The fear still threatens to choke her.

He grips her hands more tightly, vexed by her vulnerability. He has no room for caring about an Anahera, despite the increasingly nagging feelings he is having.

"Yeah but nothing. I've watched you face down those slaver shits, you gave me run for my money..." His thighs tighten unconsciously at the memory of her sharp knee. "And you hung on through a raging storm that should have killed you. You're a feisty mare and you can cope with whatever they throw at you."

Bannerman lets go of her hands and slaps his knees. "Now get some bloody sleep. We've still a way to go before we reach the Citadel tomorrow." He motions for her to lie down and to his surprise, she actually obeys.

He covers her with the blankets and lies back with an audible sigh. His muscles ache and his head spins a little. With the practiced ease of a soldier who can sleep anywhere, he quickly succumbs, the sandalwood scent of her wrapping around him.

Isabella curls up under the soft blankets, breathing in the now familiar nutmeg of the yargswool. She gazes at the Captain's sleeping form and concentrates on breathing, in and out, in and out. Slowly, her aching muscles unclench. The horrible ball of cold and loss deep in her chest begins to soften as she tries to match her own breathing with his, as if to lure her body into sleep, even though he begins to snore. He is gruff, bad-tempered, rude and capable of incredible violence, but she is beginning to gain an inkling of the kind of man he is beneath it all. There is a surprising thread of compassion running through him. She looks up at the ceiling and sighs.

I know he's a bloody nuisance, but I wish I could keep this one around.

Isabella grimaces in the darkness.

Although, [6]Stockholm Syndrome can't entirely be ruled out.

She goes back to trying to match her breaths with his and slowly falls asleep.

---

[6] *Stockholm Syndrome* - feelings of trust or affection felt in some cases of kidnapping/hostage-taking by a victim towards their captor.

5. THE HARDEST CHOICE

The Captain wakes in the early dawn, dresses and then sits, watching the Anahera breathe softly in sleep. He realises something. Although her behaviour irritates him, increasingly when she is near he feels anchored, as if she is the one solid point in a world which is beginning to make less and less sense. He has spent years being a loyal and devoted member of the King's Own Uhlan, believing the Citadel and its monarchs to be the guiding lights in a dark world and the only real opposition to the Drw-ad. He wonders when that had begun to slip, when he had first started to lose faith and a cold space had begun to gape inside him, when the few good things in his life had begun to fall into it. The fact that a simple conversation with Emmeline, could prompt a moment where he almost considered an act of rebellion plays heavily on his mind. He does not want to let her go, but he has no choice. He is almost grateful when the Anahera begins to stir.

Isabella opens her eyes to see that the Captain is already dressed, complete with snug armour. He stands and flicks a towel at her.

"Get up. I'll give you fifteen minutes to get ready or there's no break of fast." He stalks to the door and disappears downstairs.

Isabella sighs and stretches. She pulls on a pair of soft grey trews, a loose white shirt and a dark grey fitted jacket packed for her by Emmeline then combs her fingers through her hair, wincing as they catch a series of knots. Slipping her feet into the boots, she quickly shoves the rest of the clothes into the accompanying bag and scurries downstairs. She has a feeling the Captain wasn't kidding about the

84

breakfast.

Alyss greets her warmly and leads her to an outside table where Eric sits clutching a steaming mug of black chaoua, his lips already clamped around a slender cigar.

"At this time of the morning?" Isabella needles him. He ignores her, blowing a stream of smoke upwards into the wintry morning air.

The Witch appears with a plate of pastries and a mug of strong, milky tea for Isabella. She sits with them, leaning on the table and watching the Uhlan load their Anahera onto a selection of horses and carts.

Delilah strolls into view, encased in grey armour, her black braids plaited neatly over her head and laced together at the nape of her neck. She is leading two horses, including the mare from the night before. Perched upon the mare is Lianne. She clutches the pommel tightly and Isabella knows it is through fear of what lies ahead rather than any lack of riding ability. Lianne is a consummate horsewoman, having led numerous treks through the rugged landscape of Aotearoa over the years. The blonde Anahera looks down at Bannerman.

"Good luck getting her on a horse – she's a bloody nightmare."

Isabella sniffs. "Damn things are too high off the ground and they bounce." Lianne rolls her eyes.

"Not a problem – we're travelling in style." Captain Bannerman points behind them to where Proudleap is padding into view. Lianne gapes.

At the sight of the enormous beast, Isabella twists the bottom of her shirt in worry but Alyss notices and pats her hand.

"Marrons are an incredibly safe ride. You just sit there and they do all the work." At Isabella's dubious look she continues. "You can't fall out – look." She points to the marron as he pads to a halt in front of them.

Strapped to his back is an incredible contraption, part saddle, part stylishly curving chair. The harness wraps under the beast and around his chest, allowing him complete freedom of movement but keeping

85

the passenger secure. He huffs at Isabella, pulsing her an image, an instruction on how to get in.

She turns to Alyss. "Thank you…" she begins, but the blonde Witch pulls her into a warm hug.

"Remember, this is a sanctuary," she murmurs into Isabella's hair. "If all else fails, you'll be welcome here." She pulls back and speaks more loudly, indicating to Lianne to include her too. "I've attached a bag full of supplies to your saddles. It includes a moon cup for your monthlies. The instructions are with it. Good luck and don't let the Gentry grind you down." She moves to hug first Delilah, then Bannerman. "Look after yourselves."

Isabella steps closer to Proudleap and slides her hand up the half-circle of the pommel. She places her foot in the stirrup and hauls herself up, slinging her other leg ineptly over the seat. Bannerman appears beside the beast and shows her how to clip the leg restraints around her calves. He points to a pair of long gauntlet wraps hanging either side of the pommel.

"Those are for when things speed up, or you're climbing a wall. We'll be going at a sedate pace, so you won't need them today."

"Climbing a wall?" Isabella swallows.

He nods. "The Citadel is basically a series of huge terraces stretching up the mountain. If you need to get anywhere fast, a marron is the best way to do it. Sit back."

She does so and jolts in surprise as the curved seatback behind her adjusts to her body, extending enough to support her.

On the other side, Delilah has mounted up and is grinning at her reaction, her horse shifting impatiently beneath her. "Don't look so worried, it's not going to eat you. The saddle is intuitive – it's designed to keep you safe." She looks over at Bannerman.

"Jammy bastard!" She exclaims. "How did you swing a marron contract as well as a Pyre flight?"

Bannerman taps the side of his nose in response then strides quickly away, returning with a horse of his own. He mounts up, nods

86

to Proudleap and together, the group set off, joining the procession winding towards the Citadel. Isabella tries to relax.

The wide road follows the Bonhoga River as it winds its way to the sea. Spreading out before them are extensive crofts, framed by long stone walls. Each one is different; an orchard in one, a field of stubble telling of a recent harvest, a paddock dotted with small, black-faced sheep. Further back, at the base of the foothills, Isabella can see a herd of yarg cantering across the heather-covered ground. Houses dot the landscape, in much the same design as those in the city of Aith. The roofs curve over each building like an up-turned boat, dipping down to low windows and white-washed walls. Each dwelling has a garden surrounded by high stone barriers. Bannerman notices her gaze.

"We've strong winds in Hjaltland. Everything is built to withstand them...or it doesn't stand for long." He chuckles. "Just you wait 'till you experience your first Storm. That'll be an education."

"I've experienced plenty of storms before," she replies, "even the occasional hurricane. Sure, they can be dangerous but..."

"Any with winds that can strip the flesh from your bones?" He asks cheerfully. Isabella's mouth snaps shut. "No? Like I said, it'll be an education."

The wind picks up and she shivers. He catches this and tugs his scarf from his neck, handing it to her. Isabella smiles gratefully and wraps it around her own throat, pulling it up to cover her ears.

After an hour or so the fields grow smaller and the houses more numerous until finally the procession takes them through low-lying suburbs. Uhlan ride back and forth along the column, chivvying wagons and rubber-necking pedestrians out of the way. The Citadel dominates the landscape as the ground begins to slope steadily upwards and Isabella finds she cannot look away. A series of huge terraced walls snake around the conical peak. Isabella counts ten but Eric explains that some contain smaller terraces within.

"It's an old volcano. They use the energy from it to power the city.

87

They've been taming the beast for centuries." He pulls his horse sideways, avoiding a cart laden with turnips that has stopped suddenly and Isabella distinctly hears him mutter, "...the odd eruption now and then wouldn't go amiss."

As they reach the city proper, the houses change from soft curves to a more familiar block form, pressing closely together along increasingly busy streets. At intervals, covered walkways arch over the street, the weak sunlight failing to ward off the deep chill of shadow as they pass underneath. The crowds thicken, faces staring intently at each Anahera and strident voices make loud, critical assessments of them. Others push by, completely unimpressed and only focused on their own business.

This is overwhelming enough, but the thing that really gets to Isabella is the smell. She feels like her nostrils and throat are being stripped. Clashing chemical scents of manic daisy, acidic violet and cloying rose compete for attention with the nasal equivalent of baseball bats. Many of the odours are familiar, but twisted and sharpened with a chemical edge.

Bannerman hears her cough and looks up to see her covering her mouth and nose with his scarf, her eyes watering. "What's wrong with you now?"

"Eric," she gasps, "that's awful."

He has never enjoyed the reek of the Gentry but he is used to it. After the far softer aromas of the apple-scented Haven Holm and the fresh, wild scents of the Windpyre ship, he can imagine that it is a real shock for her.

"Pure, airborne poison." Isabella murmurs. A headache is rapidly filling her head and she keeps Bannerman's scarf clamped to her face, clinging to the scent of cardamom and tobacco.

Eventually they take a sharp left onto a much quieter street which curves towards the first huge terrace. As they near the enormous black wall, Isabella sees a word picked out in large brass letters stretching above the opening:

Huljun

As the procession of captured Anahera troops through the gate of the Huljun Terrace, two figures stand on the walkway of the Powder Tower high above and watch them. They are both tall but aside from this, the two could not be more different. One is clearly at ease within his environment, blond hair plaited up over his temples and secured in a braid down his broad, muscled back. His blue eyes scan the crowd with speculative amusement.

"They're a mixed bunch, aren't they?" He grins and points a tanned finger at one of the women. "But there are a few potentials." Each knuckle is tattooed with a different symbol, the ink a vivid sky blue. The sleeve of his woollen tunic falls open to reveal a landscape of blue knotwork ink snaking up his arm.

The figure beside him is unimpressed.

"Meridian, they look wretched." He rests his white hands on the rough stone parapet and leans forward. "Can you not see? Several are in chains. That does not bode well." His voice is low and measured, with little emotion.

The blond warrior snorts. "That doesn't mean they won't scrub up well. Anyway, Bryant, I like 'em a little feisty." He turns to grin at his white-skinned friend and receives a raised eyebrow in response.

Bryant's deep blue lips are pressed together, his dark eyes glittering. He focuses on the procession below, his black hair glinting almost royal blue in the afternoon sunlight. It is pulled back in a smooth ponytail which reaches to his waist, a stark contrast to the colour of his skin.

"You will no doubt enjoy finding out at the official Reception. At least the attendants will have a little time to make something presentable out of such raw materials." He misses the wicked tint to Meridian's sudden smile.

"Indeed, old friend, we will find out together." The Prince watches

89

Bryant closely. As a race, the Drw-ad are emotionally closed, giving little away and Meridian finds getting even the smallest reaction out of him an oddly satisfying challenge. Bryant freezes then turns stiffly towards him. His low voice takes on a slightly hoarse edge.

"*We*?"

Meridian raises both eyebrows and grins, unnecessarily, cheerfully.

The Drw-ad's sudden tension is revealed by an old reflexive gesture, as he runs his hand down the front of his dark blue high-collared shirt. The material is embroidered with tiny curling saurs in black thread.

"Yes, 'we'. Father has requested your presence as well." His voice mockingly echoes the stern tones of his father. "This is a prestigious occasion, not likely repeated in our lifetimes."

Bryant's voice is strained. "Meridian, you know how I feel about such occasions."

Meridian shrugs, feeling a little sorry for his raven-haired friend. As the sole Drw-ad in the Citadel, over the years the Gentry have made real efforts to make him feel as unwelcome as possible. "King's orders, I'm afraid." He turns his back on the procession and places a reassuring hand on the Drw-ad's shoulder. "Look, I'll be there with you. You won't have to chart your way through that pool of sharks on your own."

Bryant throws the Prince a look. "Aside from those moments when you will be testing unsuspecting Anahera for suitability, you mean?"

"Come on." Meridian presses on Bryant's shoulder, ushering him away from the parapet. "Let's check in with the troop debriefing and then go and get a drink."

Bryant gives a resigned sigh and allows himself to herded towards the Uhlan barracks.

Below, the shadow deepens as the marron carries Isabella beneath the arch of the gate. Her stomach twists as the bone-aching cold adds weight to her fear. She swallows and grips the leather pommel more tightly, twisting to look behind as the light and bustle of the city disappears. This is her last chance to leap for freedom. She shifts in the saddle, her muscles tensing…and can move no further. Helplessness and a series of fractured images swamp her mind – her leap from the beast, a brief scramble and then a rough soldier's hand, reaching for her throat and pinning her to the ground. Proudleap's warning is clear.

The shadow lifts as they enter a wide cobbled courtyard, ringed by tall buildings carved from granite. It is already busy with soldiers, mounts and captive Anahera. They are easy to spot, their faces drawn and fearful. Bannerman leads his horse and the marron through the crowd to the edge of the nearest building.

He dismounts and holds up his hands to catch Isabella as she slides off Proudleap, straight into a pair of waiting metal cuffs which click into place around her wrists.

She stares at him. "Eric, don't do this. Don't leave me here."

"Girlie…" His rough voice cracks. "I have no choice."

"Captain Bannerman!" A voice barks from behind them. "Glad to see you're back."

The Captain glares skywards for a moment before he turns, a more appropriate expression plastered across his face. "Commander Fallon, Sir!" He snaps out a salute.

"Leave your Anahera to the guards. Let's talk about why you used Uhlan funds to buy a Pyre flight…" The grey-haired commander turns and stalks away, followed by the Captain. His voice floats over the crowd. "And why was your Anahera on a marron?"

Isabella loses sight of him as an attendant appears and yanks her towards a heavy brass door. She is shoved against another Anahera and ordered to wait. Looking up, she realizes who it is.

Lianne bumps her with her hip. "You okay?"

"Hell no." Isabella mutters.

91

"Me neither." She nods towards the figure of Delilah. "I thought about kicking her in the knee and trying to run, but I've seen her fight and "bad-ass" doesn't even begin to cover it."

Another Anahera is shoved against them, this time a tall, dark-skinned man. He looks down at Isabella.

"Please forgive me." His voice has a deep Nigerian lilt, edged with tension.

"Not your fault, mate." Isabella looks up at him with a rueful smile. It hides her growing terror. She feels Lianne shift in front of her.

"Hey! Aw, come on." Beside her crouches a black-suited attendant. After securing a shackle to her ankle he moves on to Isabella, clipping one to her ankle and threading a chain through both. She doesn't even have time to react. Glancing along the line, she sees that each pair of Anahera are being shackled together. Turning back, she realizes that the huge brass door has opened and a line of guards wait to usher them in.

The captives are prodded forwards into a large hall set up with rows of low wooden benches. High above, a vaulted glass ceiling lets in a flood of light. They are herded into place, shuffling into lines and sitting when ordered to. Lianne and Isabella grip hands.

Filing in behind the Anahera are the Uhlan who captured them. They range themselves along the far wall, watching over their charges for the last time. Hands behind her back, Delilah leans surreptitiously towards Bannerman.

"What did the Commander say?" Her voice is laced with amusement, although underneath she is concerned for her friend. Over the last couple of months, his behaviour has begun to change, his decisions increasingly reckless. She is not sure how to broach the subject with him.

He shrugs. "There was a bit of shouting but he decided to drop the charges when I said I could get him direct access to a Windpyre negotiator." An image of Kahu flickers through his mind. He can

92

imagine the contempt the big man would have for the Uhlan commander.

A figure makes his way up the steps of the dais. He wears a tailored suit of silver-grey, with the hint of a flamboyant scarlet waistcoat beneath. His mocha-skinned head is shaved and a neatly trimmed beard gives form to a weak chin. He claps his hands sharply and the hall falls silent.

"My name is Cahuil Orda. I am the Master of Ceremonies for the Citadel." His voice is as neat and clipped as his appearance, but it echoes across the room. "You were rescued from a hideous fate and ushered here by the Citadel's finest. If not for us, you would be bound, chained, abused and your future would look very bleak."

Lianne elbows Isabella in the ribs and jangles the chain attached to her foot, rolling her eyes downward at the cruel hypocrisy of his words. Isabella's lips set in a thin line. She is trying to contain the rage and fear coursing through her, with only slender success.

"As such," he continues in a pompous tone, "you owe our Citadel a great debt."

Bannerman watches his charge's eyes narrow. He half expects her to jump up and leap for Orda's throat. He is not entirely sure he would stop her. The Master of Ceremonies continues.

"As you are fresh arrivals from another world, we do not yet know the powers and insights you may possess. You are precious few, and that makes you valuable."

"I'm not a bloody Ming vase." Isabella mutters and feels her friend shift slightly next to her.

"You'd just fall off your pedestal and damage yourself anyway." Lianne murmurs back, her gaze never leaving the man on the dais, but they both sit to attention at his next words.

"And as such, you are in high demand. Our great Citadel offers you a marvellous opportunity, with the kind of prestige you could only have dreamed about in your former world."

The two women glance at one another.

93

Opportunity?

Off to the side, Captain Bannerman tenses, knowing exactly what is coming next. His eyes do not leave Isabella. The hall is silent, waiting.

"The Gentry require new and pure gene stock, therefore, you will be given a choice – either accept an offer of marriage from one of our magnificent Gentry…" His voice takes on the hint of finickety horror. "Or be taken to the slave pits of Hamnavoe and sold to the highest bidder."

Time seems to slow and the sounds dull around her. Isabella is stunned. A deep, sludgy pool of horror begins to bubble in her stomach and her chest feels tight.

As the hall erupts in uproar, Bannerman stays silent as he watches her. Yet again she does not react the way he expects. She is completely still, even as her friend frantically clutches her arm. Then she turns her head and stares straight at him, the intensity in her green eyes stunning. Rage and betrayal swirl together, angling straight at him.

How could you lead me to this?

He cannot hold her gaze for long and he looks away, pointedly staring at the Master of Ceremonies who is flapping his arms about and demanding calm. The tight knot of guilt which has been lurking in his chest suddenly expands. The pressure makes him reach up and rub his sternum, trying to ease it.

Finally, the soldiers have restored enough order for Cahuil Orda to speak.

"Really, I expected far more gratitude than this!" He snaps. "Nevertheless, you have until daybreak tomorrow to decide. Let it not be said that we are not magnanimous." He claps his hands, signalling for the attendants to fan out around the Anahera.

The captives are hauled up and led away, trooping deeper into the mountain. It is a level containing the main barracks, storage chambers and prison cells. The cells have been freshly cleared and wait with

94

heavy iron-barred doors wide open to receive new guests. Before allowing them inside, an attendant removes the shackles from each of the captives.

Following the other Anahera into the biggest cell, Isabella, Lianne and Adejola the tall Nigerian, move to the back where heavy wooden benches sit beneath a hooded window. The light has an odd quality to it and Adejola cranes his head under the hood to see why.

"Solar tube." He pulls his head back and drops onto a bench. "The light comes from a tube in the roof." He looks at the two women. "I am…was, an architect. Now…I don't know what I am."

"How is that a choice?" Lianne snarls, holding out her hands, palms up, in an echo of the Emmeline's action days before. She flicks out her left hand. "Shitty slavery…" She flicks out the right. "Or shiny slavery?" Turning, she resumes pacing. Adejola nods in agreement but it takes the blonde woman a while to register that Isabella is completely silent and still. This is not normal behaviour for her but then, Lianne muses, 'normal' may never be part of their lives again.

Isabella feels ill, as if a gaping pit has opened up inside her and every part of her is flaking off and falling in. She scrabbles desperately to find a point of anchorage. An image of Eric Bannerman flashes into her mind, standing with the other Uhlan along the edge of the hall. He did not look happy.

There is a sudden movement beyond the bars and Captain Delilah appears, motioning Lianne to move forward. The blonde Anahera moves quickly to her and they begin talking in hushed tones. And then, there he is, strolling into the cell block with a surly look on his tanned face. Isabella rises and moves to the bars.

"Why are you here, Eric?"

He avoids her eyes for a moment, his mouth quirking as if chewing on words he shouldn't let loose. Finally, he looks up. "The troop are being deployed to the East…"

Isabella's eyes narrow and her voice is sharp. "No rest for the wicked, huh?"

He forces down a snapping retort and tries again. "I wanted to check up on you before…"

But the Anahera has no intention of letting him leave without a fight.

"Eric, *you* brought me to this. You were a slave and now you've made me one too." She watches his face shut down completely at this and she knows that the knowledge has hit him hard. She feels the burn of bitter satisfaction.

Good. Suffer, you bastard.

Through the sharp silence developing between them comes the sound of someone praying. Bannerman stares past Isabella at the woman.

"What's that silly mare doing?"

Isabella's words are clipped as she tries to hold back her rancour. "She's praying, for deliverance…or strength, I guess."

The Captain snorts. "No use in praying. None of those arrogant bitches'll listen to ya, and there's no one else." He spits. "Your time's better spent preparing for what comes next."

Isabella's stare is hard.

"Because no one's going to save us, right?"

He returns her glare. "Fact of life girlie – sometimes, we can't be saved. Sometimes, there's no one coming for us. We have to save ourselves." The vicious twin scars running down his face seem to deepen and she remembers Subtle Sands Shifting's words: "You're the One Who Survived.*"* She bites her lower lip and nods.

"True. But *you* saved *me*."

He glances towards Delilah and Lianne who are talking quietly further along the cell, then he leans in towards the bars, his rough, strong hands curling around them.

"I did, but I'm not a god and I can't keep you from this."

She steps closer, wrapping her own hands around each bar, just below his. She stares into his grey eyes and sees…sadness? Or is it guilt? The acidic resentment burning in her settles a little.

96

"I know, Eric."

At his name, he frowns and she can see the fire returning to his face.

"Listen. Actually listen." His rough voice is low and fierce. "Choose carefully: no one too pretty, too staunch, too smarmy or too rich - they're always bastards, and if you get the feeling he's even a bit of a prick, then drop 'im. This is one point where you have all the power, so bloody well choose wisely. Pay attention to what they're Offering too. It'll tell you a lot about who they are as a man. Expensive don't always mean good. Choose. Wisely."

Isabella looks at his hands, rough, calloused and capable on the heavy iron bars in front of her. The memory of them lifting and supporting her on the mountainside rises and she slides her own hands up the cold metal and over his warm skin.

Her voice is very soft. "I'm going to miss you, grumpy bastard."

And then she sees it, just for a moment – a dark flicker of pain and loss. She blinks, genuinely surprised at what his normally aggressive demeanour actually hides, but as quickly as it appears, it is gone.

The Captain slides his hands from underneath hers and around to hold them one last time. "Take care of yourself, girlie. I'll be paying attention." He squeezes her hands tightly and lets go, turning abruptly on his heel and striding out of the room.

Watching him disappear, Isabella rests her head against the chill of the bars, a heavy block forming in her chest. Her anchor is detaching and leaving her to drift through a dark ocean. A slow-burning anger wells up – he brought her to this place. He knew what he was doing, what her fate would be and despite his better judgement, he did his job well.[7]

Once the final Uhlan have left, a string of attendants file in and

---

[7] Playlist: Machineheart – Stonecold.

stand waiting just beyond the bars, hands behind their backs. They are clothed in fitted black shirts and trews, each with a cross-body sash like a bandolier, studded with pockets, scissors, combs and vials.

Isabella elbows Lianne. "I have a horrible feeling about this."

"You mean that someone's going to try and run a comb through your hair? Good luck to them." Lianne tries to keep her tone light, despite her tension.

The thirty-four Anahera ranged about the main cell look up and fresh worry ripples through them as a newcomer stomps down the stairs and across the flagstones in front of the attendants. She must be all of six feet tall, solidly built with black hair in two heavy plaits down her broad front. A black linen dress is buttoned from her booted ankles to her chin and she clutches a wooden staff topped with brass bells. She turns to face them and bangs her staff on the stone floor.

"Anahera, listen up and listen well," she booms. "I am the Matron of Ministrations. I am tasked with making sure you are prepared for what is to come. For the next three days, you are mine." She begins to stride along the length of the bars. "I will explain the process and you will listen. I will give an order and you will follow it." She reaches the end of the bars and turns, slamming the staff against them. The closest Anahera flinch.

Her gaze rakes each captive. "You are certainly rough material, but we will ensure the Gentry find you at least acceptable." A young man sitting nearby looks up at her.

"So, what's going to happen to us?" Judging by his accent, he is American. His tone is cautious.

The Matron of Ministrations glares at him. "You all need a good bath, so that is our first task." She motions to the line of people behind her. "Each of you will be assigned an attendant. They will be responsible for making sure your appearance lives up to our expectations. Everyone stand!" Her bellow rebounds off the stone walls, forcing the Anahera to their feet. The cell door swings open with a clang.

"Follow me!" She turns abruptly and marches out. As one, the attendants step forward. For a collection of individuals strung with hair clips and combs, they are strangely menacing.

Lianne shrugs. "Well, she did mention a bath." She is the first to step forward, Isabella following closely behind.

They are led along a polished stone corridor, the gradient sloping gently upwards until they reach a pair of wooden doors on either side of the walkway, each inlaid with stylized mother-of-pearl clouds. The doors slide back into the walls and steam billows out into the corridor. Isabella can almost feel her hair begin to frizz in response.

The Matron's voice booms through the corridor. "Women in here," she points her staff to the left, "men in the other. No arguments."

Isabella follows Lianne through the steam, her boots squeaking on the marble floor. An attendant leads them across the space until all the Anahera women are collected before her.

"Wow." Lianne murmurs.

Before them stretches a large pool set into the floor and lined in pale marble, the ceiling above carved into a series of curved archways. The water is crystal clear, with a blue-green tint of minerals. Just above the water, small braziers hold flickering flames and high above the last of the afternoon sunlight is channelled through a series of tiny holes in the ceiling creating dapples of light across the walls. The air has a hint of sulphur about it.

The crash of bells interrupts the calm as the Matron of Ministrations strides to a halt in front of them.

"I assume you're all capable of understanding simple instructions. If not, there will be repercussions." She jangles her staff in the direction of the pool. "Hot water. Undress, get in, wash. You will find baskets of soaps to choose from. Wash everything. You have one hour."

The women look at one another and the atmosphere becomes distinctly uncomfortable.

"What, no bikinis?" A young woman with short, tousled brown hair asks.

"I do *not* feel comfortable with this." Isabella twists the edge of her shirt. She has never been good with public nudity.

"Well, you'll have to get over it." Lianne's no-nonsense voice issues from beneath her tunic as she pulls it over her head. "No one's going to be critiquing your 'bits', they're going to be under the water." She hops backwards as she pulls off a boot.

"Maybe not, but I'll be critiquing my bits. It's okay for you, you've got a fabulous body." Even as she grumps, Isabella pulls off her own jacket.

Lianne snorts. "If you've got a body that still works, then it's a fabulous body. Honestly, I'd forgotten how much you complain." She is grinning as she says this and strolls over to a bench near the wall, snagging up two enormous white, fluffy towels and throwing one to Isabella. "Here, wrap your fabulousness in this, drama queen."

Isabella performs the age-old magic trick of removing her clothes from underneath the tightly wrapped towel and leaves them in a pile on the bench. By the time she reaches the edge of the pool, Lianne is already in. Isabella stretches down a tentative toe and swooshes it through the water. It is hot, but pleasantly so. With a reluctant sigh she drops the towel and quickly steps down into the water, sliding in with a sharp intake of breath.

It is deep enough for her feet to just brush the bottom and she swims along the edge, revelling in the sensation of water on skin. Isabella closes her eyes and tilts her face upwards, stretching her arms out and turning gently. She stays like this for some time, floating blissfully in the warmth, the heat and steam obliterating all thought until her hand bumps against the side and she looks back to see a basket sitting on a shelf just above the water. She riffles through it, wrinkling her nose at the harsh chemical perfumes emanating from each soap until she finally finds one without much scent.

"Pretty bad, aren't they?" The young woman with short brown

hair appears beside her. "Name's Mich." She leans back against the wall.

"Isabella. Where are you from?"

"Copenhagen. Had an argument with my girlfriend, went for a walk to calm down and bam! No white rabbit but a bunch of weird clouds and suddenly I'm in Wonderland." She rubs her hands over her face and sighs.

Isabella winces in sympathy and holds out her hand. "Want some soap?"

The woman smiles grimly. "Is it magical? Can it transport me back?"

"Nope, but at least this one won't leave you smelling like you've been dipped in a vat of chemicals."

"Thanks." She takes the soap and lathers her hair. She has a pleasant face, albeit tightened with worry.

Lianne surfaces beside them, long, blonde hair slick against her skin. "Floating about in here, I could almost forget we're in Hell." The other two Anahera nod, but the warm water and the low murmur of women's voices around them lulls each into a semblance of calm...until they are interrupted yet again by the clanking of bells. The Matron of Ministries appears through the steam.

"Right, out you get!" She snaps. "Back to the cells for supper then bed. You have an important decision to make tomorrow."

A string of attendants appear and proceed to chivvy the women back towards the benches, where neat stacks of clothes await them. When Isabella unfurls hers she finds that it is a long, voluminous grey dress and accompanying leggings. "Um…"

"Don't moan, just put them on." The Matron stomps past. "Your original clothes will be laundered and brought back to you." Isabella hastily pulls on her boots before anyone can whisk them away.

Back in the cells, they find the men are also garbed in long grey tunics over woollen trews. Bowls of stew filled with indefinable meat are passed around and Isabella finds a seat next to Adejola. She prods the meat suspiciously with her fork.

"Try it, it is not too bad." Adejola tries to smile. She gives him a dubious look, but takes his advice. It certainly doesn't have the rich flavour of meals at The Mutinous Piglet, but it is passable.

When they have finished, an attendant appears to show them to their sleeping quarters – a series of bunks ranged in a nearby cell.

"Oh, goody, camp." Mich climbs into the bunk above Isabella's, the bedsprings creaking under even her slight form. "I'm disappointed there's no marshmallows to toast."

The young America perched on the top bunk across the floor stares at her. "How can you joke about this? It's a prison!"

She sighs. "Listen mate, we're all dealing with the same thing, but we cope in different ways. Just because I'm making light of the situation doesn't mean I don't know what's at stake."

"Attention, Anahera." The Matron's intrudes and they quickly fall silent. "You will rise early tomorrow to make your official choice. So, lights out! No talking!"

With that, darkness descends.

6. THE RECEPTION

The next morning the attendants appear again and deliver a breakfast of pastries. Isabella, normally a fan of food in any situation, struggles to force hers down. The weight of the choice she must make presses heavily upon her and the pastry in her mouth has the consistency of wallpaper paste. It was a hard night – images of her family and friends crowding her mind as loss and fear tightened around her. Judging by the sobbing from various bunks, such thoughts are not far from the minds of her companions either.

Isabella pictures her mother's worried face and a wave of grief threatens to pour over her again, but she pulls herself upright and rubs her head, trying to focus on the here and now. She is conscious of the presence of the Matron of Ministrations sitting in a large chair just beyond the bars. The woman is simmering with impatience and as soon as the last plate has been cleared, she rises. For once, she does not bellow.

"This morning, you will be taken to the Office of Contracts and Obligations. You will be accompanied by your new Attendant. There, you will make your choice – either allow the Gentry to "Offer" for you, or be sold to the highest bidder in the slave pits." Her voice softens a little. "I am aware that this may not seem like much of a choice but understand this – the Gentry are the pinnacle of Hjaltland society. You can achieve much when you are at that level. You will achieve nothing but pain at the other."

Mich, perched next to Isabella, raises her hand.

"Yes?" The Matron snaps.

"What about those of us who aren't attracted to the opposite sex? Women are my thing, not dicks." Her voice is calm but Isabella can feel the tension radiating from her. She sees several other Anahera raise their heads, listening intently.

The Matron snorts. "What an odd question. There are plenty of Gentry women for you to choose from. Female, male, between or neither - marriage is a contract between two individuals. Who they are is no matter to us." She jangles the bells on her staff and the line of attendants steps forward again. "Now, you will wait in the cell until your Attendant calls for you. If they give you an instruction, you will follow it."

Mich elbows Isabella. "I didn't expect that at all."

"Welcome to the new world." She shrugs.

Their attention is drawn back to the Matron of Ministrations as she leans forward, a vicious edge to her words. "There is no hope of escape from this place, so don't even bother to entertain the idea. You will also be accompanied by a guard. They've been authorized to use force, if necessary. You're valuable, but not indispensable." She sits and bangs the staff on the floor. "Attendant One!"

The first attendant steps up to the cell door and calls Adejola's name. The Nigerian stands and takes a deep breath. He looks back at Isabella and Lianne, who gives him a nervous thumbs-up. With fluid grace and apparent calm, he walks from the cells to make his choice.

One by one the Anahera are summoned from the cells. None return. To stave off the tension, Isabella takes to pacing slowly back and forth. Finally, the Matron of Ministrations gives her a respite.

"You can stop that now, you're next."

Waiting at the cell door is a tall Attendant, his hair a shock of acid blond above the black uniform. It is shaved at the sides and pulled into a neat bun behind his head. From one earlobe a thin metal spike juts past his chin. He holds out a hand, indicating the stairs.

"Come on, your lift awaits."

104

Isabella follows him to a set of brass-studded double doors. The Attendant strolls up to them and slaps a glowing pad on the wall. He turns and regards her critically, his gaze raking her from the ground up.

She raises an eyebrow. "Let me guess, you're unimpressed."

To her surprise, he returns the eyebrow and smiles. "You have potential, that's why I chose you. I suspect you'll be entertaining to watch." Before Isabella can react, a cascade of tiny bells interrupts and the door slides open.

Beyond is a spacious capsule complete with a velvet-covered chaise lounge, wooden walls and a curved glass roof. A young woman with rich ochre skin stands beside a brass console topped with a larger version of the circular quires used by Emmeline and Bannerman. She is dressed in a loose white shirt and grey waistcoat, over tight grey leggings and knee-high boots.

"Morning, Bethany. The Office." The attendant ushers Isabella into the lift and the doors close silently behind him.

"Righto." Bethany eyes the Anahera, who is staring upwards through the roof at the tracks above them. "Ever been in one of these before?"

Isabella shakes her head and places a bracing hand against the lift as it sets off. The motion is smooth, but she gasps as it suddenly swings sideways and appears to travel backwards along a new track. She glances at the Attendant, who is clearly amused by her reaction.

"We're perfectly safe. Bethany's an excellent helmer." He catches her confused expression and takes pity on her. "The lifts can move in almost any direction in and around the mountain, but they each have a lift-helmer to pilot them. They know all the best routes…"

"And provide service with a smile." Bethany winks at her. "Well, most of the time. This morning I have a hangover, so you're lucky to get this." She points to her smile. The lift reaches an intersection and turns, running swiftly along a new track.

"How far do we have to go?" Isabella realises she should have been paying attention to the route. She is still determined to have enough knowledge to make a run for it when the opportunity presents itself.

"The Office of Contracts and Obligations is on the same Terrace as the cells, but on the far side of the mountain." The helmer explains. "We'll reach our destination soon."

"Do we have to?" Isabella murmurs and the helmer gives her a sympathetic look, whilst the Attendant shifts uncomfortably.

The lift begins to slow and as it comes to a stop, the cascade of tiny bells sounds again. The doors slide open to reveal a polished granite atrium, banked by enormous windows. A guard waits for them by the outer doors, his impatience obvious.

"Huljun Terrace, Port Side." The helmer intones.

For a moment Isabella is stuck, unable to place one foot in front of the other. The lift seems to buckle around her, twisting closer and closer until she cannot breathe. She jolts as she feels a hand on her arm and finds the Attendant looking down at her, sympathy in his eyes.

"Just a few more steps. I'm sorry, but you can't avoid this."

Isabella closes her eyes and takes in a deep breath.

You can do this. Nothing lasts forever, not even this.

She steps forward and together they walk to the doors. The guard pushes them open and a blast of cold air washes over her.

They step out into wintry sunlight. The view is astonishing. Curving around the mountain on either side are a series of grand buildings. They are almost Grecian in style, complete with colonnades and friezes and serve to make Isabella feel very small. Far below, a busy port teems with boats and gantries, skiffs leaving white trails between the piers. The vast, glittering arm of Weisdale voe stretches out before them, buttressed on one side by the vast mountain range and punctuated further along by the Hellister peninsula on the other. Isabella spots several Windpyre waka floating above this distant mound but she has no time to pine for them as the guard is

106

already striding across the square towards the nearest building.

The Attendant keeps his hand on Isabella's arm as they follow him. The guard skims along the side of the building and opens a discreet wooden door. A sour expression on his face, he flicks a hand, indicating they should enter and shuts the door firmly behind them.

"Don't worry," the Attendant pats her arm. "Citadel guards are a bit pissy with everyone."

A wooden corridor opens out to a sparse room. A desk sits in the middle and behind it a man with slicked-back hair and a thin moustache.

"Name?" He intones.

"Isabella Mackay." Her voice catches a little and she swallows.

"They have explained the choice?"

"Yes." She watches him tap the large circular quire in front of him.

"What is your choice?" His tone is leaden. The cold bureaucracy of it all makes her want to throw up. Instead, she speaks quietly.

"The Citadel."

He nods and points to a large square pad on the desk in front of her. "Lay your hand on the pad. It will take a sample of your skin for analysis. It also serves as your signature to contract with us." He looks up at her. "Once you agree, you are bound by the conditions."

"What conditions?" She stares at him.

"Are you going to sign or not?" He sits back. "The slave wagon is waiting if you've changed your mind. Four of your people have already chosen that path."

Isabella grits her teeth and places her hand on the pad. A light flares beneath, along with a burning sensation. She hisses and pulls back her hand.

The official gazes down at his quire screen. He lifts a hand and flicks his fingers.

"That is all. You may go."

She does not move. The feeling of heavy doors slamming down

around her holds her fast, until the Attendant gently but firmly turns her away and leads her to the outer door. She drifts out, almost as if she is caught in a dream, but as she exits the building she catches the guard's eye. He sneers.

"No trouble with this one then, docile as yarg." He looks at the Attendant, his expression sour. "Pathetic, aren't they? The Gentry'll chew 'em up and spit 'em out."

The Attendant glares at him, flicking his fringe back and moving to place himself between them. He pilots Isabella across the square and into the lift lobby where the ochre-skinned helmer still waits. Bethany quickly taps her console quire and the lift moves off.

When they reach the cells the Attendant herds Isabella back to the corridor leading to the bathing halls. He chooses a door near the far end of the corridor, revealing a suite of small rooms radiating from a central pentagonal space. At the centre sits a sunken pool in which scarlet petals float.

"Right." The Attendant claps his hands sharply, pulling Isabella from her spiralling despair. "We've a lot to do so let's get started." Three women dressed in white appear from separate rooms and bow.

"These lovely ladies are going to make you feel shiny and new. Don't try to fight it, it's good for you." He drops down onto a cream chaise lounge and crosses his long legs. He clicks his fingers and a young lad appears with a silver tray upon which is goblet. The Attendant raises it. "Off you go, luv."

He waits, directing the other attendants as she is showered, scrubbed, plucked (a difficult moment where she finds she must fight to retain her eyebrows), buffed and her hair triple-conditioned. Finally, she is deposited into a curved leather chair and the last beautician begins work on her makeup.

Isabella feels somewhat battered, but also as newly-minted as the Attendant promised. She realizes she doesn't even know his name.

"Saga." He raises the goblet again.

"In my world, that's the term for a long story, usually involving

108

heroes." She hears the man snort in response.

"I could do with one of those in my life. In the language of my home clan, Saga means 'unexpected'." He flops one long hand over the other and flicks his fringe back. "Darling, I do try!"

She laughs. "I can imagine. Well, Saga, could you do me an enormous favour?"

He blinks. "That depends."

"I really can't take the perfumes the people in this place use. Honestly mate, they give me a migraine. Now that I'm all squeaky clean, do you think you could find me an 'unexpected' perfume that's not going to make my eyes stream? I don't want to ruin this makeup."

Saga is suddenly all business, disappearing into one of the rooms and returning with a large basket filled with little bottles. He rootles through the contents, frowning, until his hand reaches the bottom and he crows in triumph, pulling out a small, golden vial.

He pulls the tapered stopper and sniffs. "Yes, this is the one." He holds it out but even at a distance, she recognizes it. She sighs and closes her eyes.

"Rose sandalwood. One of my favourite scents in all the world...s."

Saga shrugs. "I acquired this on a whim from a Windpyre tribe far to the south years ago. No one's shown the slightest interest in it but if you want to smell like a tree temple, then that's your social funeral."

He slaps his knees. "Hair's done, makeup's finished. Now to the dress!" He stands and offers her a hand up. She accepts, feeling suddenly tense.

"Aren't we moving a bit fast here?"

"Certainly not!" He stares at her. "If anything, we're behind. We have two bells before the official Reception. The Goddess knows how we're going to get you ready in time!"

She returns his stare. "A reception? Tonight?"

"Didn't our illustrious Matron mention that?" He sighs. "She

109

does like to compartmentalize." He leans forwards, a hint of kindness in his voice. "Look at it like removing a sticky bandage from a wound – it's better to get it over with in one quick rip."

"Saga, that's a terrible image." Isabella continues to protest as he leads her across the corridor to another door, which opens into the most extraordinary room.

Stretching towards the high ceiling are three mezzanine levels, each one lined with racks of costumes. The racks are grouped by colour and are tightly packed. There must be a thousand garments on each floor. At ground level, each wall is lined with shoes, sectioned into colours and styles. In the centre of the space, sit three large glass cabinets filled with jewellery, glittering in the light of water-drop chandeliers floating above them.

"Wow." Isabella drifts into the space and turns slowly, taking it in. "I know women in my world who would kill for this closet…and several men, in fact."

Most of the Anahera captives are already moving along the racks, accompanied by their individual attendants. Isabella spots Lianne high up on the third floor. The clank of bells next to her head heralds the approach of the Matron of Ministrations.

"You're late. Off you go and choose." She aims a glare at Saga as well, who shrugs.

"What can I say, she has rebellious hair." He takes Isabella's arm and pulls her towards the nearest spiral staircase. "Favourite colour?"

Isabella is tempted to quip, "black, like my heart" but instead her eye is caught by a swathe of purple. She extracts her arm from his grip and points to it. "That'll do."

After a number of rather intense discussions, they finally agree upon a dress and Isabella reluctantly strips to her underwear so that Saga can help her climb into it. It is a sheer, sleeveless gown in purple silk which follows her curves closely, before flaring slightly at her feet. It dips low enough to accentuate her cleavage and is cinched beneath the curve of her breasts with a line of pale gold embroidery.

110

Saga helps her on with the second layer - a diaphanous outer gown of iridescent heather, ringed at each elbow with a filigree golden cuff, allowing the sleeves to fall open. It too reaches the floor and appears to float around her as she moves. He pins her hair to one side, the curls tumbling over her shoulder and down her front, carefully positioning a comb dotted with tiny white gems to hold it in place.

Isabella turns slowly in front of the long mirror. She is beginning to feel strangely disconnected again – this image is not her, it cannot be.

"Not bad!" Lianne's voice issues from behind her. Her friend is dressed in a stunning midnight blue gown dotted with hundreds of tiny diamonds. Her blonde hair is pulled up in an elaborate style and she looks every inch a queen.

"Look at you, all gorgeous and glowing!" Isabella grins.

Lianne replies with a scowl, "I don't *feel* glowing, I feel like I'm going to pass out. Do you know how tight this thing is? My boobs are almost up my nostrils!" This is a slight exaggeration, although Isabella looks down and pats her own chest. Gentry dresses are certainly well scaffolded.

"Anahera, assemble!" The Matron's bellow summons the captives to the door. They shuffle before her, a motley collection of individuals. "We will proceed from here to the lifts. They will take you up to the Ostium Terrace where the Master of Ceremonies will take over from me. You will be presented to the Gentry at an official Reception which is being held in your honour, remember!" She raises a finger. "You agreed to this. There are guards stationed throughout the Terrace and the consequences for transgressions will be harsh and immediate. If you try to leave, you will be arrested and taken straight to the slave pits."

She steps into the corridor and waits as the Anahera file past. As Isabella passes her, the Matron looks down and suddenly snaps. "Stop! What is this?"

Isabella is still wearing her sturdy Sisterhood boots.

The Matron claps her hands and Saga appears at her side clutching a pair of strappy high heels. Isabella plants her hands on her hips.

"I object on principle - heels are designed to stop us running away."

The Matron of Ministrations glares down at her. "They're designed to make you look like you're skimming delicately across the dance floor." She looks Isabella up and down. "Harder to achieve with some than others." She scans the Anahera still in the corridor and raises her voice. "The Gentry have high standards and high expectations. We are NOT going to disappoint them."

Reluctantly, Isabella gives in, allowing Saga to slip the new shoes onto her feet. They are tight and she struggles not to topple over. The attendant picks up her boots with a look of faint distaste but assures her she will see them again.

The Anahera are herded into waiting lifts and taken further up the mountain to the Ostium Terrace, a level dedicated to official functions and state visits. When the lifts open, they are faced with an imposing set of closed doors stretching to the ceiling. Cahuil Orda, the Master of Ceremonies, flutters about, chivvying his attendants into arranging the Anahera into some semblance of respectable order. He wants to make an impact on the waiting crowd beyond the doors and so ruthlessly chooses the most stunning individuals to stand at the front. Lianne and Adejola are ushered forwards whilst Isabella is more than happy to lurk near the back, even if Orda had not just put her there.

Inside, a number of Gentry distract themselves with dancing whilst others mill about the edges, eagerly waiting for the doors at the top of the wide staircase to open. Some place bets, others weave between groups, spreading gossip and sharing salacious tidbits. Queen Makeda and King Sarn lounge on an enormous plush red settee on the dais at the end of the hall, surrounded by servants and Gentry hopeful of favour. High above, long shards of light drift in concentric circles, illuminating the hundreds of revellers below.

112

When the Master of Ceremonies is finally happy with the arrangement, he signals to the heralds and slips through the doors. A heavy, rippling drumbeat begins to grow, the vibration travelling through to the core of each Anahera. Isabella feels it jolt her stomach and her trepidation rises, along with the paltry remains of supper. She swallows and straightens her spine, trying to shake off her fear.

Orda stands at the top of the steps, his arms flung wide and the drumbeats cease.

"Glorious Gentry! Welcome to the event we never thought to see again." His voice fills the cavernous room, the scent of tangerines heralding the use of his magic. Under the weight of it, the crowd falls silent. "Exotic visitors from another world and you have the pick of them!"

The crowd ripples in response, still unable to utter a word in reaction.

"I give you...the ANAHERA!" The doors roll open to reveal the captives and Orda releases his hold upon the crowd. They roar and clap in response, surging towards the steps. Behind Isabella, black-garbed guards with spiral lances drawn step forward, giving the Anahera no choice but to proceed from the landing and down the steps. Isabella sees Adejola step sideways, trying to shield Lianne from the grasping hands of the Gentry eager to inspect the new specimens, before they are swallowed up by the crowd.

The sharp point of a lance prods Isabella in the ribs and she scuttles forward. The olfactory punch of hundreds of bodies drenched in chemical perfumes and colognes makes her reel and clutch the banister for support. She raises her sleeve to her face and takes a moment to study the crowd. Several hundred eyes assess and appraise her. Some look fascinated, others unimpressed. Some even appear openly hostile, whilst others leer. The lance prods her again and she hears the guard hiss a warning. She has no choice but to make her way down the staircase and into the heaving mob.

Music sparks up, a curious bass beat mixed with a soaring

melody. Members of the Gentry jostle for the chance to pull individual Anahera onto the dance floor and Isabella takes advantage of the chaos to ghost her way out and along the edge of the room. She finds a convenient pillar and leans against the cool stone, watching the throng pass by. It is a small breathing space but she decides to make it hers. Dancers swirl past in a wash of colours, silks and scent and just as she finds herself relaxing enough to take it all in, a figure appears in front of her.

He is tall and handsome, with honey-blond hair flicked back from his forehead. His smooth bow cannot hide the arrogance which seeps from him, along with the bitter scent of vinegar. He stares down his aquiline nose at her.

"You will do. Come with me." Ignoring her surprise, he takes her hand and pulls her onto the dance floor, straight into the first dance. It does not go well. Isabella cannot pick up the steps quickly enough and he is an impatient lead. She trips several times but he clearly has no intention of slowing down. More than once she feels his hand squeeze her breast and although her natural reaction would be to knee him somewhere painful, she suspects that would earn her a swift trip to the slave pens. Eventually, he deposits her back by her pillar, having suffered several bruises from her inept dancing. He regards her sharply for a moment then turns on his heel and dives back into the crowd. Isabella swears softly under her breath and resolves to stick by the pillar for safety.

The next Gentry to appear in front of her is an older man, with an extravagant grey moustache and a surprisingly warm and gracious manner.

"Care to dance with an old man, lovely lady?" He has a deep drawling voice, reminding her of cigar smoke and leather chairs. There is an air of self-confident calm about him and he has the bearing of a military man. Isabella shrugs.

"If you don't mind bruised feet, then yes, I would."

He is a far more respectful lead and as they dance she actually

114

finds herself relaxing. His cynicism and understanding make her laugh and he seems to appreciate her company. He too suffers bruises. She tells him about her 'safety pillar' and he laughingly deposits her back beside it, bowing and then leaving her in peace.

Two female members of the Gentry halt near her pillar and watch Isabella hawkishly. She smiles and murmurs a polite "hello". They each have stiff, twisting hairstyles and the flesh on their faces does not move. The near-skeletal frame of the pale one is wrapped in a tight orange sheath dress, whilst the sable-skinned woman appears to be wearing nothing but a collection of large blue bows stitched together with red twine. They do not smile back.

The one who resembles a tall, fanciful carrot stares at Isabella and leans towards her friend.

"If that's an example of what the alien world has to offer, what a dismal place it must be!"

"And have you smelt her?" Her friend replies. "Utterly vile."

Isabella blinks and her lips tighten into a thin line. She is torn between wanting to bite back with an acidic retort or melting into the shadows in a puddle of humiliation.

"Ignore those silly bitches, I think you smell fascinating." A voice issues from behind her and she turns to see a young, ochre-skinned man smiling shyly at her. He has soft features and a shaven head. Around his neck stretch tattoos of flowers etched in silver. He looks her up and down.

"I've never seen that style before, but it does suit you. Obviously, it's having an effect – two dances already!"

Isabella winces. "I'm a crap dancer and I left them with bruises."

The youth grins at her. "Well, Lord Mirl is certainly a catch, he's ridiculously wealthy. You must be doing something right to catch his eye."

Yes, my boobs certainly did.

She suppresses a grimace.

"I'm Harran, by the way." He holds out a hand and she shakes it.

115

"Oooh, look! There's the Prince." He points to the dance floor as Meridian and Lianne move past. The music swirls and the blond warrior lifts her friend into the air before setting her down and turning her towards him. Lianne glances sideways and grimaces at Isabella. Another turn and they disappear back into the crowd.

"He's gorgeous, but big, beefy warriors aren't my type. Having to scrub blood and who-knows-what from under a lover's nails before you let him anywhere near you? I just couldn't!" Harran flaps his hands in mock horror and Isabella can't help but smile.

There is a ripple in the crowd nearby and more Gentry faces set like stone. The crowd parts, not a single individual looking at the figure walking through the space. It is if some invisible force is pushing them back. Each face takes on a new expression, either pinched with distaste or stiff with fear. Isabella is fascinated to see their level of disquiet and the strange, elegant man who is causing it. He is tall, with long black hair, white skin and dark eyes glittering coldly. His midnight blue silk suit covers a powerful, lithe frame.

He pauses, looking up towards the King for a moment. Lounging on the settee next to his wife, the King is indeed watching him and inclines his head in warning. The newcomer's face shows no emotion at this, he simply turns and steps up to the pair of Gentry women nearby.

Isabella feels Harran's hand on her arm, pulling her back around the pillar. He flutters with worry and she can see real fear in his eyes.

"Is he one of those Drw-ad people?" She frowns. He nods quickly and takes another peek.

"He's the Citadel's only one. He's lived here since he was a child, as a political hostage. Can you imagine?" He leans back towards her. "He's very powerful. I heard he once ripped a servant's heart from his chest without even touching him, just because he brought him the wrong wine!"

Isabella leans back around the pillar to observe the Drw-ad. His behaviour shows a distinct absence of bloodthirsty violence.

116

He bows solemnly and asks the woman covered in big bows to dance, but she shakes her head stiffly, barely glancing at him. She looks as if she has swallowed a wasp. He turns to her companion and tries again, but The Human Carrot is even ruder and merely sneers.

"Certainly not with you! I'd faint from the stench." The Gentry surrounding them snigger at her words.

He bows politely and turns from them. In that fleeting moment, Isabella sees his expression. His dark eyes flinch under straight black brows and the posture of his body grows tense, betraying his rising humiliation. Isabella has always had contempt for bullies and she already smarts from their contemptuous treatment of her. Their insulting behaviour towards the Drw-ad prompts a flare of anger, taking over the conscious part of her brain and forcing her to step forward. Behind, Harran gasps in horror. The Drw-ad stops in his tracks.

She stands in his path and gazes at him steadily.

"Hello. Would you consider dancing with me?"

Isabella feels Harran's warning hand on her arm but she shakes it off. The stone-faced women glance at one another, clearly shocked.

Bryant is also stunned. No woman has ever asked him to dance before. He pauses for a moment to take in her appearance; her luscious curves, auburn hair tumbling down over one shoulder and the welcoming warmth in her eyes. Unlike every other soul in the room, she is smiling gently and openly at him. He finds her most disconcerting. There seems to be an aura of calm about her and the usual jarring sensation he finds when near humans is entirely absent.

"It would be an honour, Lady."

He bows and offers her his hand. He does not expect her to take it but she does, sending a shockwave through him.

Isabella takes his hand, surprised to find that it is warm and dry and she suppresses the urge to wipe her own hand on her dress first, fearing it might be a little sweaty in return. His fingers are long and deft, his skin the colour of fresh snow. It is patterned with pale whorls,

117

intersecting lines and circles, much like complex alchemical symbols. Rather than tattoos, they appear formed as a natural part of his skin.

As she moves closer to him, Isabella is aware of an immense change in atmosphere, one which brings a flood of relief. The scent of the first snow of winter flows from him and for the first time in days, she feels her headache begin to subside as the reek of the chemical perfumes surrounding them is blown away. Suddenly, she can breathe again.

Her delight fades as he leads her to the dancing space and she feels the familiar dip of sickening embarrassment. The complex steps occurring around them are a complete mystery to her. A lifetime of bouncing about on her own in clubs and at music festivals has not qualified her for dancing as a couple. As they come to a halt in the middle of the floor he turns to face her and she forces herself to admit the truth, warning him of impending doom.

"I'll be honest, I have no idea what I'm doing and, quite frankly, I'm so inept that you really should fear for the safety of your toes." She looks down at his polished black boots. "Seriously, I apologise in advance for what I'm about to do to them." She looks up again, her eyes filled with self-mocking amusement. "I may fall over."

He regards her seriously.

"You have nothing to fear, my Lady. I will guide you through the steps." His voice is as cold as his expression and nerves crunch inside her belly in response. The thrilling burn of her little rebellious stand against the stone-faced bitches has fizzled completely now that she is in this position, faced with the strangest man she has ever met. [8]Yet as the music begins and they move off, she realises that he is certainly skilled enough to navigate her safely through the crowd, holding and turning her smoothly, placing her exactly where she needs to be. Slowly, as they step and spin, her confidence begins to haul itself up from the polished marble floor.

---

[8] Playlist: Tiaan – Dive Deep.

118

As Bryant moves her gently but firmly from one side of his body to the other, he realises that she is telling the truth – she is a terrible dancer. Yet this odd woman also tried to make a connection with him using a joke at her own expense. This is very puzzling for him as jokes are usually at his expense. He resolves to make sure she does not humiliate herself in front of the Gentry and as her foot slides the wrong way along the floor, he lifts her slightly and steadies her, moving her deftly back through the crowd of dancers.

Isabella feels the strength and reassuring solidity of his muscles as he catches her and she almost begins to relax. Indeed, she hasn't stepped on his toes or tripped over once. The bright scent of snow invigorates her and the closer she moves to him, the more the reek from the surrounding Gentry diminishes. As he spins her back towards him, she breathes in and at the edge of the fresh snow she registers a hint of…copper?

The dance calls for them to step away from one another for a moment to clap and turn and she finds that when he reaches for her to move to the next step, she is looking forward to being close to him again.

Despite his apparent stoicism, Bryant is struggling. Her scent is not like the contrived, aggressively sweet, chemical aromas of the women in the Citadel, rather it wraps around him, warm and layered. As she leans into his body, her soft curls just below his nose, he inhales and in that soft scent he forgets for a moment that he is surrounded by enemies.

He keenly feels her body shift against his, the movement of her hips, the curve of her lower back under his hand, a physical awareness that begins to threaten his usual icy calm. Bryant strives to pull his thoughts from that dangerous path, for although she seems welcoming, he has no desire to feel that familiar sting once she realises who and what he is and turns a stone face to him.

Even though he has always enjoyed dancing, with precious few opportunities here in the Citadel, his only thought upon entering the

119

Reception was to be seen to do his duty and then leave, retreating back up to the solarium and his work. Now, he finds that he does not want to stop. He lifts her hand in a high arch and turns her beneath it, her body fitting back into his with ease, her arm now draped around his shoulders. Along with the other dancers, they step and sway together and as the drumbeats reach a crescendo, each lead lifts their partner into the air. At her gasp he looks up at her, dark auburn curls falling about her shoulders, green eyes filling with laughter as she looks down at him. He lowers her gently to the ground, struggling to understand his own physical reaction to her. It is immediate, intense and completely un-Drw.

As the music finishes, the crowd pauses and claps. Those around the couple openly stare, some utterly hostile. She does not appear to notice their expressions at all. She is only focused on him. An errant curl has fallen from its pin and drops down across her face so she purses her lips and puffs it upwards, before glancing at him and smiling. He is stunned. Has a woman ever smiled at him before with such genuine ease?

"That was actually fun." She laughs. "What a difference it makes, dancing with a man who knows what he's doing!"

Bryant has a difficult moment, trying to process the realisation that a woman just called time with him fun. He doubts even Meridian would admit to that. The Drw-ad takes in her flushed cheeks and slightly dishevelled appearance and impulsively asks if she would like a drink. She accepts, wincing and muttering about "nightmare shoes" which have begun to pinch. He is now bobbing into an uncharted sea, but as ever he is careful not to show his weakness. He knows with bitter certainty that the Gentry will gleefully take advantage of any lapse.

Isabella watches as he snags two curved glasses from a waiter and passes one to her. She peers down at the drink. It is a vibrant yellow with tiny bubbles which swirl in their own vortex. When she takes a sip, she blinks. It tastes of bright summer wildflowers and thyme honey, almost as if the most perfect moment of a summer's day had been caught and distilled. It is also screamingly alcoholic.

The Drw-ad watches her eyes widen and takes a sip from his own glass. He has never been fond of the Citadel's summer wine, finding the sweetness cloying. If anything, the Anahera looks more flushed as a result, so he offers her his arm, thinking to escort her out into the cool evening. It is a gesture of good manners but he does not expect her to accept.

Isabella immediately tucks her hand around his arm, noticing the solid curve of hard, defined muscle beneath the material. He stares down at her. With a sinking jolt, she realises she has inadvertently done the wrong thing yet again and hesitantly starts to remove her hand.

In fact, the pale Drw-ad is staring because no woman has ever accepted his offer of an escort. Before she can remove her hand entirely, he covers his latest lapse and ushers her towards the doors. The archway opens out onto a wide paved balcony complete with topiaries and night flowers, jutting out over manicured gardens and the shimmering lights of the city and villages far below.

Like a shoal of fish, the Gentry around them halt and stare, some actually gaping.

Who would willingly allow the foul Drw-ad to escort them? How could the Anahera even stand to be near him?

Whispers shiver back and forth around them, and having no idea why she is now being so aggressively stared at, Isabella moves closer to her dancing partner, using him as a shield.

She dives gratefully into the cool night air, feeling the heat and crush of the ballroom slide away behind them. Overwhelmed by so many people, harsh aromas and hostile expressions, her feet seriously pinching from the shoes, the crisp air and the solid feeling of the man beside her come as a welcome relief. She looks up at him, his face cold and serious as they stop near the waist-high stone parapet.

The Drw-ad certainly looks unusual and not entirely human. The

121

transparent designs in his skin end at his throat, leaving his face clear. Although his dark blue lips and black eyes against the pale skin are a little disconcerting, he is nonetheless quite handsome. The breeze catches strands of his hair, glinting blue-black in the light of the teardrop lanterns strung above them. It is perfectly straight and falls down his back like a sheet of heavy satin.

Bryant feels an unexpected drop of loss as she lets go of his arm. The Anahera sets her glass down on the parapet, slips off the offending shoes and gasps in delight as the cool stone of the balcony floor soothes her bare, aching feet. She places both palms flat on the parapet, leaning forward and peering at the view. As the night air lifts stray curls around her head, he blinks at this brazen behaviour. There is something gloriously unrepentant and completely natural about her.

"This is beautiful," she says with some surprise. "It's certainly a welcome change from stone walls and black iron bars." She looks up at him accusingly. He stares at her for a moment then shifts his gaze to the valley below.

"Does the view make up for the people?" He murmurs then looks back at her, his voice taking on a definite note of sincerity.

"My Lady," he begins, choosing his words carefully. "I am sorry this has happened to you. I know what a burden it is to have others directing one's path."

The Drw-ad's language is almost painfully formal and Isabella realises that she has yet to hear him use a contraction. His voice has an unusual quality to it, a deep timbre, as smooth-flowing as dark silk.

"Everyone here expects us to be grateful for this "opportunity". As if we should thank them for making us slaves!" She can feel her frustration rising and knows it is foolish to be so honest near one of them, even one who seems so different from the others, but she just can't bite the words back in. "Whether the cage has iron bars or golden ones, it's still a cage!"

He is silent in the face of her outrage but he knows exactly what she is talking about. Even at the age of seven when he first arrived at

122

the Citadel as a hostage, he understood the complicated state of being a valuable captive. He has had years to adjust his responses in order to survive. She has had days.

"I understand this well, my Lady, but perhaps it is better to have a cage without actual bars? One is able to at least move around more freely." His stern eyes now have a hint of compassion in them. At this, Isabella feels her anger collapse into a sinking pit of anxiety.

Bryant feels a jolt as he watches her eyes darken with it, her expression unexpectedly vulnerable. He almost reaches out to touch her but stills himself. He is utterly confused by his own reactions to her – compassion is not part of the Drw-ad design, serving no purpose in their world.

"There's no guarantee of that, is there? That all depends on the man I get as a husband."

Bryant hears a frustrated growl in the back of her throat and then she takes a gulp of the wine.

"A lifetime of female liberation and now I'm being auctioned off to the highest bidder!" Isabella feels the acidic burn of rage rise within her and struggles to contain it.

She becomes aware that he is staring at her, his dark eyes glittering, so she reins herself back in.

It does not do to let your enemies know they are getting to you.

She looks out across the gardens below, silhouettes of hedges and trees sprinkled with the lights of tiny lanterns.

Calm down. Focus on the here and now.

In this moment, she is out in the glorious night air, standing next to someone who is treating her kindly…and she is drinking wine.

Focus on the little things.

The Drw-ad watches her, fascinated as she closes her eyes, breathes in deeply through her nostrils then opens her eyes again and smiles. The way she can pull down the obvious anger and replace it with a pleasant expression is astonishing to observe.

"Sorry, mate, it was rude of me to take that out on you." She straightens her spine, lifting her chin a little. "You've been kind to me and I don't even know your name."

He places a white hand on his chest and bows.

"Bryant Lathorne, my Lady." When he straightens, there is a wry look in his eyes. "I am pleased to make your acquaintance. I have never met an Anahera before. You are certainly…" He pauses, sifting for the right word. "An interesting race."

Interesting?

This, from a man who is essentially two-tone and smells like snow. Luckily for the Drw-ad in front of her, the potent summer wine has softened the edges of her reactions, so the response he receives is at least polite.

"I also have a name y'know." She bobs a curtsey, careful to include the appropriate amount of sass. "Isabella Mackay."

He clearly does not know how to respond to this new attitude and an uncomfortable silence edges between them. She takes another sip of wine, aware that its pungent sweetness is becoming unpleasant.

"So, how about you?"

"My Lady?"

She gestures with the glass. "Do you live here?"

Bryant suddenly feels on safer ground, less liable to tilt and send him flying into the abyss of her anger and loss.

"Yes." He indicates to a stocky tower high above, perched near the top of the Citadel. "I have apartments and a research solarium in the Eyrie."

At this, Isabella grins. "The Eyrie? That sounds dramatic. Are there bats?" She murmurs to herself. "I like bats."

His dark eyes spark with amusement.

"Alas no, only dragons."

She feels herself go rigid. "I'm sorry, only what-now?"

"Dragons. They are becoming a nuisance, in fact. They nest in the eaves and make a mess of my shelves."

Her eyes have widened in shock and he wonders at this. Surely,

124

the smelly little beasts are just as common where she hails from. The upper Citadel is lousy with them. Perhaps she knows them by another title.

"Dragon is the name my people gave them. Most humans refer to them as saur."

Isabella opens her mouth to speak but is interrupted by a braying voice.

"Lathorne! You've no right to take our Anahera away from the melee!" One meaty hand clasps her elbow and the other plucks the half empty glass from her grasp and shoves it towards Bryant. "You've no right to her at all, in fact."

The newcomer's voice is completely dismissive and Isabella watches the Drw-ad's eyes grow an inky black as she is spun to face the other man. He is ruddy-faced and stuffed into a straining cream suit, with thick gold rings clamped around each finger. His thinning blonde hair ruffles in the night breeze.

"I've not danced with this one yet."

He yanks her towards him and as she leaves the protection of her companion's snow-scent, the contrived cologne of the newcomer rolls over her in a bitter-sweet olfactory punch of creosote. Her headache returns with a vengeance.

"Come girl, we can't allow you to associate with the likes of…that." He flicks his doughy fingers in the direction of the Drw-ad. "Let's see what you're made of!" His gaze practically leaps down her cleavage as he pulls her away.

Trying to resist politely, she strains to turn back to Bryant, but the blond Lord is utterly determined.

The Black Drw-ad feels the familiar sting of anger as she is hauled away squawking, "But…dragons." He is left alone, holding two wine glasses and churning with frustration at how swiftly the denizens of the Citadel are able to condemn him. He feels the darkness tighten around him. Yet again, he has been shut out.

With an unerring sense of timing, from the throng strolls

125

Meridian, flushed from the dance, his rebellious blond hair tumbling over his shoulders. He throws back his head and laughs.

"Great night!"

He pulls up short, taking in his friend standing alone with eyes narrowed and one dark eyebrow arched in simmering annoyance, still clutching two wine glasses.

"Have you taken up drinking?"

Bryant throws him a tight look then glances down and notices something.

"She has left her shoes," he murmurs. A Lady of the Citadel would never be caught looking any less than perfect, and bare feet on the dance floor are a recipe for disaster. He picks them up by the straps and considers plunging back into the ballroom to deliver them to her, but the heat from the party guests billows out through the doors, making him pause in distaste.

Meridian watches his old friend with fascination. Never has he seen him so perplexed by, or indeed *engaged* with another individual outside their tight-knit circle. The raven-haired Lord turns to him, still clutching the shoes and the wine glasses, his expression strained.

The big blond man takes pity on him. "Pass me one of those, I'm parched."

Bryant hands him a glass and watches him throw it back in one gulp. The Prince makes a face.

"Urgh, why do they insist on serving this pish? It tastes like bubble bath."

Bryant regards him seriously. "Tell me then, have you found your new queen?" He is well aware of Meridian's reluctance in the matter and he takes the opportunity to needle his friend. "Have you found that special woman to spend the rest of your long, long life with?"

The Prince glares at him.

"It's cruel to take the piss, y'know. We're supposed to be friends." His scowl softens and he flicks his eyes thoughtfully upwards. "Well, there are a couple of potentials. I have to admit,

126

they're a hell of a lot more interesting than this lot." He waves a hand towards the Gentry milling about in the ballroom beyond.

The music pulses and Bryant wonders if his former dancing companion has fallen over yet. Meridian's voice intrudes.

"So, what about you? When I saw you actually talking to a woman, I thought I was hallucinating. By the time I'd made it out here, she'd disappeared!" Meridian points to the strappy shoes dangling from Bryant's hand. "I see there's evidence of her existence, though."

The Drw-ad's expression has returned to its usual serious state and he gazes towards the party within. "She appears to be much in demand."

Yet, even before the song has ended, Isabella appears in the archway, padding quickly across the cool flagstones, her iridescent heather gown billowing gently. With a harried expression she glances behind, checking for signs of cream-tweeded pursuit.

Meridian glances from her to the pale-skinned man beside him, fascinated by the intensity with which his friend is watching her. As she catches sight of the two men, her expression changes to one of relief. Meridian grins and elbows his companion, who studiously ignores him.

"My Lady," Bryant bows as she approaches. "Are you well?"

She sighs, diving into his snow-scent with relief.

"Now that I've escaped the clutches of the human squid, yes, I think so." She glances from the dark Drw-ad to the grinning blond man beside him and back again.

The Goth and the Viking are friends?

Meridian is a little taken aback. Normally women do not dismiss him so completely. Inwardly, he shrugs. Better his friend has some positive attention for a change. Despite his outward reluctance, the Prince already has someone else in mind.

The sound of a gong reverberates from the ballroom, echoing out across the wide stone balcony and through the shadowed night-flowering gardens. Bryant holds out Isabella's shoes and she rolls her eyes.

"Now this, is some serious Cinderella nonsense. Is it midnight?"

Bryant and Meridian exchange a confused glance then look back at the odd woman from another world. Meridian is the first to rally, amusement tugging at the corners of his mouth.

"No, my Lady, but I think they're playing your tune. They're calling the Anahera back."

She smiles tightly and steps forward, taking the shoes and gently touching Bryant's hand in thanks. He looks down, stunned. It is such a simple gesture but shocking in its familiarity.

Painfully aware of this reaction, Isabella removes her hand.

"Uh, thank you for collecting them. I have a habit of accidently leaving stuff in random places."

Shoes, keys, a whole world of family and friends...

Bryant places his hand on his chest, dipping into a brief bow. His silken black hair slides from his shoulders to spill down his chest, framing his face.

"I am pleased to have been of assistance."

She can't help smiling at this stiff, formal response.

Meridian watches what plays out between them with fascination. This is the first time he has ever seen a woman respond with genuine warmth towards his friend. She is so unlike the Citadel's Gentry - less contrived, arrogant and angular, instead soft, curvy and clearly with a saucy sense of humour. No wonder the Drw-ad is struggling, he has never had to face anyone like her before.

"Oi, you!" A voice barks from behind Isabella and a guard in ceremonial green strides onto the balcony, obliterating the mood like a heavy dump of cold water. "All Anahera prisoners are to go back to their cells."

Bryant sees the woman in front of him stiffen and a flash of rage spark in her green eyes. She lifts her chin slightly, lips forming a tight line as she inhales sharply through her nostrils. Both he and Meridian watch as her relaxed posture suddenly transforms into a surprisingly regal stance.

"Despite what you think, I am not a slave. Do not command me." Her words are tight and clipped, so different from her affable manner before.

Meridian is annoyed at the rudeness of the interruption but he also feels his Drw-ad companion tense, the scent of copper rising at the soldier's tone.

"Corporal!" He snaps. "The Lady is our honoured guest. Have the decency to treat her like one."

The blond guard blanches, then pulls himself to attention.

"My apologies, my Prince, I didn't see you there." His eyes flick towards the Drw-ad and his expression sours. "My Lord." Meridian steps forward, towering over him.

"Don't apologise to me, apologise to her!"

"Lady Isabella." Bryant's soft, deep voice inserts.

"Yes." Meridian's hand flicks towards her. "Lady Isabella."

The guard hesitates for a moment, then places his fist across to the left side of his chest and tilts a brief bow.

"My apologies, Lady." He almost bites at each word. "Allow me to escort you to your…quarters?"

She nods, some of her fire seeping away. There is no way to avoid going back to the cells and the prospect of being caged again threatens to suffocate her.

Bryant watches the sudden darkening of vulnerability in her eyes and realises, not for the first time this night, that he has more than an inkling of how she feels - to appear to be free, yet in reality anchored by the heavy weights of captivity beneath, and with that understanding comes another, more unexpected feeling; an increasingly strong compulsion to do something about it.

Isabella rallies and covers her panic, smiling with crystalline brightness at the two men.

"Thank you for that." She nods towards Meridian.

Smooth as butter he takes her hand and kisses it. As he looks up, he winks at her. She can't help but grin and out of the corner of her eye she sees the soldier's eyebrows arch in surprise. She looks across to Bryant, standing stiff and formal beside the Prince. Her grin softens to a warm smile and she inclines her head.

"And thank you for making this evening far more enjoyable than I thought it would be. I appreciate how patient you were with my atrocious dancing."

Bryant wishes he could respond to her as smoothly as Meridian, but he cannot. A swirl of heat has formed in his chest at her words, but his own words are stuck. Instead, all he can manage in typically reserved Drw-ad style is to say, "You are welcome, Lady."

Behind her, the guard moves forward, reaching for her arm. Isabella turns and flicks her open hands up, glaring at him in reproach.

"I'm coming! You don't have to drag me."

He retracts his hand and instead uses it to slap a salute across his chest for his two superiors. Turning abruptly, he leads her through the doors into the crush and roar of the ballroom. She does not look back as she is swallowed by the crowd.

Meridian shakes his head. It has certainly been a night of firsts.

"Right." He slaps Bryant's shoulder. "I need a beer!"

The Drw-ad glances from his friend to the shimmering crowd beyond the doors.

"I will stay out here for a while."

Meridian grins. "Fine, I'll go get the drinks in." He plunges back into the throng and Bryant turns away, moving back to the edge of the balcony.

He takes a final sip of summer wine and places the glass on the stone wall in front of him, the 'clink' echoing across the gardens. He stands, the night breeze ruffling his hair, staring out across the city lights and the dark hills beyond. The heat in his chest has not disappeared, instead he feels it spreading, stretching through him and eating into the cold that has kept him steady for so long.

130

As they weave their way through the crowd, the guard cleaving a path for Isabella through stiff silks and unyielding bodies, she tries to ignore the stares from the surrounding Gentry. Yet again, there is the mixture of fascination, contempt and something approaching greed in their eyes. With their sculpted hair, elaborate makeup and deliberately artificial scents, they are suddenly very alien to her and she desperately strives to keep up with the guard.

They emerge from the crowd and he moves behind a pillar to open a discreet door. He ushers her through into a narrow corridor beyond and closes the door firmly behind her. The contrast between the cramped, dimly lit corridor and the brilliantly lit ballroom is a sensory shock. She pauses, inhaling the simple, musty scent.

The guard pushes past her and strides down the corridor in obvious irritation. As they move through the complex system of service corridors, they are forced to squeeze past serving staff carrying platters and crates of bottles. Each peers sharply at Isabella, making her shrink a little inside.

One minute you're chatting with two handsome men on a balcony, the next you're being stared at like a specimen in a carnival tent.

One young maidservant reaches out to touch her, as if she is some strange, holy object but the guard pivots and slaps her hand away, barely pausing in his stride.

"Keep up," he growls. They pass through several junctions and Isabella scurries along behind, almost crashing into him as he halts suddenly. They have reached a hub point for the service lifts, the walls no longer wood panelled, but rough-hewn in stone. The guard punches the pad to summon a lift and they wait. He crosses his arms and glares at the ceiling.

Suddenly, alone with him, Isabella feels the uncomfortable silence stretch. She twists one of the delicate panels of her dress around her fingers in an old nervous gesture. What does one say in moments like this? 'So, how long have you been a slave-wrangling

131

soldier then?' Or perhaps, 'seen any good movies lately?' She closes her eyes and tries to concentrate on keeping her breath calm. When she opens them, he is looking at her, his eyes narrowed. She smiles tentatively, but feels it slip away in the face of his steady glare. He turns back to scowl at the lift door.

To their shared relief, the cascade of tiny bells shivers through the lobby, heralding the approach of a lift pod. The doors open and out step three waiters, each carrying a platter laden with tiny delicacies. They ignore both Isabella and the guard and push past them, heading down the corridor behind.

"In." The guard flicks a hand towards the mouth of the lift.

Inside waits a lift-helmer, a slender man, advanced in age, his hand poised over the control screen. His white hair is brushed back from his face, complimenting the crisp white shirt over dark grey breeks. His bored expression vanishes as he sees Isabella move forward in a rustle of purple silks and resolves itself into a gently welcoming smile. He bows, ignoring the guard's sour grunt.

"Where to?"

"Where do you think? The cells."

The door slides shut behind him and the helmer caresses the control screen. "The Huljun Terrace it is then."

The guard stands to one side, one hand resting on the pommel of his sword.

Isabella glances around the lift. Flax fronds and blooms are carved into wooden panels rising to arched, clear glass windows near the ceiling. The lift lurches slightly to the side as it changes to a new track and she places a bracing hand against the wall.

"Don't worry, Mistress," the helmer says calmly. "You're perfectly safe."

She glances at him and her lips quirk with embarrassment. "Thanks. I'm just not used to lifts which can go…sideways."

The helmer pats the slender console. "This old girl can do more than that and you'll barely feel a thing." The soldier huffs a tense sigh through his nose and the helmer glances at him, his eyes narrowing. He looks back at Isabella.

"It's an honour to have you here, Anahera. We haven't been graced with your kind for over a hundred turns."

Isabella opens her mouth to reply but the guard cuts in.

"Don't waste your breath on her, helmer." He snorts. "*Graced.* They're slaves, nothing more. They're no more special than you or I. Some just manage to jump up the ladder quicker."

The old helmer nods, but not necessarily in agreement, or so it seems to Isabella. He looks at her again.

"No harm in being civil though, eh Mistress."

She smiles gratefully at him as the shimmer of tiny bells rings out, signally the approach of their destination. The doors open and the dank smell of the stone cells elbows its way into the space. Isabella's smile fades.

"Huljun Terrace, City Side." The helmer intones.

The guard grabs the top of her arm and propels her out of the lift.

"That's the last of them."

The solid Matron of Ministrations is waiting for her, one meaty hand on her hip, the other clutching her official staff like a spear.

"What took you so long?" She snaps, jowls wobbling with annoyance.

"I…" Isabella opens her mouth to speak but again the guard speaks over her.

"This one was sucking up to the White Demon and the Princeling. Can you imagine?" His face twists into a sneer.

To Isabella's surprise, the Matron turns her usual contempt reserved for the Anahera onto the guard.

"She has as much chance as anyone. Don't you have some boots to polish or something?" She stares pointedly at his feet.

He glances down then catches himself and glares back up at her.

"Teach 'em to do as they're told next time." He snaps and turns to the lift-helmer, who is watching this interplay with quiet delight.

"Barracks. Now!"

The helmer nods politely to him and touches the control screen. As the doors slide silently closed, he winks at Isabella. Her answering smile dies when she realises that the Matron is staring down at her.

"Umm…" she begins.

"Just so we're clear," the Matron of Ministries looms over her, "our esteemed Prince is not going to choose the likes of you. He'll go for someone who's far more regal and," she flicks her gaze up and down Isabella, "far more attractive."

Isabella pouts. "There's no need to be hurtful."

The Matron snorts, her nostrils flaring. "Just speakin' the truth. And as for that other one, don't worry, you're safe from his clutches." She gestures with her staff, the bells clanking. "He's not Gentry and I'm certain he's never even been with a woman, or a man for that matter. He's without feeling that one, as cold as a frozen sea." She holds up a hand and clicks her fingers, summoning two attendants. "Strip this one and launder the gown."

As Isabella moves to follow them, the Matron holds a large hand up in front of her face.

"Stop."

She turns to face the cells and Isabella takes the opportunity to roll her eyes behind her back.

"Listen up." The Matron's voice booms along the corridor and into each barred cell. The other Anahera look up, wondering what the latest bellowed edict will be.

"You have one full day before the Offering, where the Gentry will put forward their proposals. We've a lot to do, so lights will be out in five minutes. You." She turns back to Isabella, whose face has resumed a more fitting expression. "Get ready for bed-down quickly. Come on!" She claps her hands sharply next to Isabella's head until she scurries to catch up with the attendants.

Far above on the Ostium Terrace, the Reception party begins to

134

wind down, drunken Gentry tripping off to find cloaks, errant partners and lifts. Meridian wanders out onto the balcony in search of Bryant, an illicit tankard of beer in each hand. The Drw-ad almost blends into the darkness and still stands by the parapet, watching the city below.

Meridian appears next to him, plonking a tankard down onto the stone wall and slopping a little beer onto his blue silk coat. Bryant looks down with faint distaste and sighs.

"You're brooding. Stop it." Meridian picks the tankard up again and bobs it in front of Bryant's nose. "Drink. I find it helps."

The Drw-ad gives in and accepts the beer, tipping the tankard towards his lips. Before he drinks, he speaks. "There is a storm coming."

Meridian glances in the direction of his gaze, where a cloudbank blossoms over the dark mountains in the distance, edges lined with silver moonlight. "Just a little one." He takes a healthy swig of beer. "It'll be gone by morning."

"I doubt that," the Drw-ad murmurs to himself. He takes a sip of the brew and winces. "Where did you find this…concoction? I thought the Queen ordered the Reception to be more refined."

The blond prince grins at him and raises the tankard in a toast. "I know a guy."

Bryant stares down at the murky contents of the tankard for a moment then takes another sip. The flavour has not improved. "Have you made a decision yet? The King and your stepmother will not wait long before demanding an answer, you know."

It is the Prince's turn to look pensive, his gaze locked on the approaching storm clouds.

"I was enjoying myself until you reminded me." He suddenly feels very tired. "It's not the kind responsibility I take lightly." He has struggled with whether or not he is ready to Offer in the first place. "How about you? That thing between you and the Anahera was entertaining to watch."

"Entertaining?"

The Prince grins at him but his humour quickly fades when he sees the look on Bryant's face. It is one he has never seen before.

"Meridian, there is no point in dwelling on the idea. I am not Gentry, I am not even truly human. I have no legal right to Offer for her in the first place." For a moment, he feels as if the night is constricting around him. "Remember brother, my kind do not marry. There is no precedent for this."

For a while the Prince is silent, thinking. He understands Bryant's reservations, and his quiet desire. Unlike the Drw-ad, he has had his fair share of women but recently he has become tired of the games. No Gentry woman is really interested in him, rather they covet his position and what they can gain from him. Granted, the Anahera must choose someone to protect them, so their motives are not exactly pure, but he harbours the hope that they will at least approach each of them with an open mind. Increasingly, Meridian has found himself craving an ally, a woman who can match him, stand by him and fire his blood. He has a feeling he may have found her, but whether or not she considers *him* a worthy choice is entirely up for grabs.

Finally, he speaks. "Do you find her…interesting?" He chooses the word carefully. He has watched Bryant struggle as they grew up together, seen him set apart time and again and has an inkling of the vast pool of loneliness resting inside him.

Bryant nods slowly.

"If you were able to Offer, would you?"

After a moment, the Drw-ad's midnight lips form a simple syllable.

"Yes."

The Prince drops a hand on his shoulder. "Then by all that's holy, go and petition my Father for the right to Offer!"

Bryant shakes his head. "The son of his most dangerous enemy begging for the right to marry one of his precious Anahera? No, old friend, he will simply laugh at me."

"Remind him of how much he owes you." Meridian presses his

136

fingers more insistently into Bryant's shoulder. "You've dealt with far more perilous situations than this, both on the battlefield and in this place." He waves a hand to encompass the Citadel. "Bryant, you're no coward."

The Drw-ad finally looks at him, black eyes like deep alien pools reflecting the moon's light.

Meridian presses on. "What if she's worth the risk? If nothing else, she might be a useful ally and the Goddess-knows we both need more of them right now."

Bryant finally gives in, if nothing else just to stop him talking.

"I will consider it."

Meridian grins again. "Excellent! Now finish your beer."

7. THE OFFERING

The next afternoon, the Drw-ad finds himself perched on the edge of a black lacquered settee in the foyer of the royal apartments. He is sure that Queen Makeda has designed it specifically to make petitioners feel as uncomfortable as possible. He has already waited over an hour, but knows that Gentry can sometimes wait days for an audience with their leaders. Within the Citadel, Makeda's power is absolute, whilst her husband is responsible for the surrounding lands.

Finally, a purple-liveried servant appears and ushers him into the inner sanctum. Although he has seen it many times before, he is struck by the extraordinary view from this side of the peak. Stretching out before him is the glittering sea and the curve of Weisdale voe. The busy port juts out of the base of the mountain and above the peninsula along the coast, Windpyre waka float waiting to dock. They are forbidden from coming any closer.

The servant leads him through to where the royal couple are taking refreshments on the balcony, under a canopy of vivid pink flowers in the shape of tiny parasols. Queen Makeda is as stunning as ever, dark curls piled in an elaborate bun behind her head, her dusky skin dappled with light.

The King leans back in his seat and runs a hand through his grey-blond hair.

"Lathorne, this is unexpected. You don't often seek us out - we usually have to have you extracted from your tower like a whelk from its shell!"

The Queen, already several months pregnant, rests her hand on her husband's arm. "Jonat, it's lovely to see Lord Lathorne. Might we make him welcome?" She smiles encouragingly at the serious Drw-ad and motions for him to sit.

Sarn eyes him speculatively, as for once the normally stoic Lord seems hesitant. He has watched the strange, delicate boy turn into a fine man, a fittingly calm foil for his exuberant son Meridian and despite his reservations about continuing to keep the son of his most powerful enemy under his roof, at times he finds himself feeling oddly protective of him. He glances at his wife who is watching Bryant keenly.

As ever, Makeda marvels at the smooth, almost predatory way he moves and the icy calm which wraps around him and she ponders what kind of man he really is underneath.

"What's your petition?" The King leans forward, genuinely interested.

Bryant has rehearsed this request over and over during the journey to the royal apartments but suddenly that does not feel like enough. He glances between the two royals, one of whom he knows has the patience of a rooster when dawn breaks. He lifts his chin slightly and begins.

"I have served you since I was a child."

The King's patience stretches. "This, I know. Get to the point."

Makeda frowns at her husband. She is fascinated by this alteration in the behaviour of the usually reserved Drw-ad and does not want her impatient husband to put him off.

"Go on, Bryant." She uses his first name in the hope of setting him more at ease.

He nods respectfully to the Queen. "I have trained for you, fought for you, repaired the Citadel's Shield," he pauses at this memory, "used my influence to secure you intelligence and advantage against my own kind…"

The King nods, conceding these points.

139

"And in all that time I have not asked for a single thing for myself in return."

Sarn's eyes narrow. "You wish me to release you from your bond? You want to go home?" He has long dreaded this day, knowing that he has no means to stop the adult Drw-ad from leaving. The implications of losing such a powerful asset are considerable, particularly if he intends to return to the White Spires with his entire knowledge of the Citadel. He has even contemplated having him killed, should that eventuality ever arise, although killing a Drw-ad prince would be both difficult and costly.

Bryant controls his response carefully. He must not get this wrong - it is the only chance he will have.

"I have no desire to leave the Citadel or your service."

"Oh?" The King is genuinely perplexed but also a little relieved. "What then?"

Bryant's next words take them both completely by surprise.

"I wish to ask for your permission to Offer for one of the Anahera."

The Queen has just taken a sip of apple blossom tea and she splutters a little and coughs. Her husband absently pats her back.

"That is not what I expected you to ask," he admits.

Bryant gazes at them impassively but inside his tension twists like a pair of oily snakes. "I am not Gentry, I am not even truly human, so I understand if your answer must be no."

But I need you to say yes.

Every muscle in his body is tense. "However, it is something I feel I must do."

The two royals stare at him and he is sure that they are horrified by the idea.

"And First Mother has given her permission?"

It isn't often that the King is confounded. He ponders the fact that that psychotic bitch of a goddess punishes even the smallest breaks in protocol with astonishing viciousness, so why would she grant

140

something so generous, even for her favourite son? He realises that the Drw-ad in front of him has not replied. Instead, he is staring at his hands, twisting the onyx ring around his white index finger. He looks up and Sarn feels the Queen tense beside him.

For the sliver of a moment, Makeda sees the edge of the vast loneliness lapping inside of him.

"She did not." There is an unusual intensity to his voice. "I choose this path for myself."

The Queen lifts her hand and swipes it through the air. A shimmering barrier descends between the couple and the Drw-ad. He recognises their desire to speak confidentially and so turns to gaze across the voe as he waits. The screen obscures the sound of their voices, as much as the view of their bodies.

"He wants a *wife*?" Jonat Sarn struggles to take this in.

Makeda leans forward. "Isn't this the perfect way to keep him here? To truly secure his loyalty?"

Jonat looks dubious and she continues in earnest.

"My love, he's rebelling against his mother! What must it take to defy your own goddess? Doesn't that show how far his loyalty to her has frayed?"

"I know why she agreed to send him as a hostage, she clearly thought to use him as a weapon against us." Jonat strokes his beard. "But he has protected us for years and if he wants what we have..."

Makeda nods.

"There'll be uproar." He mutters. "The Gentry will be horrified."

Her smile widens to a grin. "And won't that be fun to watch."

Jonat picks up her hand and kisses her fingertips.

"You are a wicked tart at times."

"And you love it, old man." She waves her hand back again and the veil dissolves.

The Black Drw-ad sits to attention, expecting the worst.

"Fine," the King shrugs, "you may Offer. But!" he raises a cautionary finger as the Drw-ad's dark eyes widen with shock.

141

"You're on your own with the consequences of your decision."

Bryant dips his head in agreement. The fact that he has been allowed to at least try buzzes through him. The chance to join with someone who might understand his predicament, who might become a useful ally and shield, is a seductive one.

Makeda gazes at him. "The Offering is tomorrow. Have you given any thought to your choice of gift? Or your choice of words?"

"In all honesty, I did not think I would reach this far." Bryant concedes.

Jonat scoffs and rises to his feet. "This'll be entertaining then." He moves to the balcony, already losing interest. Makeda glances at him, shakes her head then leans conspiratorially towards Bryant.

He expects her to toy with him but instead she offers sound advice.

"For the gift, choose something meaningful. Not too flashy, but something unusual that suits her personally. Maybe something she can actually use."

He nods. Any points of navigation in this foreign sea might be useful.

She taps her lips. "And when you speak to her, be truthful. If she's decent, she'll appreciate that and if you're successful, a marriage based in truth already has a head start. Think about how you would wish to be treated in her position." She sits back and rubs her belly thoughtfully. "You've been a good friend to this family Bryant, but you've been alone too long. Choose wisely and don't mess this up."

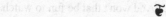

In a small corner of the Eyrie solarium, a single light glows in the darkness of the enormous glass-domed space, illuminating a desk covered in mandrels, dapping blocks, pitch bowls, soldering irons and racks of pliers. Pinned to a board above the desk are copious sketches and notes. Bryant perches on a stool as he works, his hair pulled back in a long ponytail. He wonders if a single Drw-ad has ever felt like this. Unions beyond their kind are prohibited and although the Whites and Reds are granted a little more freedom to breed amongst themselves, Black Drw-ad are expressly forbidden from joining with another. First Mother is a jealous and controlling goddess.

No great love affairs grace the pages of their books, no endearments are shared, even amongst the closest of broods. Loyalty to Mother, a thirst for knowledge no matter the cost, a sense of cold superiority and the right of domination are all classic Drw-ad traits. Mother engineers them with precision but attraction has never been part of the Drw-ad design, nor has affection. Yet here Bryant finds himself fixating on a woman from another world merely because she smiled at him and smelled intoxicating. He feels rather ridiculous.

He rubs his forehead and looks down at the object he has been tinkering with for hours. The first obstacle may have given way with almost dizzying ease, but what of the offering itself? Would this gift be enough? He runs his index finger around the smooth outer edge. It is all for nothing if he cannot find the right words.

The unbidden memory of her smile catches him yet again, along with the strange hitch at his core, pulling his thoughts back to her time and again.

Is there something wrong with me?

Some hidden mutation, pushing him away from the purity and purpose of the Drw-ad.

He closes his eyes. Her hand on his lower back as they moved through the dance, the way she seemed to breathe in and relax each time she was close to him, the flashes of both fire and vulnerability in her eyes, and how oddly warm he felt in her presence. He examines each moment carefully, remembering the feel of the curves of her body against his as they danced and the way she had hooked her hand around his arm as if being there was the most natural thing in the world. Then, equally unbidden, comes the memory of the blond Sir Lillaff, dismissing him instantly and pulling her away.

What kind of life would it be for her, joined with a pariah? Does she deserve that?

Perhaps it is a moot point – there is no guarantee she will choose him anyway.

He opens his eyes to find that one hand has clenched into a tight fist.

Why does human interaction have to be this complicated?

He picks up the delicate object in front of him and holds it up to the light, focusing on it to calm his scattered thoughts. Far to the east, dawn is breaking.

[9]The morning advances as Bryant finally makes his way down to the Huljun Terrace. The city side of the Terrace houses the cells and barracks, but stretching around the port side of the mountain are a series of elegant buildings, housing ceremonial event spaces. One such building has been repurposed for the Offering, a domed rotunda with a central corridor and small, circular, light-filled rooms attached like peas in a pod. Bryant thanks the helmer and steps out of the warm lift into the brisk mountain air, making his way to the entrance of the Offering building.

He pauses before the steps leading up to a pair of black doors studded with polished rivets. The Drw-ad runs a hand down the front of his high-collared, closely fitted coat, the gesture the only outward sign of his nerves. The material feels stiff under his hands, dark blue and shot with tiny threads of silver. Taking in a sharp breath, he strides up the steps and pushes open the doors.

The atrium inside is light and airy, covered in white marble seamed with gold. A heavy wooden desk squats in one corner next to a brass door. On the opposite side is a simple wooden bench. Perched tensely on this bench is a member of the Gentry, one Bryant vaguely recognises as being lord of one of the outer estates in the valley below. He does not look up when Bryant enters, continuing to stare intently at the door and the number display above it. A new number appears

---

[9] Playlist: Hunger – Amused.

144

and he rises, shoving the door open and striding purposefully down the corridor.

"My Lord, may I help you? Are you lost?" A voice at his elbow jolts Bryant out of his tense observations. He looks down at the small, balding official.

"I am here to Offer."

Bryant watches the man gape for a moment then hands him a slender document pod. "From the King." He places his hands behind his back and waits as the official hurries over to the desk and pops the pod into the console, peering down at the display. He glances up at the Black Drw-ad and swallows.

"Oh, I see...yes..."

A small stab of amusement prods Bryant as he watches the officious little man come to terms with the idea and is faintly impressed at how quickly he rallies, a polite expression coating his face.

"In that case, please take this quire and tap the image of the Anahera you wish to Offer for. I am not allowed to see your choice but I will be shown the appropriate room number."

Bryant scrolls through the images of the various Anahera, noting two he had seen Meridian dance with before he finds her. Her unsmiling image makes him pause for a moment before he taps the picture and hands the quire back.

The official glances at the screen and motions for him to sit.

"Room 12. Please wait for the number to appear." He points to the display above the door. "I believe you may be the last to offer, my Lord. The applications close at midday." He bows and moves back to his desk.

The Drw-ad takes a calming breath and slides a pale hand into his pocket, checking for the little box containing the gift. Unfamiliar emotions war within him - nervous anticipation and a pressing desire to run. Yet there is also that steady pull, like a scarlet ribbon snaking down the corridor and connecting him to Isabella.

145

She, in turn, has had an interesting morning. The Matron of Ministrations earlier explanation of the Offering process had not been a pleasant experience.

"Although there are a number of Gentry in this city, they rarely choose to breed outside their own caste. Marriage with those who are beneath them is ridiculed at best. You, however, are exceedingly rare and that makes you valuable. With an opportunity like this to add to their gene pool they take it, as is their right."

Beside her, Isabella heard Lianne mutter, "they seem to do a lot of 'taking', these bastards."

The Matron had glared at her and resumed pacing, gesticulating. "You are unique in this world. The Drw-ad would call you 'Collectables' and take you for their own. But we offered you a choice and you took it. Now you are granted one final choice. You will be presented with a series of Suitors. They will each make you an offer and present you with a gift. You will choose one of these Suitors and then you will be officially joined with them at the Ceremony tomorrow. You are granted this honour because you are joining the Gentry. By tomorrow evening, you will be one of them."

At her words, one of the Anahera seated on the other side of the cell had vomited and both Isabella and Lianne stared at one another in horror, their slavery suddenly deepening to a whole new level.

"Do you reckon we could lock ourselves in here?" Isabella whispered, suddenly feeling the weight of the mountain pressing down upon her.

Lianne eyed the bars speculatively. "Only if you've got a spare blowtorch down your knickers."

However, time, opportunity and underwear were not on their side and after being scrubbed, polished, shoe-horned into a dress and her rebellious hair tutted at, Isabella was deposited in the Offering room to wait. The first two Suitors were interchangeable and she couldn't even remember them from the rush of the Reception.

The next was the first man she had danced with, Lord Mirl, whose feet she had bruised with her ineptitude. He had addressed her in a haughty tone, declaring that he was one of the wealthiest men in the Citadel and that she should feel honoured to receive his offer. She smiled tightly and thanked him.

He waved away her words and deposited a heavy red box on the little table in front of her. Opening it, she found a thick golden necklace dripping with jewels, reminiscent of costume jewellery she had seen in theatres. She asked one final question.

"Why choose me?"

Lord Mirl had stared at her for a moment and then snorted out a laugh. "Because you've got wide hips - you look like you'll breed strong sons!"

She only just resisted the urge to punch him.

The fourth Suitor was more enjoyable company – her patient partner from the dance who had laughed about her 'safety pillar'. He smelt of pine forests and soft leather. He introduced himself as Sir Gellan and explained that he had worked his way up through the King's Own Uhlan to be awarded a knighthood and lands. He admitted that they weren't extensive, but pleasant. He promised her that, should she choose him, he would make sure she was cared for, for the rest of her life. On the table he had placed a beautiful, soft yargswool shawl, explaining that the winter would soon bite down hard over the Citadel and he wanted her to be warm.

Her final question made him pause to think.

"Because you seem like an intelligent, capable young woman…and you like a laugh."

The fifth to enter the Offering Room was Sir Lillaff, bringing his creosote stench with him into the tiny space. She had barely listened as he boomed his proposal at her, instead trying to control her breath and alleviate her sudden headache. He plonked a silken bag on the table, from which spilled a tiny galaxy of stones resembling

147

diamonds.

When she asked her final question, he eyed her cleavage and curves and licked his fleshy lips.

"Look at you – still tight and juicy down there, good for a few years of work in the sack before you're past it. What do you say? I've the stamina of men half my age!"

She had swallowed down her horror and politely bid him good day.

Now she sits, watching the late morning sunlight track across the walls from the patterned glass windows high above.

The gravelly voice of Captain Bannerman comes back to her: "This is one point where you have all the power." The power to choose, even if that choice is limited and contrived. To calm herself, she parcels the problem up into smaller, more manageable portions - who these men really are and how each of them has treated her. How will they treat her in the future? The overall picture? Survival, then escape and freedom. She massages her temples.

One step at a time.

Peering at the tiny sundial image on the quire in front of her, she notices that it is nearly midday.

So, this bizarre, twisted ordeal is almost over.

Isabella idly scrolls through the images of her Suitors and her heart sinks. Two nonentities, two arseholes and...one possibility. She is about to collect the gifts and pile them into the basket provided when she hears a sharp knock on the door leading to the corridor. *Another Suitor?* She takes in a deep breath, pulls herself up straighter and prepares for the worst.

"Come in."

The door slides open and Bryant steps into the room, the scent of fresh snow billowing through the air and blowing away the last shreds of creosote.

He closes the door behind him and bows to her.

148

"My Lady, I am here to offer for you." His voice is low and careful, his black eyes glittering.

"Oh, it's you!" She exclaims and instantly regrets it, for he halts at her words and drops his gaze.

"My apologies, Lady, I will leave you in peace." Bryant turns to leave, humiliation burning in his chest.

How horrified must she be at the prospect of a Drw-ad Suitor?

"Wait!" She rises, holding out her hand. He pauses, staring down at the silver door handle. "I meant, oh good, it's you."

The smoulder recedes and he turns back to face her.

"Please stay. I'm really glad you're here." She looks up at him, gentle invitation mixing with a touch of worry in her eyes. Her hair tumbles freely down over one shoulder, the dark auburn edged with gold in the late morning sunlight streaming through the windows above. Her body is wrapped in a deep red halter-necked dress, cinched at the waist with a wide golden sash dotted with tiny scarlet roses. Bryant's body reacts in a way he has never felt before, a curious pulse running through him.

Goddess, she is lovely.

It is another distinctly un-Drw-like thought.

"Please, will you sit?" Isabella motions to the curved leather chair next to him. He slides smoothly into the seat and she sits in return, taking a moment to study him properly. His long, blue-black hair, dark eyebrows and lips are in stark contrast to the white skin etched with transparent symbols. Although his appearance is striking, it is far from unpleasant. He is a handsome man, if a touch glacial in his manner, and his clothes merely serve to accentuate the taut musculature of his body. She becomes aware that the silence has stretched between them.

"So, aside from being an excellent dancing partner, what else can you offer?"

He takes this lifeline, pulling him onto more solid ground.

"I can offer you the Eyrie. It is safe and warm. I am perhaps not

149

as wealthy as many of your Suitors, but I have enough to keep you comfortable." He leans forward and she feels a thrill run through her.

Stop that! You're a grown woman with a deadly serious choice to make. Focus.

"I understand better than most the difficult position you are in and I believe that we can help one another. I will not force you to do anything you do not wish to do. I offer you protection and respect, as well as the freedom to do as you please."

Her eyes widen slightly at this. If true, the offer is precious...but can she trust him? After all, he is even more alien than the rest.

He reaches into the pocket of his coat and pulls out a small wooden box carved with tiny saurs, each tail curled around the next. He places it on the table in front of her.

"I have made you a small token, to show my commitment to this Offering."

She leans forward and picks it up, glancing at him. His cool gaze holds a sliver of uncertainty. Isabella runs her finger over the carved wood.

"Dragons." She murmurs.

Bryant's gaze does not waver but a hint of satisfaction lifts him. The dragons were a good choice.

Aware of the intensity of his scrutiny, she opens the box. Nestling on a bed of black silk is a small pendant of intricately linked silver wire in the shape of a six-petaled flower, reminiscent of Celtic knot work and dotted with seven tiny glittering crystals. She picks it up and discovers that it is attached to a long, slender silver chain. As she holds it up to the light, she feels it move between her fingers.

"Oh!" Isabella realizes that it is not a static object, rather there are several sections loosely joined together, meaning she can turn and reform them with ease, creating a new pattern to the pendant with each movement. "It's beautiful!" She looks up at him and smiles.

The worry vanishes from his eyes and he relaxes slightly.

"It is called the "Seed of Life" and it serves several purposes," he

150

explains. "One is to focus your attention when you are concerned about something. There are seven interlocking circles and a multitude of combinations you can create." He watches as she runs the glittering chain through her fingers and touches the tiny jewels carefully.

"Wait, you made this?"

He nods. "I hoped to make a gift worthy of you."

Smooth bugger.

"It is lovely. I am certainly grateful to have something to distract me in this mad place." She places the pendant back into the box. Closing the lid, she sits back and rests her chin on her hand.

"Final question then."

Bryant is careful not to reveal his tension.

"Ask."

"There are plenty of Anahera to choose from, so why me?"

He is not prepared for this candour but the Queen's words whisper in his ear, "be truthful". His gaze does not waver.

"You accepted me, without question. You tried to put me at ease, as if my responses actually mattered to you. There is an honesty about you that is rare in this world." Bryant tips his chin a fraction. "You fascinate me, confuse me, and yet I believe we could protect one another in this…'mad place', as you call it."

She cannot help but smile at this. He is a complex man. But, she reasons, not necessarily in a bad way.

"That's an interesting answer."

The sound of the heavy gong reverberates through the corridor, signalling an end to the Offering period. The moment between them is shattered and Isabella tips back her head in frustration.

"Ugh. As your friend said the other night, they're playing my tune."

Bryant rises and is about to offer his hand to help her up but she is already on her feet. The ugly thought of her trapped in those dank cells like a common criminal blazes through him and as the violent scent of copper rises, he has to pull himself inwards to hide it.

151

"Thank you for allowing me to offer." He bows solemnly, his tone cold and formal once more. He is trying to rein in his anger at her situation but to his horror, his sudden change in tone sounds contemptuous at best.

Something inside her shrinks.

Why is he suddenly icy again?

Is it the reminder that she is technically a slave? She bridles in response.

"I will consider your offer," she tilts her chin upwards, "along with all the others." It is a tiny grasp at power but it is all she has.

He is still for a moment then nods sharply and leaves the room, shutting the door firmly behind him. She feels her shoulders slump and she covers her face with her hands.

"What the hell just happened? This is mad!"

There is a sharp rap on the door behind her and a familiar voice barks, "hurry up in there!" Isabella rolls her eyes and finishes packing the gifts into the basket. She turns and opens the door, suddenly faced with Corporal Sour and Shouty, her escort from the Reception.

"Last again," he snaps. "Do I need to get you a leash?"

She opens her mouth to snap back but he is already striding away towards the service lift.

"Bastard." It is all she can manage as she scurries along behind him, her footsteps taking her back to the suffocating oppression of the cells.

Outside, Bryant pauses at the base of the rotunda steps and places his hands on the cold granite plinth of a statue. He closes his eyes and focuses on the biting chill, forcing the hot confusion downwards. One moment she is welcoming and filled with delight, the next she is cold and contemptuous, reminding him of his rivals.

How does one plot a course through such complex waters? He shakes his head. *I have tried, now I must wait.*

A tiny, insistent trilling sound intrudes upon his frustration and he opens his eyes to see a small message globe floating next to his head.

152

He is grateful for the distraction and plucks it out of the air. Work. Work will calm him. Slipping the globe into his pocket, he strides off to catch a lift back to the Eyrie.

"Well?" Lianne looks up as Isabella trudges back into the cell. The door clangs shut behind her.

"Life's an utter bastard and I want to go home." Isabella drops her basket onto a bench and plonks down next to it.

The blonde woman nods. "That good, huh?" She receives a baleful glare in return so she flicks open the basket and peers inside. "How many offered then?"

Isabella leans back against the rough stone wall. "Six. You?"

"Fifteen, including three women, which was flattering." She closes the lid.

Isabella sits up. "Well, fuck me. Or not, as the case may be. Why am I not surprised you're so popular?"

Mich, the Danish Anahera, strolls over. "Eight, and I even got two blokes in my lot too." She holds up her hands. "I promise, I was polite. No ball kicking." She shrugs and nods towards a handsome man leaning against the bars and chatting to an attendant. "I think Henri wins though – twenty three!"

"Do any of us actually win?" Isabella sighs. Her stomach rolls and she feels distinctly ill. Tomorrow afternoon she will have to make a choice which will change her life irrecoverably. She leans back against the wall, pressing against the stone and hoping for some clarity, an anchor for her thoughts. Unfortunately, the treacherous buggers turn towards her original anchor, Captain Bannerman. She closes her eyes, picturing his scarred hands, the cynical expression in his grey eyes and the scent of cardamom and cigars winding around him. The one Suitor she might have considered and he had abandoned her.

"Bastard." She breathes.

She opens her eyes and shakes off the image. Instead, she dips

153

into the basket and pulls out the yargswool shawl, wrapping it around herself. It is incredibly soft and the warmth envelops her immediately.

"Ooh, lovely!" Lianne leans over and strokes the shawl. "That's a thoughtful gift."

Isabella nods. "He seems like a nice man. He's got a good, cynical sense of humour. Yes!" She holds up a hand before Lianne can speak. "I know; he'd need it, to put up with me." She narrows her eyes. "So, did a handsome Prince Charming offer his saintly, masculine hand for you?"

Lianne's expression changes. She looks down at her hands.

"Izzy, this is horrible. How are we going to get through it?" She looks up again, her eyes filled with apprehension. "What if it's the wrong choice? We know nothing about these people. It's an arranged marriage from hell!"

Isabella blinks in surprise. She realises that her normally feisty, practical friend is actually shaking. She opens the shawl and tucks it around Lianne's shoulders. The blonde woman sighs and leans against her. Isabella has a sudden thought.

"Hey, look at this." She reaches into her basket and pulls out the little wooden box. She points to the carvings. "Dragons! And," she opens it carefully and pulls out the pendant, dangling it in front of them. "Look what it can do." She pushes the petal rings and shifts it to a new design. "Cool, eh?"

Lianne sits up. "Interesting." She peers more closely at it. "That's clever."

Isabella nods. "Apparently he made it himself." Suddenly she can see him, watching her carefully across the Offering room table, his dark eyes edged with concern as she opened his gift. And there it is, the conundrum. Who to choose, the Knight or the man who smells of snow?

154

8. THE CEREMONY

"Stop fidgeting and stand still, woman!" Saga slaps Isabella's hand down as it creeps towards her hair again. She pokes her tongue out at him in response. "Oh, that's lady-like. What's your Suitor going to think when he finds out you have the mind of a four-year-old?"

Isabella sighs and stares up towards the ceiling, trying hard to ignore the surrounding crowd. The Anahera are grouped on one side of the mezzanine level of the Great Hall. It is a luxurious space – white marble seamed with gold, plush red carpets and glittering crystal chandeliers drifting untethered high above. Attendants flutter around their respective Anahera, primping and fussing.

Saga steps back and checks the look of the ensemble. He is still surprised she chose this particular style, although he realises he shouldn't be, considering her perfume choice. It is a glittering green sari he had picked up from the southern Windpyre tribe years before. The choli is embroidered with curling paisley leaves in silver and cream, and fits snugly to her body. The rear of the tight blouse is open, the dip of her spine accentuated by silver beaded drawstrings which dangle down her back. A chartreuse sari flows to the floor and a delicately embroidered pallu is draped across her body and tucked over her shoulder. As with her outer dress at the Reception, the pallu floats behind her as she moves. Saga is quietly pleased with the outcome. He has even allowed her to wear jewelled slippers rather than the heels she detests.

As he checks the placement of the jewels in her hair, Isabella suppresses a smile. Today his formerly blond hair is coiffed into black waves, rising to wrap around a fascinator the shape of a Windpyre ship in recognition of her love of the fragrance. Saga is determined to start a new trend of Windpyre accessories, something he has never considered before. His Anahera is certainly opening up new creative possibilities for him.

On the level below, the sound of the crowd swells as the Gentry are finally allowed into the Great Hall. This presents another problem for the Master of Ceremonies as a gaggle of Suitors surges up the stairs on the other side of the mezzanine floor, heading for the corridor which will lead them to their own annex. Cahuil Orda is horrified - he does not want them to see the Anahera before the ceremony as it will ruin the drama of the moment. He quickly realises that he need not be concerned as the usual Gentry self-absorption asserts itself. All they are focused on is being the first to the door.

Isabella spots Sir Gellan waiting patiently at the back of the crowd of Suitors. He smiles as he spots her, places a hand on his chest and bows. He has aged well and is still a handsome man, with silken grey hair flicked back from his forehead and kind blue eyes. Isabella feels a distinct pang of guilt. He is a good man and she does not want to insult him. She bites her lower lip and slowly shakes her head.

For a moment he stares at her, then smiles ruefully and shrugs. Again, he bows, this time in a gesture of thanks. He is disappointed but grateful, turning and making his way back down the stairs to join the spectators in the Great Hall.

Saga touches Isabella's shoulder. "That was a real kindness. You've just allowed him to get away with his honour intact. Not being chosen would be humiliating." He resolves to spread this little tidbit around – this is certainly one Anahera to watch.

They are finally allowed to wait in a high-ceilinged antechamber. The tall, duck-egg blue doors are closed and flanked by two guards who stand with pikes. It is their task to open the doors for each Anahera.

A shimmer has been placed next to the doors, the large circular screen showing images of the enormous vaulted Great Hall beyond, the crowds of seated Gentry and the long aisle leading to a wide dais at the end of the room. Two thrones have been set up off to the side, ready for the royal couple.

The Master of Ceremonies claps his hands for their attention and waits until the Anahera are silent. "My assistants will come around with the official quire. The Suitors who chose to Offer for each of you will appear on the screen." He scans the room with a stern look. "There will be no other choices. Tap the image of the Suitor you wish to accept. When you see them move to the front of the dais, the system will call your name. You may then enter the hall and begin your new life."

One of the Anahera, a blonde girl from Norway, suddenly sobs and is immediately surrounded by attendants, cooing her into a semblance of calm and retouching her makeup and hair.

Adejola gives a heavy sigh and moves to one of the chairs along the side of the room, slumping into it and placing his head in his hands. He still wears his wedding ring, the polished gold glinting against the silken brown of his skin. Isabella walks over and places a hand on his shoulder. His voice is thick with despair. "How can I do this? My wife…"

Isabella looks at the man, so strong and capable, brought low by a nightmare journey between worlds and the weight of impossible choices. Gathering her sari, she crouches next to him and speaks in a low tone.

"It sucks, but we don't have much choice but to play the hand we're dealt. Maybe there is a way to get back, so you can be with your family again."

He looks at her between long fingers, his brown eyes heavy with misery.

"Who knows," she leans forward earnestly, "there's powerful magic here and we don't know what they're capable of. Surely, it's

157

better to survive, so that at some point in the future, we can find a way back."

"And what if there is not a way?" His deep, lilting voice remains heavy. "What if I am trapped with this new wife forever?"

She takes his hand in hers and squeezes it. "Take each step as it comes. Deal with it and move to the next. Hold onto your hope, it's a powerful thing." But as she says this, she knows it is hypocrisy – she is alone and has not lost a spouse and a child as he has. His loss is far greater than hers.

"Are you not scared?"

"Bloody terrified." She smiles tightly. "How am I supposed to know if this is the right choice or the dumbest decision of my life?"

Now it is his turn to pat her hand in comfort.

A fanfare of trumpets rolls through the hall beyond and into the antechamber, heralding the entrance of the royal couple. Isabella rises to her feet, smoothing down her pallu and tucking a stray curl behind her ear.

Cahuil Orda claps his hands again and his voice echoes across the chamber. "Places people, now!"

On the other side of the Great Hall lies the Suitors' antechamber. It has dark, panelled walls and is dotted with leather armchairs and plush chaise lounges. Large ceramic vases hold sprays of fragrant white flowers, failing entirely to compete with the manufactured perfumes and colognes coating each guest. The room is filled with Gentry Suitors, along with a number of servants moving discreetly between them offering refreshments. Some of the hopefuls are relaxed and chatting excitedly. Others are more nervous, perched on the edge of their seats or pacing back and forth near the roaring fire and the tall, mullioned windows.

When Bryant walks in, a stunned silence falls as every head turns to stare at him. He pauses for a moment, wrapping himself in his usual protective visage, appearing every inch the cold and contemptuous

Drw-ad. A young waiter, new to the role and remembering his manners, lurches forward and offers Bryant a glass of sparkling wine the colour of smashed rubies. With this, the spell is broken and a swirl of muttering rises from the Gentry.

"Why is he here?"

"Is he lost?"

"Surely that creature hasn't been allowed to offer!"

"Is he even allowed in here?"

The raven-haired man ignores each of the acidic comments, bar one.

"Why would anyone want him?"

It is a refrain he has heard so often in his own head over the years in this foreign city, that to hear it spoken aloud almost makes him spin around and stride for the safety of the Eyrie.

A figure detaches itself from the crowd and steps towards him. It is Lord Mirl, tall, blond and strikingly handsome, his aquiline nose lifted in distaste. Over the years he has made no secret of his utter contempt for Bryant, even after he had helped rescue Mirl's personal House Guard from certain death during a marauder ambush, not two years before.

"And what right have you to offer? You're not one of us." His voice drips with disgust.

Bryant does not move, staring the arrogant Lord down.

"I have the right." His voice is deep and quiet, each word carefully emphasised.

Another Suitor joins Mirl, her body sliding sinuously from behind him. Her blonde hair is twisted into an intricate pattern above delicate features and high, contoured cheekbones. She wears a sheath dress made from the glittering scales of a reptile Bryant knows to be almost extinct. Behind her head curves a high collar topped with pearls.

"Lady Wildervene." The Drw-ad tips his head politely.

Her lips form a smile entirely devoid of warmth and she raises a sharp eyebrow, plucked to within an inch of its life.

159

"Our beloved King would never grant such an honour to a feral. You must be mistaken." She flips a delicate hand as if to shoo him away. "Run along back to your filthy lair."

Already on edge, Bryant feels his temper begin to flare. Lady Wildervene loses her expression of spite in favour of alarm when she sees tiny flames dance around the edges of Bryant's black eyes. The scent of copper rises and the very air between them seems to crackle.

Mirl rears back, shoving Lady Wildervene between them as a shield. "Lathorne! You wouldn't dare!"

"He would, and you'd deserve it." Meridian's voice cracks across the room like a whip as he strides through the door. "Enough of this!"

He stands in the centre of the room, the Gentry falling back in a semblance of respect for the Prince. A potent force to reckon with, his powerful frame is swathed in a uniform of pale ceremonial gold. His hair is pulled into a neat topknot and secured with a jade hairpin and for once his beard is neatly trimmed.

"We're all here for the same purpose, including Lord Lathorne. He has my parents' blessing." He claps his hands and rubs them together. "So, let's all just relax and have a drink." He motions to the servants who busy themselves with the refreshments.

Meridian turns to Bryant, whose eyes have resumed their normal midnight shade.

"Thank you, old friend."

But Meridian places a hand on his shoulder and propels the Drwad across the room to a shallow alcove, pushing him against the wall. His muscled bulk deliberately shields Bryant from the sharp eyes of the Gentry.

"Are you mad? What are you doing?" He hisses, his blue eyes darkening with concern.

"I apologise, brother," Bryant winces. "I should not have reacted to their taunts."

"Bugger them, we should have slapped those two down years ago!" Meridian snaps, then tries to reign himself in. "And I wasn't talking about them anyway. Are you sure about this? What happens if she doesn't choose you? It won't be pretty." He crooks a thumb towards the other Suitors. "Those bastards will never let you live it down."

Bryant's eyes glitter. "I am prepared for that. I have suffered humiliation before."

"That's no reason to make a habit of it." Meridian huffs. "Look, it's not too late to pull out now. There's no shame in it."

He has known Bryant for most of his life and has long regarded him as a brother. Together they have run the gauntlets of childhood and teenage years, fought side by side in vicious battles, made a formidable team during diplomatic missions and always had one another's back. But this is one of the few moments in their entire history together when Meridian feels the sting of real concern for his friend. The consequences of failure will be harsh.

Bryant raises a calming hand. "Meridian, was it not you who advised me to take the chance? To step forward, no matter the risk?"

The Prince's eyebrows lift in surprise. "And you actually listened to my advice?" He can't suppress his smile. "Now that's a first."

"After this, I may not make a habit of it." Bryant assures him. "The choices I have made in life have led me here. I must take this chance, Meridian. This woman is important."

As the fanfare heralding his parents' entrance to the Great Hall echoes through the room, the Prince shakes his head, his grin widening. "All right, fine, throw yourself to the horde." He holds out a hand and they clasp one another's wrists in a solid shake. "Now let's go and face the bastards!"

They both turn to watch the Herald attempt to shuffle the Suitors into their allotted order, a task the Prince has never enjoyed, since organising Gentry is a lot like trying to herd saurs. Sometimes they bite.

Despite his outward joviality, Meridian's heart sinks and the weight of responsibility pushes down upon him. Has he made the right choice with his own Offer? The Anahera he offered for is like no one he has ever met before and clearly strong enough to stand by his side. But is she strong enough to survive the Gentry and their caustic jealousy?

"My Prince!" The Herald calls, stress arcing from his voice. "Take your place please."

Meridian shakes off his gloom and slips straight into his smooth, confident royal persona, moving to the front of the line.

To the north east, in the centre of an abandoned broch near the small fishing port of Freester, a projected shimmer ripples across the outside of a tent and the fanfare pulses out of tiny revolving speakers floating in the air nearby. Eric Bannerman crouches, scooping up handfuls of water from a pail and splashing it over his head and arms, scrubbing the blood away. The Uhlan troop have had a successful day and none of the blood is his. He feels the slow burn of satisfaction that only two of his soldiers were injured in the raid on the slavers' camp, whilst the marauders had been routed, several killed and two taken prisoner for questioning. They are now shackled nearby, slumped resentfully in the dirt.

"Captain, hurry up, you're going to miss it!" Artur, one of the younger soldiers, calls to him.

He grunts and carries on washing. He is interrupted again, this time by Delilah who strolls up and hands him a bowl of steaming stew.

"Don't moan, I've even added some of that screamingly hot spice you like so much, and a couple of dumplings."

He doesn't mind when it is her rotation to cook, as he knows she had lessons from Lady Kahn in her youth. Anything is better than Artur's cooking, where everything comes out raw in the middle and blackened on the outside, even salad.

"Come on," Delilah chivvies him to his feet. "Don't you want to know who your Anahera has chosen? I certainly want to know how

162

high up the chain mine will manage to climb."

"She's not *my* Anahera," Bannerman mutters, but follows her nonetheless.

The soldiers range themselves around the shimmer projection, some sitting on slabs of stone from the crumbling fort, others leaning against the remaining pillars. Bannerman chooses this option and begins to eat his stew. Delilah perches on a slab of stone, her tight black braids glinting in the light. She pulls out a slender dagger and a whetstone, examining the blade carefully.

"I hope they don't mess this up. My Anahera, the blonde one," she waves her dagger in a thoughtful circle, "seemed quite capable." She looks up at him. "D'ya know, when we were attacked by a group of slavers just shy of the Gate, she grabbed a mace from a corpse and smacked one of them in the head with it. Cracked his skull!" Her warm chuckle tumbles forth. "She looks delicate, but I'm sure she knows more curse words than I do."

The Captain's lips quirk into the semblance of a smile. "Mine too. The first thing she did was swear at me. What kind of world do they come from?"

"Oh," Delilah grins, white teeth flashing against brown skin. "So, she *is* your Anahera now?"

He ignores her in favour of watching Artur scurry about the camp, collecting plates and desperate to finish his duties and get back to watching the shimmer. The tanned warrior rubs a hand over his chin, the stubble rough under his fingers. Finally, he speaks.

"She's determined to survive, I'll give her that. She has this way of making connections no matter where she is." He shrugs. "I don't hold out much hope though – she's a contrary bitch at the best of times." This is not entirely the truth. He has nothing but hope to hang on to. Despite himself, he feels responsible for her. He could have taken Emmeline's offer and run with her, but then what? The King's reach is far and he never forgets a betrayal.

A second fanfare struts from the speakers as the figures of Queen

163

Makeda and King Sarn cross the dais to take their seats. Bannerman folds his arms across his chest and waits.

The Great Hall is filled to capacity. The Gentry gossip, craning up to catch a better view of the dais and elbowing one another for more room. Some have even brought snacks. Soaring above them, the high vaulted ceiling in the palest of blue is hung with tiny golden lights, a galaxy of stars going completely unnoticed. Instead, the crowd check their quires for the latest updates of gossip, or place bets with one another over which members of the Gentry have offered and how successful they will be. The late afternoon light streams through the enormous stained-glass windows set at each end of the Hall.

The Gentry fall silent as the trumpets sound and Makeda and Jonat enter and take their seats. The Herald follows at a discreet distance before turning and striding to the front of the dais. He bows deeply towards the monarchs and cries out in a voice powerful enough to carry to the very end of the Hall.

"Beloved leaders, celebrated members of our feted Gentry, welcome to the first Acceptance Ceremony in over a century!" He raises his arms skyward for effect and the crowd roars in response. The Herald waits for a few moments, basking in their delight, before lowering his arms, appealing for calm. "Our Suitors are on edge, as are the Anahera, so let's not waste any more time. Please give a warm welcome to the Suitors!" He flings wide an arm and steps to the side of the dais where a lectern awaits him.

Leading the pack is Meridian, the golden Prince striding across the stage to the side nearest his parents. He is followed by ranks of the other hopefuls who arrange themselves into rows around the dais. Bryant slips in near the back, hidden from view behind the other Suitors.

Meridian bows deeply to his father and step-mother then turns to the crowd and grins. They react accordingly, waving and cheering in fierce delight. Trumpets peel out again and the crowd falls silent,

164

simmering with anticipation.

The Herald clears his throat. "The rules of the game are simple. I will call a Suitor's name and they will stand before you..." Clapping ripples through the crowd. "If they have been chosen, the Anahera will walk through those doors," he indicates to the tall blue doors halfway down the hall, "up this aisle and claim their prize!" The ripple becomes a wave and again he has to motion for silence.

"But..." The Herald pauses for effect then leans forward in a conspiratorial manner. "If no one appears, with hopes dashed, the failed Suitor must slink off the dais and hide in a corner. What a humiliation!" The crowd roars again in vicious glee and in the shadows at the back, Bryant grits his teeth.

In the Anahera antechamber, Lianne has moved to stand beside Isabella. "This is just a game to them," she murmurs. "I think I'm gonna be sick."

Isabella pats her hand. "I wouldn't. You'll be surrounded by attendants like a swarm of flies before you even get a mouthful of chunks out."

Lianne stares at her. "Izzy, that's disgusting."

Isabella shrugs and forces a grin. "Made you forget the madness for a second though, didn't it?"

The blonde woman squeezes her arm tighter. "I'm glad you're here, you mad bitch."

Isabella tips back her head and barks a laugh. "Let's show the buggers. Head high, chin up in contempt, then sashay your arse off down that aisle." She peers shrewdly at her friend. "Are you going to tell me who you've chosen yet?"

Lianne, glancing at the shimmer screen, goes very still. The first of the Suitors is stepping to the centre of the dais as the Herald calls his name.

"Prince Meridian Sarn!"

Immediately the automated system in the antechamber barks, "*Lianne Silvercombe!*"

She issues a short, low growl, lifts her skirts slightly and strides forward, her head held high. Isabella is left to gape as the blue doors close behind her friend. She moves closer to the shimmer, watching as Lianne walks up the aisle, her deliberate sashay prompting an immediate bubble of pride.

Whispers flit about the crowd like tiny, manic birds. Lianne stops at the base of the shallow steps, her pale blue and gold dress pooling about her on the marble floor. She looks every inch the glamorous princess.

Isabella shakes her head. *Who would have thought she was just as at home in gumboots and a hunting shirt?*

Meridian bows deeply then holds out both hands in welcome. Lianne takes them and he leads her up the steps to stand at the side of the dais. They bow before the Queen and King, who clap in appreciation. The Gentry all scurry to clap in response.

"Bloody hell, I was only joking about Prince Charming." Isabella mutters to herself. She suddenly has the pressing urge for a stress pee. Her tension increases as one by one the Herald calls a name, the Suitor steps forward and an Anahera is summoned.

Not every Suitor is successful. After twenty minutes, twelve hapless individuals have stepped forlornly back. Isabella spots Lord Mirl, standing tall and sneering at each of the unsuccessful. When it is his turn to move, he receives an excited cheer as he strides to the front.

"Lord Mirl!" The Herald's voice rebounds across the Hall and the Gentry bubble with anticipation, but as the seconds tick on and there is no response from the Anahera room, their glee turns to confusion. The blue doors remain closed. As the silence stretches, the arrogant blond lord flicks his fringe back and glances accusingly around at the Herald, who merely shrugs apologetically. Whispers begin to spiral up from the crowd, doused when Mirl glares at them. Still the doors remain closed and the Lord's face grows flushed.

"Unsuccessful!" The Herald cries. "Step back, my Lord."

166

"No, wait!" Mirl snaps desperately.

"No one has chosen you, my Lord. Step back!" The Herald's tone brooks no argument, and with a snarl Mirl whips around and strides back to the row of the unsuccessful. The Gentry are genuinely shocked. He is one of the most popular and powerful of them all, from an incredibly wealthy family. Who could possibly have turned him down?

Far to the south, the Captain chuckles and hands a hip flask to Delilah, who returns his amusement with a grin. "Stupid bastard, for once he doesn't get what he wants."

"Couldn't happen to a more revolting bloke." Delilah raises the hip flask in a mocking toast and takes a swig. She winces at the brew but takes another, smaller, sip. "On the other hand, I'm bloody proud of my little blonde Anahera! The Prince is a good match for her. She won't let him off with any of his nonsense."

Bannerman snorts. "Good luck to him." The tension in his muscles returns as he watches the shimmer. *She* hasn't appeared yet, so perhaps there is still hope that she'll make the right choice.

In the Hall, Suitor after Suitor steps forward, either to welcome an Anahera or to slope back in shame. The rows at the back of the dais diminish until there are only a handful of hopefuls left. The Herald looks down at his quire for the next name and gasps. For a moment he looks unsure and glances up at the King. He is shocked when Sarn gives a sharp nod.

"Uh…" He stammers. "Well, this is a surprise. I give you…Lord Bryant Lathorne!"

There is a stunned silence as Bryant makes his way to the front of the dais. Across the Hall, Gentry mouths fall open, elbows jab the ribs of neighbours in shock and the silence rolls on.

In the late afternoon light in the heart of the old broch, the hip flask halts on the way back up to Delilah's lips and she gapes. "Holy shit."

Bannerman pushes himself upright, arms tightening across his chest. "Not him."

☙

The guards flanking the blue doors glance at one another. The automated system barks, "*Isabella Mackay!*"

She takes a deep breath and steps forward, ready to face the madness beyond, but she is forced to stop abruptly as two pikes clash together in front of her.

"This isn't right," the left-hand guard says, concern slapped across his face.

The guard to the right is clearly enraged. "He must have bewitched her!" He clutches his pike tightly and reassures Isabella. "Don't worry, we won't let the White Demon have you."

"But..." Isabella squawks. "I've chosen him!" She waves her hands for emphasis. "And I think I'd know if it wasn't real. Please let me through." But they are resolute, the pikes staying firmly crossed in front of her. She glances at the shimmer screen. "Oh, shit."

On the dais, in full view of the crowd, Bryant stands, resolute, unmoving, his expression cold and imperious.

The silence grows heavier, as even the Gentry hold their breath. Off to the side, Makeda clutches her husband's hand tightly. As the moment stretches and the doors do not open, the very air seems to grow sharp with the crowd's anticipation of his failure. Bryant's heart, so cautiously filled with hope, begins to sink.

In the Anahera chamber, Isabella has reached the shouting stage. "I am *not* bewitched! Get out of the way!" But instead of moving back, the sharp tips of the pikes drop forwards. She is one heartbeat away from grappling for a pike and shoving it through the nearest guard when the Master of Ceremonies appears at her side.

"What's going on here?" He barks. Everything has been going so smoothly and he is in no mood for an incident.

"They won't let me through!" Isabella appeals to him, desperate now.

"Sir, the Suitor is a Drw-ad." The guard on the left counters.

"So, what?" The Master of Ceremonies snaps. "She's made her choice, let her suffer the consequences."

Like I will, if this keeps up.

"Open the doors!"

The silence in the Great Hall begins to slip as the Gentry shift in their seats, failing to suppress their sniggers. Finally, Bryant drops his steady gaze to the floor, ready to turn and leave. He can feel humiliation begin to gnaw at him, competing with the heavy pull of disappointment.

"I'm sorry, my Lord..." the Herald begins, but he is interrupted by an enormous crash as the blue doors fly back and Isabella is propelled from the antechamber, coming to an abrupt halt at the start of the aisle.

She takes a moment to recover herself, smoothing her sari, lengthening her spine, lifting her chin a little and staring down the aisle at the figure waiting on the dais. In his long, close-fitting midnight blue robe, he looks icily calm and regal.

Bryant, however, feels like he is about to choke. She is stunning. Her auburn hair is free of all constraint, tumbling down over one shoulder and flaring in the breeze from her movement. Her beautiful curves are wrapped in glittering green, each wrist wreathed in bracelets, and down the front of her dress swings the silver pendant he had given her in the Offering room.

Shock ripples across the room as every head turns, some Gentry standing for a better view of the Anahera who is mad enough to choose a Drw-ad. Although she is terrified, the little spark of rebellion deep within her flares and becomes a roaring flame. Her lips twitch into a serene smile and she sets off down the aisle, lifting her sari slightly to avoid tripping and adding just a hint of sass to the movement of her hips.

169

Beside Meridian, Lianne breathes, "that's my girl!"

As she reaches the steps, Isabella dips in an inept curtsey and Bryant bows solemnly in return. When she rises and looks up at him, her smile has changed from carefully sculpted to soft and genuine. Deep down, the hard-wired Drw-ad in him snarls at his weakness, but he cannot stop. That smile and the welcome in her eyes cracks open parts of himself he didn't even know were there.

He holds out a pale hand and she takes it, allowing him to guide her up the steps as she moves gratefully into his snow-scent. Together, they turn to face the monarchs and bow. Both the Queen and King clap, Makeda looking particularly delighted. A smattering of clapping from the crowd flourishes briefly in response, before being doused by embarrassment.

Bryant leads her to the back of the dais to wait with the other successful applicants as the Herald clears his throat and calls another name. A Gentry woman steps forward and the blue doors swing open again.

They stand a little apart and he releases her hand politely. Isabella is aware of the surreptitious glances from the other Suitors and Anahera but they are not what distracts her. There is a kerfuffle off to the side, where the unsuccessful Suitors stand. Lord Mirl is being ushered away, pushing and snarling at the attendants. His words can be heard echoing across the dais.

"She chose the White Demon over me? He's glamoured the whore, I tell you! It's an insult. Let me go!"

Whilst Isabella gains a sense of quiet satisfaction from his self-righteous tantrum, she realises that the man beside her has gone very still. She looks up at his stark profile, noticing the muscles near his jaw flex.

Reaching out, she slides her hand around his. He looks down at her, his black eyes so cold she almost jerks it back again. For a moment desolation swamps her until she feels Bryant's fingers curling around hers in response.

170

The Drw-ad finds his tension abating a little as she moves closer, her rose sandalwood scent drifting up to him. Her simple act of solidarity gives him an anchor and he watches her relax at his touch, turn and smile vaguely at the crowd, as if nothing is wrong.

The final Anahera has accepted his Suitor and as they move to join the others, the Herald bows deeply to the two monarchs who rise and bow in turn to the crowd. The Ceremony is over.

Delilah looks up at Bannerman. He is frozen in place, his face holding the kind of expression she has seen often enough before, but usually when he is about to head-butt someone in a fight.

"Eric…" she begins, but he shakes his head tightly. It has been some time since he has felt anger this intense. Finally, he drags his gaze from the shimmer and glares at Delilah.

"I didn't put my balls on the line for her to go and do something this fucking stupid!" He snarls. He can feel the rage surging upwards and it propels him forward, striding past Delilah and towards the entrance of the broch. As he passes the marauder prisoners, one of them makes a mistake.

"What's your problem, ya cunt?"

Bannerman is on him in a moment, hauling him to his feet and punching him hard. He hammers into the man, his fists splitting skin. Hands and feet still bound, the marauder cannot defend himself. He crumples to the ground beneath the onslaught and is only saved by the combined efforts of Delilah and Sergeant Doric as they wrestle Bannerman off him, yanking him backwards and out of the broch, propelling him into the frigid evening air.

"Alright, alright!" He snarls as he shakes them off. He takes a few more steps to the edge of the mound and stares out across the nearby voe. The warrior pauses for a moment, planting his hands on his hips and breathing hard, more from anger than exertion. "Fuck," he mutters.

Delilah and Sergeant Doric look at one another. They have never seen him react like this before and each is unsure how to deal with it. Delilah tips her head back, indicating towards the broch entrance.

"Check on the prisoners."

The Sergeant taps his fist to his chest in salute and strides back through the opening. He is the troop's medic, a foul-mouthed and messy individual who has known the two Captains for years.

Bannerman finally turns and walks back to the broch wall, dropping down onto one of the abandoned stones and resting his elbows on his knees. He pulls a small cigar from a pocket inside his leather wrist vambrace and stares down at it.

Delilah stands with her hands on her hips. "That was a pretty extreme reaction. What's going on, Eric?" He looks up at her, his eyes still holding a fierceness which makes her want to take a step back.

"Of all the choices she could have made, she chose him." He shakes his head and looks down at the hardbolt scars on the back of his hands. "If he doesn't kill her first, I will when I catch hold of her." After a moment he clicks his fingers to generate enough spark to light the smoke, jamming it between his lips and inhaling.

Delilah stares at him. She has known him for years but this is something new. He has always made a show of being utterly unconcerned for others but in truth she has watched him guide and defend his comrades and subordinates time and time again, even at the cost of his career and physical well-being. She watches him struggle to pull the usual cynical glower back over his face and she realises that his briefly unguarded expression was one of real confusion and pain. Could he actually care for the Anahera? If so, this was not good news.

The new couple linger behind the crowd, the Drw-ad unwilling to take her through them. Both the Anahera and the Gentry stare at them as they pass and Bryant sees that Isabella is as uncomfortable with this as he is.

They progress into a large room filled with long tables and high-

172

backed chairs. The room is packed with Gentry and their new Anahera mates, the latter certainly more subdued. Long, slender lights like spears hang from the vaulted ceiling above and servants weave between tables refilling goblets held aloft by demanding Gentry.

Bryant can feel the tension in the Anahera beside him, mirroring his own. In truth, he detests Gentry banquets, not least because every move he makes is assessed for weakness by the crowd. Now there is an added pressure – the presence of the woman by his side. Within the space of twenty minutes he has become wholly responsible for her well-being and there are already too many people paying attention to them. He ushers her to their allotted seats along the wall nearest the top table, the latter reserved for royalty. He may be considered a pariah by the Gentry, but to the royal family he is one of their most trusted advisors. Nearby, Lianne and Meridian have joined the royal couple. The Prince looks cheerful, although Bryant can see the tension in his friend as he leans to explain something to his new wife.

Isabella is painfully aware of the cold, silent man beside her, so tries to distract herself by taking a sip of wine. It is a potent red, heavy with the taste of black tea and blueberries. Servant after servant enters, each carrying a new platter and Isabella leans forward to peer at the plates in front of her. The nearest appears to be a fresh crab and fennel salad with the added aroma of lemon and green apple. In front of Bryant sits a platter laden with sea bass, roasted with thyme, lemon and little potatoes on the side.

"Wow." It is a little overwhelming.

"Is something wrong, my Lady?" Bryant's deep voice and measured tone cuts through her daze.

"Uh, no," she gulps, "I'm just not sure where to start."

"May I?" He holds out his hand and she passes him her plate for him to deposit a portion of the sea bass and potatoes onto.

Bryant eats a little of the nearby scallop and mussel salad but in truth his attention is elsewhere. Without appearing to, he scans the room, searching for anyone who may be paying them too close attention. He is determined to ward off any threat before it even arises. As the feast progresses, the Drw-ad also begins to wonder how he will deal with the traditional end to the wedding feast, where revellers accompany the couples to their apartments to encourage the union. He suspects his new wife may not take kindly towards it either.

Finally, Jonat and Makeda rise and bid the crowd good night. An enormous cheer goes up and as soon as they leave, a group of Gentry surge towards Meridian and Lianne at the top table. The blonde Anahera has time to throw Isabella a horrified look, before she is hoisted into the air along with her new husband, and carried from the hall.

Groups of revellers converge on each new couple, lifting them up and carting them away. One particularly drunken trio turns towards Isabella and Bryant, slamming into the table and scattering plates. Bryant is ready for them. The combination of a cold Drw-ad glower and a sudden flare of bitter white light is enough to shake them from their foolishness and they fall back, arms raised against the glare. They recover quickly, shrugging it off and moving on to the next couple. As Bryant pulls in the pulse of light, he looks down and discovers that his new wife's hand is curled tightly around the handle of her knife. Clearly, he judged her reaction correctly.

She breathes out. "Thank you."

Bryant rises and motions towards the doors behind the royal table. "There is a lift point just beyond. Shall we retire to the Eyrie?"

Isabella takes in a deep breath and nods, her stomach twisting. She follows him to the doors and they wait in awkward silence.

The trip in the lift is uncomfortable and strained as both try not to look at one another but remain polite at the same time. Unconsciously, Isabella begins to twist the edge of her pallu around her fingers. The helmer responds to the silence by pretending to focus on a phantom problem on his console screen. There is a sense of palpable relief when the cascade of tiny bells heralds their destination.

When the lift slides to a halt, the helmer bows and intones, "The

174

Eyrie." He is tempted to add his usual "have a good night!" but suspects that may not be the most appropriate thing to say, given the circumstances. Bryant thanks the helmer and ushers Isabella out of the lift.

They step out onto a stone landing leading to a pair of tall, heavy doors. Bryant solemnly offers Isabella his arm and she takes it, far more tentatively than before. They walk up the steps and pause before the entrance. Isabella realises that a smaller door sits inside the left hand one. She swallows, as the reality of her new situation threatens to choke her.

He turns to her.

"Do you remember the gift I gave you on Offering day?"

She nods and slips her hand from his arm, reaching under her pallu and pulling out the length of silver chain until the intricate pendant hangs between her fingers. Through his tension, he feels a kernel of pleasure. She is still wearing his gift.

"You said it had several functions."

He nods and indicates towards the doors. "When you wear it, the doors will recognise you and open. Try it." Hesitant at first, she pushes on the door and it opens soundlessly.

"Oh." She smiles softly, looking up at him and something in his chest contracts. He distracts himself by leading her through the door and into the atrium. The walls are hidden in shadow as a single lamp glows above the far door, illuminating the tell-tale sparkle of a crystal chandelier above. Bryant opens the door and leads her through into the inner sanctum of the Eyrie.

It is a substantial room, with a vaulted ceiling and flagstones beneath, covered with thick woven rugs. To the left, flames leap and crackle in a large stone fireplace and three comfortable, high-backed couches and a collection of easy chairs are arranged around it. Wide bookcases stretch up the walls on either side of the fireplace, stuffed with books and map scrolls. Bryant waves a hand and lamps flower into life above them, floating in the air. To the right, a large wooden

175

table sits near high, balcony doors. When Bryant steps aside, Isabella spots an enormous four-poster bed at the far end of the room. Her stomach twists further.

She is completely at sea, having no idea what to expect. She is barely holding her fear in check, her muscles aching from long-held tension. But when she looks at Bryant, she realises there is a kindness in his normally cold eyes.

"My Lady." His voice is soft, deep and careful. "I want you to know that you are safe here." He gestures to the room. "I will not force you to do anything you do not wish to do."

Her eyes widen in surprise.

Bryant takes a step forward and suddenly she is wary again. He sees this and stops.

"I promised you protection and respect. I will not go back on that promise."

She has not moved, nor spoken and he sees now the smudges of exhaustion under her eyes. He points to a discreet wooden door in the far wall.

"That leads to the servants' quarters. I have engaged a maidservant for you. Millie will be along shortly to assist you."

Finally, Isabella finds her voice, albeit one which cracks with both fear and fatigue. "And you?"

Bryant places a hand on his chest. "I have work to complete in the solarium. I will leave you to settle and bid you a good night." When she still looks hesitant, he tries again to reassure her, his frustration at his failure to do so biting at him.

"You may sleep in peace here. No one will harm you."

Her tension is obvious and it is beginning to get to him. He is trying his hardest but he has no idea how to proceed or what to say, so he bows and strides to the far end of the apartment, slipping through another door and up the twisting staircase to the solarium.

Isabella is left alone in the middle of the room, feeling as if a whirlwind has just roared through and taken all the air.

"Right. Umm…"

She looks around, unsure of what to do, when a soft tap sounds from the servants' door. It opens to reveal a young maidservant who enters clutching a tray laden with a glass jug of steaming liquid and a patterned mug. She has tanned, rosy skin dappled with freckles and her red hair is pulled back into two neat buns. She must be all of seventeen.

"Evening, my Lady. I'm here to help you with anything you need." She places the tray on a low table near the fire and moves closer, frowning. "You look exhausted."

In the face of Millie's unrelenting normality, Isabella pulls herself together.

"It's been an interesting day." She replies dryly and holds out a hand. "I'm Isabella."

Millie regards the proffered hand with confusion. No Gentry would ever greet a servant like this. She remembers his Lordship's earlier cautions: "The Anahera are very different. They will have strange customs and will not understand ours. You will need to be patient."

She takes a chance and shakes the Anahera's hand then proceeds to look her up and down.

"That's a beautiful dress, my Lady."

Isabella smiles ruefully.

"It is, but I managed to spill sauce on the pallu during the feast."

Millie narrows her eyes at the spotted stain. "Don't worry, I can deal with that." Suddenly she is all practical business. "We'll get you changed and settled then I'll take it to be laundered."

Isabella allows herself to be led to a heavy blue curtain behind which is a door. It slides open to reveal a large bathroom and she pauses, her mouth falling open.

[10]The vaulted stone ceiling is covered with a canopy of tiny lights

---

[10] Playlist: CloZee – Secret Place.

177

drifting slowly in the air. A large, arched window looks out over the dark landscape below. To the right is an enormous, circular wooden bathtub with steps running up the side. A narrow platform runs around the top, complete with a pile of soft fluffy towels and a basket of bottles, vials and soaps.

Millie sees her expression and shrugs. "His Lordship wasn't sure what kind of fragrances you would prefer, so I think he ordered half the shop."

To the left is a large, open shower lined with iridescent blue fish-scale tiles. Three wide-mouthed water chutes jut out from the sides, ready to dispense waterfalls of hot, mineral-rich water. Isabella turns to Millie.

"I think this may be my dream bathroom."

The maidservant visibly relaxes. She had viewed the Ceremony with the other staff in the kitchens, biting her thumbnail as she watched her new Lord stand waiting on the dais. She has no idea what kind of woman would choose such a creature and her gut has been twisting with worry in the hours since. A new Gentry mistress would be terrifying enough, but this woman is from another world. Yet the Anahera standing in front of her looks pleasant enough, if a little unsure. At least she likes the bathroom.

"Which would you prefer, my Lady?" She indicates each in turn. "Bath or shower. The bath won't take long to fill."

It has been a long and complicated day and although Isabella craves the relaxation of a bath she also has a burning desire to scour off the pervasive reek of the Gentry's chemical scents and the stress of the Ceremony from her body.

"Shower, I think. I don't want to put you to any trouble at this time of night." She smiles tiredly at the girl, who stifles her surprise. A Gentry mistress would never take a servant into consideration when choosing anything.

"It's no trouble, my Lady," Millie bobs a curtsey, "but if that's what you'd prefer, I'll prepare the shower." She strides over to the

178

wall where a series of levers are attached. She pushes one down and a cascade of water spills from each chute, the steam rising quickly. Millie pivots to look at the exhausted Anahera and taps her lips thoughtfully. Turning back, she twists two smaller levers and the water flooding from the chutes takes on a slightly green tint, the scent of a fresh herbal soak billowing into the air.

Isabella closes her eyes for a moment and breathes it in, the fresh burst softening her headache a little. Millie turns back and catches the blissful edge of her new mistress's expression. She moves towards her, ready to help the woman off with her clothes but the Anahera's eyes fly open and she steps back.

"Whoah there, missy! I can undress myself, thank you."

Millie pulls back her hands in surprise and takes a moment to process this.

"My Lady, Gentry never dress themselves. That's one of the duties of a servant." Millie bites her lip in worry, wondering if Lord Lathorne will react angrily if he finds she is not treating his new wife as she should. The Anahera in front of her raises an eyebrow.

"Not dressing yourself is ridiculously lazy. I am not a child. I can get undressed on my own." Isabella feels both irritated at the custom and a little sorry for the worried girl in front of her. "Thank you for preparing the shower. Could you give me some time to undress and wash on my own?" She smiles tightly. "Please?"

Millie swallows and then nods. "Of course, my Lady. If you leave the dress on the towel chest over there, I will collect it when you're finished." She curtseys and moves to the door where she pauses. "Are you sure you don't need any help?"

Isabella tenses. "Thank you, but I'm fine."

Please leave, I can't keep this up for much longer.

The girl nods and leaves, shutting the door softly behind her.

Isabella breathes in deeply, holds it for a moment then slowly lets it out. She undresses, and runs a hand down each wrist, sliding the bracelets off and dropping them on top of the clothing. Feeling a little self-conscious, she stands naked in the middle of the room, glancing around. It seems secure enough.

She raises her arms and breathes in again, tipping her head back and stretching, then she walks into the shower space and gasps. The water from the chutes crashes down over her body, shutting out all thought. She merely stands, letting it buffet her and wash away the stench of the Citadel in a primal union of water and skin.

Eventually, Isabella pulls her head from under the stream, runs her hand over her face to clear it and glances around. Recessed into the wall to her left is a shelf stuffed with glass vials and soaps. She riffles through them, pulling open stoppers and sniffing. Some have the familiar chemical punch of Gentry perfumes, making her wince, others have a softer scent and she finally settles on a small bar of soap which smells like mimosa. She runs it over her skin, before diving back into the waterfall.

When she emerges, feeling slightly battered but clean and more relaxed, she pads across the floor, snags an enormous towel from the pile and wraps it around herself. She moves to the door and cautiously slides it open.

Millie has been loitering nearby, worrying. She points towards the bed.

"I've laid out some nightgowns for you to choose from." She pauses and bites her lip. "Um…"

Isabella's lips quirk into a smile, genuine this time.

"Don't worry, I really don't need help getting into one." She steps forward. "It's late and you must be tired. Would you like to finish up and go to bed?"

Millie rides another wave of confusion at the Anahera's generous behaviour, however, she swallows it and curtseys, moving quickly to the bathroom to collect the sari.

"I've left you a calming tisane." She nods to the tray on the low table near the crackling fire. "If you need anything, press that pad by the servants' door."

180

"Thank you, Millie." Isabella smiles. "I appreciate your help."

The girl blinks at her, shakes her head and then departs.

Isabella chooses a silken nightgown in deep blue and pulls it on, adding the matching robe over the top and tying it to the side. She stands with her hands on her hips and surveys the bed. It is enormous, piled with soft covers and a collection of fat pillows.

She glances towards the door in the corner, the one her new husband took to the solarium and decides. Snagging the folded blanket from the end of the bed, she picks up a pillow and marches to the couches ranged in front of the fire, choosing the most comfortable one. She lies down, fluffing the pillow before laying her head upon it and facing the fire.

The high back of the couch behind her and the warmth in front give her some semblance of comfort but she can feel the suppressed tension rising inside her, creeping up her throat and threatening to choke her. For the first time in days, she is truly alone. Biting her lip, she tries to hold it down but it is too strong and it overwhelms her. Tears begin to slide down her face and a sob escapes her, deep and primal. In the depths of the night, in the high stone tower, she sobs out her grief and loss. Eventually, as unfamiliar stars wheel above her in the darkness, she falls asleep.

Hours later, the arched wooden door to the solarium stairs opens quietly and Bryant appears. He steps cautiously into the room. Although he swore he would leave her in peace, he cannot sleep and feels compelled to check on her. When he stands before the bed, he feels his stomach clench into a hard ball. The bed is empty – she has run from him. The familiar feeling of betrayal bites into him and he strides swiftly towards the atrium door.

As he reaches up to wave it open he is caught by a sound he has not heard in the Eyrie before – the soft inhalation of breath in sleep. He turns back, finally noticing Isabella's form curled on the deep couch by the fire. She has not run, but why is she there and not in his bed?

He moves to stand above her sleeping form. Her tumble of dark auburn hair is edged with gold in the glow of the firelight and her face is relaxed in sleep. Isabella's arms are wrapped tightly around her and her knees are pulled up. Bryant feels the twisting ball in his stomach slow and begin to ease. She has not left him yet.

He covers her with the blanket and then eases himself into a nearby chair, watching her with a mix of anticipation, worry and confusion, the unfamiliar feelings layering together. He realises that in this moment in front of the fire, with his new wife asleep near him, he feels more hopeful than he has in years. Lulled by these new thoughts and by the warmth of the embers, he falls asleep in the chair.

Just before dawn breaks, Bryant rises and leaves before she wakes. He does not wish to cause her alarm, particularly as he knows he has intruded where he promised he would not.

As he strides up the staircase, he feels more refreshed and rested than he has in years. He realises that he has actually slept, without the usual nightmares which plague him. Instead, that same odd, blissful calm he feels when near her seems to have extended to his dreams.

9. FINDING YOUR FEET

Isabella wakes to the clink of a tea tray. She opens her eyes to find Millie hovering beside the low table in front of her, looking worried.

"Are you alright, my Lady?" The maidservant's hair is now in two low braids and she twists one around her finger nervously.

Isabella nods and pushes herself upright, wincing at a crick in her neck. The couch is very comfortable, but it is still a couch. She realises that someone has covered her with the blanket.

"Thanks, Millie." She looks up gratefully but the girl frowns.

"I didn't put that there, Lady." She points to the tray. "I've brought a tisane to refresh you. There's toast and jam if you would like to break your fast."

Isabella pulls the blanket more tightly around her. The Eyrie has a hint of morning chill and when Millie notices her movement, she turns and stokes the fire into life.

"Millie, does Lord Lathorne have breakfa...I mean, 'break his fast' down here?" Isabella feels a wobble of nerves at the thought.

The girl shakes her head. "He hardly ever spends time here – he's either working in the solarium or out with the Uhlan." She perks up. "Having you here gives me something to do!"

Isabella smiles at this. "Have you had something to eat this morning?"

"I will eat after you've finished and have no more requests for me." Millie watches the Anahera's expression change, dropping into something distinctly unimpressed.

"That seems pretty unfair. Have a seat and we can break our fast together."

Isabella is unprepared for how horrified the girl looks.

"No, my Lady, I couldn't! It wouldn't be right. Servants don't dine with Gentry. Ever."

Isabella narrows her eyes. "Well, I'm not Gentry, so those stupid rules don't apply." She deliberately softens her voice. "Please share the food with me."

Millie shakes her head vigorously. "I couldn't, my Lady." She looks towards the solarium door. "What if his Lordship were to see me?"

"If he doesn't like it, then tough. He'll have me to deal with. Sit down."

"But…"

"Millie, SIT." Isabella barks and the maidservant's backside bounces onto the nearest chair.

"Yes, my Lady." She gulps, her eyes wide. She continues to look mortified as Isabella leans forward and pours tea for each of them, passing over a steaming mug then sitting back.

"Relax. If it makes it any better we could call this a 'request'." She sighs. "To be honest, I'd rather not spend my first morning here completely alone. I appreciate your company."

At this, the girl visibly relaxes. She leans forward and rubs her hands together, much like Captain Bannerman did when he created sparks for the fire on the mountainside. She places her hands on the top and base of the covered plate containing the bread and frowns, concentrating. After a few seconds, the smell of fresh toast seeps from the plate and Isabella sits up in delight.

"Millie, that's fabulous!"

The girl tips her head slightly. "Tis nothing. But warm toast is better, don't you think?"

They eat in companionable silence and before Millie can clear away the dishes, Isabella holds up a hand. "Will you stay for a

184

minute? I have something I need to discuss with you." She watches the girl grow tense again. "It's nothing bad, I just need to explain something."

She is not quite sure how to approach the issue, so she pours another cup of tea for them both.

"I know I'm going to be a bit of a challenge for you." Isabella looks sideways and mutters, "I am for most people." Taking a sip of tea, she looks back at the girl perched on the edge of her seat. "I'll admit, I'm not comfortable with this situation. I've never had a…servant before. Where I grew up, we were all expected to pitch in and work alongside everyone else."

To Isabella's surprise, Millie's expression becomes quite steely.

"Forgive me, my Lady, but now you need me. There are public occasions you'll need to be dressed for and you cannot be expected to fetch your own meals all the way from the Rivin Terrace."

Isabella regards her steadily. Apparently, she is just going to have to deal with the set-up. She sighs.

"Okay, I'll concede that point, but how about I propose a slightly different arrangement? I have no idea how anything works, so I am very grateful for your presence. What if we agreed to be colleagues?"

Millie mouths the word as if it is something very strange to taste, suggesting there is clearly no Hjaltland equivalent so Isabella tries another tack. "Perhaps advisor would be a better term. You could advise me on how to deal with all these new situations. I know I'm going to get an awful lot wrong over the next few weeks, so your counsel would be very useful."

Millie smiles. "That sounds like a good idea, but you must understand that Lord Lathorne may seem far more reasonable than the Gentry in his treatment of me, but things are done in a particular way in the Citadel and I don't want to incur his wrath if he finds I haven't been fulfilling the duties I am contracted to do."

As she is also not sure how he will react, Isabella gives in on this point also. She rises to her feet and holds out her hand. "So, we are

185

agreed then? You will be my advisor."

Millie stands and shakes her hand then sets about clearing away the dishes. As Isabella moves to help, she straightens abruptly and plants her hands on her hips. "My Lady, as my first piece of advice, I think you should change into your day clothes."

Isabella smirks at her sudden change in attitude and shrugs. "Yes Ma'am." She throws up a hand as the maidservant steps forward. "No! I don't need help. I can dress myself. If…" She glances around, suddenly unsure. "You tell me where my clothes are?"

The girl grins and points to a large armoire in the corner of the room. "There's a selection in there to start with."

Once she is dressed, Isabella begins to explore the inner sanctum. As well as the central room and the bathroom, there are servants' quarters and guest rooms along a hidden corridor. At the end is the servants' lift point, allowing them to come and go without having to walk through the Eyrie inner sanctum. She makes her way back to the central space and realises what lies beyond the large glass doors – a balcony. It is wide and paved with pale flagstones, overlooking an astonishing view. The city stretches far below, eventually easing into the vast sweep of the valley cut by the snaking progress of the Bonhoga River. Far beyond, twin mountain ranges rear either side, the tips dusted with snow.

Isabella is delighted to find the stone parapet is covered in trailing jasmine and large pots overflow with marjoram, thyme and sweet mint. A pergola juts out from the Eyrie wall giving shade over a large settee. It has clearly not been used for some time as it is empty of cushions and dotted with moss. Passionfruit and grape vines twine around the pergola struts above, the remains of their leaves littering the floor. Millie explains that Lord Lathorne had them all planted years before because he said they reminded him of his home in the White Spires.

Isabella's fingertips brush a spray of jasmine blooms. "It must be very beautiful there."

Millie shrugs in reply, not trusting herself to speak. She realises it would be imprudent to voice her immediate response, considering it contains the words, "I've heard the streets are painted with the blood of their slaves." She looks up to see her new Lady, hands planted firmly on hips, frowning at the abandoned furniture.

"Let's see what we can do with this."

It is not until early afternoon when Bryant emerges from the solarium. He finds the Eyrie empty and has another unpleasant moment, until he notices the balcony doors have been flung wide open. He discovers that Isabella and Millie, after a tussle over whether or not Isabella should be allowed access to cleaning implements, have scrubbed down the settee and covered it with plush, embroidered cushions. His new wife is curled up reading a book, with a tasselled rug tucked around her legs to ward off the chill of the mountain air.

"I hope you don't mind, I raided your bookcase." She smiles up at him. "It's astonishing that those little nantine bug things we were injected with translate the written word too."

"You like to read?"

She laughs and it strikes him that it flows naturally from her, not contrived and deliberate as it is with most Gentry women.

"I love reading! To dive into a story and immerse yourself, drifting away into whole new worlds..." She pauses and a shadow crosses her eyes. "Although actually traveling to a new world is far more traumatic and messier than I ever imagined."

He watches her carefully, unsure how to respond to this. She gives a little sigh and then smiles again.

"So, what are your plans for the day?"

He takes a moment to answer. No one has ever bothered to ask him before. "I have a meeting with my banker to grant you access to my accounts and then I must lead a training session for new Uhlan troops in the afternoon." He looks at her sternly, his eyes growing cold again. "Please stay in the Eyrie. You will be safe here."

Isabella's skin prickles in response to this attitude. "O...kay. I'm nobody. What exactly is out there that could possibly want to do me harm?"

He stares at her for a moment, his flinty gaze pinning her to the seat. "*They* are." With that, he turns on his heel and stalks away.

Isabella takes in a deep breath and looks around the empty balcony. "What the hell am I supposed to do now?"

10. EXPEDITION

This uncomfortable state between them continues for several days. The Drw-ad leaves in the morning and does not return until late. Each time he greets her solemnly and then takes his leave, retreating to the solarium to work and only returning deep in the night to check that she is warmly covered, before falling asleep in a nearby chair.

Isabella fills each day by working her way through the bookshelves, interspersed with long periods of pacing back and forth or sitting on the balcony wall, staring out across the city and the valley below. The grief of losing her family and friends is immense and she feels a heavy blanket of grey fog encroaching as her world contracts, suffocating her. Staying in one place has always been a challenge for her, let alone being unable to leave the tower, no matter how pleasant it is. She begins to wonder if her new husband is exaggerating the threat beyond the walls, merely to keep her there.

Millie watches her new Anahera mistress with growing concern. Over the days since the Ceremony she has become less and less communicative, no longer asking questions but instead smiling tightly whenever Millie approaches and refusing all offers of assistance or food. She seems to be existing mostly on cups of tea.

She recalls the last proper conversation with Isabella, in which she asked, "What exactly do the Gentry do with their time?" Millie had struggled to answer, knowing the truth lay somewhere between 'going to parties' and 'feuding'. She is not sure how to discuss her concerns with Lord Lathorne but to her surprise he comes to her

189

instead, appearing one evening when she is clearing away yet another uneaten meal in the alcove beyond the servants' door.

"Has she eaten anything yet?" His voice is deep and cold, but there is an edge of tension in his eyes.

"Maybe a couple of olives today, but nothing else, my Lord."

He nods and stalks away, but his concern is clear. Millie realises that he has no idea how to deal with this, so when she takes the tray back down to Lady Kahn in the kitchens she decides to ask for her advice. The cook regards her seriously. She has seen each tray come back untouched and is perturbed. Lady Kahn has known Bryant since he first arrived in the Citadel as a child and is well aware of his situation.

Thus, on the fifth evening of marriage, when Bryant has still not returned from a meeting of the King's Sallet Council, Millie appears in the Eyrie with a tray. The delicious aroma of chicken soup and freshly baked bread wraps around Isabella, rousing her from her funk. She pulls herself from a slouch and sits up. Millie leans down and plucks a handwritten note from the tray, passing it to her.

Lady of the Eyrie,
Kindly take this replenishment - it will do you good.
L.K.

Isabella looks up at Millie. "Who is L.K?"

"Lady Kahn. She governs the Citadel kitchens. She made this meal especially for you." She bites her lower lip. "Please try it."

Isabella feels the grey fog crowding back around her but after so many days, the smell of this particular food is intoxicating. She sighs and picks up the spoon. Her first mouthful is tentative, but the taste of the hot broth, salty with a hint of garlic and herbs, is enough. Within minutes the soup and bread have disappeared, closely followed by a slice of cherry cake for dessert. Isabella sits back and rubs her hands over her face.

"That was delicious. Thank you for bringing it up, I definitely feel a little less 'ugh'."

The girl in front of her sags with relief. "I shall tell Lady Kahn. She will be pleased!"

Isabella waves a hand. "I'd like to thank her myself. Will you take me to the kitchens?"

Millie stares at her. "My Lady, the Gentry never…"

"…visit the kitchens. Yes, I can imagine. But once again," Isabella points to her chest, "not Gentry."

The maidservant is swiftly coming to recognise that particular tone and the pointlessness of resistance. She bobs another curtsey, fetches a warm cloak, wraps it around the Anahera and leads her along the servants' corridor to the service lift.

When the lift arrives, the helmer is initially reticent. "My Lady, Gentry never take service lifts. They seem to think servitude is contagious."

Isabella smiles at him. "Well that's all right then, mate, 'cos I'm not Gentry, I'm just me. Your lift is lovely and warm and I appreciate your help in getting me there."

He looks at her shrewdly. He has heard of this new wife of the White Demon and the word in the shafts is that she is odd, even for an Anahera. Now that she is in front of him, he can see why. He has only seen the other Anahera at a distance or on a shimmer and every one seems cowed by their experience. Not this one. She looks tired and a little drawn but she holds herself upright and the warmth in her attitude towards him is without guile.

Eventually the lift doors open as the helmer intones, "The Rivin Terrace." The two women step from the lift onto a wide gantry high above a series of open kitchens. Each one holds a separate station – fish are being prepared in one, shellfish in another. Further along, ovens steam, tables are laden with pastries being rolled, pots bubble, joints of meat turn on spits and crates of produce are wheeled back

191

and forth. Scores of staff bustle through the spaces between, each one clearly focused on a specific purpose.

Millie leads Isabella to an open-sided wooden lift which takes them down to the floor below. She pilots her through the gaps between the kitchens until they reach a wide, arched doorway. Beyond, is a spacious room with a large fireplace, several comfy chairs and a dining table. It is an oasis of calm in the heart of the heat and steam.

"Isabella Mackay! I'm glad you decided to grace us with your presence." Lady Kahn raises an eyebrow and smiles, teeth white against silky brown skin. She is seated in an easy chair, yet it may as well be a throne, judging by her posture. Heavy curves are wrapped in a glittering blue sari and her wrists and throat drip with gold. Isabella can't help herself – she curtsys.

Lady Kahn laughs, a deep, throaty chuckle. "Oh, I like you already, little Anahera! Sit." Her warm voice takes on a layer of command and Isabella slides immediately into the seat in front of her.

"I'm glad you finally gave in and decided to eat. I was one step away from coming up there and force-feeding you myself. People do not generally turn down my food." Her eyes narrow. "I was tempted to take offence."

Isabella looks down at her hands, the heavy fog threatening to return. "I'm sorry. It just…all got a bit much." She looks up. "I didn't mean to insult you."

Lady Kahn nods and clicks her fingers. The scent of cinnamon blossoms forth and a plate of sugar cookies slides onto the table between them, followed by two cups of something which smells suspiciously like coffee. "Do you take cream in your chaoua?"

Isabella nods, wrapping her hands around the cup when it is ready. She feels tears prick her eyes. She had not thought to smell coffee ever again.

The cook leans forward, her tawny eyes serious. "I'm glad you came to see me, little Anahera, I wanted to speak with you." She motions to the plate of cookies. "Eat. You'll need to keep up your strength if you're going to survive that lot," she nods upwards, indicating the general direction of the Gentry, "and he'll need you to be strong."

Isabella sighs. "Look, I'm trying but it's pretty overwhelming. I feel so lost. And anyway, Lord Lathorne spends most of his time in the solarium or out training. He's not interested in me as a person at all."

Lady Kahn raises an eyebrow. "Really? He gambled everything on you! The Gentry are incensed that he was allowed to offer in the first place. He's not had much experience with this kind of thing and he's trying to navigate through it as best he can, trying to do the right thing. He is giving you time and you should allow him time in return. It's hard for him to soften his guard."

She sits back and her voice takes on a new tone, one that draws an audience in and keeps them spellbound. Isabella realises that the woman in front of her is a natural storyteller.

"I remember the first time I saw him." She shakes her head. "A skinny, white seven-year-old with hair so black it flowed like the deepest night. He was standing on the cobbles of the Huljun courtyard. The Black Drw-ad guard escorting him from the White Spires just turned and left him alone, without even a word of goodbye." She takes a sip of chaoua.

"I knew it wouldn't be long before the Gentry boys set about him, they couldn't resist. There had never been a Drw-ad in the Citadel before, at least, not a live one, and now they had an official Hostage in their midst! For months he put up with their taunts, giving them nothing in return, until one day they cornered him and tried to seriously hurt him. My third son was a stable boy at the time and he saw it happen. The Drw-ad bested them all; spun and kicked, sliced and punched, until every one of them was a groaning heap on the ground. He nearly killed young Sir Liffin with that blood magic of his." Her voice takes on a deeper tone.

193

"Their families were livid and demanded reparations. The King had no choice, he had to assign a punishment. So, the little Lord was whipped, strung out in the main courtyard in front of all the families in nothing but a short pair of trews. Fifteen lashes to his back and legs was the punishment. Eight lashes in and he didn't make a sound. Just hung there and took it. The Gentry howled at him – they like to see you publicly suffer."

"But this was too much for young Prince Meridian, bless him, and he ran forward, stood before the Punisher and declared that as his father was elsewhere, he was the voice of the law in his stead. The Gentry were stunned," she cackles, "and he took advantage."

She leans in and waves a finger. "Never mistake him for being just a big blond oaf who likes his ale, that's what he wants people to think. That lad has a mind like a whip and he knows how to command."

"He called Sallamon Dae, the head of his father's House Guard and Captain Delilah's father, and didn't even have to *ask* for him to cut the boy down. My oldest son, Manvir, was there as Sallamon's assistant. He said that the Commander was livid with the Gentry and the King himself. Sallamon is a good man - he saw the punishment as dishonourable as Bryant had stood up to bullies and won. But he was gentle and lifted the little Lord over his shoulder. The Gentry were enraged but he carried that boy through the crowd, with the royal House Guard clearing a path for them."

She motions to the room. "He brought him straight here, because he knew I would protect him and he could not guarantee his safety in the hospital wards." Her eyes narrow and a dangerous look slides over her face. "The Gentry have no power here. These kitchens are mine."

"We made a nest for him on that table," she nods to a heavy table near the fireplace across the room, "and I tended to his wounds. His back was torn to shreds. Not once did he cry out – not even tears. But late in the night, as I sat with him…" She taps her chair. "He turned his head and said, 'I was just trying to survive. Why do they hate me,

194

Lady?' And the look in his eyes was different, not cold and glittering like the lost galaxies, instead he just looked like a sad little boy and very, very alone."

Isabella covers her mouth with her fingers at the image. Lady Kahn continues. "All I could tell him was that some people fear what they don't understand, and that fear can turn to hate."

"Sallamon would not let Meridian stay that night but the Prince slipped down first thing in the morning and sat with the little Lord as he slept. When he woke, I made their break of fast and although the Lord was silent, the Prince kept talking to him."

"I can still remember his words." Her voice takes on the timbre of a young boy. "He said, '*Those ratsnakes deserved what you did to them. When I heard how you'd beaten every one, I laughed and laughed! I wish I could fight like you – will you teach me?*' The Prince clearly decided that the Drw-ad was going to be his friend, whether he liked it or not."

Isabella cannot suppress her horror at Bryant's treatment. "How can anyone think that's acceptable punishment for a child?"

Lady Kahn shrugs. "They did not consider his age when they demanded that price. To them, he was merely a violent, bloodthirsty Drw-ad and they took their own bloodlust out on him. Not known for their self-awareness are the Gentry."

She leans forward. "And perhaps they had a point. It was practically a kindness compared to the punishments meted out by his own people. If you have angered a Drw-ad, you'll not survive it."

It occurs to Isabella that despite his apparent civility, she really knows nothing about the individual she chose to marry and not one single person has had anything positive to say about his race so far. Lady Kahn reads her expression clearly.

"Oh, don't worry girl, he's not a threat to *you*. Remember, he's put everything on the line for you." She undercuts this with a mutter. "His mama's reaction is going to be interesting, for a start."

She clears her throat. "Anyway, you'll need your wits for other things. You must understand that for the Gentry, reputation and their standing in the game is everything. If you cross them, they'll find a way to hurt you and they don't have many boundaries. They're also disturbingly creative."

"Which is why they demanded a small boy be whipped and humiliated in front of them because he stood up to their bully-boy sons?" Isabella frowns. A little piece of the puzzle that is Bryant has clicked into place. No wonder he expressed an understanding for the difficult position of an Anahera.

When you're an outsider, you're fair game.

"So, did things improve after that? I mean, if a prince was on his side?" She fervently hopes the answer will be positive, but the cook shrugs.

"Perhaps a little. The Gentry have certainly made things difficult for him over the years, purely out of spite. But he's no weakling – he is one of the Citadel's finest warriors. Even watching him train can be terrifying."

Lady Kahn smiles. "And he's not completely alone. Over the years, a few others have befriended him, mostly hostages from other lands and tribes – outcasts really, like the Lordling. Just wait until you meet his friend Vallan. He mostly smells of 'horse', but he'll make you laugh!"

The scent of cinnamon rises briefly in the air as she taps the table three times. In response, another plate of biscuits appears and settles between them.

"Lord Lathorne's a good lad, if a little odd." Lady Kahn leans forward. "But you're also very odd, Anahera. I know you had other Suitors who were worthy, but you chose him. Think about why."

Upon her return to the Eyrie, Isabella asks Millie what Bryant might eat for a late supper. The maidservant grins and then disappears, returning some time later with assorted dim sum and shao mai in small bamboo baskets and leaves them on the corner table, gently steaming.

Bryant returns in the darkness, tired of the bickering and obstinacy of the Gentry. There are rumours of unrest and increased marauder raids to the north east, but the Council refuse to investigate any further than sending a small party of Uhlan to patrol the area. He and Meridian are concerned but aside from Sallamon Dae, they have little support on the Sallet Council. Instead, the discussions inevitably return to commerce and internal wrangling within the Citadel.

He expects to see Isabella asleep on the couch but instead the room is filled with the delicious scent of steamed buns and she is still awake, reading a book by the fire. She rises to meet him with a hesitant smile.

"I'm glad you're back. You must be exhausted."

Bryant inclines his head. "It was a long debate."

"Have you had anything to eat?"

He shakes his head, though at the intoxicating scent of food, hunger begins to gnaw at him.

"Will you share a meal with me then?" Her eyes have an uneasy look to them, as if she is afraid he will say no.

"Of course, my Lady." He is surprised by her offer and relieved that she is finally eating something.

She moves to the low table near the fireplace, pouring a glass of wine and holding it out to him. He takes it as she pours one for herself. It has a lightness and a hint of sweet cherry to it, yet it does nothing to ease the uncomfortable silence which grows between them.

Isabella covers herself by opening the bamboo lids and picking out a selection of tiny dim sum parcels with slender wooden chopsticks. Bryant rises and fetches a platter packed with little bowls of sauces. They eat in silence, each concentrating on their selection and not one another. Isabella is working up to something and finally she cannot contain it. She places the plate beside her.

Bryant looks up, his expression wary.

"Lord Lathorne," she pauses then huffs out a little sigh. Knowing the right words to use is a struggle. "I wanted to...thank you."

He frowns. "For what, my Lady?"

"Offering for me." Isabella tilts her head. "You've taken a big risk for this, haven't you...for me?" She watches him go very still. He does not speak and the silence grows again. She looks down at her hands.

"This experience, this world, is so strange to me. I don't know how to deal with..." She waves a hand, indicating the two of them. "This, at all," Isabella looks up, "but I want to make the best of it and that's why I chose you."

Some of the stiffness leaves his posture. She bites her lip, "and...I want to help."

He waits, but this seems to be all she can manage. In the Citadel, an unsolicited offer of assistance is never what it appears. There are always layers of obligation to be wary of, but she is an Anahera and has only been in the Citadel a few days. Perhaps her intention is genuine. It is difficult for him to judge honesty and even more difficult for him to trust. He sets aside his own bowl and sits straighter.

"Lady, I appreciate your sentiment." He does not know how to put his feelings into words, instead he feels strangled by them. "I must apologise if I do not behave as you would expect. This is also uncharted land for me."

There is a fleeting moment, no more than a flicker, when she sees the hint of struggle in his eyes, before he resumes his flinty expression. In that tiny moment, she has the flash of an image - a young boy, white skin torn red by the lash, black hair hanging down over a face determined not to show weakness before his enemies.

Breaking through is going to be harder than I anticipated.

Then he does something unexpected, something which takes even the Drw-ad himself by surprise. "I realise that I have not treated you well, my Lady." She opens her mouth to protest but he barrels on. "I have left you completely alone, in a place you know nothing of. As reparation, may I offer you a tour of the Citadel? At least," he pauses,

198

his expression turning sardonic, "the acceptable parts."

She smiles. "I would like that."

Why did I offer that?

His own impulsiveness surprises him. He rises quickly to his feet. "I will come for you after the first break of fast tomorrow."

He bows stiffly, turns and strides to the door, slipping quickly through and taking the steps to the solarium two at a time. Isabella is left, sitting on the couch, her mouth open.

As Bryant reaches the solarium doors he throws them open, frustration rippling through his usual calm.

Why can I not speak to her normally?

He realises that, yet again, he has left her too abruptly. A Drw-ad would never be concerned with such human manners, but he has lived long enough in the Citadel to acquire them. Lady Kahn taught him better than that. He leans on his work table and grips the edge. Tomorrow, he will try again.

The next morning Millie makes sure Isabella is equipped for her tour – good boots, leggings, a simple yet elegant grey halter-necked dress and a warm coat. She also presents the Anahera with a green velvet bag into which she slides a small flask of lemon water and a pair of red leather gloves. She pins Isabella's hair up into a loose bun and is just teasing out a few tendrils when Bryant appears in the inner sanctum.

Isabella smiles nervously as he bows before her. This morning he is wearing a dark green coat over a cream shirt and trews. The tension in his eyes mirrors her own as he straightens and holds out a circular, leather-bound quire.

"This contains maps of the Citadel and its lift links. There are the hub points where the lift-helmers whom I particularly trust may be found." He nods to Millie in thanks and offers Isabella his arm. She takes it and they make their way to the outer lift.

Their first stop is the Mechanica Terrace. Bryant explains that this level contains foundries and engineering factories on one side of the mountain, and artisans and jewellers on the other. When they step from the glass lift hub, it is straight into a bustling crowd. After so many days of isolation it is a little overwhelming for Isabella but exciting nonetheless. The Drw-ad pilots her as deftly through this crowd as he did through the dancers at the Reception until they reach a quieter lane. Here the buildings lean close over the walkway, mullioned windows at street level allowing a view into each atelier.

"Forgive me, but I need to check on the progress of a commission. Do you mind?"

She shakes her head, fascinated now as she peers down into the rooms around them. As they walk along the narrow, cobbled lane she watches artisans and smiths working, hunched over desks, adjusting with instruments, pouring hot metal into moulds, tending gyroscopes or fashioning bubbles of light, their power glittering in the air. Finally, they stop at a workshop, above which hangs a sign of crossed hammers. Inside, a collection of machines thunder and drone. A smith appears beside them, coveralls smeared with oil stains and a cheerful look on his round face as he pushes back his safety goggles.

"Lord Lathorne! Excellent timing, we've just finished it." He motions for them to follow him into an office beneath the stairs and perches on the edge of a desk, picking up a part and handing it to the Drw-ad. Isabella is intrigued – this is as pleased as she has seen Bryant so far, even if no hint of a smile crosses his face.

"Let us test it then." Together they huddle over another machine and Isabella folds her arms and looks around. The office walls are covered in sketches and schematics. Through the window she can see a shower of welding sparks spew from a gantry. As the daughter of an engineer, she suddenly feels quite comfortable here.

Bryant is pleased. "That should reduce the vibration. It is miniscule at present, but I do not wish to risk the potential for resonance."

The smith turns to Isabella. "So, what do you think of our

200

Terrace, Lady? Hot enough for you?" He winks.

"It's brilliant! I could explore for days." She grins. "I am surprised though, I didn't think the Gentry worked for a living."

The smith barks out a laugh, looking to Bryant.

The Drw-ad explains. "Ivar is not Gentry. Thankfully they do not infest the entire Citadel. Most of the people you see around these terraces will not be. Ivar and his kin are citizens of the Citadel – they are called the 'Folk'."

Ivar holds out a hand, which Isabella shakes. It is a firm grip and she tries to return it.

"Aye, unlike those layabouts, I actually craft for a living."

Bryant hands back the metal part. "Thank you, Ivar. I will need thirty more." The smith grunts, lifting a quire and tapping it. "Isabella, shall we move on?"

After a shorter lift ride than before, their helmer intones, "Kishie Terrace, Port Side" and the doors slide open to a rush of scents. This terrace is comprised of markets, the first of which is the fish market. As they proceed along the wide street, Isabella peers into shallow circular troughs filled with assorted fish and eels, each one sliding through clear, aerated water. On tables beside are stacks of crabs, boxes of iced shellfish and baskets of herbs and flowers which are used in many of the local dishes. The air is incredibly fresh and Bryant explains that this is because the tanks and boxes are constantly emptied and replenished, straight from the boats.

"Citadel cooks prefer their produce to be as fresh as possible and will visit before each meal. Lady Kahn for instance has very high standards." As he speaks, Bryant nods to various vendors who wave in return. "She used to send me here regularly to collect orders when I was a child."

Eventually, they move from the Sea Quarter to the vegetable market, where the air takes on an earthier scent. The stalls either side of them snake into the distance and from there they progress into the Quarter of Trees, where long lines of pots hold bonsai trees and

201

ornamental palms. Isabella touches the fronds as they pass and peers at the statues beneath. Snarling dogs and bizarre creatures are carved from granite and sit waiting on thick pallets.

Bryant motions to her and they turn onto another street, this one wide and no longer edged with covered stalls. Instead, it houses apparel shops and it is teeming with people. More ordered and up-market than the previous quarters, this is where Isabella feels the atmosphere change. Whereas before the couple had been shrewdly observed by the stallholders as they passed, their expressions keen but not unfriendly, now the citizens around them begin to stop and stare. Isabella cannot help but hear the barely-hushed whispers.

"How can she even look at that vile creature?"

"I know, let alone marry him?"

"Is she mad?"

Someone spits on the cobbles near her feet and a woman pulls her children back as Bryant passes them. He is used to ignoring such reactions but now he is forced to acknowledge them again because he is suddenly very aware of the woman beside him and what she might think. A number seem to believe she has been bewitched.

Their reactions disturb Isabella but she tries not to show it for fear of offending him. He appears stoic and unconcerned but during one encounter she realises he has turned slightly, using his body to shield her from the aggressor. Even though he is the target of their bile, he is still trying to protect her.

With relief, they reach a lift hub and catch a ride to the next stop, the Plantiecrub Terrace. Here, an aura of calm descends and Bryant leads her along paths of crushed lime which separate enormous greenhouses. They remind her of the glasshouses at Kew Gardens, white-painted metal curling into elaborate designs at their tips. Each structure holds a different crop; fruit trees in one, greens in another, along with whole sections of what looks like purple wheat. Bryant explains that they are heated by geothermal energy, allowing for a much longer growing season. They are even able to grow redberries in winter. He adds that the other side of the Terrace is filled with fields for livestock.

Isabella feels herself relaxing but even here the stain of his reputation seeps forth. As they pass a group of workers, one notices him and instantly reacts, her laughter drying up. She turns to stare at them, or more specifically, the Drw-ad. One by one they notice, stop and turn. Bryant is so used to such wary reactions that he barely notices, instead he watches Isabella. She registers the change, looking faintly confused.

The group are left behind as the couple stroll along the gravel path through more formal gardens, flanked by high, manicured hedges and topiaries. They walk silently until Isabella works up the nerve to ask the serious man beside her a question. Finally, as they pass an oval fountain which creates a hub point between greenhouses, she speaks.

"Bryant, does that happen to you often?"

He walks a few more steps, seemingly oblivious to her question then comes to a halt, looking away from her. She can see the muscle in his cheek flex and she feels a tiny trill of fear, still unsure as to how this odd man will react to things. He sighs.

"Alas, that is something you will have to grow used to. I am not...popular."

Isabella moves to stand in front of him. "What is their issue with you exactly?" She tries to keep it just light enough not to be pushy, but serious enough to warrant a reply.

He looks down at her. "They fear my kind. We are very different. My appearance marks me as an outsider, and it is difficult for them to accept and trust a Drw-ad. We are not always...kind, to humans." Her expression urges him to continue. "Generally, if a Drw-ad lets a human live, it is because they are saving them for later."

She tries not to react to this, keeping her expression steady as her mind squawks.

What?

203

He pauses and when he continues there is a hint of regret in his voice.

"And I am not...demonstrative, as they are. As you are." He finishes with a dry tone. "Apparently this makes me untrustworthy." He watches her process this, brows dipping slightly over thoughtful green eyes. She purses her lips then huffs out a sigh and looks up at him again, a lopsided smile tugging at her lips.

"Well, we'll just have to work on that, won't we?"

Despite his surprise at this, Bryant becomes aware that they have been walking for some time without a break and he remembers her issue with the shoes at the Reception. He asks if she needs to rest, as they have walked quite a distance.

She smiles. "I'm fine, look." She lifts her skirts to reveal the boots.

Bryant frowns. "How did you acquire Sisterhood boots?"

"When I came through the Gate I was wearing slip-ons – fine for a party, not so great for a hike over a mountain. My feet were ripped to shreds. When we reached the Mutinous Piglet, Alyss fixed me up and gave me these." She waggles them and taps her heels together. "And a lecture on the importance of always being prepared."

He stares at her.

"You suffered?" A chill wraps sharp fingers around him. It had not occurred to him that she may have experienced hardship or distress in her journey to the Citadel. He struggles to identify the feeling, for it is an unfamiliar one.

Guilt.

She shrugs. "It is what it is. At least I had help to deal with it." The image of Captain Bannerman flickers across her mind, followed by the scent of cardamom and cigars, but she shoves it roughly away. She doesn't want to think about the bastard who brought her to this place.

Yet despite her cheerfulness, Bryant sees she is beginning to flag a little. "I have a surprise for you. One more Terrace to go."

When they arrive on the Rivin Terrace, he leads her down a

204

cobbled street to a light blue door. It is decorated with bright blooms which remind Isabella of the paintings on canal boats. Bryant knocks and the door is instantly opened by a small waiter wrapped in a white apron. He grins up at them.

"Welcome!" He bows and ushers them through a whitewashed corridor to a large, sunlit courtyard beyond. It is enclosed in a three-storeyed building and covered with a glass roof. The space contains large potted palms and a shallow pool in the middle, while patrons lounge in plush couches and high-backed chairs, nibbling on delicacies delivered on silver trays. The waiter leads them up a wide wooden staircase and they finally emerge on the top mezzanine floor. Seated in large chairs near a cast iron fire-pit, are Lianne and Meridian.

The blonde woman leaps to her feet and throws herself at Isabella. It has been barely a week but the Anahera cling to one another. Lianne has been struggling with the situation herself but considering Isabella's predictably mad choice, she has also been desperately worried about her friend. She steps back and looks at Isabella closely. She seems fine, if a little tired. She glances towards the Drw-ad standing silently beside her, his stark appearance disconcerting.

Her husband clasps Bryant's wrist in greeting, slapping his arm and laughing. "What took you so long? I'm starving!"

Bryant raises a dark eyebrow. "I refuse to be beholden to the demands of your stomach, brother."

Meridian snorts and turns to Isabella. "Good to see you've remembered your shoes this time." Isabella grins and lifts her skirts, revealing the sturdy boots.

"Yup." She catches Lianne's look of confusion. "At the Reception, I accidently left those bloody awful shoes behind."

The blonde Anahera sighs and nods towards Bryant. "You might be plagued by Meridian's stomach but I'm plagued by her feet. Honestly Izzy, what is wrong with you?"

"At this point? Hunger." Isabella plants her hands on her hips.

"The smells in this place are driving me mad."

Lianne rolls her eyes. "You can always tell when things are really bad for her – it's the only time she'll turn down food!" She misses the shadow that passes across Isabella's face, but Meridian certainly notices his old friend's gaze settling on his wife. He knows exactly why Bryant asked for this meeting.

The diminutive waiter appears beside Meridian's elbow and bows deeply. "Your table is ready, my Prince."

They are led to a balcony where a low table and a heap of large cushions sit. Before them is the vast sweep of Weisdale voe and the mountain ranges on either side stretching into the distance. Waiters begin to arrive, setting down platters laden with fried squid served with caper sauce, tiny deep-fried sardines scattered over salad leaves, aubergines stuffed with minced lamb, tomatoes and peppers served with rice. Bryant is not sure who looks more delighted, Meridian or Isabella.

Between mouthfuls, the Prince waves his fork at Isabella. "This was his idea, and not a bad one, I have to say."

Bryant can feel her gaze but he concentrates on his plate. He examines his own reaction to the meal, for it is an odd mixture of comfort and distance. He is doing something most would consider to be completely normal - two couples enjoying a meal together - but it feels very strange to him. Again, he is fascinated by the Anahera. Her quips cause Meridian to roar with laughter, she is at ease with her friend and she even tries to include him in the conversation. Only his closest friends have ever done that, yet she has known him only a few days. Meridian shares stories of their past and the two women listen avidly.

At one point, Isabella offers Bryant a taste of something from her plate. He does not know how to deal with this at all. "Why would you want me to eat your food?"

She smiles encouragingly at him. "I want to share something I've enjoyed with you and I'd like to know your opinion."

"My opinion?"

"Of course, your opinion is important to me. Why wouldn't it be?" She waves a laden fork in front of his nose and he gives in, taking it from her. Cautiously he chews, his dark eyes narrowed. It is delicious, although he still finds the notion odd.

Lianne hides her smile behind a sip of wine and beside her, Meridian finds the whole thing entertaining. But he is also making his way with his new wife. Every so often there is a jolt of miscommunication or uncomfortable silence but this eases as time, and wine, progresses.

Meridian asks if Isabella likes the Eyrie. She smiles and glances at Bryant before answering, aware that the Drw-ad has suddenly grown still, waiting for her answer as he stares down at his plate.

"It's lovely. Honestly, Lianne, you should see the bathroom! And the balcony is covered in jasmine which smells divine at night," she pauses for a moment and pulls in a deep breath, "but…"

Beside her, Bryant's eyes flick up to meet Meridian's steady gaze. Isabella turns to look at the Drw-ad.

"It's not that I don't appreciate what you've done for me, it's just that…" She glances at Lianne, knowing she will understand. "All my adult life I've worked, studied or travelled. I've always had a purpose. Without it, I'm just drifting. I'm just…lost."

Finally, Bryant looks at her. "I assumed you were unhappy because I am not what you expected, because I do not behave as others do."

Both Meridian and Lianne glance at one another, suddenly uncomfortable with being witness to the tension of the conversation, but it is Isabella who breaks through it.

"No! That's not it at all." She places a hand on his arm. "I just need something practical to focus on."

Lianne leans forward. "Bryant, believe me, Izzy has a short attention span and she's a nightmare when she's bored. But," she leans forward and taps Isabella's arm with her fork, "I may have a solution."

Beside her, Meridian smiles. "She's quite a force to be reckoned with when she wants something. I knew there was a reason I offered for her."

Lianne shrugs. "I've been feeling the same way as Izzy, so I began thinking – what is it that the Anahera need right now?"

"Protection." Bryant regards her sternly.

"Er, no." Lianne continues, frowning at him. "Knowledge. We know almost nothing about the Citadel or about Hjaltland itself, and without knowledge we're at a real disadvantage. So, I petitioned Makeda for an education programme for us all, since she's in charge of the Citadel. She's agreed to provide us with rooms and tutors."

Isabella perks up at this. The chance to study again is certainly an alluring thought, however she is aware that the Drw-ad beside her does not look happy. She fervently hopes he is not about to try and forbid her from attending the classes, as a reaction involving flipping the table and threatening to stab him with her fork might upset the surrounding patrons.

"It is a good idea." Bryant's tone is deliberately careful. "I do not want you to be unhappy, Isabella. However," he looks at Meridian, willing him to understand, "I am nonetheless concerned for your safety, particularly in other parts of the Citadel."

Meridian nods. "You have a point. There have been two assassination attempts on Anahera already and we're not even a week past the Ceremony."

Isabella glances between Meridian and Lianne, the latter of whom looks decidedly uneasy. "Assassination attempts?"

The Prince frowns at Bryant. "You didn't tell her?"

"She was not…well, Meridian. I did not wish to concern her further."

Isabella waves a hand. "Hello, I'm still in the room. For the record, I'd rather know than live in ignorance. Who was attacked?"

"One of the female Anahera was injured when her horse was shot, and your friend Adejola was forced to fight off a knife-wielding assailant in the gardens as he walked with his wife." Meridian shrugs. "Apparently he's had some martial training before."

Bryant taps the table for emphasis. "This is exactly why I asked you not to leave the Eyrie." Yet, when he looks into her eyes, he can see the haunted look beginning to return. He does not want to be the reason for that expression. "Meridian?"

The big warrior shrugs. "I suppose we could supply a guard detail for the Anahera. That should keep them safe to and from the training centre."

Lianne watches the Drw-ad's cold expression in response and wonders if he understands the perils of trying to forbid Isabella from doing anything she chooses. He wouldn't be the first to incur her wrath. Considering what she has heard about his people, she wonders if Isabella will survive it in turn.

Bryant is aware that all three of them are staring at him, expectantly. He grits his teeth and acquiesces. "As you wish."

"Excellent!" Meridian bangs the table. "Now let's have dessert." He summons the waiter.

When dessert arrives, Isabella's is a tamarillo tart served on a platter with a goblet of fresh cream to drizzle over the top. She dives in with delight. Bryant has never tried it before and she encourages him to accept a spoonful. He finds it agreeable and then finds himself sharing it with her. She tries not to look smug at this little victory.

As they wait in the courtyard for coats and cloaks to be fetched, Meridian takes the opportunity to speak with Isabella.

"I'll admit, I tried to convince him not to offer for you. Not," he barrels on as he sees her frown, "because I thought badly of you. I just didn't want him to suffer such public humiliation if you didn't choose him."

Isabella relaxes a little. "I think it's going to take us a while to be comfortable with one another. How long did it take you to break through his walls?"

209

"About twenty years," Meridian smiles ruefully. "And I still have to bully him into speaking even now." He shrugs. "But that's who he is. We just have to deal with it."

He lays his tattooed hand on her shoulder, "but in the space of one evening with you, he decided to attempt the impossible, so I don't reckon it'll take another twenty years before he cracks." Meridian's expression grows more serious and his voice drops until only she can hear it.

"He's a good man, despite what you might hear. Please, give him a chance to thaw out."

Isabella swallows and nods in reply, not trusting herself to speak. The reality of this utterly mad experience suddenly weighs heavily upon her again.

On their way back to the Eyrie in a lift, she becomes aware that Bryant is watching her. She looks up.

"Meridian spoke to you."

She pats his hand then curses herself as she watches him consciously fight the flinch.

"Don't worry, he was being a good mate and checking I understood how important you are to him. Next time we meet, I'll threaten him in return." She grins.

Bryant stares at her. "You intend to threaten the Prince?"

"Of course, that's what you do when you meet a good friend's intended. You threaten them with grievous bodily harm if they dare hurt the person you care about. He may be a big, tough warrior, but I will find a way to kick his arse if he hurts Lianne."

Bryant looks towards the lift helmer who is clearly eavesdropping. "Is this normal human behaviour?"

The helmer nods. "I'm afraid so, my Lord. The night before my wedding, my wife's best friend threatened to impale me if I ever let her down."

The Drw-ad frowns as he processes this. "It seems a strange way to behave."

210

A shiver of tiny bells heralds their destination as the lift slows.

"The Eyrie," intones the helmer. He watches his two passengers leave the lift, both thanking him on the way out. As the doors close and the lift turns and smoothly makes its way along a new track, the helmer considers how steep the learning curve for the Drw-ad Lord must be. He smiles and shakes his head.

Once in the Eyrie, Bryant takes his leave and makes his way to the solarium. There he works deep into the night until his body aches for sleep. Then, as he has done every night since her arrival in the Eyrie, he walks down the twisting staircase to the inner sanctum, checks Isabella is resting and warmly covered, then settles himself into a chair nearby and finally allows sleep to claim him. Once again, the nightmares do not come.

11. RETRIBUTION

Over the three weeks following the Ceremony, two Anahera die in separate incidents, one toppling from a Terrace rampart, the other poisoned. Their spouses are distraught but ultimately, the general Gentry attitude is that they lost the game. Even Meridian expresses concern, and whilst assassinating the Prince's wife would be foolish, there are some particularly unpleasant and equally foolish Gentry. Although Lianne experiences more regular bitchiness, it is Isabella who becomes the next target.

After a pleasant lunch of game pie and a salad dotted with tiny, peppery red flowers, Isabella sits at the large wooden table reading a book. The weak winter afternoon light dapples over her through the large window above. In the comfort of the Eyrie, with Bryant working in the solarium above, she has dispensed with the elaborate costumery of the Gentry in favour of a loose linen shift dress in pale cream. She turns a page, tucking an errant curl behind her ear and crossing her bare feet. Her refusal to wear shoes in the Eyrie has already caused Millie and Bryant some consternation. Growing up in a surfing community on the Pacific coast, Isabella spent her childhood essentially shoeless and even in adulthood prefers the freedom of bare feet.

The shimmer of bells alerts her to a presence at the Eyrie's entrance, so she stands and pads through the lobby, pulling open the small door at the end. In the distance, the retreating form of a servant hurries down the steps. Isabella frowns. Although she is learning to ignore the Citadel citizens' unpleasant attitude to being anywhere near her Drw-ad, it still rankles. As she turns, she notices a large box sitting on the flagstones beside the door. She shrugs and carries it inside.

Placing it on the table near the balcony doors, she checks to see if there is a note attached. On the other side of the room, Millie bustles about, fluffing pillows and collecting up clothes for the laundry.

Isabella touches the top of the box and it opens to reveal a spray of flowers. They are astonishing - deep black in the centre, the petals and stamen edged with bands of sunset orange, their shape reminiscent of orchids. Tiny motes of pollen drift from them, glittering in the air. Isabella smiles and calls across. "Millie, I didn't know sending flowers was a Drw-ad thing. Aren't they stunning?"

[11]As Isabella leans over to inhale their fragrance, Millie looks up and her face changes, abject horror crashing over her.

"Lady, no!" She drops the bundle of clothes and races across the room, snatching up the flowers and hurling them out onto the balcony, slamming the doors shut behind them.

"Millie, what the hell?" Isabella gasps. As the maidservant turns to her, Isabella realises that the whole room is revolving with her. "Ugh." She places a hand on her forehead. Tiny prickles spread across her skin, the sensation turning to pain as they develop into sharp needles. Flashes of intense cold begin to pulse across her body, alternating with screaming heat.

Millie reaches her and wraps an arm behind her shoulders as she starts to slump. "Crap." She grunts. "Milady, we have to get you back to the bed and I can't carry you."

Isabella nods muzzily and takes a shaking step. Together, they shuffle over to the canopied bed and she sinks into it. The room is spinning and the flashes of extreme temperature increase in frequency.

---

[11] Playlist: Nox Arcana – Night of the Wolf.

213

She groans and Millie swithers with indecision. She should run for his Lordship up in the solarium but can she really leave her Lady alone? Then she notices that the pendant Isabella always wears has slid free of her bodice and has begun to glow.

High in his solarium, Bryant absently rubs the fleshy part of his right palm. It itches. He ignores it for a moment, concentrating on the schematics in front of him, until the spot begins to burn, demanding his attention. He turns his hand to inspect it and finds that the new sigil of interlocking circles has turned red. Shock pulses through him and he rears to his feet, the chair flying back, scrolls and quires scattering. He throws himself across the room and races down the stairs to the inner sanctum, tearing open the door.

As he bursts into the room, Millie jolts upwards. "My Lord…"

"Isabella!" He is by her side in an instant.

Perching on the bed, he holds a cool hand just above her forehead. It is scorching. When she rolls her head to look up at him, her pupils are enormous.

Bryant twists to look at Millie. "What was it?" He snaps.

"Flowers, my Lord." Millie quails for a second then pushes forward. "Nightfevre Orchids. Someone sent a bunch of them!" She watches him close his eyes for a moment, his powerful shoulders dropping slightly.

He knows the poison well - it is fast acting and devastating and for all his power and skill, Drw-ad magic was never designed to heal. He cannot save his own wife. Frustration bites into him as he feels Isabella begin to shiver.

His eyes snap open.

"Summon the Witch. Tell her to make haste. We do not have long."

Millie picks up her skirts and runs for the desk containing empty message globes, plucking one up and fashioning the message. The globe pulses an urgent scarlet and zips away, out through the hatch above then dipping down towards the Mutinous Piglet far below, its

214

speeding progress followed by a tiny sonic boom.

Bryant places his hands either side of Isabella's shoulders, trying to calm her but the shivering has intensified. "Millie, blankets." He orders.

She scurries to the large wooden chest at the foot of bed and pulls out two yargswool blankets, throwing them across the bed and tucking them around her mistress.

"Isabella, can you hear me?" Bryant leans towards her, concern crunching in his chest.

Through gritted teeth she manages to speak. "Yes. I feel like I'm about to fly apart." Her eyes flick towards his, pain and terror swamping them.

Seeing this, rage begins to grow within him.

Someone is going to suffer for this.

He reaches out tentatively and strokes her forehead, trying again to soothe her. It is the first moment of touching any part of his wife other than her hand, and it is tainted by poison.

"All will be well, my Lady." He tells her solemnly, trying not to let the immensity of his concern show. "We have sent for the Sisterhood Witch. She will be here soon."

Isabella screws shut her eyes as a spasm of pain rattles through her. The Drw-ad looks up at Millie, fretting beside him. "Where is she?"

But before she can reply, the message globe has returned, bobbing and trilling before her. She taps it open and reads the message. "She's coming by marron. She'll arrive on the balcony in a few minutes." Millie sees the same relief she feels reflected in the Drw-ad's dark eyes, before her own eyes widen in horror.

"Oh! I threw the flowers out onto the balcony!" She turns, ready to retrieve them, but Bryant is on his feet, one hand raised.

"I will deal with them. Please stay with my wife." He does not need another casualty.

As he strides towards the balcony doors, Bryant pulls his poniard

215

blade from his sleeve and flicks it across a tiny sigil on his index finger. Pinpricks of blood pop up and infuse the shape. He focuses and in response, his fingertips begin to glow a soft blue. The Drw-ad circles his hand in front of his face, creating a mask of light which drifts to nestle into his skin, ready to protect him from the pollen. He claps his hands together then draws them slowly apart, a new skein of blue light stretching between them. Manipulating the light, almost like a pizza chef stretches dough, he creates a wide, glowing net. A quick glare at the doors causes one to pop open in response. Bryant slips quickly through the gap and the door shuts firmly behind him.

To the left he spots the flowers, sprawling in a heap near the balcony wall and surrounded by the glinting shards of the vase. Despite the stiff breeze, Isabella's beloved jasmine is beginning to wilt and blacken along the wall near the Nightfevre orchids and the flagstones are stained with their sticky nectar. The Drw-ad feels the prickling of their pollen over his exposed skin.

He fashions the net of light into a size capable of encompassing the polluted area and hurls it over the flowers. As it settles to the floor, it begins to solidify, sticking like glue to the flagstones. The poisonous scent is extinguished, and just in time. The sound of claws locking onto stone then releasing, issues from the wall below.

With a grunt, a huge black and gold marron clambers over the balcony wall, breathing hard, and in his saddle perches the Sisterhood Witch, Alyss. Her fountain of luscious blonde hair has been pulled up into a thick braid and her eyes are covered with a pair of almond-shaped goggles. A brown leather jacket is laced tightly around her ample chest and her usual flowing skirts have been replaced with trews and leather ankle boots. She slides from the beast and pulls off her goggles.

The marron snorts and shakes his huge head, his nostrils flaring once, then shutting tightly. An image of seeping black appears in each of their minds, along with a brief feeling of sickness.

"Yes, old friend," Alyss pats the marron's shoulder.

"Nightfevre." Dispensing with formalities, she grabs a pack from the saddle and strides over to the glowing net covering the flowers. Her eyes narrow with contempt. "That's a jade's trick." She spits.

Bryant touches his mask and it dissolves, the skin of his finger almost healed. "Thank you for coming so quickly." He bows to her but she is already striding past him.

"You're lucky, I was on the Mechanica Terrace running an errand when the globe found me. Where is she?"

Bryant flicks his fingers and the balcony doors open. When Alyss reaches the bed, she shoos Millie out of the way and leans over Isabella, making a *tsking* sound. As well as increasing convulsions, vivid cadaver-purple lines have begun to snake across Isabella's skin, following the course of her blood vessels as the poison evolves within her.

"Damn." Alyss mutters, and as she turns, her elbow clashes against the Drw-ad who is standing right behind her, static with worry.

She glares at him. "Since the Drw-ad can't heal anyone but themselves, you're no use to me there. Make yourself useful and get a washbowl and some hot water. That pollen's still on her skin and we'll need to get rid of it."

As he moves off, to her surprise doing as he is told, she delves into her bag and pulls out a syringe tube and a tiny vial of green liquid.

"Well, my dear," she muses as she pops the vial into the tube and shakes it briskly. "This will feel like a supernova going off inside you, but needs must."

As the latest convulsion shivers away, Isabella's head lolls sideways to look at her imploringly, her arm lifting briefly then falling open over the edge of the bed, inviting injection. The Witch raises an eyebrow.

"Eric's right, you really do have a bloody-minded determination to survive." She takes the proffered arm and makes ready to press the tube firmly into the soft skin.

217

As Bryant appears on the opposite side of the bed with cloths and a brimming bowl, he sees his wife begin to relax at the witch's touch, but Alyss barks at him. "I need you here! Once this serum hits her heart, we'll need to pin her to the bed or her spine could snap."

He deposits the bowl and clambers quickly across the sheets to kneel next to his wife. His stark Drw-ad face shows no emotion as he concentrates on the Witch's instructions, his long black hair falling in curtains as he bends over Isabella.

"Millie!" She calls. "Come up here and sit astride her lower legs." The girl is there in an instant, clambering onto the prone woman's ankles and leaning in, ready to push down on Isabella's thighs.

"You." Alyss motions to the Drw-ad. "One hand on her forehead, your other arm across her chest. I'll take her hips. Ready?" Her two attendants nod and she presses the silver tube against Isabella's flesh, the sharp needle within piercing her skin. Her arm jerks as the chill of the serum flows into it and for a moment her muscles relax. There is a pause and Bryant frowns.

"Wait." Alyss commands, watching her charge carefully.

As the serum makes its way quickly through her veins, Isabella feels it calm the convulsions and quash the temperature spikes. "Oh," she manages. And then it reaches her heart.

It is as if the very substance of life has exploded inside her.

Is this what the first living cell felt like?

The sensation rips through her, an intense punch of fertile energy hammering into every muscle, every cell. Her mouth gapes open and she feels her body contract and buck.

Bryant leans into her, pressing down and hoping not to hurt her further but even he, stronger than any normal human, struggles to pin her against the bed. Alyss grunts with effort, using her full weight to suppress the convulsions and Millie hangs on to her mistress for dear life. Isabella screams, her body arching, and Alyss watches Bryant screw his eyes shut at the sound.

Abruptly, the scream dies and she collapses back into the bed.

218

Slowly, each of them releases her, sitting back. Alyss busies herself checking Isabella's vitals. The cadaver purple in her veins falls back before a flare of brilliant green, the poison dissolving, replaced by a pure punch of life.

Isabella takes a shaky breath and then opens her eyes. "What the hell was *that*?" She croaks.

"Sap from Piglet's Yggdrasil tree[12]. Only the best for my most wealthy clients." She winks at Bryant but he is staring intently at his wife. His hand moves slightly as if he wishes to touch her again but as Isabella tilts her head to look at him, his fingers curl into a fist and he presses it into the sheets next to her. Despite her utter exhaustion, she smiles softly up at him and his chest contracts.

She lifts a heavy hand and waves it vaguely. "Thank you, everyone." Her voice is husky from the scream.

Bryant looks up and catches the Witch's eye, his black eyes glittering.

"Yes," she says, in reply to his unspoken question. "She should recover now. I will sit with her." She stands up and plants her hands on her hips. "Go. Do what you need to do." Venom begins to drip from her words. "And when you find the cowardly bastard who did this, make them suffer."

Bryant's face has set, cold and hard. "May I borrow your marron?"

"You'll have to ask him." She shrugs. "His name is Night Hunt."

The huge marron is curled in a contented heap in front of the roaring fire. His deep fur rises and falls as if he is asleep but when the Drw-ad approaches, his eyes are open, glinting in the firelight.

"Night Hunt." Bryant bows politely. He forms a picture of the offending flowers in his mind, and infuses it with the feeling of a

---

[12] Each Sisterhood "Haven Holm" has an Yggdrasil tree. It is a source of immense power and feeds the life in and around the Holm.

219

chase. Night Hunt responds with the image of a shard of glass.

Bryant walks quickly to the balcony doors and slips through them. In the time it has taken for them to cure Isabella, night has fallen. He murmurs a word and a tiny ball of light appears above him. Scanning the flagstones around the protective net, the Drw-ad spots the glint of a stray fragment of the vase. He is about to pick it up when he feels hot meaty breath fluff the hair behind his ear in warning. The marron is right behind him, having moved with astonishing speed and silence. Bryant opens his hands and steps back in acquiescence. The beast dips his head to the shard and inhales. Marrons are curious creatures, in that they can smell intention as much as the layers of actual scent.

Night Hunt raises his head, flicks his black tufted ears and sends an invitation image of his saddle. Bryant nods in thanks and climbs up into it. At the marron's thought, the saddle adjusts itself to the Drw-ad's body so that he can lie securely on his front along the beast's broad back. He clips his legs into the long stirrups and the high padded back of the saddle seat curls over the top of him and clicks itself into place, holding him fast. It is designed to automatically adjust itself to the form and motion of both the rider and mount, even while vertical.

As the marron pads to the parapet, Bryant fits his arms into the secure gauntlets, readying himself for the first jump. With ease, Night Hunt pulls himself up onto the parapet and balances there for a moment, scenting the air. He can already sense the general direction of the trail and pulses a feeling of readiness.

Bryant pictures his agreement but the beast is already in motion, plummeting down through the icy air, heading straight for the pointed spire of the roof far below. The Drw-ad's black hair streams in the wind and his eyes tear up from its pull but he keeps them open, revelling in the speed of the fall. Strings of lanterns light the streets beneath them, growing closer with each second. They are about to plummet past the spire but at the last moment Night Hunt reaches out a paw, claws lengthening. They catch along the long metal tip of the

220

spire and with a teeth-aching screech, allowing the lithe beast to swing around and land on a flatter roof below. He pauses for a moment then lifts off again.

As they make their way from roof to roof, wall to wall and along the terraces, Night Hunt muses that he has never carried a Drw-ad before, so he shields his thoughts more carefully than he normally would from the two-leg sitting astride him. The pale man has a surprisingly feline feel to him, certainly sharper and more clinical than the humans, who tend to be quite scattered in their thoughts. The marron recognises the familiar prickle of a predator offended by the intrusion of another onto his patch. Someone has invaded his home and threatened the life of his mate. Night Hunt can feel the Drw-ad's thoughts like long blades in the night, and knows that he intends to exact a painful revenge.

The marron reaches the edge of a tiled roof and leaps again, stretching easily for the far side and the next claw hold. Below, the city glitters, its inhabitants with no idea of the progress of the assassin above them.

Bryant has slipped into the ages old Drw-ad hunting trance; the sting of the chilled air, the movement of his body as he holds fast to the beast beneath him, the steady spin of power deep within him, preparing itself to be unleashed, mind focused only on his prey. All thoughts of the distraction that is Isabella have been ripped away by the night wind and by the acidic burn of rage. It is one thing to face a man on the battlefield and attack him, it is entirely another to sneak about and destroy what is his. The words of the Witch slip back into his mind.

That is a jade's trick.

With a scrape of claws, the marron halts. The roof on which they perch housing a bakery, judging by the flavour of the air. Night Hunt ignores it, searching instead for the faint hint of the scent he had found on the vase shard. Tipping his huge head upwards, he closes his eyes and inhales, his nostrils flaring. Now he has it. He scans the high

221

terraced wall above him.

The Drw-ad cranes his head to follow the line of his gaze: The Araneid Terrace, home to the wealthiest, most powerful families in the Citadel. There is no surprise at this. Nightfevre orchids are hard to source, not least because the Queen placed a ban on their importation years before in her determination to stamp out the rampant application of poison in Gentry disputes. Like Bryant, the Queen prefers to face her enemies and although most Gentry are loyal to her, she also prefers not to take chances.

Night Hunt pulses a picture of the gap between the roof and the nearest buttress supporting the Terrace wall. It is a considerable distance but the marron needs but the tiniest claw-hold to attach himself. Bryant replies with a feeling of agreement. The fire within him has moved on, tipping over and becoming a deathly cold, churning ball at his core. He has a feeling he knows where the scent trail leads.

When the marron is sure that his passenger is ready, he takes the leap, his keen senses automatically judging the trajectory and angle. They sail through the air, a glorious mix of wind and muscle, fur and skin. Night Hunt's claws connect with the edges of the buttress, sliding into small grooves in the stone and holding fast. They are almost vertical and Bryant presses his head against the marron's shoulder, willing his own lithe and powerful body to be part of the beast's form so as not to throw him off balance. They hang for a moment above the sleeping city, before the Drw-ad feels the huge muscles bunch beneath him and the marron takes the final leap up on to the top of the Terrace wall.

Although Night Hunt breathes hard, he flips a feeling of satisfaction towards his passenger. Bryant pats the marron's flank and sends back a pulse of appreciation. High on the Terrace wall, they are hidden from view by the shadows of a large ash tree, allowing Night Hunt a moment to catch his breath.

The Drw-ad scans the courtyard below their perch. Although it is

222

empty, a party is clearly going on in one of the apartments above, the light spilling from the open doors of a lengthy balcony. Frenetic music and the pounding of feet peels forth from the space, along with the cackling of drunken Gentry.

Bryant's heart sinks a little, but the marron sends him a light mental slap to pay attention. He lifts his head, tipping it slightly to indicate the direction of his gaze. On the level above the party, an elegant white balcony juts out, its doors flung wide and a soft light glowing from within. A picture forms in Bryant's mind, the silhouette of a solitary human.

His prey is alone.

Night Hunt pivots and trots along the wall until he is parallel with the last of the bottom-tier balconies. Stretching over, he uses it to propel himself silently up to the parapet, balancing for a moment then dipping to a crouch on the pale balcony flagstones. His huge black and gold body blends perfectly into the shadow of a small arboretum in the corner. Bryant slips his arms from the gauntlets and carefully unclips the leg braces. The saddle peels back smoothly, allowing him to slip down to the cool stone. The marron notes with interest that the Drw-ad is as silent as one of his own kind. A true hunter.

Long white curtains move gently in the breeze, shielding Bryant from the attention of the figure within as they pace back and forth across the room. They pause for a moment next to a dresser, picking up a glass and swigging back the liquid inside. Lord Mirl sniffs, the nostrils of his aquiline nose narrowing with discontent. He flicks his blond hair back from his eyes and resumes pacing. From the party below comes the crash of a bottle hitting the marble floor and a flurry of laughter flies up after it. He frowns in irritation. He had thought to cover himself this evening by holding the gathering, but it may turn out to be even more expensive than anticipated, given the behaviour of his guests. Behind the curtain, Bryant watches him like a serpent.

The man halts again, this time beside a small table near the balcony doors. He stares down at the plush red box resting upon it.

Reaching out, he opens the lid gently, belying the bitter sting of rage burning in his chest.

She chose him. The enemy.

He stares down at the heavy gold necklace, completely unable to fathom her choice. The thickset jewels glint in the light, mocking him. All this wealth, all the prestige of his family name offered up on a plate and it was still not enough for her. A traitorous voice inside him whispers.

You aren't enough for her.

Mirl slaps the lid down sharply. Nonsense. She is mad, or bewitched by the White Demon. The humiliation twists inside him as he remembers the crowd of his peers stretching out before him in the Great Hall, the aisle empty between them and the bark of that bastarding Herald, ejecting him from the dais when she did not appear for him. Having to watch from the side as that disgusting Drw-ad took her by the hand instead was the icing on the foetid cake. He pulls in a deep breath and resumes his pacing.

In the shadows, Bryant feels his rage build at the fresh memory of his wife writhing in agony on his bed, and the way she looked at him with eyes filled with terror. A woman wholly innocent of the vicious games the Gentry play and who, for the simple act of choosing to be with him, had nearly paid for it with her life. All because a hateful, spoilt lord wanted what he could not have.

Mirl stops, mid-pace. He sniffs again. Looking down at his glass, he holds his nose over it. He frowns and pulls at his shirt, taking a cautious sniff, his long nostrils quivering. There it is again - the scent of copper. His blue eyes flick sharply about the room as he turns, but he is alone. Yet, he has the distinct feeling he is being watched. Suddenly, the white curtains billow in the breeze, bringing in the sharp scent of fresh snow from the mountains.

Surely, it is too early in the winter for that?

Mirl strides to the doors and steps out onto his wide balcony, pushing aside the curtains as they swell around him. He scans the space but it is as shadowed and empty as it should be. Below, the tempo of the music increases and he hears the thump of the dancers' feet as they throw themselves into a frenzy.

"Nonsense." He mutters to himself. Why should he be worried? Few will suspect him of having sent the flowers and even if they do, they will be powerless to do anything about it. The Mirl family retains more wealth and influence than the rest combined.

Spinning about, he pushes the curtains back into the chamber and pulls the doors shut, locking them securely. He turns and halts, shock pinning him to the spot.

Standing next to the table with the red box is the Drw-ad, calm and still, as if he has always been there. His form is wrapped in a simple black shirt and trews topping high leather riding boots. Although he makes no move, there is something deeply disconcerting about him. His normally inscrutable eyes have a new edge to them, as if Lord Mirl were nothing but a piece of errant prey. In his gloved hand hangs the heavy golden necklace.

Lord Mirl gapes.

"How did you get in here?!"

The Drw-ad ignores the question, running his thumb over the necklace.

"It is little wonder that she turned you down." His voice is low and calm. "This gaudy dross is far from a fitting Gift for her." He places the necklace back into the box and closes the lid. For such a simple action, it is filled with menace.

"How dare you!" Mirl snarls, as outrage threatens to choke him. "You, a seeping stain on our mighty city. You were a hostage, a slave! You have no rights here!" His voice drips with disgust. "What could you have possibly offered the bitch that was better?"

The Drw-ad moves with astonishing speed, closing the space between them. Mirl raises his hands to ward him off but finds them immediately covered by a sheath of blue light. With horror, he watches the flesh of his fingers stretch like melted cheese and meld

225

into one another, sticking fast. He cannot move them. Bryant catches him by the wrists, shoving him hard, forcing him to stumble backwards until his back hits the central stone pillar.

Recovering himself, Mirl snarls in response but before he can react, Bryant brings his knee up sharply, hammering into his groin. Pain explodes through the man, along with a powerful need to vomit. The Drw-ad gives him no time to crumple into a ball of pain, instead lifting the man's arms high above his head. The energy cuff around his hands stretches, wrapping itself tightly around the pillar and holding him fast. He has been staked out, stretched, awaiting the butcher.

Bryant regards him for a moment, inspecting his work. Satisfied, he moves closer to the man gasping in pain, a hard stare pinning him to the stone. Mirl's eyes drop to the Drw-ad's midnight blue lips, only an inch from his cheek, and the words they are softly forming.

"Respect, Mirl. That is what I offered her. You know nothing of respect, only dishonour." Bryant can smell the bitter stench of the man's fear welling up around them.

The last vestiges of the Mirl's rage and arrogance kick in and he grasps at a final threat.

"The King forbade you from using magic on us! You will not get away with this!" He screws shut his eyes, the pain from his groin and wrists tearing at him.

The Drw-ad's white hand slaps hard against the stone beside Mirl's head and the man's eyes jolt open.

"Idiot human." His black eyes narrow and he leans ever closer, hissing. "I chose to agree to that. Equally, I can choose otherwise. You think I am a pet on a leash, to be yanked back at your pleasure? I could burn the flesh from your bones and *no one* could stop me."

Despite the pain, Mirl goes very still. He is not used to the fear that now courses through him, loosening his bowels and disabling his muscles.

Bryant suddenly leans back, his head tilted to one side.

226

"You would kill an innocent woman, merely to get at me? You lost the game, yet you would burn *my* world to cover your failure. After all this time, do you really hate me that much?"

Through gritted teeth, Mirl growls a reply. "You? You're nothing. It's *her*." He coughs. Even through the pain, that disgrace still burns. "She humiliated me!" He finds a tiny kernel of rebellious strength left at his core and he spits it out at the Drw-ad.

"So, tell me, did the whore suffer? Did she spew black blood all over your dirty sheets as the poison ripped her apart?"

Bryant's eyes widen and with a snarl he is on the man again, as close as a lover, whispering in his ear. "She lives, you bastard."

The man bucks in shock.

How could she have survived that?

"Drw-ad magic only brings death!" He gasps. "How could *you* save her?"

Bryant pulls back, suddenly calm again. He purses his dark lips and gently blows a stream of breath into Mirl's face.

"What the...?" The lord's confusion is immediate. Then he inhales and is astonished. Far from being the corpse-like fumes Mirl had always imagined, the Drw-ad's breath is like plunging into a fresh, clear mountain stream. Its effects are swift, racing through his body and quenching every last shred of pain.

Bryant steps back and reaches up to pull his long hair into a tight ponytail.

"Th-thank you." The lord stammers, relief loosening his usual spiteful arrogance.

"I did not do it for you. I need you to be clear of pain for this."

With those ominous words, Bryant stands, regarding Mirl speculatively. "I must admit, I am surprised that it was you who attacked the heart of my domain. I did not think you were bright enough to arrange such an elegant assassination."

The pain now completely gone and with a feeling of invigoration suffusing his body, a shadow of Lord Mirl's treacherous self rears in

227

response.

"You should go after that Wildervene bitch, not me! She suggested the flowers!" It takes a moment for him to realise that this is a mistake.

"You spoke of killing my wife with her?" Bryant's visage of icy calm is almost cracked open by the sneer which threatens to reveal itself. "Then you are even more of a weakling than I imagined, if you needed help to slaughter a defenceless Anahera."

Mirl grits his teeth. The Drw-ad has pulled his poniard blade from his wrist pocket, drawn it across a sigil on his left hand and is now spinning the resulting energy between his palms. Instead of his usual blue, the skein is a harsh yellow, the colour of bile. The scent of copper rises, scraping at Mirl's nostrils and throat.

"What are you doing?" He croaks but the Drw-ad ignores him, twisting the light into the shape of a short, narrow tube.

"Did you think," the raven-haired man takes a step closer, "that I would merely let you go?" His hands turn the sickly light, tiny sigils appearing as shadows within it.

"That I would not punish you for what you have done to me...to us?"

Something about the sigils makes Mirl feel suddenly queasy.

"Please..."

The Drw-ad takes another step forward. The air in the narrow gap between them begins to crackle.

"Since I cannot trust you not to attempt another assassination," he gazes steadily at Mirl, "and killing you would be inconvenient..." He flicks a finger, a tear opening in the man's shirt near his belly. "I will have to ensure your obedience by other means."

He places his hand over the man's mouth, pressing down hard. Mirl's eyes widen. The Drw-ad leans into him, the pulsating tube of light lengthening to a point and piercing the flesh of his belly. Under the steady white hand, Mirl screams in agony. Bryant drives the contagion into him, until the man's body has absorbed it all, then

228

holds tight as he bucks and howls. Mirl can feel pieces of it crawling through his veins, sinking into every fibre, spreading the agony and corruption to every part of his being.

Suddenly, there is a hammering on the inner doors of the chamber.

"Mirl, you bugger! Are you in there? You can't leave your guests to celebrate without you!" A drunken voice barks from the other side. "Mirl! This is bad form!"

The man in question cannot reply, he merely drifts through crashing waves of torment. Finally, when Bryant is satisfied that the spell has reached every part of his enemy, he leans back and blows softly into Mirl's nostrils. The man inhales and sags with relief as the Drw-ad's breath soothes the pain. He removes his hand from Mirl's mouth.

The hammering begins again.

"Mirl! Are you drunk? Open the damned door!"

He hangs, exhausted and stunned. Bryant cups one hand around Mirl's chin and lifts his head.

"I have given you a gift." There is almost a hint of a smile on Bryant's dark lips. "The gift of continued life." Mirl gapes at him, drool pooling at the corner of his mouth. "If you ever threaten her again, if you even *look* in her direction, my gift will flower within you, and every tiny seed will disperse sweet agony." He tips his head slightly. "You will die, screaming."

Mirl's lips close and part again, his eyes imploring.

Beyond the chamber doors, the drunken voice is now demanding that a servant open the door. Keys rattle furiously around the lock.

Bryant raises a cautionary finger. "If you behave, you may live a long life, but you will never be free from its pain. Understand, should you try to continue your line, your seed will sicken and die."

He lets go of Mirl's chin and straightens.

"I am nothing, if not generous."

With a flick of his fingers, the flesh of Mirl's hands slides back into its natural place and the energy cuff holding him to the pillar

229

evaporates. The once proud lord crumples to the ground with a grunt.

The doors fly open and the guest stumbles through, followed by a concerned manservant. Mirl can do nothing but concentrate on breathing, his hair hanging in rat's tails in front of his face, his skin slick with sweat.

"See! I told you he'd had too much to drink, the sot!" The guest, a distant cousin, grabs him by the shoulders and pulls him up into a sitting position, smacking his head into the stone pillar in the process.

Mirl scrabbles at his shirt, peering desperately down at his belly. There is nothing but a tiny red pinprick. He looks up and stares across the room, searching for the Drw-ad, but all he can see are the billowing curtains and the yawning black of night beyond.

Night Hunt and his passenger are already in flight, bounding across the rooftops. The marron is impressed. The Drw-ad toyed with his prey just as he would have, inflicting the type of punishment that could drive a man to suicide. There is something quite elegant about that. Yet as he moves, revelling in the night wind and the easy work of his muscles, he can feel that the two-leg is not as pleased as he should be. This piques Night Hunt's curiosity and he slips into the edge of the Drw-ad's thoughts. The lord is thinking of his mate, a swirl of concern and hope moving through him, and instead of the white-hot rage of before, there is now a sullen anger. There is someone else he must deal with before the night fades. Out of a growing respect for his passenger, Night Hunt speeds forwards.

High in the Eyrie, Alyss is admonishing her recalcitrant patient. Isabella is curled into the corner of the large sofa near the fire, wrapped in a blanket.

"Keep drinking." She points to the steaming tisane clutched in Isabella's hands. "It'll flush your system of any residue. Mind you, you're going to pee, a lot."

Isabella makes a face. "It's disgusting. It tastes like you've boiled

230

old socks and then thrown in some dirt for good measure."

The Witch sniffs. "The worse it tastes, the better for you." Despite her apparent irritation, she is starting to like this Anahera. She is fascinating to watch.

"You mean my body will get better more quickly, just to avoid ingesting any more of this stuff?"

Interrupting her grumbling, Millie returns from the servants' quarters with a small, leather-bound quire. She holds it out to Alyss.

"Your payment has been authorized, Sister. Please place your mark and it'll be transferred."

Alyss nods and holds out her hand. She pinches her thumb and forefinger together, then pulls them apart to reveal a tiny glowing apple. It seems to dangle from her finger by an invisible thread. She moves her finger to the quire and the apple drops, hanging above the device briefly before being absorbed.

Isabella gapes.

"That's your signature?

Millie frowns. "Yes, my Lady. Is this not how you seal transactions?"

The Anahera shakes her head. Beside her, the Witch twists around to peer at the balcony doors.

"They've returned." She leans forward, checking that all her belongings are back in her bag.

The doors open and Bryant strides in, bringing the scent of snow with him. For a moment, he seems particularly alien. His hair is pulled tightly back and his face seems almost pinched as he surveys the room. However, when he spots Isabella, his expression relaxes a little in relief.

"Is it done?" Alyss stands, picking up her bag and turning to him.

He nods sharply and moves forward, his eyes never leaving the crumpled form of his wife by the fire. Although she smiles at him, he detects a hint of uncertainty in her and he wonders what the Witch has been saying in his absence. The Sisterhood have never been friends of the Drw-ad, and will grab gleefully at any advantage they see in an effort to undermine their old enemy. The irritation he has nursed on the way back to the Eyrie burgeons.

Unaware of this development, Alyss leans over to Isabella and, to the Drw-ad's shock, hugs her.

"Thank you for looking after me…again." Isabella smiles ruefully.

The Witch laughs in reply. "Let's not make a habit of it." She nods towards the glowering Drw-ad. "Good luck with that one."

Failing to catch the gentle amusement in her voice, her words merely cause a spike in his annoyance. He may be tired but he cannot let this slide.

As the blonde woman walks towards him, instead of thanking her, he holds up a hand for her to stop. She does so, confused.

"Your money's gone through, if that's what you're wondering about." She begins.

The Drw-ad steps closer, lowering his voice so that Isabella cannot hear him.

"I wish to be clear. I jumped to your bidding because I needed you to save my wife. Do not think to command me again, Witch. You will find no advantage here." The scent of copper rises around them in unambiguous warning. However, the Sister is not swayed and she merely regards him steadily, hands firmly planted on her hips.

"And if you want my help again, you'll keep a civil tongue. Your magic doesn't scare me, so calm it down." She stares up at him, unflinching. The rivalry between the Sisterhood and the Drw-ad is ancient and bitter, and the residue of that long-held rancour sticks to the two of them even now. Alyss' power ripples out across the room, the table and wooden doors creaking in response to the sudden influx of living magic as her signature scent of apple rises. As it touches the leading edge of Bryant's copper, the very air begins to fizz.

A worried voice from the sofa behind them interrupts.

"Ah, people…should the table be doing that?"

At his wife's voice, his gaze never leaving the Witch, Bryant allows his threat to subside, the sharp scent of copper evaporating. In turn, Alyss pulls her own magic back.

"Do what, lovely?" She asks, her light tone belying the hardness in her blue eyes.

Isabella feels she has had enough Wonderland-style nonsense for one day and is in no mood to deal with their rivalry. Having witnessed feuds in many of the far-flung places she has lived, she has always considered them an utterly ridiculous waste of time and energy. She decides not to take this particular one seriously at all.

"Well, apparently the sap is rising. Where am I going to put my teacup now?"

The heavy wooden table, once so solid and polished, is now completely covered in tiny new leaves of almost transparent green. Apparently, it had started life as a proud oak tree, judging by their shape. There is certainly no flat space left for a teacup.

Alyss grins. "Whoops."

Bryant turns to regard his once-proud table and frowns. "Whoops? I have had that table for years." He looks at her reproachfully. "Please change it back."

The blonde Witch shrugs. "I'm afraid I can't. Once the process starts, there's no going back. Really, that's Life for you."

Bryant suddenly feels very tired and his wife's gentle interjection has taken the wind out of his sails. He places a hand over his chest and bows.

"My apologies, Sister, that was rude of me. Please accept my gratitude for your swift actions. I will thank your Yggdrasil tree for its sap, the next time I pass that way."

Alyss nods. "You're welcome. I was happy to help." She looks around. "I've always wanted to see the inside of this place." She snags her goggles from the side pocket of her bag and pulls them on, walking to the balcony where Night Hunt still waits. Glancing down, she notices faint claw marks carved into the flagstones. She smiles

233

and pats his shoulder. As ever, her old friend had been ready to come to her aid, should she call.

Bryant leans against the balcony wall, watching her climb up into the saddle. He pulses a feeling of thanks towards the marron who stares at him a moment, before grudgingly sending an acceptance back. Turning with sinuous ease, Night Hunt pulls himself onto the parapet, pauses for a moment, then woman and beast are gone.

[13]The Drw-ad stares out across the night towards the mountains in the distance, a deeper silhouette against the royal blue of the sky. Breathing in, he turns and pulls the doors shut behind him.

At Isabella's request, Millie has retreated for the evening, having left a platter of bread, cheese, tiny vitamin-rich flowers and cold meats for Bryant's supper.

Bryant breathes out, finally catching a moment alone with Isabella. She is still ensconced in the corner of the high-backed couch, the cream blanket wrapped around her and pooling at her feet. He stops at the edge of the firelight, all his rage and venom spent, tentative now in the presence of his new wife.

She looks up at him and smiles with a soft warmth that is rapidly becoming a vital part of his daily life. He hesitates, caught in a sudden flaring image of what he has done to Mirl and how Isabella might react if she finds out. She holds out her hand, inviting him to come closer and he finds he cannot resist.

He takes her hand, feeling the slight tremor still lurking within her. He speaks quietly. "Are you hungry enough to share the platter with me?"

She crooks an eyebrow. "Always. I thought you'd never ask."

He fetches the platter and sits on the couch near her, placing the food between them. They eat in silence but Bryant begins to feel the tension slip away and each time he glances at his wife he feels relief that she is still with him. In turn, Isabella takes surreptitious glances

---

[13] Playlist: Astrid S – Hurts So Good.

at her odd new husband. She has a question, but she doesn't want to ruin the mood that has developed between them.

When they have finished eating, Bryant brings her the steaming tisane that Alyss has prescribed, designed to bolster her energy and immune system after the ravages of the poison. Isabella is quietly pleased when he resumes his seat next to her and so takes the chance to ask her question.

"Bryant."

"My Lady." He feels the question he dreads rolling towards him like a tidal wave.

"Where did you go? Alyss wouldn't tell me. She said you had an important errand to run and that my concern should be recovery."

The Drw-ad is silent, surprised at the Witch's discretion.

"But when you came back, you were…" she scrambles for the right word. "Wired. I mean," she points behind her, "you picked a fight with the Witch and now we have a living tree for a table."

Instead of the anger he expects from her, he sees amusement. Perhaps she will understand his actions. Again, the Queen's words press in on him. *Be truthful.* He looks down at his hands, the white skin layered with pale symbols. Eventually, he speaks.

"I did not wish to leave you, but I was honour-bound to find the person responsible for your pain before the residue of the trail disappeared."

She raises her eyebrows. "Honour bound?"

He glances up and sees her expression. "I was also very angry and I wanted to punish the person who did this to you."

"Oh, well, I can appreciate that." She smiles, tightly. "So, did you punish them?" Her eyes narrow.

"Yes, my Lady, they will suffer for a long time."

"Good," she murmurs, nestling down into the cushions, her head on a pillow near him. Yet again, this odd creature from another world surprises him.

"Would you not prefer to sleep in the bed?" He cannot understand

235

why she chooses to sleep on the couch, night after night.

"No, I would prefer to stay here," she says firmly, her eyes closed. She opens one eye. "Will you stay with me for a while?"

"Of course, as long as you need." Being in her presence is like a balm and he too feels the pull of fatigue.

"In that case, may I use you as a pillow?" Tiredness has stripped away most of her feelings of caution and she resolves to disregard his stunned-mullet response.

"As you wish."

She pushes herself up slightly and he shifts closer to her, placing the pillow on his lap. She lies back down facing the fireplace and he pulls the blanket more securely around her. Initially careful not to touch her, he does not know where to put his hands, eventually settling on one beside his thigh and the other along the back of her. Despite his obvious discomfort, she finds herself relaxing, exhaustion pulling her down. As her breathing slows and she slides into sleep, his steady gaze moves from the fire to her. He lifts his hand and gently strokes her hair, the sandalwood scent of her wrapping softly around him.

As he slowly relaxes and closes his eyes, Bryant hopes that this power she has to ward off his nightmares will remain. Yet it is not a bad dream that arrives to haunt him but an unasked-for memory.

You should go after that Wildervene bitch, not me! She suggested the flowers!

Lady Wildervene. After all these years, her cruelty has not diminished.

How beautiful the young Alinna Wildervene had been to the lonely sixteen-year-old Drw-ad. They had shared many of the same classes and although she had mostly ignored him as he pined for her, her treatment of him was initially more civilized than the others. But she was as mesmerizing as a forest fire is, until you realize the devastation it brings.

One afternoon, out of the blue, she had asked him to her chamber

236

and despite the furious warnings of Meridian and Vallan, he had foolishly gone. Her hair was butter blonde at the time and it flowed freely down to her waist. Surrounded by its glow, she had welcomed him with surprising warmth and plied him with sweet wine. Despite his reserve, despite his heavy natural caution, he had let his guard down and in that moment, she had kissed him. She tasted of sour, chemical strawberries, but he gave in to her.

High in the Eyrie, Bryant opens his eyes and stares at the embers as they pop and settle in the fireplace. He rubs a hand across his forehead, trying to crush the memory before it reaches the cracking point. But it is no use.

His mind slides towards the moment where, having asked him to undress and wait as she prepared herself in another room, he was stunned as the chamber doors flew open and Mirl and his vile friends piled in, hooting with delight. But it was not this humiliation that lanced him the most, rather it was the sound of her words as he struggled to gather his clothes.

In delighted horror the young Mirl had barked, "the filthy bastard didn't kiss you, did he?"

Her reply had shattered any hope he ever had of fitting into the normal human world and shoved him back, far down inside himself.

"Ugh, yes! He tastes disgusting – so cold, it's like kissing a corpse!"

Bryant shakes his head to clear the memory but he cannot shake the concern it brings. If his new wife ever kisses him, will she react the same way?

He looks down at her. Isabella's breath is steady, her head a comforting weight in his lap. For a moment, her breath hitches and he lifts his hand from her hair cautiously. Instead of waking, she shifts slightly, nestling closer into him then her face relaxes again into sleep.

He lowers his hand and resumes caressing her soft auburn curls, closing his eyes and focusing only on the motion of her breathing and her calming scent. Slowly the worry ebbs and he falls asleep.

12. COMPLICATIONS

Several days later, Bryant sits at his desk in the solarium, sketching out a new design. He is engrossed in his work, the winter sunlight illuminating the lines in front of him. He becomes aware of a muted trilling approaching from across the room. Without looking up, he plucks the message globe from the air and places it on the desk beside him, keeping his focus on the sketch. Unusually, its clamour does not cease. He sighs in irritation and picks it up, tapping it open. As he reads, a sinking feeling drags at him and he sits back, trying to take it in. The implications are enormous.

He rises and makes his way down to the inner sanctum. Millie is clearing away Isabella's break of fast and preparing a morning tisane for him. He asks her to fetch the household accounts quire then moves off to find Isabella. She is drinking tea and sitting on the balcony parapet, her legs dangling over the edge.

"My Lady." He inclines his head in greeting and then stands looking out at the view, not speaking, but rolling the message globe around in his hands.

Isabella glances sideways at him. "Something you wish to say, Lord Lathorne?"

He looks down at the globe and continues to turn it. "I would like to try an experiment, if you would consent to it."

Intrigued, she swings a leg back over the wall and faces him. "What kind of experiment?"

He looks at her. "A magical one."

"O…kay. That sounds interesting." She smiles, although the

238

edges slip a little as she realises that he does not seem pleased.

He places the message globe on the parapet and pulls another from the pocket of his coat. Tapping it open, he composes a message and then murmurs, "Lady Isabella Mackay." He opens his fingers and the globe rises into the air, drifts sideways and floats next to Isabella, trilling quietly. "Please tap it. It will open for you."

She does as he asks and the globe curls open, revealing his message:

Good morning, my Lady.

Isabella smiles. "Thanks?"

"Now take it in your hand and compose a message in return."

As she curls her hand around the globe it instantly becomes a weight, no longer hanging in the air. "How do I do that?"

He does not answer straight away, but instead stares at her more intently. "You will need to use your magic."

She frowns. "People in my world don't have 'magic'. I wouldn't know where to start."

"Try."

Isabella shrugs then focuses, squinting at the globe in her hand. "Go on, *compose*." It remains resolutely blank and heavy. She shakes it and tries again. Still nothing. She looks up at her husband, in time to see a flicker of concern cross his dark eyes.

Millie appears through the doorway. "I have it, my Lord." She holds out the requested quire, aware of the sudden tension. Bryant does not take his eyes from Isabella.

"Millie, please activate the household account."

Holding her hand just above the curved screen, a tiny green open book symbol appears from her palm and flares briefly before dropping onto the glass and disappearing.

"It is open, my Lord."

Isabella sits straighter. "That's what Alyss did after the orchids

239

episode! That's like your signature, isn't it?"

Millie nods and Bryant holds out his hand for her to deposit the quire into. He passes it to Isabella.

"Please close the household account by making your mark."

Isabella swallows and a crunching feeling of dread begins to grow inside her. Nevertheless, she tries, holding her hand above the screen and concentrating. Nothing appears. Isabella swallows and looks up at him.

Bryant sighs, hands the quire back to Millie and then picks up the original message globe from the parapet. "This comes from the Office of Contracts and Obligations. Do you recall giving a sample of your flesh when you agreed to the Offering?"

Isabella nods, remembering the sting as the pad on the official's desk glowed beneath her hand. It seems like a lifetime ago.

"Each of your fellow Anahera did the same. Your cellular sequence was recorded so that the message globes might find you, among other things. The Office then passed the samples on to a laboratory, to be tested for abilities and deformities. The results have just been published and they are most confounding. When the Gate last opened, we did not have the technology to assess the Anahera, so we had no idea this might be an issue." He looks down at the globe and when he looks up, his expression is tight. "My Lady, you are all entirely without magic."

I could have told you that, mate.

Isabella resists the urge to say this out loud but her understanding does nothing to cover the feeling of dread. It continues to grow.

Bryant is surprised at her lack of reaction.

Does she not understand the implications?

He purses his lips, struggling to find the right words to explain. "Never, in all my studies, have I come across an issue like this. Not one, single Hjaltlander of any race has ever been identified with the absence of magic. It is simply…not."

"And in my world, there has yet to be one single irrefutable piece of proof that 'magic' actually exists. Plenty of people think it does, or certainly wish it, but…" She shrugs.

"My Lady," he tries again, stressing the words. "This presents us with a number of problems. You cannot access our accounts to pay for what you need, nor can you send a simple message. Even the doors to the Eyrie will not open for you without the pendant. That is challenging enough, but even worse, you cannot defend yourself against an attack of power. You are completely defenceless."

Isabella holds his gaze. "Yeah, I did wonder about that."

"And you are not concerned?" He struggles to understand her reaction.

She twists her lips and then answers. "Of course, but I can't change it, can I? I take it there's no magical injection for something like this?"

He shakes his head. "Alas, we are each born with our abilities. Power can be enhanced but it cannot be acquired, it is innate."

"Well then, we'll just have to find ways around it. Millie, I'm afraid you're going to have more secretarial work to do, if I can't even send messages myself." Her voice is nonchalant but inside, she screams in frustration.

A grown woman reduced to the capabilities of an infant! If I didn't feel like a freak before, I certainly do now.

Another unpleasant thought intrudes. If her husband is as powerful as she suspects he is, what must he think of her now? She looks up at him again.

Bryant keeps his reaction to her glance tightly controlled. The look in her eyes is suddenly painfully vulnerable. Even then, he does not expect her next words.

"Do you regret offering for me?"

He is floored by the question, so much so that he steps forward and takes both her hands, for once not even stopping to think about it.

"I do not. This is merely another challenge, and an interesting one at that." He holds her gaze for longer than he ever has before, until he

241

becomes aware of how close his body is to hers. He lets go of her hands and steps back.

"I will consult with my banker to devise an alternative way for you to access the accounts. Millie and I will discuss the practicalities of her new duties. Please, do not fret." With this he turns and strides from the balcony, flicking his hand for Millie to follow. Yet again, Isabella is left alone in his wake.

She crosses her arms tightly, staring out across the valley far below, fighting the mixture of horror and anger which tumbles inside her. Having to rely on a spouse for money and security is humiliating enough after so many years of independence. A lifetime of standing on her own two feet, earning, paying her way and now she is reduced to this? Grey despair threatens to swamp her again.

"Well...shit."

The next morning, Bryant leaves early for the Huljun Terrace and Isabella begins her routine of taking tea on the balcony. She is once more perched on the parapet with her legs dangling over the edge when a message globe appears in front of her, trilling. She glares at it, mindful of the unpleasant revelation the day before but the trilling grows louder and Isabella sighs, tapping it sharply. It curls open and the message floats before her.

This is shit, isn't it? I can't even text you! Had to get a servant to write this. Want to know what our blokes do all day? Meet me at the Training Grounds on the Huljun Terrace at 2ⁿᵈ breakfast – I mean, break of bloody fast. Oh, and add that it's me, her friend Lianne.

Isabella cannot help but smile at the message, picturing Lianne's frustration as she dictated the message to a servant who clearly took her words literally. Apparently, she is not the only one struggling with the lack of magic in a world where it is the norm. She is, however, intrigued by the chance to catch a glimpse into another part of Bryant's existence.

"Millie!" She swings her legs back over the wall and hops down, striding back into the inner sanctum.

By mid-morning Isabella finds herself stepping out of the large, glass lift-hub onto her least favourite terrace, Huljun. She walks to the edge of the platform and looks down over the large courtyard below. It is almost devoid of people, a far cry from the last time she was there. She recalls the moment she slid from the marron, straight into a pair of metal wristcuffs held by her Captain.

No, not my Captain, my captor.

She pulls her scarlet coat more tightly around her. Each day the weather grows colder and she fervently hopes that wherever Eric Bannerman is, he is freezing his balls off.

Grabbing the railing for support, she makes her way down the steps. At the bottom she stops a young soldier and asks where the Training Grounds are. Sensing an excuse to evade [14]KP duty for a little while longer, he agrees to escort her there. After all, who is he to say 'no' to a powerful Lady? As they walk, he explains that there are extensive grounds ranging around the Terrace, each one allotted to a specific type of training.

"Were you looking for a particular group, my Lady?"

She nods. "Prince Meridian and Lord Lathorne's training session."

"That'll be the Taapster arena then." As they continue, he glances at her surreptitiously and when they reach a large, circular two-story pavilion, he suddenly stops and turns to her.

"I remember now! You chose the White Demo…" His mouth snaps shut and his eyes widen.

Isabella sighs. "Lord Lathorne, yes. I sense you have an

---

[14] Kitchen duty. A punishment.

243

opinion?"

"Don't we all?" The soldier grins. "I was in the training ring with him yesterday in fact."

"And?"

"And that's why I'm on KP duty today, because I fell over in front of Prince Meridian in the melee, and then he tripped over me and nearly impaled the White Demon. He wasn't best pleased. Apparently, I'm 'just as dangerous as the enemy'." He sees her sudden amusement and shrugs. "I'd rather peel tatties than be hit by him. No one gets through his defences!"

Isabella rolls her eyes. "I know the feeling."

He points to a large wooden door at the base of the pavilion. "Through there and up the stairs is the viewing gallery. You'll have a good view from there. Alas," he sighs, "the tatties are callin' me." He taps his fist to his chest and bows before striding away.

Isabella pushes open the door and climbs until she reaches the mezzanine gallery on the second floor. Although it is roofed, the space above the central training pit is open to the sky, letting in plenty of light. Below is a wide, oval sparring arena covered in coarse sand. Lianne leans against the wooden railing of the mezzanine, staring avidly into the pit. She looks up and greets Isabella with a fierce hug.

"How does it feel to be a freak?" She grins.

"Unsurprising. It's not the first time in my life I've been the odd one out." Isabella shrugs and then sighs. "But it does make things more complicated for us. It's bad enough that I have to rely on someone else for money and a roof over my head, let alone protection from being flash-fried or turned into a frog."

Lianne frowns. "I don't think they do that here." She is interrupted by a bellow and the clash of weapons. The two Anahera lean over the railing to see Meridian, encased in padded practice armour, throwing a hapless recruit backwards into three of his fellows. They crash to the floor of the pit in a chaotic heap.

"What did I *just say*? Spread out! Work together! Don't leave him to do all the work." Despite his harsh tone, he is clearly enjoying himself. "Now, AGAIN."

Lianne is also clearly enjoying watching her husband train. "He's big and fast, they've got no chance." She points to the far end of the pit where a line of soldiers wait. "They're nearly falling over themselves to go up against him but none have managed to touch him yet." There is a definite hint of pride in her voice as she speaks.

The next group to step up are more organised, led by a young woman with coppery skin and tight braids. She confers with the others and then all four spread out, wooden staves ready. Meridian nods and they begin to circle him. With lightning speed, the black-haired man behind him moves in and Meridian spins to deflect the blow. As he does so, the blonde woman to the right tries to take his legs from under him. The Prince leaps sideways, landing to trap her stave beneath his feet and punching forward, sending her flying.

Suddenly, the stave is in his hands and he spins it behind him, winding the second man. He reckons without the copper-skinned soldier who leaps on his back, one arm around his throat, the other covering his mouth and nose with a shimmer of power. Caught off guard, he staggers and struggles with her for a moment before contracting his body and flipping her over his head, tearing the mask from his face and using his own power to widen it into a net which he flings over her. It shrinks, pulling her limbs in tightly and rendering her defenceless. The Prince straightens, grinning.

"Better!"

Isabella looks at Lianne, whose expression has become more thoughtful. "That was intense." The blonde Anahera nods, then points to the other end of the pit.

"Look who's up next."

The Black Drw-ad moves smoothly into the space. His hair is tied back in a long braid and he wears a dark blue panelled [15]*hogu*, his

---

[15] Protective practice armour for the chest.

finely muscled white arms bare to the wrists, which are encased in leather gauntlets. His black eyes are calm, one hand lightly balancing a metal-tipped spiral lance. In loose blue trews and leather boots he does not make a sound, lifting the weapon and aiming it in a stinging blow towards the back of Meridian's head. The Prince ducks sideways, turning with ease and knocking the lance aside.

"Nice try, brother." He laughs and Bryant nods in reply. Meridian turns back to the soldiers. "Right, you lot! Lord Lathorne's next tutorial will be with spiral lance and base powers. Listen to what he has to say and watch how he moves. The aim of the exercise is to gain an understanding of what you'll be up against with a Drw-ad opponent. My Lord." He bows respectfully to the Drw-ad and strides from the pit, making his way quickly up to the viewing gallery. He slides an arm around Lianne, who smiles up at him.

"Impressed?"

She shrugs. "You didn't have to work very hard." But she relents when she sees the beginnings of a pout. It looks odd on a big warrior. She pats his cheek. "Yes dear, you were very impressive."

[16]Below, the atmosphere amongst the recruits has changed. Whereas before there was a certain good-natured competition, those who step into the pit now appear more focused and Isabella senses a bitter edge to several. Bryant shows no sign of concern, he merely adjusts his stance, balancing lightly on his feet.

"This should be interesting." Meridian speaks quietly. "They all want the chance to make a name for themselves, taking down the Big Bad Drw." He bumps the suddenly worried Isabella with his elbow. "They're in for a bit of a shock."

The first to step up is a sharp-faced man with short black hair. His spiral lance at the ready, he moves in, aiming for the Drw-ad's head. Bryant tilts easily sideways and bats the lance aside before using his own lance to sweep the man from his feet. He pivots and presses his

---

[16] Playlist: Two Steps From Hell – Chase the Light.

boot onto the man's throat, the sharp tip of his lance pointed just under the hapless soldier's left eye.

"Too obvious." Bryant's voice reaches the edges of the pit. He raises his head to stare at the waiting opponents. "Remember, the Drw-ad consider humans to be slow and predictable. Your moves are easy to foresee. You must be more creative, or you will die." He takes his boot from the man's throat and offers him a hand up. The soldier glares at him, struggles to his feet and spits into the sand. Bryant merely nods. "Next."

One by one, recruits race towards him, each trying to get close enough to do damage. Bryant moves about the space with astonishing speed, his spiral lance flicking with devastating efficiency. His movements are tightly controlled and close to his body, unlike the desperate flailing of many of his opponents. He leaves a trail of crumpled, groaning bodies in his wake and Isabella can see what Lady Kahn meant when she said that even watching him train could be terrifying. He is deadly calm and lethal.

There is a short break, where the more bruised recruits stagger back to the safety of the sides. There is no shortage of volunteers, despite the high attrition rate. Clearly, the chance to attack a Drw-ad is a powerful one.

Bryant stands waiting in the centre of the pit. As he catches the unexpected scent of rose sandalwood he frowns, scanning the arena then looking up to the gallery, finding Isabella immediately. She is wrapped in scarlet, her dark auburn hair piled behind her head and a watchful expression on her face. Bryant flicks the lance up behind his back, the sharp metal point towards the sky and bows deeply to her.

Looking down at him, Isabella feels a curious shiver of anticipation. His eyes hold intelligent amusement and something akin to a challenge, a contrast with his usual completely cold expression.

Taking advantage of his apparent inattention and not even waiting for him to turn, three recruits charge at him. Without taking his eyes off his wife, Bryant flicks the lance to the side, smacking the

247

first soldier in the head. He drops like a stone. The Drw-ad slides into a crouch and spins, his boot taking out the second recruit at the knees. As she crashes to the ground, a flair of power erupts from Bryant's open hand, stretching to cover her head and pinning her to the ground.

He looks up at Isabella again as the final soldier swings his lance around and thrusts it forward, the lethal tip aiming for the Drw-ad's belly. Without even looking at the man, Bryant leans backwards away from the thrust and spins his own lance around his back, reaching out and punching the base end upwards into the soft space under his opponent's chin. The soldier flips backwards and drops to the ground, coughing and choking. The Drw-ad spins the lance back behind him, stepping aside as medics trot up and carry each opponent away. He bows again to Isabella, turns and strides towards the next group.

Isabella tips slightly towards Meridian. "He's showing off, isn't he?"

"Mm-hmm." Meridian frowns. "I've never seen him do that before. Until today, he's always considered these training sessions to be a solemn duty. He could at least give the impression that he's taking it seriously, or even trying." His tone is disapproving. "But if he keeps this up," he looks down at her, "I'm going to have to ban you from the training arena."

He is even less impressed when she grins up at him, completely unrepentant. He turns and whistles sharply. Bryant immediately breaks off from the melee and strides to stand beneath them.

"Pay attention to *them,* not her. They'll think you don't care."

The Drw-ad raises a dark eyebrow, touches his fist to his chest in salute and bows. "Yes, my Prince." When he straightens, he angles a smouldering glance at Isabella then turns on his heel and re-joins the fray.

"There's a surprising amount of sass in that man, isn't there?" Isabella finds that she is genuinely impressed and not a little turned on.

Meridian rolls his eyes. "It takes most people years to notice

248

that." He looks down at her. "I had high hopes for you y'know, but now I'm starting to think you might be a very bad influence on him."

They look down as a body sails across the ring and slams against the wall beneath them. The soldier groans and mutters a curse, before hauling himself to his feet.

"Better!" Meridian barks, then looks to Lianne. "We'll be at this all afternoon. I will see you later." He kisses the top of her head then glowers at Isabella. "And you, stop distracting my best warrior." With that he strides back along the gallery and down the steps.

Lianne places a hand on her shoulder. "Shall we go and get some lunch? Meridian's set up accounts for me in a number of eateries on the Rivin Terrace." She catches Isabella's sudden shadowed expression. "I know, it's not ideal, but until we can work out a way to make our own money and access accounts, we'll just have to deal with it. And I need to talk to you about the content of our next tutorials. They start tomorrow."

Isabella sighs. "Fine." She perks up. "And if Meridian's paying, I'm in the mood for cake."

❦

As evening settles over the Citadel, Bryant finally reaches the Eyrie. When he steps into the inner sanctum, he finds it empty.

He pulls off his coat and stretches, his muscles aching a little from the exertions of the day. Stoking the fire, he drops onto Isabella's favourite couch and leans back. Above him, the lights float slowly through the air. He raises a finger and idly swishes it in a circle. In response, the lights high above begin to swirl. He changes the pattern and they respond again. It is a simple action he uses occasionally to calm himself and avoid thinking. Bryant drops his hand and closes his eyes, thinking to rest for a moment, but instead he drifts into sleep.

Isabella is in fact in the bathroom, having showered and then spent some time wrestling with her hair. She looks in the mirror and sighs, giving up. Flicking it forward over her shoulder, she ties a green yargswool wrap dress around her body and smooths it down over her

249

leggings.

She pushes open the door to the inner sanctum and then stops. The lights are behaving strangely, swirling in an increasingly tight vortex above her couch. The motion is slow at first, but accelerates, tiny bursts of energy crackling between each lamp. Bryant's dark head is directly beneath the twister. He does not stir.

Isabella moves slowly towards him, glancing up at the lights. Her hair, always attuned to the presence of static, begins to frizz. She looks down at the Drw-ad.

He is asleep, his usually stern face now softened a little. He still wears the padded vest, his white arms bare and the transparent tattoo-like markings more obvious this close up. Lines intersect circles like the ripples on a pond, layered next to patterns reminiscent of Viking knotwork. His chest rises and falls slowly and he appears relaxed, but the lights above spin faster and Isabella can feel the electrical charge building. It does not feel…right.

She moves to the samovar in the corner, making a loud show of rattling the cups. Bryant's breathing changes as he wakes and she looks back to see him pull himself upright. He glances at her in surprise and rubs his hands over his face. Now that he is awake the vortex of crackling lights slows to a halt, each lamp drifting back to its usual place. Isabella turns back to the samovar, resolutely telling herself not to freak out.

"My apologies, I did not realise you had returned." Bryant twists to stretch the muscles in his back then rises. "I will leave you in peace." There is a definite note of regret in his voice. He is tired, his muscles ache and the room is warm and comfortable. Isabella turns to him with two goblets of wine in her hands and the smile he now looks for each day is back.

She moves closer and passes him a goblet. "I know you have work to do upstairs but would you consider sharing a meal with me before you go? Millie has promised me a dish called, 'Amok Fish' this evening." She realises she actually feels nervous about asking

250

him. Indeed, he looks genuinely surprised.

"I would like that, my Lady. However," he looks down at his soiled clothes, "I fear I smell of the arena. If you will permit me, I will wash first." He dips his head in a bow and moves to the bathroom.

Isabella takes in a deep breath to calm her nerves. In reality, they have only spent short stretches of time together, usually in the presence of others. The idea of making conversation with a man who doesn't give much away is daunting. She taps the pad by the servants' door and Millie appears soon after. The maidservant is delighted when Isabella explains that his Lordship will be joining her and hurries away to prepare the tray. When she appears again, it is just in time for Bryant to emerge, freshly clothed and rubbing his long black hair with a towel.

The couple sit across from one another and Millie places a covered bowl in front of each. When Isabella lifts the lid, the delicious smell of spices billows upwards. She realises that Bryant is watching her.

"This is a good choice. It is one of my favourite dishes." He appears to be waiting for her to try it.

She digs in with her spoon, scooping up a piece of flaked white fish covered in a pale-yellow sauce. Her eyes widen in delight as she tastes it, as the fresh lift of lemongrass and lime leaves mixes with fish sauce, palm sugar, turmeric paste and spices, all pulled together with coconut cream.

"Wow."

Bryant nods and begins to eat. For a while an uncomfortable silence hangs between them. He does not know what to say and he curses himself for it. Over the years he has studied the human interaction around him and puzzled at their need and ability for 'small talk'. It is a skill he has never mastered.

Suddenly, Isabella points her spoon at him. "I nearly forgot! You got us into trouble today."

Bryant's own spoon pauses part way to his mouth. He places it

251

beside the bowl and stares at her, his black eyes glittering.

"What do you mean?" He is confused. She does not seem worried or annoyed and he cannot fathom what he might have done to incur the ire of the Gentry this time.

Isabella quirks her lips to one side. "Meridian told me off for distracting you. He actually got quite huffy."

Bryant's voice is mild when he replies. "He does have a penchant for the dramatic. However, I fail to see how this is my fault." The issue is not what he imagined at all and he is becoming aware that she finds it amusing. Slowly, he begins to relax.

"Husband, dearest, I know exactly what you were doing. I was standing in the gallery watching and you were showing off." His expression turns flinty and she wonders if she has pushed him too far.

"I was merely illustrating a point to the new recruits and paying you proper respect at the same time. I believe it is called 'multi-tasking'."

And there it is again, subtle but present – a level of sass she didn't expect to see.

"Meridian seemed quite surprised by it," she offers.

Bryant shrugs. "He is an immense show-off; he has no right to complain." He picks up his spoon and finishes his meal, aware that his wife is smiling at him again.

"I have to admit, I enjoyed watching you work. You move ridiculously fast – they didn't have a chance!"

He nods. "That is kind of you. It is but the first stage in a long process, however I do not think it will be enough, despite Meridian's hopes." He leans over and pours them each another glass of wine.

Isabella accepts the glass, pleased that the Drw-ad is beginning to relax enough to speak. "What do you mean?"

Bryant sits back. "It has been thirty years since the last clash between the Citadel and my people. None of the new Uhlan have the slightest idea what facing a Drw-ad in true combat is like."

"Terrifying?" She hazards a guess.

252

"Indeed, and usually fatal. However," he shrugs, "it may never become an eventuality. The Gentry seem particularly keen on establishing financial links with the Drw-ad. Apparently, the promise of great wealth can smooth over many apprehensions."

He takes a sip of wine and waves the glass slightly. "Tell me, what will your next set of lessons be covering? Are your tutors up to scratch?"

She takes this change in direction easily. "The lift system. Actually, I have a suspicion that one of our tutors is on the run…" She regales him with her madcap conspiracy theory about the oldest tutor, who hides in the supply cupboard whenever a member of the Gentry appears in the study rooms. Bryant does not smile at her tale but his expression softens and he leans forward, engrossed in her words.

"And your fellow Anahera? They seem a rather…diverse group."

She grins. "Well…"

As she speaks, Bryant finds himself relaxing further. She has an odd way of seeing the world but it is nonetheless entertaining and astute. No wonder the other Anahera gravitate towards her whenever she leaves the Eyrie and even the lift-helmers speak highly of her. There is a warmth and an openness to her that is rare in the Citadel and he finds himself pulled towards her like a moth to a lamp. He realises just how much he has learnt from her in such a short space of time. They talk well into the evening; the painful silences almost entirely absent for once. It is with considerable reluctance that he takes his leave of her and returns to the solarium to work.

Isabella watches him go and finds that, instead of being cheered by the evening, she is merely confused. He appeared to be enjoying their conversation and then bam! He leaves again. To calm her irritation, she sets about gathering the dishes, carrying them through to the servants' alcove where Millie is clearing up.

The maidservant takes the goblets from her and as she begins to clean them, she speaks. "I hope you don't think I'm being too forward, my Lady, but you and Lord Lathorne seem to be getting on much better now."

"I suppose." Isabella frowns. "But until this evening, he's avoided me like the plague when night falls."

Millie regards her carefully. She is reticent about admitting the truth but there is a loneliness to the woman in front of her that she cannot stand to see persist. "Please, my Lady, don't tell Lord Lathorne I told you this…"

"Of course not. Just spit it out."

"Every night, he waits 'till you're asleep, then he comes down from the solarium. He checks that you're covered and warm, then he sits reading or staring at the fire until he falls asleep. He leaves before you wake so as not to scare you."

Isabella doesn't quite know how to take this. "How long has he been doing this?"

Millie takes a deep breath. She can't read her Lady in this matter, which worries her. "As far as I can tell, from your first evening here."

Isabella stares at her. "How do you know?"

The maidservant winces. "I was worried about you so I came back to check you were okay. Just as I was about to sneak through the door, I saw him." She touches her fingers to her lips. "Please don't think badly of him. I know he was worried about you too. Although…" She bites her lip and winces again, realising she is about to reveal something else she should not.

"Millie." Isabella takes a step forward, narrowing her eyes. "Although what?"

"I promised I wouldn't tell." Millie realises she is fighting a losing battle as her Lady leans forward, suddenly very menacing. She sighs. "A little while after the Ceremony, Prince Meridian pulled me aside. I couldn't believe he even knew who I was, much less want to speak to me."

"Millie, get to the point." Isabella has moved even closer. Her maidservant swallows.

"He told me to pay close attention to Lord Lathorne if he ever

254

came to sleep with you."

"What?"

Millie hurries on, knowing how bad that sounded. "He told me that sleeping near his Lordship is dangerous. Apparently, he's had terrible nightmares since he was twelve years old and when they come, so does his magic. But because he's not conscious it's not controlled, so it can have terrible effects!" She takes a breath. "Prince Meridian said that even now when they're out on deployment with the Golden Uhlan, his Lordship won't sleep for days just so he doesn't accidently hurt anyone."

"Holy shit." Isabella folds her arms tightly across her chest and leans back against the table. She wonders if the odd behaviour of the lights earlier in the evening was an example. "So, he's been sleeping near me for several weeks? In all that time, have you seen any of this...mad magic?"

Millie shakes her head. "No. If anything, he seems to sleep soundly when he's near you. He looks more refreshed than he ever has before." Again she bites her lip. "My Lady, I know it may be hard to believe but I really think he means no harm by it. Until you came, he hardly ever spent time in these apartments, he mostly kept to the solarium. Although he has several friends, including Prince Sarn, I think he must have been very lonely before you arrived. He seems more...relaxed, now."

Isabella pats Millie's arm. "Don't worry, I won't tell him what you've said. In fact, I don't think we should let on that we know his little secret. He's not done me any harm and if doing this helps him sleep, who am I to ruin that?"

Deep in the night, however, she finds herself still awake. Eventually, she hears the tell-tale swish of the solarium door and she closes her eyes, deepening her breaths to mimic sleep. She deliberately left the yargswool blanket slung over the back of the couch and has been cursing herself for the artifice as the heat from the fire diminished. However, now she feels the blanket being lifted and

255

carefully placed over her. She almost breaks her act as she feels his fingers gently stroke a curl back from her forehead, the action unexpectedly intimate. Yet he moves away and she can hear the chair across from her creak as he sits in it.

Still maintaining her steady, slow breaths, Isabella opens her eyelids just enough to see him, but not be obvious. She watches him, elbow perched on the armrest, his hand over his face as he lets out a heavy sigh. It is a moment which catches Isabella completely unaware. The desire to stand up and...what? Touch him? Wrap her arms around him? It is sudden and intense and she only just manages to shove it down. She can just picture his mortified reaction.

In the soft glow of the fire, he shifts so that he is leaning back and slumped a little in the chair, staring at the embers until he falls asleep. When she hears the depth of true sleep in his breaths, Isabella decides to take a chance. She sits up and looks at him more closely. This incredibly powerful individual, who is not even truly human, who has protected her and made connections with her despite his deficiencies, really is as Millie suggested – a lonely man who is trying to do his best.

She stands, padding quietly to the bed and snagging another blanket. Very carefully, she takes her own, still-warm blanket and places it over him. At this, he shifts in his sleep and she freezes, but he settles again. She takes a deep breath then moves back to her couch, pulls the blanket over herself and eventually joins him in sleep.

Later, as the light of dawn drifts into the room, Bryant wakes. He feels surprisingly warm and the scent of sandalwood wraps around him. Sitting up with a start, he glances around but Isabella is still in her usual spot. He touches the yargswool blanket covering him. He must have been tired, as he does not remember pulling it over himself. Bryant sighs and rubs a hand across his face. It is foolish to push himself so far without sleep. Once more, he leaves the inner sanctum before she can wake.

256

13. AN EVENING OUT

"Millie, is this really necessary? I can't breathe."

"If you can speak, you can breathe, my Lady. And if you want to make an impression on the Gentry during your first proper soirée, this is the best way to do it." Millie's no-nonsense voice issues from behind as she tugs on the fastenings of the dress, almost yanking Isabella backwards.

Isabella flicks her gaze to the ceiling and mutters. "Soirée. What a pretentious load of shite."

The dress is stunning but she has never worn anything so tight in her entire life. It is a Saga original, specifically designed for her body and she is rapidly growing to resent both the Attendant and her maidservant for it. Millie, taking her advisory role increasingly seriously, had travelled to the Attendants' Quarter on the Kishie Terrace earlier to consult with her former aide for advice. Saga welcomed her with considerable delight and they had spent several hours discussing and discarding options before they finally settled on the perfect ensemble. Saga's parting words, relayed by Millie, stick firmly in Isabella's mind: "If this doesn't instantly twist their undergarments, I don't know what will." She fervently hopes this is worth it.

The material is made up of appliquéd lace leaves over a black silk sheath dress which pools at her feet. It is topped with a halter-neck basque, leaving her arms bare and wreathed in black and gold bracelets. They echo the inner lining of the skirt, split to above her knee to show a flash of burnished gold satin. Her hair is piled in an intricate wrap of curls atop her head and dotted with tiny golden bees.

"Lord Lathorne has declined every invitation so far." Millie's voice is muffled by a mouthful of hairpins. "He said he wanted to wait until you were stronger before he let you face the Gentry again."

"Are they really that bad?" Isabella bites her lip, nerves beginning to gnaw at her.

Millie shrugs. "Some are, some aren't, but you'll have to restrain yourself, my Lady." She moves around to stand in front of Isabella. "I know it'll be hard but you'll do us all no good by impaling one of them with a cake fork." Her expression is stern.

"Millie!"

"I'm sorry, but you did say "advisor" and that's what I'm doing. You have to keep in mind that they'll be judging both of you from the moment you enter. This," she waves her hand up and down Isabella's body, "is going to make an impact. After that, you'll need your wits about you. They play the game, my Lady, all the time. They'll be testing you for weaknesses, just as they've done to him," she nods her head towards the solarium, "for years."

She teases out several curls from Isabella's up-do and stands back, her hands on her hips. "But I know you can do this. I remember the look on your face when you walked down the aisle at the Ceremony. The way you moved! You need to show them that you're not just prey."

Isabella's lips quirk in a smile. "Millie, I do believe you'd make an excellent general. I'd follow you into battle!"

The girl in front of her grins. "I'll go and fetch the wrap that goes with the dress. It's chilly outside tonight."

As she trots through the servants' door, Bryant emerges from the solarium staircase to see his wife standing by the fire. Her silhouette highlights her ample, hourglass figure and as she looks over her shoulder and smiles, an odd feeling surges through him. She turns and places one hand on her hip.

258

"So, do you think this will be acceptable to the Gentry?"

Bryant swallows before he answers, painfully aware that the surge has centred somewhere in his body that is really not helpful at this point. He grips the top of the couch in front of him, glad of its position as a barrier between them.

"I cannot speak for the Gentry, but you look very pleasing to me." He wishes she would stop looking at him like that. It is not helping.

She is impressed. He is actually wearing colour this evening in the form of a high-necked fitted shirt, open at the throat and embroidered with copper peonies over black silk and topping his usual dark trews. His long, blue-black hair falls smoothly back into place as he runs a pale hand through it. Despite his elegant appearance, he seems out of sorts.

"Are you alright?" She asks, taking a step forward.

He moves further along the couch away from her. "Yes, my Lady. I...do not enjoy these events. They can be tedious at best."

"Well," she shrugs, "at least we can deal with it together." She turns as Millie reappears and places a long, tasselled wrap around her. It is made of thin wool but instantly warms her.

Bryant takes this distraction gratefully and moves towards the door. "Shall we?"

Isabella sighs. He is suddenly icy cold again, for no conceivable reason. She realizes that she is going to have to have a conversation with him about that at some point. She thanks Millie and follows him out to the lift port.

When the lift arrives, it contains a welcome warmth and an inordinately cheerful lift-helmer. He is somewhat portly and seems very pleased to see them.

"Finally! It's taken me weeks to win the race to transport the Eyrie couple." He grins at them. Isabella and Bryant glance at one another and then back at him. "Please, Lady Mackay, sit." He motions to the white chaise longue behind her.

She does as requested, and takes a moment to look around. Every

259

lift is different, decorated to the individual helmer's tastes. This one has black lacquered carvings of leaping fish, topped with a curved glass roof revealing the tracks above. The helmer himself has a white camellia tucked into the pocket of his grey waistcoat. As she looks up, the lift switches seamlessly to a new track and slides diagonally downwards.

"I like the carvings," she smiles and their host's look of pleasure intensifies. "What did you mean by the 'race' to transport us?"

"You two have become the talk of the Citadel, my Lady." He eyes her keenly and she realises that his joviality masks a sharp intelligence. Apparently, it is not just the Gentry's assessment she needs to be aware of. "The word on the tracks is that you are quite an unusual woman." His smile falters a little when he glances at Bryant, who is staring at him coldly.

"*Up-swing* or *down-swing*, helmer?" The Drw-ad's tone is icy. There is no mistaking the danger in his question.

Isabella glances between them, confused. "Is that code or something?"

The helmer nods, unable to tear his gaze away from Bryant's. "It is, and you need not be concerned, Lord, she is unreservedly up-swing. Of all the citizens of this Citadel, you have been the most gracious towards us, and your wife is no different. She is actually interested in us." He looks at Isabella, his expression more measured now. "The Gentry assume that they are the centre of everything and barely notice the rest of us. We're like parts of the great machine of the Citadel to them, unworthy of attention. But without us, they would have to hike everywhere." He grins. "And we hear and see everything."

Isabella nods. "I can imagine. So, is up-swing good?"

The helmer places a chubby hand on his chest and tips a bow. "Yes, my Lady. For us it means that you might be considered potential allies - passengers to lend support to. Your husband has been up-swing for years. Lord Lathorne's people may be ancient enemies of

260

the Citadel but he has never left a lift without thanking the helmer."
He leans forward.

"There was an accident, years ago, when the lift system faltered.
Several helmers died in the pile-up and many more of us would have
perished but for him. Along with Prince Meridian and Lord Vallan,
your husband put himself in mortal danger, climbing through the
shafts to pull helmers and passengers out, and not one of those Gentry
bastards even thanked him. But *we* remember."

Bryant nods. "That was indeed a dark day."

"Each lift-helmer who has transported me so far has assured me
these things are safe." Isabella frowns. "Is that not true?"

The helmer smiles. "It is now. That incident led to many changes,
a number of which were designed by your husband."

Isabella taps her lips with a finger. "Our Anahera study group is
learning about the lift system at the moment. May I ask you a few
more questions?" The helmer's face creases with delight.

"Of course! Ask away."

Isabella rises to peer at the quire console. The helmer explains
how he navigates through the system and just before the cascade of
tiny bells heralds their arrival on the Araneid Terrace, Isabella has
convinced him to let her into the most hallowed part of the lift-helmer
world, the Common Room. Bryant looks on in fascination.

Eventually the lift reaches its destination. Unlike most of the lift
hubs which are airy and understated, the Araneid Terrace's hub is a
confection of gold bas-relief and glittering marble. Several lift ports
disgorge Gentry passengers in a steady stream and Bryant feels his
wife's hand clutch his arm as she moves closer. He wonders how she
can be so confident talking to a complete stranger like the lift-helmer,
yet so overwhelmed by the crowds. Nonetheless, he is pleased to feel
her body move closer. It makes him feel a little less alone as he faces
the hordes.

In fact, Isabella has also moved closer to her Drw-ad because the
olfactory assault has begun again in earnest. Each individual Gentry

appears to be trying to out-do the others with the strength of their manufactured scents. The closer she moves to Bryant, the stronger the shield of his snow-scent. She is grateful for the speed at which he manoeuvres them through the crush and out onto a wide stone walkway which runs above the main Terrace wall. It is open to the elements along one side and there is enough of a night breeze to whisk the chemicals away.

The soirée is being hosted by Lady Morrimar in apartments which jut out from the port side of the Terrace. As the landscape below comes into view, Isabella slows to a halt. Far below, the lights of the port jitter in the frosty air and the voe is dotted with waiting boats. Above, the last shreds of sunset are overtaken by the deep blue of night and the first stars reveal themselves. Isabella pulls the shawl more tightly around her shoulders.

"My Lady," Bryant's smooth, deep voice issues from beside her. "May I ask you a question?"

She tears her gaze from the view. "Mmm?"

"How do you do that?" His eyes grow an inky black.

"Do what?"

"You are more…foreign, than almost any other being here, you have no magic and you know virtually nothing about this place and yet…" he tilts his head, "you seem to be able to navigate your way through almost any situation. You know what to say to each individual and they respond to you."

He looks away. "I have been here for years and I cannot do that."

She attempts a smile and places her other hand on his arm. "I think you'll find that I also have a talent for upsetting people, but I've travelled through my own world enough to know that most people are generally decent and given a chance they can be worth the effort. Even here, I've found that to be essentially true."

But under Bryant's gaze, she cannot help but admit the truth. "After all, what am I supposed to do? Give up? Curl into a ball and die? I shove down the fear and speak to people as if nothing's wrong, as if nothing fazes me. You have to keep going, keep connecting with the world around you."

She smiles sadly at him then her gaze flicks away to the silhouette of the Sandsound Mountains in the distance. "I suppose one day it'll all boil to the surface and I'll just start screaming and never stop."

He stares at her. There is a real turbulence in her eyes, a yawning void of loss. Yet it is momentary and like a spring storm is gone in an instant, hidden again. She runs her hand up his arm and around his bicep, clutching him tighter and making to move off. "Shall we get this over with before this bloody dress asphyxiates me?"

The Drw-ad marvels at her ability to take things in, rapidly process them and move on. He wishes he could let things go so easily.

As they step back into the stream of party-goers, the scrutiny begins in earnest. Each Gentry appears to have their own distinct style. An onyx-skinned woman tottering past on six-inch Geisha-style sandals stares down at Isabella, her slick green hair topped with a Windpyre ship fascinator. Clearly, Saga's accessory line is doing well. An elderly man with an elaborate moustache bustles past Bryant, leaving the Drw-ad to brush the drift of glitter left in his wake from the sleeve of his black coat.

Ahead, the crowd of guests elbow their way through an archway edged by two enormous golden tusks. Potted palms line the walkway and, lurking beside the fountain of a small, pudgy child peeing on a leaf, are Lianne and Meridian. The Anahera is wrapped in a low-backed dress of the most intense ruby red, the bodice studded with hundreds of glittering scarlet gems. The long, chiffon sleeves drift gently in the evening breeze as she pulls Isabella into a hug and then punches Bryant lightly on the shoulder.

"Mate, actual colour!"

He bows, eyeing her fist. "I shall take that as a compliment, my Lady."

Meridian grins. His hair is tied back in a topknot and his short beard is uncharacteristically groomed. "The missus thought it would

263

be a good idea if we entered together."

"The *missus*? Do you enjoy sleeping on that couch, Meridian Sarn?" Lianne narrows her eyes, her voice suddenly sharp.

"No. I take it back." He holds up his hands. "Please don't make me go back there, it's colder than your heart, woman." She laughs and they look at one another fondly. "Right, enough of this. I know we'd all rather be down the pub, but let's get it over with and face the bastards."

Together they walk through the entrance and onto a wide landing where they wait to be announced. Below stretches a long, white ballroom, the walls studded with the trophy heads of enormous animals dipped in gold. At least two hundred Gentry already crowd the room. An attendant takes Isabella's shawl and as Meridian turns to mutter a rude comment about a passing lord he stops, staring at her. He gives a low whistle and looks at Bryant, who merely regards him coolly.

Lianne laughs at the two of them and takes Isabella's arm. "Can you actually breathe in that thing?"

Isabella makes a small, desperate noise and shakes her head. Before she can speak, a Herald announces them, his voice echoing above the clamour of the guests below. As one, they fall silent and turn.

The weight of their stares presses against Isabella and she is grateful for Lianne's presence. She is keenly aware of the raking gaze of each guest, sharply appraising her. A number of faces shift from surprise to something approaching appreciation, whilst others crimp unpleasantly. She feels Bryant's arm move behind her back to steady her, his other hand reaching for hers.

"This way." He and Lianne turn her and she looks at their route with horror.

"Oh shit, steps." With a dress this long and tight, and her lifelong talent for falling over, panic threatens to swamp her. She instantly pictures herself tumbling to a crumpled heap at the bottom of the sweeping staircase in front of the crowd.

"Fear not, my Lady, we have you." Bryant's deep, smooth voice reassures her.

"Just take a step, Izzy." Lianne is still attached to her arm and Meridian has moved to a couple of steps in front of her, so at least she will have something soft to fall onto.

Giving no outward sign of turmoil, they move steadily down the steps and Isabella is able to exude the appearance of elegance, mostly because Lianne and Bryant are holding her up. The Drw-ad is also watching the reactions of the crowd and he realises what Lianne and Meridian are trying to do. Their collective entrance is a deliberate, public show of unity and acceptance.

As they near the bottom, Lianne murmurs, "I'm glad you're finally here, I hate these things. I can't even get drunk to cope, just in case one of them takes offence and tries to kill me."

Remembering her own near-fatal night, Isabella feels the crunch of fear but shoves it roughly downwards. Once they reach the relative safety of the floor, Isabella tries to do as Millie suggested, lengthening her spine, chin lifted slightly and a confident, imperious expression slapped across her face. The scrutiny continues but the Gentry are easily distracted and soon return to gossiping.

"Kitchen Thieves!" A familiar voice arcs above the nearby crowd and from it steps the Tuatara ambassador, Subtle Sands Shifting. Their six curved horns are now adorned with silver rings, their powerful body encased in an elegant, cobalt blue suit and a waistcoat embroidered with silver lacewings.

"Sandy!" Meridian grins and hugs them roughly. The Tuatara's green eyes flicker and their tail snakes up to clap the Prince on his back. "We haven't had a chance to catch up yet." He steps back and introduces Lianne, who holds out a hand. Subtle Sands Shifting cocks their head to one side, horn adornments clinking, and regards her sharply before ignoring her hand and dragging her into a hug.

"Lianne Silvercombe, happy to squish you!" Subtle Sands

265

Shifting pulls back and appears pleased when the blonde woman laughs, a little breathlessly. They look sideways at Meridian and smirk, revealing razor-sharp teeth. "Knew you would pick this one." They turn their attention to Bryant and bow.

"Good to see you out and about, Quickblade. I've been busy-busy, but I miss your counsel."

Bryant bows in return. "As I have missed yours, Subtle Sands Shifting. Allow me to introduce…"

"Isabella Mackay, friend of The One Who Survived!" The Tuatara's tail darts forward and lifts the bottom of Isabella's dress to one side. "No fluffy slippers? They were a good look."

The Anahera stretches down to unhook her dress from the tip of the tail. "Hello again, ambassador. No, no fluffy slippers anymore, I have proper footwear now." She narrows her eyes. "And he is *not* my friend!"

As the Tuatara shrugs, their expression shrewd, Bryant frowns. "You have met before?"

Subtle Sands Shifting nods. "On the pirate ship. New wifey was being repaired by the Manaroa family."

Bryant feels his chest tighten. He has not given much thought to what Isabella may have endured before she arrived at the Citadel, but the Tuatara's words concern him. What else does he need to know?

"Ambassador," Lianne breaks in, "why did you refer to these two as 'kitchen thieves'?"

Meridian laughs. "Lady Kahn's kitchens were a haven for us growing up. Sandy came here as a youth and lived for years, studying under the old Tuatara ambassador. Many a pie or a slice of cake went missing, I have to admit."

"You were shit at stealing things." Subtle Sands Shifting points a taloned finger at the Prince. "If it hadn't been for Quickblade here, you would have felt the sting of Food Lady's fire bees every day!"

Bryant nods. "You've always lacked subtlety, brother."

"Oi!" Meridian protests. "Quit ganging up on me in front of the wife!" His expression changes as he hears Lianne's mutter of, "*the couch.*" He curls his arm around her. "Sorry, dearest; in front of Lianne."

The Tuatara's eyes hold real amusement and they clap their scaled hands together. "So good to have us all together! But," their expression turns serious, "I have something quiet-quiet to discuss." They bow. "Would wifeys mind if I stole the males for a moment?"

Lianne sighs. "Since I'm feeling very '1950s housewife' at the moment, go ahead." She takes Isabella's arm. "We have some Anahera to catch up with anyway." The blonde woman tugs sharply on Isabella's arm, pulling her away from the group and towards a more secluded area, fringed with large potted palms.

"I'm not sure about that one." She murmurs. "They have a strong history together, but..."

"But the Tuatara clearly has their own agenda? Yeah, I noticed." Isabella frowns, but her expression lightens when she sees the Danish Anahera, Mich, approaching with her new wife. The tousle-haired woman grins and hugs her fiercely.

"I heard someone tried to kill you!" She leans back and her eyes are filled with concern. "Are you okay?"

Isabella nods and splays her hands. "Still breathing. Well, just – I swear this dress is trying to crush the life out of me."

"But it's worth it, you look stunning." The Gentrywoman beside Mich arches an eyebrow. She is tall and willowy, with honey-blonde hair, ochre skin and an astute twinkle in her brown eyes. "And I can see why the others find you such a conundrum. You chose the White Demon, did you not? It is either a brave choice or a sign of accelerating madness."

"This is Karo, my wife." Mich smiles and Isabella is relieved to see how happy she is.

Lianne lets go of Isabella's arm. "We've met before. It's lovely to see you. Izzy, Karo's offered to take some of our classes when we start on the commerce section of our course. She runs several companies. Actually, I have a few questions, if you don't mind?" She indicates to the couches nestled in the alcove and Karo nods, moving to sit.

Mich slides her hand around Isabella's arm and they stroll away.

"I got the impression that the Gentry are an unmitigated shower of bastards, but you seem to have found a decent one." Isabella nods back towards Karo.

The Dane smiles. "She's pretty special. Through her, I've met a few who aren't too awful. It's weird, they fight like feral cats amongst themselves but they're surprisingly loyal to Jonat and Makeda. Maybe it's because their governance has made the Citadel obscenely wealthy."

She points to a collection of Gentry lords off to their right. They are huddled together and arguing vigorously. "Those are members of the Flying Corps Collective. There's no actual 'flying corps' yet, but they're constantly nagging the King to force the Windpyres to give up some of their technology in order to create one."

As they slowly amble around the edge of the ballroom, Mich continues to point out various factions and individuals to watch out for and Isabella realises just how sheltered her existence has been, far above it all in the Eyrie.

Eventually, they come to a halt near a fountain. The statue is that of a stag being brutally slaughtered, crystal clear water gushing from its various wounds.

"Delightful." Isabella grimaces.

Mich suddenly turns towards her and hisses. "Fuck, she's here."

Isabella stares at her. "Who?" Mich's eyes have narrowed, her pleasant face twisting with disgust.

"Look, over by that staircase. See that woman who looks like a human glitter ball, surrounded by idiot flunkies? Henri, the French guy, chose her as his Suitor. Just watch what she does."

The woman is stunning, with luscious blonde hair piled in an intricate style above her head, the glittering gown hugging smooth, golden skin. She is holding court as a collection of Gentry hang on her every word. When she pauses to stare at an approaching young woman, they all fall silent. The girl is clearly nervous, holding up her skirts to walk on heels which appear to be made of glass. As she passes the group, the Gentrywoman smiles insincerely at her and her hand flicks to the side. The air ripples with her power and instantly the shoes shatter, bringing the girl crashing down in front of the crowd, her feet ripped and punctured with shards of glass.

"Holy shit," Isabella gapes and instantly moves to help her, but Mich's hand bites into her arm, holding her firm.

"Not a good idea."

They watch as the surrounding Gentry merely titter and stare, until a flock of servants appear and lift the sobbing girl, helping her away and sweeping up the glass. One young servant kneels on the floor to wipe up the spatters of blood and Isabella watches the blonde woman reach out a delicate foot and push him forwards, straight into the remaining shards. As he gasps and lifts his newly-sliced hands, she and the group cackle with laughter.

Isabella stares at Mich. "What the hell?"

Mich makes a face. "That, my lovely girl, is Lady Alinna Wildervene. She's a consummate player of this ridiculous 'game' they all keep going on about. She's pretty much untouchable, as far as I can tell." She snorts. "Lianne calls her 'the Wilderbitch'. And look," she nods to a man standing unhappily at the edge of the group, "how bloody miserable Henri is!"

The Frenchman, previously so classically suave and gentlemanly, is staring morosely at the floor. He looks oddly crumpled. His wife glances sideways and spots him, barking a command and clicking her fingers to summon him.

Isabella's rebel heart kicks in and she plants her hands on her hips, narrowing her eyes and glaring at Mich.

"Fuck it, let's have some fun." She turns, her glare resolving into a stunning smile as she sets off across the floor. The Gentry crowd

269

parts before her.

"Aw, crap." Mich swallows and glances around for support, spotting Bryant in the distance. She knows an "I'm going to fuck you up" smile when she sees one.

Isabella's anger finally pulls her to a halt in front of Henri, who looks up in surprise.

"Henri, mate! How are you?" She grins, resolutely ignoring the woman beside him.

"Isabella." Henri's face creases into a smile. He is a handsome man, with floppy caramel hair and warm brown eyes, although now they retain a haunted look. He embraces her and they kiss one another's cheeks several times. His wife's eyes narrow and her group falls silent, stunned. Henri holds her at arm's length, looking her up and down. "You look well."

"I feel great. Is this the famous Lady Wildervene?" She glances at the woman and turns on her warmest smile. "How delightful to meet you." As she catches the shadow that passes across Henri's face, her anger flares again.

Lady Wildervene's gaze rakes her up and down, rising to a look of barely concealed contempt. She does not even bother with a polite reply.

"You chose the White Demon. As a creature far less than human, he has never been able to grasp our ways, so it is no wonder that you are sorely in need of instruction." She leans forward. "I am more than happy to act as your mentor in domestic matters."

Isabella feels herself momentarily pulled off-kilter. "Domestic?"

The woman's expression resolves into one of pity. "I hear that you refer to your maidservant as an 'advisor'." She speaks more slowly, as if Isabella is a little dim. "It is entirely inappropriate. The lower orders cannot be allowed to get above themselves. Do not give them false hope of advancement, they're really not capable of it. Such dull, bovine minds. We are each born at our own level and that is an end to it."

270

Isabella raises an eyebrow, pulling herself together. "Millie is not a 'lower order'. She is a young woman who works very hard, does an excellent job and deserves respect."

Behind Henri, the servant who has been hanging around waiting for Lady Wildervene to choose another drink stares at Isabella. He burns to share this insolent disruption to the normal social order when he returns to the servants' section and his eyes widen with vicious delight when he spots an approaching figure over Isabella's shoulder. Mich has finally attracted Bryant's attention and he rapidly makes his way across the ballroom to pull her away. The servant decides that he cannot possibly leave his current post; this promises to be too juicy.

Lady Wildervene, about to snap back at Isabella, becomes aware of the Black Drw-ad's approach and her expression changes instantly, a crystalline smile coating her face.

If Isabella didn't know any better, if her natural instinct for artifice in women wasn't already buzzing, she would swear the bitch was happy to see him.

"Lord Lathorne, such a surprise to see you here! We all thought after that awful moment at the Ceremony where your wife obviously had second thoughts, that you had been thoroughly put off appearing in public for good!" Behind her, Lady Wildervene's coterie of associates titter. They remind Isabella of fruit flies, hanging around a rotten apple.

"Alinna." Bryant places a hand on his chest and bows. "You look...bright, this evening." His low voice sounds complimentary but his gaze takes in the way Henri winces as the light reflecting from her dress flashes across his eyes.

"Thank you." She curtseys prettily. "It was simply fascinating to see you enter with our Prince and his new whor...wife. It's so sweet of him to have kept you as a *pet* all these years. It's really done you good." She tips her head to one side, blinking at him and completely ignoring Isabella.

Bryant goes very still, but then his wife does something he does

271

not expect. She moves closer, placing her hand on his lower back in an obvious show of solidarity. He glances down to see her exchange a significant look with Henri, who rolls his eyes.

Isabella is fighting a vicious battle to control herself. Not only has the Wilderbitch insulted her oldest friend but her deliberate viciousness towards Bryant makes her want to tear the woman's throat out. She feels very sorry for Henri, so she uses him as a way to send Lady Wildervene a verbal left hook.

"Henri, you look very tired. I hope she is treating you well."

The Frenchman regards her steadily, wondering what she is up to. "I am well, Isabella. I merely find the air here…disagreeable. It gives me a headache. Do you not suffer from it too?"

Isabella smiles, deliberately appearing relaxed. "Thankfully, not often. The air is blissfully clear in the Eyrie and," her smile widens to a grin, "I have a secret." She motions to him. "Come closer and breathe in."

Henri frowns and looks at his wife. Her expression falters a little and she shrugs. He steps forward, closer to Bryant and inhales. The Drw-ad's fresh snow-scent wraps around him and Henri's eyes widen. He takes in a deeper breath.

"C'est incroyable! If I were married to him, I'd never let him go!" Reluctantly he steps back and Bryant and Isabella watch him wince as the Gentry perfumes settle over him again, in particular Alinna Wildervene's trademark chemical strawberry scent, which is powerful enough to strip the nostrils. Henri gives a Gallic sigh. "Perhaps you could hire him out."

Bryant glances between the two Anahera. He has no idea what they are talking about and Alinna appears equally confused, and not a little annoyed that her husband appears to appreciate the Drw-ad. He hopes he smells acceptable, as Isabella has yet to complain about his scent, unlike the rest of the Gentry.

Henri, invigorated by Isabella's rebellious attitude and Bryant's scent, suddenly asks about the assassination attempt. Isabella is aware

272

that Lady Wildervene is suddenly watching her like a hawk.

"Indeed, I would love to hear how you survived it." Her tone is warm but her gaze is like acid sizzling on flesh.

"My husband is an exceptionally talented man. It was merely a little problem, swiftly dealt with," Isabella replies archly and rests her other hand on Bryant's wrist, smiling up at him.

He looks down at her and despite his tension, he realises what his wife is doing and what an impact it is clearly having on Alinna Wildervene, a woman who is usually unflappable. Her vicious smile slips and she glares at him. The words 'a little problem' appear to have hit their mark.

"It was a particularly cowardly attack, Alinna."

"Really?" She arches an eyebrow. "I thought it rather artful. Whoever devised it had a sense of style." She flicks a delicate hand. "We should bring it back, make poisoning chic again. It's most entertaining." She gives a little laugh, echoed by the Fruit Fly Coterie behind her.

Bryant narrows his eyes. He has no desire to play it this way. "Strange, your companion Mirl is not here. He never misses an opportunity to inflict himself upon others."

Alinna frowns. "He has been ill recently. He will not even leave his rooms." She shrugs a delicate shoulder. "Perhaps it was something he ate."

Bryant's control slips for a moment. "Or perhaps it was something he did. How many lives have you destroyed, Alinna, in pursuit of the game?"

She smiles brightly. "Not enough, Lord Lathorne." She waves a hand vaguely, glancing away and fluttering her fingers at someone in the crowd. "So, do you know who might wish to harm your wife?"

He nods. "I know exactly who is responsible and they will each suffer for it in time."

Her gaze flicks back to him and she almost balks, taking in the way his dark eyes begin to glitter.

273

"Did you think I would let such an act go unanswered, Alinna?" He gains a little satisfaction in the way her mouth gapes at this before quickly snapping shut.

"Dearie me," Isabella leans forward. "If other lords like Mirl are indisposed, perhaps such toxicity is catching. You should be careful, Alinna." She looks to Henri, dismissing Lady Wildervene entirely. "Henri, do take care of yourself. If you ever need a break, you are more than welcome to visit us."

He smiles tightly. "Thank you. Your company is a breath of fresh air." He glances up at Bryant. "I am pleased to finally meet you, Lord Lathorne. You are not as I had been told. Clearly, Isabella made an excellent choice." He resolutely ignores the look of outrage which crosses his wife's face, even though he knows he will suffer for it later. He had all but given up rebelling against her but now he feels an ember of resistance begin to flare. Henri resolves to keep it burning.

The Drw-ad bows. "Come, Isabella, the evening grows late." Together they move away, leaving the Fruit Fly Coterie to whisper behind them.

As they leave, Alinna Wildervene is suddenly struck by how the two look together. Isabella's arm is still around the Drw-ad's waist and they fit easily into one another's shape. He looks down at his wife with an expression which shocks Alinna. It is a brief, unguarded moment and he quickly covers it, but it makes the Gentry woman grit her teeth. Her own husband has yet to look at her like that. If anything, increasingly he seems to be trying not to look at her at all. Even when she pins him to the bed and rides him hard, he barely makes eye contact. And the Anahera beside the White Demon? She looks relaxed, as if she is actually enjoying his company.

How could she? He is a disgusting mutation.

But then, a far deeper truth emerges. Yes, she finds him utterly repellent but for that one, small memory. When she had kissed him all those years ago, he did not taste as she expected, and as she had

274

crowed to countless others afterwards. Instead of the bitter taint of death, his kiss had invigorated her and was like none she had tasted since. Her hatred for him surges and she turns to snap at her husband, for he is yet again staring longingly into the distance, the attention she craves far from his mind.

When they reach the top of the staircase, Isabella gasps. "What the hell just happened?"

Bryant looks down at her. "You did well, my Lady." And to himself he murmurs, "I did well."

Isabella squeezes his arm. "You did do well! They're all still alive, aren't they?"

She swears that he almost smiles.

As they walk along the corridor towards the lift port, Isabella turns the whole conversation with Alinna Wildervene over in her mind, anger growing with each step. She halts near a fountain of leaping fish and turns to him. "Bryant, will you be honest with me?"

He nods, cautiously. "Of course. What is troubling you?"

"You and the Wilderbit...Lady Wildervene, appeared to be having an entirely different conversation from us. What were you really saying to one another?"

Bryant marvels once again at how astute her observations are. He does not wish to tell her but she asked for honesty and he has tried to give her that. He ushers her around to the far side of the fountain so that the sound will mask their conversation from the passing crowd.

"Isabella, on the night of the assassination attempt, I left you." She nods and he looks towards the ground. "I did not wish to leave but I had to follow the trail of the orchids before it disappeared."

"And you found its source."

"I found one of them. It was another Suitor, Lord Mirl."

Isabella's mouth drops open. "The arrogant sod who threw a tantrum when we were on the dais, just because I turned him down?" Bryant nods and takes her hands in his.

275

"Mirl wanted to punish you for choosing me but although he is a vindictive man, he is not an inventive one. I knew the orchids must have been someone else's choice."

"Alinna Wildervene? Why did she have an issue with me? I'd never even met the woman until tonight!"

Bryant looks at her with an expression which makes her stomach twist. When he speaks, his voice is quiet.

"She wanted to punish *me*, Isabella. She wanted me to feel powerless, to remind me that even now she can destroy any chance of happiness I might hope to have."

The cruelty is breath-taking and Isabella suddenly realises that the Gentry are like spoiled children, smashing things up merely because they can. "Bitch," she snarls.

Bryant squeezes her hands. "She is dangerous, Isabella. Please stay away from her. Let me deal with her instead."

Isabella smiles tightly and nods, watching him relax slightly. As she takes his arm and they stroll towards the lift hub, she knows that she has absolutely no intention of doing so.

14. A SPANNER IN THE WORKS

Several days pass and Isabella spends most of them riding the lifts and interviewing helmers. Her understanding of the Citadel continues to grow and she finds she is enjoying her studies. One morning, after a tutorial and nearing the second break of fast, she arrives back in the Eyrie to find Millie on a mission.

"I'll be with you in a moment, my Lady." Millie balances the covered break of fast tray on her hip and opens the door to the solarium stairs.

"I'll take it up." Isabella holds out her hands. "It's the one place in the Eyrie I haven't been yet."

"That's true, but," Millie manoeuvres the tray out of Isabella's reach, "we both know your track record for carrying things successfully isn't great, so I'll take it up for you."

Isabella pouts. "I'm not *that* bad!"

The maidservant gives her a steady look. "Beg pardon, but since you've arrived in the Eyrie you've broken eight cups…"

"Yes, but…"

"You've tripped over the step out to the balcony more times than I can count."

"Look," Isabella folds her arms across her chest. "In my defence…"

"My Lady, you even wear jewelled slippers to events because you're frightened of 'falling off' heels." Millie's gaze flicks to the smudge of a bruise on Isabella's arm. "And where did that come

277

from?"

The Anahera's lips become a thin line. Millie nods.

"You tripped over the rug again, didn't you?"

"Fine." Isabella sighs. "You got me, I'm a klutz. Can we go up now?" She is suddenly desperate to escape the conversation.

Millie turns, feeling vindicated, and leads the way up the stairs, oblivious to the fact that the woman behind her is poking out her tongue.

The stairs curve steeply and finally end at a large, embossed metal door. Millie passes Isabella the tray and holds up her hand, the tiny, green open book symbol appearing from her palm and sinking into the lock. The door swings open and the maidservant steps back, allowing the Anahera to enter before closing the door behind her.

The solarium is enormous, with tall windows stretching high above to a glass-domed roof. It is lined with bookshelves and tables cluttered with globes, alembics, vials and tools. Curved metal structures loom at the far end beneath a gantry and a complicated harness system. In the middle of the room, the Drw-ad perches on a stool at his desk, his hair pulled back in a workman's braid. One hand is raised in front of him, palm upwards, a diagram formed from light floating above it, reminding Isabella of a holographic projection. The other holds a stylus, the point flicking over the circular quire on the desk.

"You may leave it on the table, Millie." He does not look up as he speaks, concentrating on the slowly rotating images before him.

Isabella glances around at the clutter and feels at a loss. "Where? The only clear space appears to be the floor."

Bryant turns, waving his hand to disperse the symbols. "My Lady, I did not realise it was you. Please, give me a moment." He rises and begins to clear the desk in front of him. As well as the quire, it is covered in large sheets of paper, measuring tools and open books.

Isabella places the tray on the newly available space and steps back. "I'm sorry to bother you." She smiles at him. "But I realized

278

that I haven't been to visit you here. If you're busy, I can leave."

"You are not bothering me at all. Welcome to my workshop." He spreads his hands and bows. "I am pleased you are here."

Isabella turns slowly in a circle, taking it all in. "What an extraordinary space. I can't believe I never asked before, but what is it that you actually do here?"

"I have a number of advisory roles and the King has specifically tasked me with refining the weapons the Uhlan use. However," he indicates with a broad sweep of his hand, "my true interest lies in the creation of new Shields for other settlements."

Isabella frowns. "What kind of shield?"

Bryant leans back against the desk and clicks his fingers. A curved leather chair suddenly bumps the back of Isabella's knees and she sits in surprise. "Hjaltland is often beset by storms. They can be dramatic but they clear the air. However, every so often a much larger system will form, powerful enough to destroy."

"Powerful enough to strip flesh from bone?" Isabella remembers the Captain's words on the way to the Citadel.

"Yes." He nods. "However, certain forms of life have evolved over the millennia to be resistant to a Storm. For instance, an Yggdrasil tree protects each Sisterhood Haven Holm from both Storms and attacks by creating a barrier of energy which it projects outwards. This disrupts much of the wind's force." He perches on the edge of the desk, his cool voice becoming more animated.

"Just over a century ago, an engineer working alongside the Sisterhood devised a way to harness the geothermal power in this mountain and use it to create a "shield" which could act in much the same way as an Yggdrasil tree. When activated it can encompass the entire city." He looks down at his patterned hands and a shadow seems to cross his face. "Unfortunately, the design has a number of flaws." He is silent for a moment and she watches him swallow uncomfortably, before suddenly standing up.

"It is also the only one of its kind and its design is closely guarded by the Citadel." He motions towards the windows and the landscape stretching far below. "Everyone else has no choice but to batten down the hatches and hope to survive. It seemed…uneven to me, so I have been working to refine the basic design and create smaller units which can be fitted into any settlement. Please," he indicates behind her to the huge workspace cluttered with welding kits and large, spherical metal cradles.

Isabella rises and follows him across the floor to the nearest one. "The cradle is designed to contain the power core and regulate the energy, directing it to the inner pillars which anchor the energy of the Shield. I have had some success." There is a distinct look of satisfaction on his face.

She smiles. "That's impressive, and pretty cool too."

"What do you mean?"

"Well, you're giving other people the chance to protect themselves. Didn't you say it wasn't just a way to ward off the Storms?"

He nods. "That is true. As it stands, they must rely on a Citadel response to any threats, including marauders, and that takes time to deploy. I have had a number of enquiries from outlying settlements."

An odd sound interrupts and he looks down. It is the grumble of Isabella's stomach, protesting at the lack of attention. She colours slightly. "Will you join me for the break of fast?"

She grins and they move back to the desk and lift the cover to find that Millie has put together an impressive spread. Isabella eyes the leather chair suspiciously and then opts to perch on the stool. Bryant drops into the chair and reaches for a plate. The tray is laden with a selection of cheeses, slabs of smoked mackerel, slices of freshly baked bread and oatcakes, grapes, fruit quarters, tiny dark green capers, olives and little peppery flowers. Bryant suggests she try a thin slice of pear with the blue vein cheese and then ruins the moment entirely as he pulls the top off a small, squat dish. The most extraordinary stench of ammonia-soaked armpits erupts into the air.

Isabella slaps her arm over her mouth and nose and rocks backwards. Her muffled voice is laced with horror. "What the hell is that?"

Bryant regards her with restrained amusement. "The Stinking Marauder is a very fine cheese, I will have you know." He dips his knife into the dish and lifts a sickly yellow smear from inside, spreading it onto an oatcake and holding it out to her. She stares at him, so he picks up a grape and drops it on top, as if somehow this will improve it. She shakes her head furiously and he shrugs, popping it into his mouth with one hand and putting the lid back on with the other. He waves his hand and a window in front of the desk opens, the stiff breeze blowing the horror away. Isabella tentatively comes out from beneath her arm.

"That's wrong on so many levels, Bryant."

He quirks a dark eyebrow. "Meridian always complains too. Humans have no taste." To appease her, he loads a slice of bread with a less offensive cheese and a dollop of relish and hands it to her. She sniffs it suspiciously, but after the first nibble devours it.

They eat in companionable silence until a shadow flickers over them. Isabella looks up to see that several tiny saur have gravitated to the metal beams above, or perch on instruments and machines nearby, staring at them in a hopeful fashion. One, covered in iridescent blue feathers, twists around the brass lamp beside her and blinks, winsomely.

"Dragons," Isabella breathes in delight and holds out a piece of cheese. The little beast eyes her beadily, then snatches it and gobbles it whole. It drops to the table and taps its tail on the wood, demanding more. She hands over an olive.

"That is foolish, my Lady. You will never be free of him now." Bryant shakes his head, watching the little creature spit out the olive pit onto one of his books.

"Isabella," she murmurs.

"I am sorry?" He is confused.

"You're always so formal. Surely we've known one another long enough for you to call me by my name." She scratches the saur behind his head and he shivers happily.

"I apologise, I thought only to treat you with the proper respect."

She smiles softly. "You have, and I appreciate it. But you can relax a little."

The Drw-ad eyes her thoughtfully. "I admit, I did not expect things to be like this."

"What did you expect?"

He shrugs, his voice matter-of-fact. "That we would merely use one another as a public shield, then eventually you would grow bored, take lovers and I would be alone again."

Isabella stops scratching the saur and stares at him. "Bryant, that sounds dire."

"I did not expect to enjoy your company so much." He looks down at his hands. Perhaps now is the time to tell her. Perhaps she will understand.

"Isabella." He almost seems to taste the word as he says it. "There are reasons why this kind of interaction is…complex, for me." He watches the disgruntled saur flap away. "First Mother designs my people in very specific ways, but affection is not one of them. It serves no purpose for us. Until two hundred turns ago, Mother kept our creation entirely to herself – no one was allowed to breed."

He tries to maintain eye contact, striving for honesty. "Drw-ad are forbidden from mating with anyone outside our race, although for some time now Mother has relaxed the rules for Reds and Whites, and they may apply for her permission to join with one of their own kind." He pauses. It is a fact, so why should it be difficult to admit? But he struggles with it, and with the look in Isabella's eyes. "Black Drw-ad like myself are still expressly forbidden from joining with another. We belong completely to the Goddess."

She stares at him. "Did you ask her permission to marry me?"

"No." He watches her process this and worry twists in his gut but yet again, she does not react the way he expects.

Slowly, she speaks. "Bryant Lathorne, am I a rebellion for you?"

He frowns. "There is much more to it than that…" To his surprise, she throws back her head and laughs, a throaty sound which heralds true amusement. "My La…Isabella?"

When she finally calms down, she explains. "I've never been used as an excuse to rebel before. Usually I'm the one being shouted at for misbehaving!" She looks at him fondly. "Every day you surprise me. I think I respect you even more now that I know that!"

She is not the only one surprised. That she appreciates defiance is confusing enough, but he is oddly reassured by her reaction. He watches her become serious as another thought hits her. It is a thought he had hoped would stay hidden.

"Will there be repercussions for your actions?"

He does not reply.

"Bryant?"

He speaks quietly. "I do not know."

Isabella taps her fingers on the desk. If this is another potential threat, then it is a long way off and not worth worrying about yet. She sits up, deciding that the mood has been dampened enough.

"Never mind. Here and now, it doesn't matter." She sees relief flooding his dark eyes. Glancing around, her gaze falls on the large design sketches he had shoved aside earlier. "I have a question."

Bryant tenses again. "Ask."

"How are your new shields powered?"

The Drw-ad feels himself relax, appreciating her change of subject. "So far, the only settlements I have considered establishing shields in are the ones with drillable access to geothermal power."

Isabella points up towards the weak sun high above. "Do you have solar technology in Hjaltland? In my world, people are starting to make real headway with wind and wave turbines. Surely, with the windscape here and so much coastline, you wouldn't have to be tethered to just geothermal?"

283

Bryant stares at her. How could he not have thought of that? A never-ending source of power, easily managed by the townsfolk themselves? He pulls a piece of paper towards him, snags a stylus and begins to sketch a design. Mid-line, he pauses and looks up.

"Will you stay with me a while? I will have questions."

"No problem. If you need me, I'll be over there, hunting dragons." She picks up a piece of cheese and wanders away, trying to tempt another saur down from the beams.

Outside, a winter squall begins to hurl sleet at the windows.

To the north, halfway between Aith and East Burrafirth, a storm of a different kind is brewing. Captain Eric Bannerman has been cursed with a new commanding officer. A Gentryman fresh out of officer training, Lord Ethel holds a very definite set of opinions about how things should be done.

Bannerman and Delilah's units have been amalgamated and their orders are to patrol a stretch of coastline often beset by marauders. The newly arrived Lord has other ideas, demanding they move further along the coast towards lands owned by his family, including a mining facility he wants protected. It already possesses its own guard unit and both Captains are increasingly frustrated by this, for there are unguarded settlements all along the coast which require their support instead.

They ride in a long line near the ridge of a low hill. To one side, miles of heather-covered moorland stretch and to the other, rocky coves dip in and out along the coastline. A series of fish farms dot the water in the distance, the sea reflecting the grey tips of scudding clouds overhead.

Further along, Sergeant Doric can be heard berating two new recruits and chivvying them into order. With scruffy brown hair, dark eyes and a lined, unshaven face perpetually creased into a cynical scowl, he is probably Hjaltland's roughest medic, but he is also a thoroughly capable soldier and a staunch ally of the two Captains.

Lord Ethel glares at him in disgust and spurs his mount to catch up with Eric and Delilah, who ride side by side.

"Captain Dae!" He snaps as he pulls alongside. "Is that scruffy, bawling excuse for a Sergeant one of yours?" He flicks his ash blonde hair back from his pale eyes and glares at Delilah. "He's a disgrace! Either he is deaf and therefore unfit for duty, or he is deliberately ignoring my requests."

Delilah regards him steadily. "My Lord, Sergeant Doric is probably the best medic in the Uhlan and he's an excellent soldier." She shrugs. "Sure, he's a bit rough, but…"

"I didn't ask for your opinion, Captain, I asked if he was your responsibility." The commander sniffs derisively, his long nostrils quivering. "The best medic in the Uhlan? That doesn't say much."

Delilah's mouth falls open but it is Bannerman who responds first.

"There's not a trooper I'd rather have by my side in a scrap, saving Captain Dae here, my Lord." He watches the commander's gaze rake him up and down, clearly sneering at his scars, and decides that this is possibly the most "punchable" Gentry officer they've had yet.

"Yes, a bunch of *scrappers* is what the Uhlan have clearly become. No wonder the King has tasked the Academy with whipping you people into shape. Still," he lifts his chin, "you may be of some use if the refinery is attacked. At the very least you can provide a distraction."

Delilah glances sideways and notices the tell-tale muscle clench in Bannerman's cheek. Her gaze drops to see his knuckles whiten as he clutches the reins more tightly, wrestling for calm.

"I wanted to talk to you about that," Bannerman somehow manages to keep the insolent edge out of his voice. "The refinery is already well defended. It makes more sense to track the progress of the marauder group that was spotted two nights ago near the port town of Scarvataing. The scouts reported a drifting village nearby which might be too much of a temptation for them."

The commander snorts again. "A drifting village? Those worthless bastards? Moving from place to place with neither croft nor profession? What loss would they be?"

Delilah notices that one of Bannerman's hands has moved to the hilt of the dagger at his far hip, so she urges her mount closer, giving him a warning bump. "My Lord, they're still the Citadel's subjects. It's our responsibility to protect them."

"Captain Dae," the man glares at her, "it is up to me to decide who we are responsible for. You, on the other hand, need to take more responsibility for your troops, starting with Sergeant Doric. I expect to see him cleaning out the latrines, where he belongs, when we reach the refinery."

He leans forward, glaring at the man beside her and clicks his fingers. "You there, Bannerman. Do not forget what you are. You will not undermine me in front of my troops again." With that, he spurs his horse forward towards the front of the line.

"I really want to hit that man." Delilah's dark eyes glare up at the clouds pooling above them. To her surprise, Bannerman remains silent. She glances at him. "Eric?"

He shakes his hands out, trying to ease their clenched tension. "I don't think that'd be enough." He rasps. "That one's clearly a danger. Who knows what bloody stupid ideas he's going to throw at us. We'll have to step lively…"

Bannerman is interrupted by the thunder of hooves, heralding the return of a scout. The young man pulls his pony to a halt beside them.

"You were right about the drifting village, Captain. That marauder rabble are almost upon 'em." He pulls his mount around and together they move to catch up with Lord Ethel, where the scout delivers his report.

Ethel huffs, his mount shifting skittishly beneath him. "Well, there's nothing we can do for them now. Let's press on."

"My Lord!" Delilah stares at him. "The village is just over that rise. We can be there in moments if we move!"

The Gentry Lord is acutely aware that the rest of the troop have caught up with them and are watching him with barely concealed frustration. He opens his mouth and then closes it.

"My Lord, this is what we're here for." Bannerman growls.

"But…" Ethel stammers. "The refinery…it's safe there!"

"Not for them." Bannerman realizes that the man has no stomach for the fight at all and his eyes narrow. He tries a different approach. "My Lord, how will it look if a whole village is slaughtered on your first day of command?"

Lord Ethel stares at him like a rabbit in lamplight, his pale eyes blinking rapidly. "I…"

"Right, good choice, my Lord." Bannerman stands in his stirrups, turning to the troops and raising his voice. "Uhlan, prepare to engage." He points over the rise. "Down that hill and a split-unit pincer, crush them from both sides. Go!" He spurs his horse on and beside him Delilah does the same, splitting off with her own unit as they crest the rise. Behind him, Lord Ethel struggles to control his mount and his shock at the Captain's actions.

The Uhlan thunder over the low hill and down towards the shore, where a ragged collection of makeshift huts and tents huddle together. Several are already aflame and screams rend the air. Marauders move between the huts, slaughtering the old or infirm and collecting the rest. Two cell wagons wait on the road running alongside the rocky beach. So intent are they on enjoying themselves, the bandits are oblivious to the approach of the Citadel troops until they are upon them.

Leaning low over his horse, Bannerman targets a tall, skinny marauder, opening up his back with a sweep of his sword as he canters past. From the opposite end of the village, Delilah throws herself from her mount, straight onto the back of an enormous, horned warrior. Her blade at the ready, she tears it across his throat, riding him to the ground as his blood sprays across the dirt. She rises and turns, racing to assist one of the young recruits as he wrestles with a snarling female. Around them, villagers duck and scurry.

The Uhlan are experienced but this particular marauder band is sizable, comprising nigh on forty warriors, each one hungry for plunder and violence. After dispatching three more bandits from on high, Bannerman slides from his horse to pull a sweat-soaked raider away from a little girl, cornered against the door of a hut. She cowers as the Captain throws him against a nearby hitching post.

"Fuck off, soldier. She's mine." The man sneers and then produces a wicked, serrated blade. He seems a little taken aback when the scarred Uhlan in front of him merely rolls his eyes.

Bannerman makes a fist with one hand and flares his power within it. Short sword in the other hand, he feints left and as the man reacts, thrusting with the serrated blade, the Captain flings a handful of sparks at his eyes. The marauder's sword arm wavers and his snarl of pain turns to a howl as Bannerman twists to the right, slicing open the man's belly. His sword flashes back, punching through the warrior's throat and pinning him to the hitching post. For a moment, the Captain struggles to remove his blade but hearing a noise behind him, yanks harder and extracts it just in time, flicking it under his arm and thrusting backwards, impaling the raider moving up behind him.

Sergeant Doric jogs past, directing two Uhlan towards another knot of fighting. Artur is just behind him. Bannerman whistles and they both turn, making their way across the muddy ground towards him. He crouches in front of the little girl, who jambs her fists against her mouth in fear. The Captain forces his muscles to relax.

"I know we look scary but we're here to help you." His rough voice is low and calm and his grey eyes hold only softness. His scent of cardamom and cigars wraps around her. "See this young lad," he indicates to Artur, "he's going to look after you and help you find your family." Artur's pale, young face nods and he bows to the little girl. "Will you let him help you?"

The child regards him seriously for a moment, then uncurls one fist, holding it out to Artur who reaches down to lift her up. Doric points to the top end of the village.

"Take her past the edge and wait for us to finish clearing these bastards. I'll be back in a minute." He jogs back along the track to where a group of Uhlan are hammering into the last remaining marauders. His bellow echoes across the hill. "Don't kill 'em all – we need one alive!"

Bannerman follows Artur and the child back up the hill, checking each hut for marauder stragglers until something catches his eye. Lord Ethel's horse is tethered next to a shack which sits at the back of the huts. He realizes that he hasn't seen the man since the Uhlan came down the hill so he slaps Artur on the back and orders him to keep going. He stalks towards the shack, stepping over the body of an old man lying crumpled in the mud.

He spots another body lying just beside the gaping door. It is a young woman, her throat slit, the wound still fresh and her blank eyes staring up at him. He crouches and scans her body. Behind him in the darkness of the interior of the shack comes the sound of movement and a muffled cry.

Bannerman rises, his short sword ready. He eases in through the doorway, his eyes adjusting to gloom. A rough kitchen lies in front of him, a small wash basin upended on the floor beside a scattering of vegetables. Separating the kitchen from the sleeping space at the back is a curtain, the folk embroidery now faded and fraying. The material rises slightly as someone moves behind it.

Blade at the ready, the Captain reaches out and tears the curtain from its pole. The sight that greets him leaves him momentarily frozen.

Lord Ethel stands with his back to him, his trews down around his knees, bending a small blond boy over the table in front of him, his hand pressing the child's head against the wood. The Gentry commander snarls back at him. "Wait your turn, Captain."

As he turns his head, Bannerman sees fingernail marks across the man's cheek and he realises that the woman bleeding into the dirt

289

outside more than likely died trying to protect her child. Rage punches through him and he reaches out and tears the Gentryman away from the boy, hauling him backwards and punching him hard in the belly. As the man folds forward the Captain grabs his head, pulling it down hard into his rising knee. Lord Ethel's nose breaks with a crack.

Grabbing the man by his shirt, Bannerman hurls him bodily out of the shack and into the mud outside, following closely behind and hammering his boot into the Gentryman's back, aiming for the kidneys. As he dives forward to haul him to his feet again, a woman's voice finally cuts through the mist of rage which engulfs him.

"Eric! What the fuck? Stop!" Delilah grabs his shoulder and pulls him backwards, nearly earning a fist to the jaw for her effort.

Jerked out of his frenzy, Bannerman finally becomes aware that the Uhlan troops have returned from their marauder clean-up and are now staring at him, several open-mouthed.

"Look!" Bannerman snarls and points to the half-undressed state of the Lord in front of them and then spins on his heel and strides back into the shack, Delilah following closely behind. He snags a ragged blanket from a cot in the corner and wraps it around the boy, picking him up. The lad flails feebly against him for a moment before giving in. Bannerman looks down at him, his grey eyes once again calm and steady.

"I'm not going to hurt you, I give you my word, and he…" he points outside, "isn't going to hurt you again, I'll make sure of it." There is something about the Captain's voice which calms the child and Delilah, watching in stunned silence, feels strangely lulled by it herself. The smell of cardamom grows a little stronger for a moment.

Bannerman exits the shack, holding the boy so that his head is over his shoulder. He does not want him to glimpse Lord Ethel again. "Check the woman." He nods to Delilah who crouches next to the body beside the door.

She too has seen the claw marks on Ethel's cheek and when she checks the woman's right hand, she sees fresh blood under her

290

fingernails. She turns to glare in disgust at the Gentry Lord.

"Doric!" Bannerman rasps. The Sergeant appears and moves to take the child, who upon seeing the rough soldier begins to breathe rapidly. Doric cups the lad's head in his hand and begins to hum, releasing a soft energy which calms the child. The scent of peaches wafts into the air. He carefully takes the boy from the Captain.

"Don't fret, little one," the medic murmurs. "I'm an ugly bugger, but you're safe with me. I'm only scary to bad men." He glares at Lord Ethel and then carries the boy a little distance away where he can begin to assess him.

Through all this, the officer on the ground continues to shout, his voice rising to a shriek. "Look what he did! Look what he did to me!" He staggers to his feet, hastily pulling up his trews. "I want him arrested! I want him flogged!"

Delilah pulls a message globe from a pouch on her belt and turns away, quickly composing a report and letting it fly, then she turns back and steps between them. Bannerman's grey eyes flash and he starts forward as Lord Ethel screams at him, albeit slightly muffled thanks to the broken nose.

"Eric, stop and think." Delilah tries to keep her voice reasonable, even as Bannerman turns his dangerous glare upon her. "Continuing an attack on a superior officer isn't going to take you anywhere good. Calm down!"

Suddenly the Gentry lord stops screaming and the two Captains realise he too is composing a message. Delilah takes a step forward but he holds the globe triumphantly aloft and lets it fly.

"The Uhlan Commander will hear of this! You will be court-martialed and I will demand the rope! Captain, arrest this man." He flicks his fingers at her.

Delilah glares at him, struggling to rein in her own anger. For a moment she wonders if they could make his death look like the result of an unfortunate encounter with a marauder. That has certainly been done before, when Uhlan troops have been led into peril by useless commanders. But it is a foolish thought, quickly quashed as her eyes flick across the assembled soldiers. There are too many of them and she cannot be completely sure of where each of their allegiances lie. She grits her teeth and moves towards Bannerman, tugging her wrist cuffs from her belt and imbuing them with deadbolt magic to make them more secure.

Bannerman stares at her. "Del..."

"You know I have no choice; you saw him with the globe. He's sent it now, so we're fucked. Hands."

His rage dissipates before the crashing wave of the consequences of his actions. Too many eyes witnessed what he did, no matter how legitimate the reason. Reluctantly, he holds out his hands and she cuffs him.

Rumbles of dissent issue from soldiers in both units and Doric, who has finished ministering to the child nearby, mutters loudly. "This is such *shit*." He glares at Lord Ethel who wheezes in vicious, self-righteous delight.

Delilah leads Bannerman to the cell wagon they have liberated from the marauders and secures him inside. When he looks up, he realizes that it is already occupied. One solitary raider has been left battered but alive, ready to be transported back to the Citadel for questioning. He is a lanky fellow with a sly grin and a rank stench. He looks delighted to have company.

With considerable reluctance, Sergeant Doric passes the traumatized child to one of the remaining families and ducks his head as the villagers stare at him mutely. There is no thanks, only conspicuous fear and mistrust. As the Uhlan move out, ready to make the long trek back to the Citadel, the sergeant is sure he isn't the only one who feels stained by Ethel's actions.

15. BLOSSOMING

On the Læran Terrace, Isabella leans against the wooden desk in the Teaching Gallery, trailing a finger across the circular screen of her chronicle quire as tiny flags of information rise to the surface. The tutors have managed to find a stock of old devices, untouched by magic-specific technology for the newcomers to use.

Around her, other Anahera perch on high stools, hunching over their quires in pursuit of information for their own research projects. The tutor, a tall man with short grey hair, moves between the students to discuss their progress. Sunlight streams in through the carved panels of the doors, several of which have been flung open to let fresh air in from the courtyard garden beyond. Isabella is deep in concentration, tracing lines of information about the four Living Goddesses when she becomes aware of an intrusive presence.

She looks up to see a message globe floating beside her, trilling quietly. She wonders how long it has been there and when she glances across at the tutor, he is already glaring at her. She taps the globe and it slides open to reveal the message:

I require your presence on the Verdelais Terrace, immediately.

Isabella sits back, her eyes narrowing at the breath-taking demand in those words. All Bryant's careful assertions about the importance of respecting her and, in reality she is still a slave, to be commanded at a moment's notice with a curt snap. Her stomach contracts and a feeling of nausea rises. She considers ignoring the globe but it begins to pulse bright red and emits a high-pitched whistle, demanding an acknowledgement.

"Alright!" She snarls and taps it again, sharply. The globe zips shut and whisks away through the nearest window, rising through the air towards its sender. She slaps the quire closed and shoves it back into her green velvet bag. The other students turn and stare.

From the neighbouring desk, Lianne frowns at her as she rises. "What's up?"

Isabella snorts and flips a hand towards the upper levels of the Citadel. "I'm being summoned by his Lordship. I mean, really? I'm expected to drop everything and scurry all the way up to some random Terrace, never mind that I'm in the middle of something!"

She can feel her ire rising like hot lead as she speaks. "It's the wording. Did he design it specifically to piss me off? Is 'please' such a difficult word to squeeze past those blue lips?"

Isabella barely pauses for breath as her friend opens her mouth to speak. "And I hate being interrupted when I'm doing something!"

Lianne is well acquainted with her old friend's reaction to being ordered about. There is a deeply stubborn, rebellious streak running through her that was evident even when they were toddlers. She has long relished the looks of astonishment on the faces of the unsuspecting when the 'feral' in Isabella emerges.

"I'm almost tempted to come with you, just to watch the fireworks," she offers.

"It's just that…" Isabella fiddles distractedly with the strap of her bag, struggling with the flood of anxiety which threatens to choke her, "I thought he respected me. This just makes me feel like…property, again." She bites her lip to contain the intense wave washing over her.

Lianne is surprised. This is one of the few times in the whole mad experience that she has seen her friend falter. But true to form, Isabella rallies, her fear rapidly replaced with righteous anger.

"He's Meridian's closest friend, so please don't dent him too much. I'll never hear the end of it." Lianne sighs.

Isabella pats her friend's shoulder. "I make no promises." She spins on her heel and strides from the room.

The thoroughfare outside is teeming with people. The pale stone of the low buildings glows in the afternoon light and the bunting on the awnings jutting out above each shop flutters and snaps in the breeze. Here the Citadel Gentry mix with a multitude of other races, all clamouring to buy, sell and trade salacious gossip.

Latching on to a passing tuft-eared marron and using him as a shield, Isabella dives into the miasma of sharp chemical perfumes and riotous cooking smells. The marron's striped orange fur ripples as it moves, his huge paws making steady progress along the crowded street. His saddle is empty and he turns his massive head towards her, the nostrils of his muzzle flaring. A picture of the saddle appears in her mind along with a feeling of enquiry. Isabella shakes her head and politely declines. With a shrug he pads onward, the crowd closing round him like waves around a rock.

Isabella skims along the edge of Sundhamar Way until she reaches the glass gates of the Oversund terminus, the main lift hub for the Læran Terrace. A lift pod slides into place and she steps in, nodding to the helmer; a young woman with auburn hair in two tight buns perched atop her head and a smattering of freckles across her nose and deeply tanned cheeks.

"Where to, my Lady?" One hand is poised above the screen, the other resting lightly on her hip. Her crisp white shirt and pale grey jodhpurs are neatly pressed and her black knee-high riding boots are highly polished. A spiral lance is strapped across her back.

"The Verdelais Terrace please, wherever that is."

The helmer's eyes widen with delight. "That's an extraordinary part of the Citadel!" She taps in the destination and tiny blue track lines snake across the screen. The lift rolls forwards and lurches to the right. "You might as well take a seat, this one will take a while."

Isabella lowers herself onto the plush crimson cushions of the couch. She can still feel the anger fizzing in her chest and she plucks up the trailing ribbon from her open wrap blouse and curls it back and forth around a finger. The helmer notices her agitation and folds her arms, leaning back against the curved wall of the lift.

"Have you ever been to the Cloud Terrace before?"

Isabella frowns. "The what?"

The helmer smiles. "The Cloud Terrace is the common name for it. Not many of us ever get the chance to visit." She glances towards the glass ceiling wistfully. "I was taken there once as a child. Goddess knows how my father secured a pass."

Isabella stops twisting the ribbon for a moment. "What's so special about it?"

The young woman blinks. "You must be from very far away if you've never heard of it!" Then she pauses, leans forward and sniffs. "Ohhh, I thought you smelled different! You're an Anahera!"

Isabella's expression solidifies. "Nothing quite says 'you're a freak' like someone sniffing you."

The helmer leans back quickly. "Oh no, my Lady, I didn't mean to cause offence! You smell lovely. It's such a soft, clear scent. It's just that I've never had one in my lift before!"

"One…" Isabella murmurs, her lips setting into a thin line.

The helmer opens her mouth to backpedal but closes it again when she sees Isabella's expression. The lift slows to a crawl, prompting the young woman to check the screen.

"We're approaching the Upper Hub." She turns back and regards Isabella. "You do look familiar." She takes in Isabella's dark auburn hair, piled messily on top of her head and now edged with scarlet in the bright afternoon light shifting through the glass panels of the lift. Her speculative gaze notes the unusual cut and colour of her dress and finally her narrowed green eyes. Her own eyes widen in recognition.

"Are you…? Did you choose…?"

She has taken on a rather guppy-like appearance and Isabella

296

sighs, resigning herself to the now depressingly predictable conversation.

"Lord Lathorne, yes."

The helmer slaps her hand across her mouth, muffling an "...oh my!" Her expression suddenly brightens, shock replaced with enthusiasm. "We all watched the Ceremony on the shimmer in the Common Room. I pulled two extra shifts just to be able to get off early to watch it!"

Isabella stares at her. "You all...how many people watched the Ceremony?"

The helmer shrugs. "Most of the Citadel at least, but who knows how many across Hjaltland." Her face darkens into shadow for a moment as the lift pod races through a tunnel. The lamps hanging in each corner glow brighter in response.

Isabella feels the hot lead of her anger grow cold and solidify in her stomach. "Oh goody, I'm famous."

The young woman nods, oblivious to the feelings of horror currently washing over her passenger. "When Lord Lathorne stepped forward, I was so shocked! I mean," she grimaces, "He's always so stiff and cold and…" Her voice grows hoarse as she remembers who she is talking to. "Foreign…"

Isabella is regarding her more calmly now, so she rallies. "No one ever imagined he would offer in the first place! He doesn't seem to like anyone, and he's not even truly human." She stops and bites her lip, clearly worried that she has gone too far but Isabella lets her continue, interested to hear the perspective of someone outside the bitchy Gentry.

"My heart was in my mouth when he stood at the end of that dais waiting. All those people staring at him, expecting him to fail. Imagine how scary that must have been!" She sighs, unnecessarily wistfully, Isabella thinks. "But when the trumpets sounded and you stepped out in that gorgeous green sari…I know I wasn't the only one feeling relieved!"

Isabella shrugs ruefully. "It was pretty stressful for both of us. Have you ever met him?"

The young woman nods. "Once. I took him from the Mechanica Quarter to the Upper Hub." She pauses. "He was very...imposing. He's an odd fish, isn't he?"

She speaks in short bursts of enthusiasm; a habit Isabella is beginning to find weirdly endearing. There seems to be little guile about her, a refreshing contrast to the usual Citadel citizens.

"True," Isabella concedes. "But I've always appreciated a bit of 'odd'."

"I remember he was very polite. He thanked me for my service. Hardly anyone does that. Most Gentry barely notice me at all." The helmer glances at her passenger. "So, he can't be all bad, can he?"

Isabella grunts. She is determined to hold on to her anger at his treatment of her and isn't about to be derailed by talk of his manners, which clearly haven't been deployed for her this afternoon. The sudden descent into captivity is still a fresh trauma and the resulting anguish and loss bubbles away in the deep pit where she has shoved it in order to progress.

She stands and peers out of the oval window. The lift emerges from a tunnel into the light again and an enormous grey wall stretches out ahead of them. Isabella feels her stomach clench - another wall, another enclosure contracting around her. She has never been good at staying in one place and has always prided herself on being able to escape, to move on. But this true captivity is different and she realises that the feeling of suffocation is steadily increasing in strength once again. She closes her eyes and concentrates on breathing in and out, trying to wrest control over the growing panic.

An image of her husband blooms in her mind - his deliberately careful movements whenever he is near her, his dark eyes constantly searching for understanding. Fresh anger flames up through her panic. She was starting to trust him and like an unexpected slap, suddenly he treats her like property! Her eyes snap open and she stares straight at the helmer. The young woman gulps.

"Are you alright, my Lady?" A tiny bell chimes and she glances out the window. "The Ramparts! We're nearly there." She smiles encouragingly, despite Isabella's dark expression. "Don't worry, I promise you won't be disappointed."

Isabella softens in the face of the helmer's unrelenting enthusiasm. "Really? Because that's a bloody ugly wall."

The helmer laughs. "True, but it's what's inside the wall that's special. It's there to keep them safe." The lift slows to a halt and clicks into place.

Before Isabella has a chance to ask about "them", the doors open into the enormous vaulted foyer of the Verdelais Terrace hub, its steeply sloping walls made of clear glass with streaks of bright copper framing each panel, allowing light to flood in. Isabella blinks in the sudden glare and turns back to the helmer, who bows.

"The Cloud Terrace."

Isabella feels apprehension fizzing through her body and it almost swamps her. But then she remembers that she is an adult and that hiding in a corner is generally frowned upon, so she forces a smile and bows back to the young woman.

"Thank you for the trip and for the conversation. It was... interesting."

The helmer's eyebrows shoot upwards in surprise. "Thank you, my Lady. I hope I didn't offend you."

"Certainly not." Isabella grins suddenly at her, the action genuine this time. "That's a lot harder to achieve...unless you're my husband, apparently."

She holds out a hand and the increasingly astonished woman takes it. The Gentry never behave like this.

"I'm Isabella. It has been very nice to make your acquaintance...." She pauses, waiting for a response.

"Nixalia...Nix for short." The helmer stammers.

"Well Nix, here I go." She steps out of the lift onto the polished black marble floor of the foyer. "If you hear any explosions and screaming, it's because I have lost my temper with my husband." She glances back over her shoulder and winks at the helmer, who lifts a hand to wave uncertainly at her.

The arched brass door slides silently open as Isabella approaches. In front of her lies a courtyard paved in polished stone and dotted with low block marble benches and burnished cobalt pots holding puffball topiaries. The huge Ramparts wall rears from the right, curving inwards at its peak. A hedge stretches from the wall, along the back of the courtyard, forming the edge of a garden corridor off to the left. Members of the Gentry lounge in small groups, chatting raucously with one another and rather conspicuously pretending to ignore the Black Drw-ad off to the side.

Bryant stands quietly, watching the polished brass entrance to the terminus. He hears the commentary between the Gentry but refuses to focus on it. Allowing their vicious gossip to slide over him has become second nature over the years. He reaches across and adjusts his dark grey robe, running his fingers down the cream edging embroidered with interlocking knots and camellias, and smoothing the folds of the pale grey tunic beneath. He feels a strange disquiet bubbling beneath his outward calm. The fingers of his left hand drift again over the message globe in his pocket and he glances up at the sky, an arc of solid blue high overhead. There is still time.

The door slides open and Isabella steps out into the courtyard, blinking in the sunlight. Her curves are wrapped in a long, pale green halter-necked dress, topped with a diaphanous white blouse. It billows around her in the fresh breeze and she catches the ribbons and wraps the blouse securely around her body, tying a bow off to one side. As one, the Gentry turn to stare at her. Bryant feels a surge of pride as he watches his wife raise her chin and one imperious eyebrow in response then turn towards him, pointedly disregarding them. He has been looking forward to this afternoon for some time and the delight he hopes she will feel when he shows her the secret of the Cloud

Terrace. He bows and moves forward to meet her.

She stares at him for a moment. The top half of his black hair is pulled back in a ponytail and secured with a silver hair pin, the rest falling like a sheet of silk down his back. As he approaches, she feels the familiar jolt of tenderness but shoves it roughly down in favour of outrage.

I will not be distracted from this.

She strides forward.

"Isabella…" He falters as he sees her expression.

"You," she jabs a finger at him, "need to work on your manners." She gains a certain satisfaction from seeing his eyes widen. "I am not a slave. I am not a servant at whom you click your fingers for immediate attention."

His blue lips fall open. "My Lady…" He tries again. "Isabella, what is it that so offends you?"

How can this have gone wrong?

He had planned the afternoon so carefully.

Isabella crosses her arms tightly. "Your message. You just expected me to drop everything I was doing and race to heel. Not even a simple 'please' to take the edge off!" She glares up at him. "I really thought better of you than that."

Bryant forces himself to remain calm in the face of her onslaught. He had not expected her to be so judgmental without knowing all the facts first.

Is her true nature finally revealing itself?

A heavy little ball of anger forms in his chest.

Have I been foolish to trust her?

He becomes aware that they are being closely observed by a number of spectators.

"Isabella, will you sit for a moment?" He motions to a marble block off to the side. When she makes no move, he tries again. "Please!"

She gives a small snort, rolls her eyes and stomps to the seat,

301

dropping down onto the cool marble with a huff. He sits, careful to leave space between them.

Staring down at his hands, he is unsure how to proceed. Human men he finds hard enough to deal with, but this is so far outside his limited experience with women that he is sure there isn't even a map.

"I have offended you." He glances up to see an unimpressed eyebrow shoot upwards at this glaring observation.

Fool.

Isabella watches the Black Drw-ad struggle, his usual icy calm rippling with frustration, and gains a certain acidic satisfaction in seeing him squirm.

He glances away for a moment and closes his eyes, sifting through the images of the last few moments. Why would such a simple request upset her so? *"I am not a slave."* Where does rage come from but pain? Where does his own anger stem from? Captivity and betrayal.

"Ah."

He opens his eyes and turns back to her. Isabella's sour smugness evaporates in an instant, for his eyes hold understanding and regret.

"I apologise. I summoned you without explanation, as if your opinion and independence were of no consequence. That was not at all my intention but I understand now how my message appeared." He holds out his hand, palm upwards, the sigils in his skin translucent in the light. "Please forgive me. I am still learning how to chart my way through this new world between us."

Although a tiny, feral part of Isabella is still kicking her ankles and squawking at her for giving in, she softens towards this strange man. She shrugs and takes his hand.

"We both are," she smiles ruefully. "I may have overreacted. A little."

"Perhaps, perhaps not. Like me, you are a stranger in a strange land. It can be difficult to navigate at times." He glances up at the sky then back down at her. "I intended something very different for this day. May I show you now?"

"Your message said this was the Verdelais Terrace, but my lift-helmer called it something else – the Cloud Terrace?"

He nods and within the deep black of his hair, hints of blue glint in the afternoon sun. "The common name is more appropriate, as you will see." He crooks his arm in invitation and she takes it. "Shall we?"

Their footsteps crunch along the white path, following the curve of the hedge forming a garden corridor. It is a little cooler in the shade and Isabella feels more of her tension ease. Bryant's arm under her hand is comfortingly solid.

"There is something very special about this place. It is where I come when I need to relax and I have been waiting to introduce you to it." His voice has lost much of its former intensity. "This is one of the few places in the world where they grow."

"They?"

As they round the final corner, she gasps. Before them is the most astonishing sight; a forest of trees with foliage like fluffy cumulus clouds, all in shades of pearlescent white, pale rose and soft violet. Billowing puffs drift back and forth in the breeze and soft fat petals swirl through the air like snow. Isabella walks forward slowly. Heady scents, reminiscent of orange blossom, mimosa and jasmine draw her in. She stops under the nearest tree and peers up at the branches arching above. The bark is dark copper and gnarled, but each bough is swathed in masses of flowers like cherry blossoms, topped with dense wisps of fine, pale tendrils, a little like the Smoke Tree she had played under in her grandmother's garden as a child. The steady, undulating hum of bees' pulses through the air as the tiny workers zip back and forth high above her.

Bryant watches her response with some satisfaction. He may have had to work a little harder than he expected to achieve this but he is glad he can finally share this with her. She turns to him, smiling with delight.

"They're beautiful! And that scent…"

303

"It is certainly different from any other scent you will find in the Citadel." This is a pool of immense calm within the frenetic cacophony of the hard-edged city, sheltered by the thick, jutting protection of The Ramparts. "The guardians of the Cloud Forest are fiercely loyal to their trees. It is difficult to secure a pass and even then, many Gentry avoid this place." *Thankfully*, he adds quietly to himself.

Isabella is surprised. "Why would anyone want to avoid it? I would happily camp here just for that scent alone."

"It is a wholly natural scent and most Gentry find it unpleasant. They prefer to use chemicals to create their own..." he searches for the most appropriate word. "Aromas?"

Isabella wrinkles her nose at his choice. "Stench is more like it. Or perhaps 'reek' is better." She inhales again and realizes that the familiar headache she always develops when in the city has vanished.

Bryant moves closer and she hears the thrum of the bees swell with intensity in response. He reaches out a hand and individual bees drop from the blossoms to land lightly on his skin. One particularly flirty worker begins a waggle-dance on his palm.

"You're a bee-whisperer now?" Isabella laughs. She has always been fond of bees.

"The Drw-ad and the bees have long been connected. Every Drw-ad city hosts a multitude of hives." He lifts his hand higher and tilts it. One by one the bees leave, zipping back to their work amongst the blossoms.

"Let me guess, everyone's related and there's one Queen to rule them all?"

His dark blue lips part in surprise and he raises an eyebrow. "Lady Mackay." She grins up at him. He shakes his head and then glances up at the sky again.

"Somewhere you need to be?"

"Yes." He nods. "Will you walk with me?"

Isabella takes his arm and they move off, strolling under the drifting clouds of blossoms. A stream tumbles over rocks and is channelled alongside the path before curving away out of sight.

The path slopes upwards, following the rise of a mound until they reach a wooden platform at the top, nestled under the canopy of a maroon cloud tree. Spread upon it is a cream rug piled with cushions. Two identical servants wait next to a low table laden with delicacies.

Isabella gasps. "Woo! I'm starving." She steps forward, ready to dive in but Bryant's hand on her arm stops her.

"Before we dine, take a look behind you." His voice holds gentle amusement.

The platform juts out from the highest point in the terrace. Stretching out before them are the soft folds of the Cloud Tree tops, drifting gently in the breeze. Late afternoon is turning to twilight and each tree takes on a soft golden glow in response. Suddenly, a flash of colour explodes from one of the puffs and a tiny, iridescent saur shoots into the sky, barrel rolls and then drops, skimming over the tips of the trees. Isabella throws back her head and laughs, stretching her arms wide and spinning on one foot.

"This is glorious! It's as if we're floating above it all." Her spin takes her perilously close to the edge and Bryant catches her on the way past. He is already well aware of her talent for tripping over.

"Shall we eat?" He ushers the slightly dizzy woman over to the cushions and they sit. Each servant delivers a new dish until they are surrounded by choices; plates piled with buttery pastries, wooden boards laden with wedges of cheese and thinly sliced cold meats, tiny fruit pies topped with glistening berries and a tiered stack of little cakes. Finally, a carafe of autumn wine is delivered and Bryant pours a glass for each of them.

In between mouthfuls of food, Isabella sips her wine and as the heady liquid burns through her, she gazes out across the tree tops. The soft gold of twilight has intensified, deepening to a burnished copper. The folds and peaks of the cloud forest below are edged by the contrast of sunset and shadow. She feels the Drw-ad shift and she glances at him.

"This is beautiful. I feel ridiculous now, for doubting your intentions."

"To be fair, I did not give you much to work with." Bryant leans forward. "May I ask what you were studying when I interrupted?"

"We were learning about the Living Goddesses." She reels them off, uncurling a finger for each. "First Mother, Midnight Mother, Mother of Monsters and The Hag. In my world, people are expected to believe in gods without any proof of their existence, but here…are they actually real? I mean, living, breathing, life-creating goddesses?" She is still having trouble coming to terms with the idea.

He nods and raises his glass to the north, his expression hard to read. "My mother is one of them, remember?"

Time seems to slow and Isabella finds it momentarily hard to breathe, choked by the implications of marrying the son of a living deity. Reading information on a screen about the origins of the Drw-ad is one thing, but the reality feels very different. She wonders if First Mother is as terrifying as she appears in the chronicles.

"You've not really talked about this aspect much before because…?" Isabella regards her husband with caution.

"She created me, but I will not let her direct my life." He finishes his wine in one gulp. "We have not spoken for some time and I prefer it that way." His gaze remains on the sunset.

Not wanting to ruin the blissful mood of the evening, Isabella changes tack.

"So do all these '*Mothers*' get on with one another?" She pops a tiny blueberry tart into her mouth.

Bryant raises an eyebrow to illustrate his confusion so she continues. "I mean, do they meet up every so often for drinks? Take scones with tea? Go on goddess-only cruises together?"

"I believe they communicate on occasion, although it is rare. I suspect that they do not agree on many points." His response is stern, covering the fact that he finds the images she paints of Hjaltland's

306

deities amusingly absurd. Whilst Isabella's words can be confusing at times, he finds he is increasingly enjoying the way she speaks. A picture of the Mother of Monsters cheerfully handing his mother a teacup full of eyeballs leaps into his mind. He shakes his head and rises, offering both hands to help Isabella up.

Evening has drifted in, along with a chill breeze. The royal blue of fresh night covers the sky and the distant hills are gilt-edged with the last of the disappearing sun. The Ramparts and the Cloud Trees within have a muffling effect on the raucous sounds of the city, so that they are only a gentle buzz in the distance. A small cart and pony have arrived at the base of the mound and the servants collect up the dishes and cushions, roll up the rug and stow them away. They return and bow.

"Your work is appreciated." Bryant bows in return and leads Isabella away.

Together they make their way along the paths under the trees, blossoms glowing softly above them. Little balls of light appear along the edge of the path as they walk. Rounding a corner, they come across a tree guardian, dressed in khaki coveralls and pushing a wheelbarrow, a spiral lance strapped to his back. Tiny lights similar to those along the path bob around him, illuminating his work. He nods to Bryant but eyes Isabella suspiciously.

She lets go of Bryant's arm and strides over to speak to him. The man looks alarmed but as she greets him and begins to talk, the guardian visibly relaxes. As Bryant approaches, he is surprised to see the man laugh. He had not realized that the guardians had a sense of humour, as they always seem so dour.

"My Lady, it's only a small thing."

"It is not!" She points to one of the bobbing lights. "Mate, that's extraordinary." She turns to Bryant. "This wonderful bloke is responsible for lighting all the pathways."

The Drw-ad is tempted to say, "of course, it is his duty", however he is stopped by the look of wonder on her face. To his surprise, the

307

nuggety guardian begins to blush.

"Thank you for your work. Your efforts are certainly appreciated." Isabella holds out a hand and looks at him expectantly. The guardian stares at it as if it were a snake about to sink its fangs into his flesh then he glances up at Bryant. The Drw-ad merely regards him steadily.

"Isabella Mackay."

The man shrugs and shakes her hand firmly in reply. "Tuwhare." He comes to a decision. "You are always welcome in our groves."

Isabella grins. "Thank you, Tuwhare. This is the only other place in the Citadel besides the Eyrie where I feel I can actually breathe."

The guardian nods. "I suspect your husband is the same." He glances at Bryant. "I was impressed, my Lord, with the speed of your reaction before. I was sure she was off that platform the way she was whirling about."

Bryant shrugs. "She has a talent for falling over. I was merely ready."

The man shakes his head and chuckles. His tone becomes more serious. "There are still a number of Gentry walking the paths near the Hub. Earlier there was some sort of…party." He utters the final word with considerable distaste. "I can smell 'em from here."

Bryant bows. "Thank you, Guardian, for your cautions. We will proceed nonetheless. I am sure the trees would not thank us for taking up more of your valuable time."

Isabella curls her hand around his elbow and gives the Cloud Tree guardian a little wave as they move off. As she turns away, something catches her eye and she has to fight hard to suppress her reaction. The Guardian has a tail. It drops from beneath his coverall, the white tuft at the end flicking gently.

As they proceed along the pathway lit by Tuwhare's gently drifting orbs, Isabella feels a fizz of excitement running through her. The combination of lights in the darkness, the scent of the trees and the sound of a distant party is a heady one. On impulse, she climbs up onto a low wall and balances along it, the edge of her dress in one hand, Bryant holding her other to steady her. The Gentry strolling by stop and stare, clearly confused by the sight.

The Drw-ad holds her hand up high as they walk along and he can't quite believe he is doing it. She, balancing like a precarious child, he with his usual stiff, cold expression. He tips his head and looks up at her.

"Why are you doing this?"

She grins. "Do you never just do something on the spur of the moment? Just for the craic?"

He shakes his head. "No. There are always consequences to be considered, for every action."

"Hmm." She hops over a gap in the wall. "That must be exhausting."

He steadies her on the other side and considers this. "It is right to do so. The consequences of one's actions can be far-reaching."

She glances at his white hand holding hers and then along to the extreme contrasts of his features. She also takes in the wary and occasionally hostile expressions of the people around them. "I can imagine that the consequences for you growing up here have been quite... significant."

Eventually, she reaches the end of the wall and the pathway opens out into wide formal gardens with long, shallow steps leading up to the portside lift hub.

Bryant turns in front of her, holds out his other hand for her to grab then steadies her as she jumps down. Her boots crunch on the gravel and she grins as she looks up at him. His expression stays the same but his pupils widen slightly.

She keeps hold of both of his hands and squeezes them gently. "But maybe a little spontaneity now and then might not be such a bad thing?"

He is aware of people slowing down around them to gape at their closeness but he finds he does not care. Isabella's eyes hold a good-humoured challenge, drawing him in and setting off a heated feeling in his chest…and an echo lower down. He lifts her hands and bends down to kiss them. Her eyes widen in surprise.

Bryant straightens and tips his head upwards to look at the sky. She glances up too, wondering what he is looking for. His gaze drops back down to her, one black eyebrow slightly raised.

"Nothing. No lightning bolt nor meteor. No apparent consequence. Perhaps you are right."

Has he just made a joke?

She swallows. "Well, it's a start."

Upon their return to the inner sanctum, he once again excuses himself to continue work in the solarium. Deep in the night, Bryant falls asleep and for the first time since Isabella's arrival in the Eyrie, he dreams. Straight away he slides into dreams of the lash, tearing into the skin of his back and legs as the crowd of Gentry bays for his blood. His wrists are torn by the bite of the restraints, shoulders burning from the pull of his body on outstretched arms. Black hair slick over his face, the taste of blood as he bites into his cheek to stop from crying out. The Gentry howl in delight and the lash snaps through the air, ripping the skin from his back over and over again. He can barely breathe, choking as the lash descends, his blood rising into the air in a fine spray and the crowd screams.

Bryant wakes with a choked gasp and clutches the desk in front of him, coughing wretchedly, his eyes streaming. Each lash scar on his body burns. He opens his eyes and pushes his hair back, shoulders slumping when he sees that every piece of paper on the table in front of him has turned to ash. Hours of work ruined. The solarium is cold, the bitter chill seeping into his body through a shirt damp with sweat. He stands, a compulsion without thought propelling him out of the solarium and down the stairs of the Eyrie.

[17]He pushes the door open and strides into the inner sanctum, the warmth in the room wrapping around him instantly. His impetus spent, he comes to a halt in the middle of the room. He is breathing roughly, every muscle clenched tight.

Isabella sits curled in her usual spot on the couch near the fire, wrapped in a blanket and reading a book. She looks up, the firelight lending her a soft glow.

"Oh, hello."

She sees his expression as he swallows painfully.

"What's wrong?" She is instantly on her feet, throwing off the blanket. "Bryant?"

He clutches the back of the armchair in front of him. "I..." He closes his eyes for a moment. "I fell asleep in the solarium and I had a dream." He swallows again.

Why did I come down here? She will see my weakness.

Isabella takes a step forward.

"A bad one?"

He opens his eyes. "Yes. There are no others for me."

She moves to him and before he can react she wraps her arms around his neck and shoulders, pulling him close. At first, he resists, as usual bristling at being touched, but she is not going to give in this time and waits, eventually feeling his muscles soften as he gives in to the warmth of her embrace. He closes his eyes, breathing in the honeysuckle scent of her hair and his stressed, ragged breaths slowly even out.

Isabella becomes aware that his shirt is wet, smells strongly of bonfires and his body feels painfully cold. Reaching up, she gently brushes his hair from his temple with her fingertips.

"Come and sit by the fire."

As she steps away and her warmth leaves him, he feels the loss. But she takes his hand and leads him to the couch. He sits, holding

---

[17] Playlist: Lindsey Stirling – Between Twilight.

himself tightly upright.

"Take your shirt off."

He glances up at her, confused.

"It's soaking wet and it smells like you've torched something."

"My work." He murmurs. "The flames came as I slept." He peels off his shirt and she takes it, dropping it in the linen basket before moving to a chest of drawers and pulling a night robe from it. Bryant feels the warmth of the fire touch his bare skin but go no further. Cold seems to seep from his very core.

As Isabella returns to the couch she sees his back – the lash scars livid against the pale skin. She places her hand on his shoulder. He looks up.

"May I?" She asks, her eyes flicking behind him. After a moment he nods and feels her warm hand slide over his shoulder and down to the first scar across his back. He winces as she touches it. Although his skin is cold, the scar is not. "Wow."

She removes her hand and opens the robe, helping him into it then sitting down next to him. "Will you tell me about the dream?"

He does not want to share yet another humiliation with her but the dread has risen up to his throat, threatening to choke him if he does not let it out. He has never allowed himself to betray this weakness before.

"When I arrived at the Citadel as a political hostage, I was seven years old. Many had never seen a Drw-ad before, but all had heard stories of us. To have one in their grasp was...a boon."

Isabella takes his hand in hers. She can see the memory stifling him.

"The other children in our training group had quite an unpleasant welcome for me and they were unrelenting."

She remembers Lady Kahn's story of her first meeting with the young Drw-ad and has a horrible sense of what is to come.

"I did not wish to fight them. I knew they were no match for me and the consequences of my actions would be far reaching, but they would not stop. In the end, to prevent them from killing me, I had no choice. I hurt them badly and the King's duty was to punish me." He pauses for a moment, staring at the fire.

"My dream was of that punishment. They tied me between the whipping posts, stretched out before the crowd like some sacrifice." His voice has grown cold, as if trying to distance itself from the memory. "Understand, my own people are not gentle in their punishments, but here the Gentry crowd were baying for my blood and the lash…I can still feel the way it tore the flesh away from my back." He swallows, the dream images flooding back. "I was seven years old. What could I do but take it?"

Finally, he looks up to see her green eyes heavy with sadness and a touch of anger. Again, she reaches up and brushes back his hair.

"You shouldn't have had to. You should have been protected from all of that. You were a child!"

He straightens a little. "At least I gave them nothing, not even the smallest whimper of pain."

She can see that he is trying to hang on to the cold, unfeeling visage of the Drw-ad, pulling in some semblance of pride. There are shadows under his eyes and he looks exhausted. Clearly his dreams are taxing for him and for the landscape around him when the unrestrained power leaks out. She wonders what she can do to help ease this for him.

"Bryant, will you stay with me for a while?"

"Of course, my Lady." He cannot yet admit the truth.

I have no desire to leave your side.

Isabella sits back for a moment.

"Do you remember the night with those bloody horrible orchids?" She asks and he nods, his expression growing darker.

"When you returned from your… 'errand', you let me fall asleep on your lap." She smiles at him gently. "I know you've been sleeping down here each night." His expression freezes with the knowledge he has been caught but she continues quickly. "And I know it's because

313

for some reason my presence suppresses your nightmares."

"That is not the only reason, Isabella…" He stops himself in time. Even now, he cannot yet bring himself to admit it aloud to her.

I stay because I wish to be near you. I cannot stay away.

"So, I was wondering, since it worked so well for me after that trauma, perhaps this time you might benefit from the same thing?" She looks at him with tentative invitation. He frowns, not quite understanding, so she picks up a pillow from behind him and places it on her lap, patting it.

He looks down at it, then back up at her and makes his decision, pulling his long legs up onto the couch and lying down, placing his head on the pillow and facing the fire. It feels very odd for the restrained Drw-ad, but not unpleasant.

Isabella pulls the blanket from the seatback, throwing it over him. His body is rigid, still unaccustomed to such closeness but yet again she ignores it. She reaches down and begins to stroke his hair back from his temple, running her hands through the heavy silken strands. She trails her fingers across his forehead as he closes his eyes. Slowly, she feels his shoulders relax and his breathing become steady. On the edge of slumber, he speaks.

"Thank you, Isabella. I am glad you are here."

She smiles, her other hand coming to rest against the top of his head, her fingers splayed through his hair, surrounding him with comfort. "You don't have to survive all this on your own anymore," she murmurs, and feels him drop into sleep, his breaths becoming deeper.

But she cannot shake off the image of the small boy, alone in a huge, dangerous city, being tortured in front of a screaming crowd just because he dared to stand up to bullies.

"No," she whispers, "you're mine, and I'm not going to let those bastards hurt you again."

314

[18]Bryant wakes to an Eyrie filled with morning light. His head rests on two pillows and he feels surprisingly comfortable. As he inhales, the fresh scent of mint clears his head a little.

Perched on the low table in front of him is his wife, clutching a green-glazed mug. She holds it out to him.

"Peppered-mint tisane?" A soft smile plays on her lips. "How are you feeling?"

"Better." His words are betrayed by a wince as he pulls himself upright. "I did not dream again."

"Thank goodness." The smile expands. "I've become quite fond of that couch. I'd rather it didn't end up in flames."

He takes the mug from her, breathing in the punch of scent and taking a sip. "That is cruel, Isabella." His tone however, is mild. He is slowly coming to recognise her humour and not take offense as he normally would.

Bryant sits back and looks at the woman in front of him. Her tumble of dark auburn curls are flicked over her shoulder and down her front, leaving her neck and far shoulder bare. Her silken nightdress is wrapped in a cream robe, neither doing much to hide her curves. One leg is crossed over the other, yet his eyes are drawn to the soft curves of her breasts beneath the silks. He looks up to see that her eyes hold a mix of affection and humour.

Unbidden, the image of the incinerated pages upstairs begins to nip at him.

"Alas, my Lady, I must go back up and rescue what remains of my work."

"My dear husband," Isabella begins and Bryant's mug pauses halfway to his lips. "Normally I enjoy the scent of you but right now I would like to suggest you take a shower first. You smell like a doused forest fire."

He grimaces. "Is it really that bad?"

---

[18] Playlist: Hazey Eyes – Untitled.

She nods. "Anyway, it'll make you feel better and wash away some of the stress of last night. I'll have Millie bring us the break of fast while you freshen up."

Bryant allows her to take the mug from him. Apparently, she intends to leave him no choice. He rises and makes his way to the bathroom. Noticing that she has left the window open yet again, he sighs and closes it, wondering why she needs to have so much "fresh air" in the middle of winter. As he leans out, the cry of gulls and the scent of the sea far below spiral up around him, a hit of pure morning.

He removes his clothes and the stink of burning wafts upwards. She is right – he does smell. Skin prickling in response to the cool air, he rolls his shoulders one at a time, loosening his muscles. The burn of his lash scars has diminished to a dull ache but he feels clammy and soiled.

Moving to the shower he pulls the main lever, releasing a torrent of water from all three chutes. He steps beneath it, allowing the heat and the power of the water to strip away all thought, along with the grime of the nightmare. After a few moments Bryant steps back and reaches towards the shelf, selecting a bar of eucalyptus and menthol showermelt. He massages his muscles as the sharp scent clears away the last of his headache then he dives back into the stream. His black hair slicks to his pale back, the trailing vestiges of bonfire stench washing from it.

With considerable reluctance he pulls himself out of the water and flips the lever back up, wrapping himself in a robe and returning to the inner sanctum.

Isabella is busying herself with plates and cutlery but she looks up and pauses for a moment, appreciating the sight of her husband in nothing but a robe. The shadow of the dip at the base of his throat, the hint of strong pectoral muscles in the gap at the top of the robe, the steady look in his eyes, all conspire against her. As time goes on, she is finding it increasingly difficult to stop herself from looking at him in a lascivious manner.

316

The break of fast is a pleasant one. Millie has brought up bowls of creamy yoghurt piled with lush berries and a pot of mixed nuts, seeds and oats sits ready to sprinkle over it. Alongside this rests a plate piled with golden crumpets, a crock of yellow butter and a selection of crystal jars filled with dark honey and marmalade.

Isabella hands Bryant a bowl and sits next to him. Once again, he struggles with her closeness. Where before it was that he wasn't used to any kind of gentle touch or contact, now it is because he has begun to want far more than he promised.

Into this moment bustles Millie, balancing a tray of cups and little canisters of tea. Her Lord and Lady are perched on the couch, knees almost touching. The look Lord Lathorne gives Isabella as she slides her yoghurt spoon from her lips and licks the tip of it causes Millie's eyes to widen and she turns away, focusing desperately on the bubbling samovar.

She wonders if they've done it already but then shakes her head. No, there is still that build-up of tension in the air that makes Millie's teeth itch. The way one will stare longingly at the other when they think they're not looking is a ridiculous way for adults to behave, so she thinks. She fervently wishes they'd just get it over with, not least because she is sick of Lady Kahn elbowing her sharply in the ribs every time she visits the kitchen and asking, "any Eyrie babies yet?"

Millie becomes aware that her Lord is staring at her coldly. Clearly, he wishes her to hurry up and leave. She collects the dishes and beats a hasty retreat into the servants' alcove.

"Isabella," he begins, although he does not know quite how to broach the subject. "In regards to my rather unorthodox sleeping arrangement, I wish to apologise. I broke my promise to you that you could sleep here in peace."

"You covered me with a blanket and then fell asleep in a chair. That's hardly a vicious attack." She shrugs.

"It was inappropriate and on that first night I put you in danger." His voice has become unconsciously stern and he curses himself for

317

it. He tries again, determined to explain. "Yet when I awoke the next morning, I felt calm and rested as I never have before. Every night I tried to keep my promise, but I could not."

"I understand you didn't want to freak me out but we've started to get along well recently. You could have discussed this with me y'know. Look," she waves her hands, "not freaking out."

"Isabella, please. After so many weeks, how could I possibly admit to this?" He frowns. "How long have you known?

"Just over a week." Isabella shrugs. "Who do you think has been covering you with a blanket?" She watches him grow still.

"I thought…oh." He lifts his head and changes the subject. "Why will you not sleep in the bed? Is it not comfortable?"

"To be honest, it was because on that first night it was huge and cold and lonely. I desperately needed some sort of 'nest' to make me feel a little more secure, so I made one here. Like you, once I started doing it, I just couldn't stop."

His expression softens a little. "I admit I was confused. Meridian and I discussed whether sleeping on couches was something common to your world."

"What did he say?"

"He agreed that it must be. Lianne made him sleep on the couch for some time after the Ceremony. He had to work very hard to woo her."

Isabella tips her head back and laughs. She can imagine Lianne doing just that. Now her occasional mutterings of the word "couch" make sense.

Bryant looks down. "I feel a little ridiculous."

She takes his hand. "At least we've been ridiculous together." Her voice takes on a more serious tone. "But you know, now that we've both been honest with one another, it can't continue this way. We're going to have to change things."

Bryant feels a familiar block form in his chest. He knows it is true but he does not want to spend his nights alone in the solarium again.

More than that, he does not want to be separated from her. "I understand that but, in all honesty, sharing this space with you has become important to me..." He trails off, suddenly aware that she is not paying attention to him. Instead, she is peering out through the balcony windows behind him.

"What time is it?" Isabella feels a crashing realisation wash over her.

He frowns. "It is nearly the second break of fast. Is something wrong?"

Isabella gapes at him. "Oh crap, I'm going to be late!" She leaps to her feet and scurries to the armoire in the corner, tearing it open, pulling out garments and muttering to herself. Once she has an armful she disappears into the bathroom, emerging a little while later clad in Sisterhood boots, leggings and a long tunic, her movements punctuated by the sound of her muttering, "crap, crap, crap." She pulls on her grey coat and begins to twist her hair into a loose bun.

Through a mouthful of hairpins, she explains. "I'm supposed to be meeting my Anahera project group on the Kishie Terrace at lunch...bugger...second break of fast. We're studying the market traders' links with other cities."

She pulls her green velvet bag across her body and slips the map quire into it before moving towards the door. Suddenly she stops and spins around, striding back to him. Still in his robe, he is a little taken-aback.

She leans down and strokes her fingertips across his temple again, brushing back his hair. For the first time, he does not flinch.

"When I said we had to change things, I didn't mean in a bad way. I would really like to spend more time with you. It's important to me too." She watches the tension ease in him a little. "Why don't we talk about it over dinner this evening?"

"Shall I meet you at the restaurant where we dined with Meridian and Lianne?" He feels the block in his chest dissipate, replaced by something far more pleasant: Anticipation.

"Excellent idea! I'll see you later." With that, she turns on her heel and strides from the Eyrie.

16. INTO THE STORM

In a thoroughly good mood, Isabella makes her way down to the Kishie Terrace in time to have her Anahera group make mocking fun of her predictable tardiness. Her amusement is dimmed somewhat when the two Citadel guards detailed to escort them step forward. One is a fresh-faced young recruit, already blushing as one of the women winks at him, the other is her old nemesis, Corporal Sour and Shouty. He glares at her but for once says nothing.

The group in front of her is a mix of four Anahera, including Maksim the Estonian and the Japanese woman, Akiko. Her hair is now in a sleek bob, the ends of which flick as she leans over to take Isabella's arm.

"Let us go." She smiles as they move off. "It is a lovely day but there is a storm coming later. We should hurry and complete the survey before it arrives."

Behind them, Maksim laughs. "What she means is that she would like more time to go shopping."

Akiko shakes her head. "This from a man who has just asked me to help him choose a new wardrobe because he is bored with his current one!"

Their banter continues as they make their way through the Sea Quarter, stopping to quiz selected stallholders and peering into the shallow, circular troughs and iced crates filled with sea creatures. At one point, Isabella notices a small, plump grandmother wrapped in a floral head scarf cackle at a saucy joke from a handsome young stallholder and then point to a glass bowl filled with small, live eels. He nods and fishes out her choice, deftly slapping the creature onto the board in front of him. In one fluid motion he raises a cleaver and slices the eel's head off. A spurt of blood hits his already stained apron as the head shoots into a waiting pail.

Isabella stares at it for a moment, feeling distinctly ill. Normally blood and gore have no effect on her but for some reason this sudden act of execution is a shock. She feels momentarily dizzy and clutches the strut of a stall for support. The old woman and the young man turn to stare at her, a little contempt at her weakness lacing each expression. She runs a hand over her face and then frowns, realizing that the others have moved ahead of her. As she follows them, the disconcerting feeling of darkness refuses to disperse.

The survey group has only one more trader to interview in the garment quarter and they turn down a quieter lane, trailed by the two guards. It is very near one of the Terrace gates, yet the hubbub from the main thoroughfare is muffled by the surrounding buildings. At the end of the lane is a small square where a stall covered in bright, embroidered silks sits. The fabric drifts in the wind, rippling like water. Several girls are already there, sifting through the delicate cloth and chatting happily. The younger guard wanders over and is quickly drawn into their conversation, his blush returning with a vengeance.

"There is a tailor just around the corner." Maksim offers Akiko his hand. "Would you come and give me some advice?"

The Japanese woman smiles and glances back at Isabella. "Will you come too?"

"No thanks," Isabella returns her smile, "I'll just go with…" She turns, but the other two Anahera have already disappeared around another corner to their target trader's boutique. She shrugs. "I'll just check out the silks."

Akiko nods and moves off with Maksim. The sour guard stares after them and then looks at Isabella.

"I'm going to get some food. Don't go anywhere." With that, he stalks back towards the main street. Isabella glares after him and then turns to the group of girls at the stall, her mood lightening when she sees them gently teasing the young soldier. He looks like he is thoroughly enjoying himself. One of the girls, her blonde hair tied into a short ponytail, beckons her over and they fall to chatting.

Isabella begins to relax and leans towards the silks, her hand drifting over the soft fabric. As she looks up at the stallholder, she realizes his expression has changed, fear crossing his face. He is staring over her left shoulder.

"Well, ain't this a pretty sight?" A rough voice issues from behind her. "Don't you think so, Caelin?" Something about the voice makes Isabella's muscles tense and she shivers as a cloud crosses the sun. Even the colour of the silks dulls before her. The stallholder steps back.

Isabella turns to see four men arrayed in front of her. Behind them, a covered wagon now blocks the exit to the busy main thoroughfare. They are each dressed in rough brown leather and sport identically shaven heads. One steps forward, his lined face resolving into a sneer which reveals broken teeth.

"Aye, fancy a drink with us, girls?" He reaches out and caresses the long braid of the youngest, who must be all of fifteen. She recoils and he laughs, turning to the others. "I think she's shy."

Isabella frowns and is about to open her mouth to speak when the young guard steps forward, his face flushed with anger.

"How dare you! Step back." His hand reaches behind to unhook the spiral lance from his back and the young women around him shift nervously.

"Aww, Billa, I think he likes you." A second man strolls forward, positioning himself off to Isabella's right. He inhales and suddenly leans forward, his nose an inch from her throat, then sniffs again. "Ooh-hoo! What have we here?" He straightens and grins at his mates. "It's a fucking *Anahera*." The others share significant looks and Billa cocks his head.

323

"Then her name'll be on the List." He slaps his hands together. "A good haul then."

"I told you to step back," the guard snaps, rolling his lance from under his arm, the point close to Billa's middle. The scarred man tips his head, a strange smile pulling on his thin lips.

"Shut the fuck up," he drawls. Without warning, his arm flicks out, his dagger burying itself in the guard's soft throat up to the hilt. The youth's hand drops the lance and his wide eyes stare at the man, his mouth gaping, a hideous choking gurgle issuing from it.

Before any of the women have a chance to react, the men snake forward, each throwing a handful of energy at their prey, the ripples in the air coalescing around each target. Isabella is stunned as each woman falls even before they are touched. The magic appears to render them senseless in a moment. Behind, the sound of the stallholder ramming down the shutters pulls Isabella from her shock.

She darts sideways but she is not fast enough. Time seems to slow, or perhaps it is that *she* is slow. Each man is bigger, faster and stronger than her and the knowledge of her weakness horrifies her. Billa appears in front of her and opens his hand, the air rippling with the progress of his power. But it slides past her and she snarls at him, trying to take another step. He stares down at his hand, gives it a shake and then shrugs, nodding behind her. She has forgotten about the man to her right, the one who had sniffed her.

A calloused hand grabs her around the throat whilst his other arm snakes around her waist and lifts her off her feet. He grunts as she struggles but he holds her fast as Billa lurches forward, jamming a cloth over her nose and mouth. The cloying solvent reek of chemical sedation quickly pulls her down, rendering her muscles useless. Although she remains conscious, she is powerless to resist as they lift her into the back of the wagon with the other girls and pull the cover back over it. She can do nothing but stare up at the canopy as the wagon jerks forwards and moves off, blending into the traffic of the main thoroughfare and heading down through the next terrace wall, towards the outer ring of the Citadel.

Bryant has spent the afternoon with the head welder of the Crossed Hammers on the Mechanica Terrace and as he makes his way towards the lift hub, he feels satisfied at the progress they are making, with yet another part for the new shield design finished and tested. He is looking forward to telling Isabella, considering they had worked on the design for this particular part together.

Once on the Rivin Terrace, he strides quickly to the restaurant, glancing up at the clouds gathering overhead. They are dark grey in the belly and have smeared edges, a sure sign that they carry ice. Upon reaching the blue door, he is welcomed by the diminutive waiter who leads him to the covered courtyard and hands him a glass of hot apple tea. The Drw-ad sits in one of the wicker chairs and takes a moment to relax. He has yet to see Isabella make a single appointment on time, so her absence comes as no surprise. A shadow falls across the space and a sudden rattling issues from high above. Bryant looks up to see hail hammering against the glass roof of the courtyard.

But as time moves on, he feels a spongy disquiet grow.

She should have arrived by now.

He knows she is often late but as the minutes stretch and guests come and go, he feels increasingly annoyed and not a little hurt by her behaviour.

Surely, she could have made an effort for this?

He stands and paces to the opposite side of the courtyard and back, finally leaning against a marble pillar near the entrance, his arms folded tightly across his chest. He had thought the evening would be important to her as well, seeing as she had promised a discussion of their sleeping arrangements. Eventually his frustration boils over and he gives up, making his way back up to the Eyrie, his mood mirroring the growing tempest outside.

He throws open the door and strides into the inner sanctum, pulling off his sodden coat and dumping it over the back of the chair.

325

He glares about him but Isabella is nowhere to be seen. Instead, Millie enters from the bathroom, already aflutter.

"Welcome back, my Lord. I've drawn a bath for Lady Isabella." She picks up his coat. "Can you believe it? Slavers have struck the Citadel! Have you ever heard of such a thing?" She stops and looks around. "Is my Lady not with you?"

Bryant stares at her. "She is not here?"

"No, my Lord. I thought she was having dinner with you."

A strange sensation grips him and he opens his mouth to speak. He is interrupted by the appearance of a message globe, glowing with the scarlet light of warning and trilling madly. Bryant snatches it from the air and taps it. The globe is from Meridian.

"Where the fuck are you?! Isabella is one of the abducted. The Eldhestar stables! NOW."

It is not until he is halfway to the Huljun Terrace that the Seed of Life sigil on his right hand begins to burn.

Once the wagon has reached the outer ring, it turns onto the hill road leading north. Two stout ponies are urged on through the lashing rain with the aid of an ergon whip wielded by the wagon master perched behind them. The wagon is comprised of an enclosed cabin at the front, where two of the slavers take refuge from the storm, and the cell section at the back. Its base is wooden, with heavy iron bars stretching over the top leaving it open to the elements. The final slaver is detailed to sit with the captives and he hunches in the corner by the door, wrapped in an oilskin cloak and nursing a covered lamp. The weather is foul, with heavy rain and squalling wind battering the wagon as it skids along the muddy road.

The wagon lurches and Isabella, who has been propped in a stupor against the side, crashes against the other girls. Two are sobbing, the others hunched and silent. She shakes her head muzzily and grabs the iron bar next to her, the chill of the metal biting into her hand. The bitter rain helps to revive her at first, washing away the last of the sedative. Her muscles tense as she pulls into the side of the wagon, sheltering against the wood holding up the bars. She is terrified but that cold, immobilising fear is rapidly melting as rage flames through her.

Another bloody abduction, another fight to escape yet another bastard of a man.

Her head has been resting against her wrist but now she raises it to glare at the slaver sitting next to the door.

Rain splashes down his pock-marked face as he bends over the covered lantern, his teeth tearing at a rough piece of bread. The wagon jolts violently again and he looks up, grinning at her with broken teeth and gummed bits of bread. She shifts slightly against the wood, steadying herself.

"What are you looking at, bitch?" He sneers. "Want some?" He waves the bread in front of her. She merely glares at him and he laughs.

"That attitude ain't gonna help you where you're goin'." He waves the bread to make his point. "They'll be pleased with another Anahera to play with, they will. I hear they make you scream for days before they end you."

He eyes up the girls behind her, licking his lips. "Which is exactly what's going to happen to these little sluts when we get to the Hamnavoe slave pits. But you," he waves the bread at her again, "you're going somewhere different. You're on their Special List." He leans forward and leers at Isabella.

[19]It is as if a white veil has descended over her vision and everything around her slows as all the rage, the hurt and the loss of her old life surges through her. She pulls her body upwards with the

---

[19] Playlist: Grimes – Medieval Warfare.

bar, her leg shoots out and she kicks him hard in the face, the tough Sisterhood boot breaking his jaw. Blood, spit and bread fly from his lips. His head slams against the bars and before he can react she is scrambling over him, locking her legs around his back and shoving him to the floor. She grabs the heavy lantern with both hands and rams it into his skull over and over again, screaming. There is nothing in her head but rage and the white mist.

Once he stops moving, for it is hard to move with so much brain matter on the outside, Isabella looks up, breathing hard, to see the other girls staring at her in horror.

"Fucker." She gulps.

The wagon lurches again as it thunders through the night. The two slavers safely ensconced in the front cab show no sign of having heard, the storm is so loud and violent around them, and the wagon master has never been one to pay attention to the screams of women. Isabella reaches down, riffling through the man's pockets until she finds the key.

With shaking hands, she struggles to unlock the cell door, dropping the key through slick fingers. She forces herself to stop, breathe slowly and then try again. The door clangs open and the road yawns dark behind them. For a moment it is illuminated, stark and cold, by a stab of lightning from above.

She turns and reaches out for the nearest girl, the one with the braids.

"We're going to have to jump!"

The girl cowers and shakes her head. "I can't." She gasps.

Isabella strives for patience, but it is too hard. "For fuck's sake, it's that or what they've got planned for you. Did you hear what he just said? Choose!" She snarls.

The girl blinks at her, sobs once and then grabs her hand. Isabella helps her drop and watches her roll away into the darkness, then one by one helps each of the others. Finally, the last girl turns at the door, her short ponytail slick against her neck, and she sees the Anahera clinging to the bars and looking speculatively back at the cab.

Isabella clambers over the body of the slaver, gagging at the smell of him, and picks up the lantern. A ball of flaming fuel spins inside it.

"Go!" She barks at the girl and she drops, rolling away before scrambling to her feet and peering after the wagon. She watches Isabella grin bitterly and swing the lantern hard against the cab of the wagon until it cracks open. The burning fuel spills and splashes over the wood of the cab, its fire spreading quickly. Within moments, the wagon disappears from the girl's sight.

Isabella scrambles back towards the door just as the flaming wagon slews sideways, the flames having eaten into the front wheel. She reaches the door and throws herself into the night, hitting the ground hard and rolling. The slide continues as the horses struggle against the momentum of the heavy wagon. The front crunches down into the dirt and it tips, throwing the wagon master from his perch and landing on top of him.

Ignoring his screams of agony and the desperate shouts from inside the cab, Isabella tries to pull herself upright but can only manage to roll onto her knees. She struggles to pull in breath after being winded and her left ankle burns from the twist as she hits the ground. She is covered in mud and leaves, her hair slicked to her skin. Raising her head to see the wagon consumed by flames, for a moment she feels relief, however short lived. The door is flung open as one of the slavers manages to kick it outwards. He crawls out and drops to the ground before reaching up to haul his companion, the vile Billa, from the wreck. Even through the storm Isabella can see that he is badly injured as his companion drags him away from the flames and props him against a tree.

"Roan, look." Billa rasps, his head lolling in Isabella's direction. "There's one left."

She snarls and grabs a nearby sapling, using it to haul herself upright. When she puts weight on her left ankle, a shooting pain makes her hiss but the joint holds and she hobbles across the muddy road in the direction of the Citadel.

Isabella makes it to the far edge before she hears movement behind her and Roan grabs her arm, spinning her around and letting fly a salvo of power at close range. It ripples through the driving rain but seems to slide away from her, instead ripping a branch from the skeletal tree behind her. She kicks him hard in the shin and he bellows but unlike Isabella, he has been in many fights before. He backhands her, spinning her to the ground. Dazed, all she can do is lie in a crumpled heap, tasting her own blood. The slaver reaches down and grabs a fistful of hair at the nape of her neck, hauling her to her feet. He leans in close.

"You stinking bitch! You're not worth the money." He spits into her face. His eyes are filled with rage and a terrifying inevitability. He grapples with her, managing to wrap both hands around her neck as he shoves her hard into the tree behind, lifting her from her feet. Isabella kicks and claws at his hands but she cannot break free.

The pain and desperation grow intense and she clutches at his shirt, struggling to find some way to distract him. For a moment she can barely believe it when her flailing hand contacts the hilt of a small dagger at his belt. Her freezing fingers slip twice before she manages to snag it, but she wastes no time, pulling it from its sheath and ramming it into the nearest part of him – his belly.

He grunts and pulls one hand from her throat to touch the wound. He looks up at her in shock but before he can react she jabs out with the blade again, this time a little higher. The vice grip of his other hand lessens and she slides to the ground, twisting her ankle yet again. With gritted teeth she punches upwards, the hilt of the dagger slick in her fist. The blade finds its mark, this time opening a deep gash in his groin. He roars in pain and rage and lifts her bodily, flinging her sideways towards the edge of the steep slope.

As she descends, she finds nothing but air and then branches, crashing through them on the way down towards the edge of a sheer drop. She scrabbles desperately at a sapling but the slope is unstable

330

and it pulls away from its tenuous grasp on the soil. Finally, just before the edge, her hands connect with a stouter tree root and she slides to a halt.

Far above, the slaver drops to his knees, bleeding into the sodden ground. He can barely believe it but the stupid, worthless bitch has hit a major artery. He can hear Billa's voice calling his name but he cannot move. His head feels heavy and he slumps forward, the pain from his wounds tearing at him. Slowly, he topples over into the mud.

Back in the Citadel, Bryant has reached the eldhestar stables, bursting in as Meridian and his squad are preparing to leave.

"Is it true? They have taken my wife?"

Meridian moves to him, clutching his shoulder and squeezing. "I'm afraid so brother, but we'll find her." He can smell the coppery scent of power as his friend's rage rises and he is already worried about where that might lead. He has never seen him so agitated, so far from complete control.

[20]The Prince has readied the Golden Uhlan horses, eldhestar from their friend Vallan's personal stable, and the two men climb into their saddles, ignoring the wary glances of the Uhlan around them. They trot through the Powder Gate, cautious on the cobbles slick with rain and sleet. The rain grows heavier as they turn and ride along Breiwick Rise, breaking into a canter and curving around the voe before leaving the last shreds of the northern suburbs and up towards the Girlsta Hills.

The eldhestar have been designed to be fleet of foot and unfazed by either storms or battle and normally on a hunt Bryant would relax into the experience, sharply aware and focused, but comfortable. Now his breath is ragged as he struggles to control the power building under his skin. He has never felt rage like this before. The bare, wintry trees offer no protection from the storm but the maelstrom barely

---

[20] Playlist: Two Steps From Hell – The Fire in Her Eyes.

touches him. Instead, the hard, cold ache he felt before Isabella's arrival in the Eyrie has returned and rooted itself deep inside him, twisting like a snake around his spine.

After two hours of hard riding, he hears shouting in the distance. The scouts ahead have found the shivering form of a girl in the middle of the road. As the rest of the unit catch up, three more young women emerge from the undergrowth. They have managed to find one another, although one still lies propped against the trunk of a tree, her ankle broken from the fall.

Bryant slides from his horse and strides up to them. "Where is she? Where is my wife?" His intensity is too much for the first girl and she can do nothing but shake and sob.

Meridian steps between them. "My Lord, this is not helping." He turns to the girl and throws a spare cloak over her, speaking over her head to the young woman behind her. "What happened?"

Another Uhlan wraps a cloak about her shoulders as she explains through chattering teeth that the Anahera had attacked the slaver in the wagon cage and beaten him to death with his own lantern, before flinging open the door and ordering them all out.

Bryant lurches forward but Meridian's gauntleted hand stops him. "Do you know where Lady Mackay is now?" he asks.

She looks fearfully at the Black Drw-ad straining behind him, his eyes an intense and inky black, his white skin glowing in the lamplight, and she gulps. "I'm sorry, she was still in the back of the wagon." She sags in exhaustion. "The last I saw of her after I jumped, she was smashing the lantern against the wagon's cab. She was trying to set it on fire."

"That sounds like her," Meridian mutters wryly, aware that Bryant has already swung himself back into the saddle and is off, urging the eldhestar into a gallop.

An old, familiar, heavy cold spreads through Bryant's body with every stride of his eldhestar and the darkness twists around him. However, it is not long before he spots a flicker through the darkness

332

and the grasping trees; the wagon, turned on its side and burning despite the rain. When the eldhestar skids to a halt, he sees that the scouts hold a man in front of them, kneeling and injured.

Before Meridian can reach him, Bryant slides from his mount and strides forward, grabbing the slaver by his dirty jerkin and lifting him to eye level. The man grunts in pain but his face is defiant in the face of the Drw-ad's rage, even as he sees sparks of copper fire flare around the deep black of Bryant's eyes. The two scouts step back.

"Where is my wife?" He demands, through gritted teeth. Behind him, Meridian senses the danger but cannot move quickly enough.

Bryant raises him higher. "Where. Is. She?"

The slaver, too dumb and too arrogant to even imagine the consequences, coughs out a laugh. "She fought back right enough. Killed Roan." He nods to the slumped figure at the edge of the road. "But he did for her 'n all." He flicks his head in the direction of the trees…and the cliff.

"Threw that bitch over the edge."

The soldiers behind Bryant feel an odd sensation, as if all the sound and fury of the storm has suddenly ceased and nothing but silent rain falls. The Drw-ad's eyes widen and the tiny copper flames spread over the black of his pupils. He lets go of the man, who floats backwards through the air, his mouth opening in a soundless howl of agony, his back arching. The air seems to pulse and the pressure builds to the point where several Uhlan clap their hands over their ears in pain. In silence, the floating slaver's flesh splits open, long fissures tearing through his clothing and dirty skin. His skin peels back, revealing white bone through the mess of red and without a sound, the pressure reaches its peak and the man bursts into a fine red mist. Tiny scarlet droplets coat each Uhlan before the storm swirls the rest into the night. Bryant spins on his heel and strides towards the tree line.

Meridian clutches his head to clear the dizziness. "Shit."

At the edge of the slope, Bryant stares down into the darkness

333

below. After a moment, he holds up a cupped hand and opens the Seed of Life sigil on his palm, creating an orb of bright light. He stretches his hand out, his body tense and listening. Rain sizzles around the orb. In the darkness, through the burling storm and sheeting rain, he hears the whisper of his name.

Clinging desperately to the root of a small gnarly tree on the steep slope below, Isabella gasps out a sob. She knows she cannot hold on much longer. Her hands are numb from the freezing rain and her muscles scream. She is so very tired that she wonders if letting go might, after all, be the best thing to do. But as the root creaks ominously, she feels a warmth grow just below her breasts. A soft, white glow emanates from the pendant Bryant had given her as a marriage Offering. She has enough strength left to whisper his name but to her despair, receives nothing else in return. The root creaks again.

Then, in the darkness above her, she senses movement. Someone is slithering and crashing through the shrubby trees and for a moment she wonders if it is the slaver, come to finish the job. She contemplates letting go, until suddenly she can hear Bryant's voice.

"Isabella, hold fast, I am coming for you."

Her head has been pressed against the slope in an effort to stay still, but now she cranes it upwards in time to see his white hand reaching for her through the rain.

Bryant has dived down the slope, slipping in the mud and deep leaf mould. Grabbing a lichen-covered tree branch he stretches until he touches her hand, gripping tightly and hauling her up before falling back against the slope and pulling her up alongside him.

"I have you."

"Don't let me go," she whispers, utterly exhausted, her body a patterned cloak of pain and numbness.

"I promise, I will not." He replies, pulling her soaking body tightly to him, stopping her from slipping backwards. The ground beneath them is unstable, leaf mould sliding over dark, peaty mud and he is forced to hold them both still until Meridian and another soldier reach them, helping to pull them back up the slope.

The Prince takes her shivering body from Bryant and holds her as he swings onto his horse. Meridian lifts her up in front of him, one of the Uhlan passes them a fresh cloak from her saddlebag and the Drw-ad wraps it around Isabella then pulls his own about them both. Having felt her deathly cold even through the thick yarg fabric before lifting her upwards, now when she lolls against Bryant and looks down, Meridian realizes that she is staring straight through him.

He has seen the onset of hypothermia before and he barks at Bryant. "The Piglet is closer. Take her to the Witch." Climbing onto his own mount he takes a moment to fashion a message and lets the globe fly before following his friend into the squalling night.

Although the road is lit by flashes of lightning and the eldhestar knows the way, Bryant finds the darkness pressing around him. Isabella is not holding on, she merely slumps against him, so he clamps his arms tightly around her and urges his mount to move faster. He is unaccustomed to the sensation which bites into him but as he rides he realizes what it is – the deep, vicious ache of fear. This is the closest their bodies have been since they met but instead of a heightened connection, all he can feel is her slipping away. He wants to reassure her, to call her back, but all he can do is hang on and ride through the darkness and the storm.

Finally, through the driving sleet, the lights of the Mutinous Piglet appear in the darkness. The riders pull to a halt outside the main door and Meridian is off his horse first, moving to lift Isabella down. The Drw-ad slides off his mount and takes her back, lifting her to the door.

Having received Meridian's message globe, Alyss is already there, waiting with a large, warm towel and the pub lights low. Her usual wild waves of blonde hair are pinned up in a no-nonsense knot behind her head and she glows in the soft light, radiating a practical calm. She has them take Isabella to the wooden lift which rises to one of the top balcony rooms where two of her acolytes wait.

The room smells of fresh astringent herbs and even Bryant feels more energy course through him as he inhales. Alyss sends Meridian back down to the pub to be fed and dried out along with the Uhlan who have accompanied them. She has Bryant lift his wife into a cubicle set up in the corner of the room – a healer's bed with layers of warmed towels and surrounded by crystals which radiate a specific temperature. There they begin to clean sections of her, patching up the cuts and grazes and anointing her with restorative salves.

Alyss shoos Bryant into the corner of the room where he drips, fretfully. The burning cold has infused every part of him. The Witch pulls the curtain around the bed and begins her own magic work, the room glowing with iridescent golden light. She hums, a subtle song of power which curves and grows and the Drw-ad finds himself starting to relax, muscle by muscle, and his eyes begin to close.

He jerks awake to find Alyss, arms folded, standing in front of him. Isabella has been placed in the large main bed, with fresh white sheets and a soft duvet around her, the air now infused with the heady scent of apples. The Witch's expression is thoughtful.

"She's alive and warming slowly, although I'm still very concerned about her." Her blue eyes are stern. "When you brought her in, she was close to death. She'll have to be watched carefully." She nods to the chair. "There's a fresh shirt and a pair of breeks for you."

When he opens his mouth to protest she raises an eyebrow and admonishes him. "Your wife needs you and you can't be there for her if you're suffering from pneumonia. Also, you're dripping mud on my floor."

Bryant nods stiffly in acceptance and she moves to the door as he begins to remove his cloak.

"I'll have soup and bread sent up for you." She glances back to see him frown. "Eat it – you need your strength too. I've laid her in a deep sleep, so go." She motions to the bed and the yargskin-covered

336

chair beside it. Her tone brooks no argument. "I'll leave you to change."

The diminutive woman turns abruptly and strides from the room, closing the door quietly behind her. She leans on the wall of the corridor outside, taking in a deep, calming breath. She has no intention of admitting the truth to the Drw – that his wife did not respond to her healing magic at all. Not once, in all her years of practice, has the magic failed. The Anahera's body responded to the herbs, the honey and the warmth of the crystal but not to the Hum and the Song, the principle means of Sisterhood healing. Alyss runs a hand over her hair, straightening her bun. Her thoughts turn to her library and the medical archives within. Perhaps an answer lies there.

Bryant removes his armour, laying the pieces on a table near the window. Exhaustion tugs at his muscles and his thoughts slide away, only actions remaining as he peels off his sodden clothing. He glances up at the sudden clatter of rain against the window as the storm rages through the night beyond. Drying himself, he pulls on the fresh clothes, grudgingly admitting that the Witch is right – although the actions are automatic, at least he feels a little warmer.

He eases himself into the chair beside the bed and gazes down at his wife. Her face is grazed and pale, with bruises darkening across her cheek and around her throat. When he looks at her hand, the knuckles have dressings on them. He can only imagine the fight she put up and he feels a fierce pride flare.

She is breathing softly and he senses she is a long way from the surface. He takes her hand, caressing the undamaged skin, tracing his finger along her wrist where her veins show blue beneath the skin. He breathes out a heavy sigh and rubs his other hand across his face before holding his fist against his mouth to stop the well of tension rising up and spilling out.

"Isabella, stay with me," he murmurs. "Do not leave me here on my own."

She has become such an integral part of his life that the possibility

337

of not having her there creates an intense pressure in his chest. He never imagined he would feel this way about another. He is no longer just defending his territory as he had the night Mirl and Alinna Wildervene tried to kill Isabella with Nightfevre orchids. Instead, he has an overwhelming desire to protect her, to please her, to touch her. Whenever she is near, he feels calm, safe, anchored. His chest aches with the pressure and he rubs a hand across it.

There is a soft tap at the door and an acolyte enters bearing a tray of chicken soup and bread. The girl's hair is pulled into a high braid and the sides of her head are shaved and covered in tattoos of ocean waves. Bryant accepts the bowl she proffers.

"You could lie next to her, you know." Her golden eyes are filled with sympathy. "It will do her good to feel your presence."

Bryant nods but when she leaves, he finds he cannot bring himself to do it. What if Isabella wakes and finds him there? He has no idea how she might react but a screaming woman in a Sisterhood teaching complex would be a recipe for disaster. He finds he is struggling to read the situation and how to respond appropriately. Just because they have grown closer recently does not mean she will welcome him in her bed. So, he remains in the chair.

Instead, he reaches out and takes her hand, lifting it to his lips and kissing the tops of her fingers before holding them lightly against his mouth and nose, inhaling her delicate scent. Against her skin he murmurs, "Do not fear. I will not let anyone hurt you again." He looks down at her battered knuckles. "I will find a way."

He drinks a little of the soup and then settles back. As the rain hammers across the window outside, Bryant slowly falls asleep.

Deep in the night, Isabella wakes. She is gripped with terror and struggles to breathe. She has no idea where she is, everything hurts and her dreams are of violence and suffocation. But there, in the glow of the firelight, she sees her husband. He is slumped in his chair, still holding her hand. As she stares at him, she slowly gains control over her ragged breaths. Even in slumber his face looks drawn, but his presence calms her. She wonders if he realises that he has that effect on her? Before she can even think to fight it, exhaustion pulls her back down into the void again.

Morning comes and she does not wake. Nari, the acolyte from the evening before, appears at the door and informs Bryant that Prince Sarn is asking for him in the pub below. Reluctantly, he places Isabella's hand back on the bed and makes his way to the ground floor where he finds Meridian ready to depart for the Citadel.

He places a tattooed hand on the Drw-ad's shoulder. "How is she?"

"I do not know; she has not woken yet." Bryant replies stiffly.

The Prince can see that although the Drw-ad's usual icy calm has reasserted itself, beneath lies real concern. "I have appraised Father of last night's events and asked him if you can stay with your wife while she recuperates."

Bryant opens his mouth to reply but Meridian raises a hand.

"Bugger your 'duty', she needs you here and she's in no state to be moved. Anyway, Father has granted you extended leave. You've not even had such a thing as a day off in years, so just take some time, Bryant."

The Drw-ad nods tightly. "Thank you, brother."

Meridian slaps him on the back and strides away. Bryant watches him leave then turns to find Alyss standing right behind him.

"Come this way. I'd like a word with you."

In the healing chamber above, Isabella jerks awake to the sound of a tea tray clattering against the bureau next to her bed.

"Oops, sorry." A young woman smiles sheepishly down at her. "I was trying to be quiet."

Isabella takes in a deep breath and winces. Every part of her seems to contain an aching bruise. "You look familiar." She grimaces, for it is painful to speak.

339

"I'm Nari – we met when you first came to the Piglet. You looked almost as rough as you do now."

"Thanks," Isabella mutters dryly.

"Rough, but wonderfully stubborn." Nari grins at her. The Anahera tries to push herself up but gasps in pain. The acolyte looks at her with concern. "It's a bit early to…" But Isabella is already on the move.

"I really need to pee!" She tries to stand but buckles, dropping back onto the bed.

Nari sighs and helps her to the adjoining bathroom, waiting while she uses it. She expects to help her back to bed but the Anahera has other ideas, tottering to the door, determined to 'get some air'.

For Isabella, the feeling of claustrophobia is intense. The room is pleasant but she feels the walls constrict around her. Once she is in the corridor however, she has to cling to the door frame for a moment, suddenly feeling light headed.

"Isabella!"

She turns to see Bryant's dark figure striding along the corridor and so she takes a couple of steps, diving into him.

He is heartened to see his wife awake and upright but he is also worried by her crumpled state. She clings to him ferociously. He does not know how to respond to this and he glances along the corridor to where Nari is hovering. Having studied the Drw-ad race extensively over the years, she is well aware of their emotional shortfalls. She mimes stroking Isabella's hair with one hand and holding her with the other. Hesitantly, the Drw-ad does as she suggests, wrapping his arms around his wife as she slumps into him.

Isabella is shaking but the solid mass of his chest and the strength of his arms encircling her gives her something to focus on, even if his movements are painfully stilted. Her initial stubborn determination has worn off and now she merely feels ill, battered and exhausted.

"You should be in bed. Please." His voice is stern.

"No." She grips his shirt tightly to pull herself upright. "I really

340

need some air. I can't breathe in here."

Behind her, Nari speaks. "The veranda is just along here. There are comfy seats and blankets."

Against his better judgement, Bryant agrees and Isabella allows him to support her back along the corridor. Nari opens a wooden door carved in the shape of a tree to reveal a long veranda, dotted with seats and leafy potted palms. The internal shutters have been pulled back to reveal a view across the gardens and orchards and a gentle but chilly breeze drifts in. Bryant lowers Isabella onto a chaise longue covered in deep blue velvet and Nari brings a yargswool blanket to tuck around her.

"I'll bring the tray Alyss sent up. She said to make sure you drank the tisane…or else." She plants her hands on her hips, endeavouring to look serious.

Isabella makes a face. "Yes, I've tasted her 'restorative' concoctions before. I'm not sure I can cope with another one this early in the morning."

"It's midday." Nari's expression is unimpressed. "I'll go and get the tray." She strides off to fetch the offending item and Isabella sighs, gazing dolefully after her.

Bryant pulls a high-backed chair alongside the chaise and sits. Isabella looks at him, her gaze travelling from his black boots all the way up to his dark eyes. He looks remarkably regal sitting there, as if he is perched on a throne. Silence stretches between them until Isabella clears her throat. It is badly bruised and it hurts to speak.

"You came after me."

He regards her steadily. She looks down and picks at the tassels along the edge of the blanket.

"Of course, Isabella. They took you from me."

She looks up to see the edge of a dangerous glitter in his eyes.

"Thank you." Her voice is soft yet filled with tension. Feeling the pinch of pain in her scraped hands, she has a vivid memory of clinging desperately to the roots of the scraggy sapling. "I didn't think I could

341

hold on any longer… and then I heard your voice in the darkness."

"That is the reason I gave you the pendant – so I would know if you were in pain or peril." He shows her the corresponding sigil on his palm. She takes his hand and runs her thumb lightly over the mark before looking up at him.

"You hurt yourself for me? Bryant…" she murmurs, frowning. She impulsively reaches out and cups his jaw, caressing his skin. She feels him freeze under her hand then force himself to relax. His eyes half close as he leans into her hand and a sigh leaves him.

"Isabella…" Bryant begins, but he is interrupted by Nari shoving open the veranda door with her hip. Isabella removes her hand.

Nari spots the tender moment between them and curses herself for interrupting. She has been fascinated by this union from the moment she watched the Anahera step onto the dais with him at the Ceremony. The entire staff of the Haven Holm had packed into the student common room to watch the event on the shimmer. She busies herself uncovering the tisane and passing the steaming mug to Isabella.

The Anahera sips it reluctantly. Its flavour comes as no surprise – an earthy punch of peat moss and bitter herbs. A tiny mushroom floats to the top.

"Ugh." Isabella shivers as the first mouthful bullies its way down her bruised throat but within seconds the pain begins to fade. She becomes aware that the Drw-ad and the acolyte are watching her expectantly. She shrugs. "I'll survive."

The veranda door opens and two vaguely familiar faces appear. Mara, the tall redhead who had been the first to greet Isabella in Alyss's recovery room, strolls forward. On this occasion she wears a grey leather jacket over a white blouse and grey breeks and her fiddle is once more strapped to her back. Her eyes are the colour of amber, gazing at them keenly over cheeks covered in freckles. Her expression, when she makes eye contact with Bryant, is not friendly.

She places her hands on her hips. "So Drw, are you going to

342

behave?"

The young man next to her frowns. "Mara, that's not exactly polite." He runs a hand through his short red hair and looks apologetically towards Bryant. "She's only just returned from a long scout, so she's a little tetchy."

Mara turns to glare at him. "Don't make excuses for me, Foddi," she snaps. "We haven't fought their kind for millennia for nothing you know. We have to be sure." She looks at Isabella, whose eyes have first widened in surprise, then narrowed at her words.

The acolyte points towards the Drw-ad as she speaks. "*He* knows why I'm cautious. I have good reason to be."

Bryant, who has gone very still, looks at his wife. "I do. To my knowledge, this is an unprecedented experience. No Drw-ad has ever been allowed to set foot in a Sisterhood Haven Holm before. Our people have been at war for a very long time." His tone becomes curiously mild. "If the roles were reversed and this were the White Spires, she would already be strapped to a table to be drained by now."

"Bryant!" Isabella frowns at him, aware that Mara has bristled and even Nari's hand has drifted to the dagger at her hip. "Now who's being rude? Look," she swallows painfully and her fingertips stray to her throat, "can you all just calm down? I've had a very rough night and if you're not going to stop all this needless aggravation, I'm going to ditch the lot of you."

She pulls off the blanket and pushes herself to her feet but before she can take a step, a wave of dizziness crashes over her and she turns pale, almost keeling over. All four of them immediately jerk forward, ready to catch her. The nearest is Foddi, who grabs her by the elbows, keeping her upright as Bryant stands to support her from the back.

"See," she gasps, "it's more natural for you to work together." She allows the acolyte and the Drw-ad to lower her back onto the seat and Foddi covers her with the blanket again. Isabella rubs her forehead. "Anyone got a bucket, just in case I throw up?"

343

Nari opens a small jar on the tray and picks out a handful of herbs, dropping them into the teapot and caressing the sides. The scent of nectarines rises as she concentrates her magic and the teapot begins to steam in response. She takes Isabella's mug and pours some of the mixture in. "Try this, it should calm the nausea."

Isabella takes a sip. It tastes of ginger with a hint of liquorice. She looks up at the others. "So, can you have a civilized conversation with one another, while I sit here and try not to barf on anyone's shoes?"

Mara and Bryant regard one another for a moment then the acolyte lifts one auburn eyebrow and smirks. "You moved fast Drw, to catch her. Any other of your kind would have let her fall. Perhaps there is some good in you after all." She grabs a wooden chair from the side and swivels it so that the back faces the Drw-ad, and sits. Bryant gives a brief nod and returns to his seat.

"Well," Mara sighs, "your presence is certainly causing a stir. Sister Alyss has the ultimate say over what happens in her Holm, but I know many of the other Sisters are concerned. She dealt with a barrage of messages this morning, from all over Hjaltland."

"She looked like she was enjoying it though." Foddi breaks in. "Alyss likes to push the boundaries."

"Says one of the few male Sisters in the Order." Mara smiles at him fondly.

Nari perches on the end of Isabella's chaise. "That's why each of us was placed with Sister Alyss to begin with – we don't quite fit anywhere else. But I'm very grateful for that."

Mara nods. "We couldn't ask for better training."

"And the food's great." Foddi grins.

Mara rolls her eyes then looks at Isabella, a more serious expression settling across her face. "You're welcome here, Anahera, but your Drw will have to be careful. Many of us have lost loved ones to the blood-lust of his people. I'm surprised though," she glances at him, "they're never this well behaved."

Isabella huffs out a sigh. "My husband has treated me with

nothing but civility and respect from the moment we met. I don't think he's quite what anyone expects." She is aware that Bryant is now staring at her. She reaches out a hand and takes his. "You never know, maybe you can work together."

The acolytes exchange glances.

"Well, actually," Mara leans forward, "that's what we wanted to talk to you about." She seems to struggle with the next words. "Would you consider…training with us?"

Bryant lifts his chin and regards her gravely, then nods. "Your Holm Sister made it a condition of my continued presence here. However, I would be honoured to train with you. I am sure we can learn from one another."

Mara blinks. She is genuinely surprised.

Nari claps her hands and bounces to her feet. "That's brilliant! Shall we start tomorrow morning? Fod, how about you?"

The young acolyte looks to Isabella. "I'd like to offer the Anahera my assistance instead." He opens his hands. "My interests lie in healing and research, not martial skills. Plus, I really hate running. Perhaps I could help you with your recovery?"

"And in doing so you can study me like Alyss did before?" However, Isabella smiles at him when he stammers a protest. "It's okay Foddi, I appreciate your offer." He sags with relief.

"Right!" Mara slaps the chair and rises. "We'll go and draw up some suggestions for the training and prep the arena for tomorrow." She nods to Isabella. "Heal quickly, Anahera." With that, the acolytes file out of the veranda, Nari giving a cheerful little wave as she closes the door behind her.

Isabella glances at Bryant. His expression appears even more stern than usual. "Are you really okay with this?"

His fingers tighten around hers and he glances away, staring out across the gardens. "I am trying, Isabella. I never expected to find myself at the very heart of enemy territory without…"

"Without having to carve your way in, amid torrents of blood and

345

screaming?" Isabella finishes for him and he glances back. The tension in his eyes has been replaced with amusement.

"Something like that." He strokes her fingers with his thumb. "You have a surprisingly astute view of things for someone so new to this world."

She shrugs. "I think I'm just getting better at reading you." They gaze at one another for several moments before Bryant blinks and looks away, almost shaking himself to regain his stolid composure. Isabella can't help but smile.

He turns back and looks at her closely. "How are you feeling, my Lady?"

She sighs. "In all honesty? Bloody exhausted. I think I need to lie down again." She accepts his help to rise and they make their way back to the chamber. Bryant stokes the fire and she climbs into bed, quickly succumbing to sleep. He picks a book from the nearby shelf and returns to his chair.

[21]Deep in the night, Bryant wakes to the sound of a harsh cry. Isabella shifts, clawing at the covers, her body twisting and he realises that she is having a nightmare. It is the first he has seen in all the time he has spent with her.

She gasps and her face contorts in fear, yet he hovers at the edge of the bed, not knowing what to do and once again feeling frustration at the shortfalls in Drw-ad training. He feels the desire to lie next to her, to take her in his arms...but is that the right thing to do? Her hands curl into fists and she moans. Clearly, she fights in the dream.

Bryant decides and perches on the edge of the bed. "Isabella, do not fear." He takes a clawed hand in his. "I am here. Nothing can hurt you." He reaches up, performing the same action she has for him before, stroking her forehead, trying to soothe her.

At his touch, she wakes with a choking gasp, clutching at his arm.

---

[21] Playlist: Myàr - Thunderstorm

When she becomes aware that it is him, Isabella takes in a shaking breath and he helps her sit up. She rubs her hands over her face.

"Oooh, that was horrible. I felt like I was being suffocated, crushed." Her voice catches and she coughs. Bryant reaches to the nightstand and pours a glass of honeyed lime water, handing it to her. She sips and then sighs, pushing up the pillows behind and leaning back. "I'm sorry I woke you."

Bryant squeezes her hand. "It is no matter, my Lady."

Isabella winces as gust hammers past the windows, the wind outside rising to a shriek. Another storm stalks the night above them. "I don't think I'll be able to fall asleep again."

Bryant looks thoughtful then picks up his book.

"I noticed that one of my favourite books from childhood is here. Our Brood Aunt would read to us whenever a true Storm hit the Spires. I do not know why she had books filled with human stories and poetry. They are not something the Drw-ad consider worthy." He glances at her, his dark eyes uncertain. "May I read a little to you?"

She smiles. "I would really like that. But," she pats the bed beside her, "could you sit next to me?"

He regards her cautiously for a moment then does as she asks, propping himself up with a pillow. He is rigid at first but then she picks up his hand and manoeuvres his arm around to rest along her shoulders as she curls into the side of him. He tries not to react.

As he reads, Isabella sinks into him, occasionally glancing up to watch him. His voice is calm, deep and soporific. She takes in a breath and relaxes, her hand moving to rest upon his chest. Slowly, her eyelids grow heavy and close, sleep claiming her.

Bryant pauses in his recitation as he hears a deeper tone to her breaths and he looks down. He feels the familiar pressure in his chest as it strikes him again how lovely she is. At first, he thinks to leave, to extract himself from her embrace, but he does not want to wake her. He struggles with himself, reasoning that she invited him to share the bed with him in the first place, so perhaps she will not begrudge him his continued presence. He looks up to the ceiling and sighs, frustrated at his own reticence, then freezes as her breath hitches and she suddenly turns over in her sleep, her back to him. He stares down at her and then makes a decision.

Sliding down, he lies beside her and pulls the covers over both of them. Isabella wakes briefly as he moves and, in the darkness, her smile grows. She reaches behind as he secures the covers and takes his hand. Again, he tenses but she ignores his reaction and pulls his arm across her so that he is curled against her back. Slowly, she feels him relax and with exhaustion still haunting her, she quickly falls asleep.

Bryant struggles with such closeness for some time and then gives in. He feels cocooned in the warmth of their shared bed and, with the storm outside and the woman under his arm breathing softly, he feels the aching cold within slip steadily away. Despite his determination to stay awake and enjoy the moment, he quickly follows her into sleep.

Bryant rises early, changing into the simple black sparring clothes left out for him the night before by Mara. He twists his hair into a ponytail and pulls on his boots. He is almost ready to leave when he hears Isabella shift and stretch.

She looks up at him. "You're leaving?" There is something more focused about him this morning.

"We will begin with a run and then spar. Please do not push yourself this morning, you are still healing." For a moment he stands, uncertain, then bows to her and exits the room.

Isabella rolls her eyes and growls, thumping the bed with her fist in frustration. "Ow." The scrapes on her knuckles sting.

There is a tap on the door and Nari enters. "Morning. How are you feeling?"

"A little better. But I know if I don't move I'm going to seize up." Isabella pulls herself upright.

"Good point. I've come to help you dress before I join them on the run. I'll take you down to Alyss and she'll show you around."

Isabella waves a hand. "It's okay, I can dress myself." The young woman regards her sceptically for a moment and then shrugs. She points towards the corridor.

"At the bottom of the steps turn right. Alyss is tending the raised beds in the garden out the back." She steps out of the chamber. "Wish me luck in beating your Drw!" She calls as she hurries down the corridor.

It takes Isabella far longer than she anticipated to shower, pull on clothes and make her way down to the garden. Once she reaches the first raised bed she is forced to perch on the wooden edge to catch her breath. Fennel fronds drift in the breeze behind her, their heady scent lifting her mood. She closes her eyes and tilts her face upwards, revelling in the weak winter sunlight. It is an unexpected moment of peace.

She hears the crunch of footsteps on the path nearby and opens her eyes. Alyss strides to a halt beside her, leans down and pulls her into a hug. Isabella sighs contentedly and hugs her back. When the Witch steps back, she looks Isabella up and down.

"A little better, but we've still work to do." She checks the bruises around Isabella's throat. "I'm impressed you managed to survive that. Eric was right – you are a ridiculously stubborn woman."

The shadow of a cloud momentarily crosses the sun and Isabella is struck by its dramatic timing. The mention of the Captain dampens her mood somewhat but when she looks at the Witch, she cannot help but smile. She stands with her hands on her hips, golden hair tumbling down her back and a tiny yellow-feathered saur clinging to a couple of curls.

Alyss shrugs. "Snuff likes to hang out with me when I garden, on the off-chance that a sizable bug might present itself. I just wish he wouldn't eat them whilst still attached to my hair." She ambles over to a large stone bowl which forms the base of a water feature and dips

349

her hands in to wash them. "I come out here as often as I can. There's something very therapeutic about digging your hands into soil, don't you think?" She dries her hands on her apron and then holds them out, helping the Anahera up.

She slides her arm around Isabella's. "Shall I give you the tour?"

Together they wander through the kitchen garden then through an arch in a dense hawthorn hedge. Isabella pauses at the sight beyond. A massive wall of greenery stretches along the base of the cliff and an astonishing mix of scents rises from it. Isabella realizes that there is order to the vertical garden – lavender hanging from one section, sage from another, basil, thyme, marjoram, cumin, turmeric, ginger… She knows that each requires different growing conditions, but here they flourish together. She ducks as something buzzes past her ear and curves away towards the wall. Snuff chitters at it and launches himself into the air, giving chase.

"The saur are trained to harvest the herbs but they also like to show off." Alyss points upwards and Isabella realizes that the iridescent flickers zipping in and out across the vertical garden are in fact tiny dragons.

"Well, that's just…cool." Isabella falls back into a childlike response. It seems appropriate.

They move on, strolling along the base of the wall until they reach an orchard. There is an odd atmosphere in the air, almost as if the trees are watching…and judging her. Alyss takes hold of her hand and lays it on the nearest trunk. The bark is warm – far warmer than it should be in such weak sunlight. When she speaks, the Witch's voice is serious.

"I need to introduce you to them. These trees are very special and if we don't do it right, the repercussions will be unpleasant to say the least." She begins to hum, a low sound which steadily takes on a resonance, almost as if several people are humming at once. The ground beneath Isabella's feet seems to pulse for a moment and she struggles to keep her feet. Finally, Alyss's hum subsides and the

350

atmosphere softens, becoming much lighter and more welcoming.

"Um..." Isabella stares at her and she smiles.

"Welcome to the Orchard, Isabella Mackay. The trees have shared your energy signature amongst themselves," she taps her foot lightly on a root to indicate the line of communication, "and they will recognize you when you come again." She smiles. "There are trees from all over Hjaltland here and many grow nowhere else. Some of them can get a little...defensive at times."

"Defensive?" Isabella frowns.

Battle trees?

Alyss gives a wry smile. "If they sense an intruder, they will kill it. Others will take in the bodies of the fallen and transmit them into pure energy, ready to be born again. In a Sisterhood Haven Holm, when one of our number dies, we gift them to the trees to continue the cycle of rebirth."

"Oh." Isabella has no idea how to take this, so she decides to shift the conversation in a different direction. "So what else does this fabulous Holm hide?"

Alyss turns her around, facing back towards the circular buildings. She points off to the side. "Over there lie a series of fishing ponds, the woodland behind provides us with game." She indicates a squat white tower at the edge of the complex. "That's my husband Neb's design lab and next to it are the acolytes' apartment tower, study rooms and the training grounds."

Isabella points to the enormous tree off to the side and the Windpyre platform attached to it. "What kind of tree is that? I've never seen one so huge."

"That is an Yggdrasil tree. Each Haven Holm is built around one. It is a wairua ora. I suppose you might call it a 'soul tree'. Its roots go very deep into the earth and it protects the Holm from both Storms and attacks. Actually," she adds, "you'll have a good view of the runners from up there."

Together they wander back through the gardens and Alyss helps

351

Isabella to climb the wrought iron steps to the platform, taking her leave to go and present a morning lecture. Left alone, Isabella scans the landscape and finally spots the two acolytes and the Drw-ad. Even at this distance she is impressed by how fast and lithe he is. Yet again, exhaustion drags at her and she leans against the trunk of the Yggdrasil tree for support.

Every single leaf momentarily ceases its movement and then a scattering of tiny flowers bloom into existence near her. The tree extends the branch to head height and although she does not notice it move, she is suddenly surrounded by an invigorating scent. She looks up, touches a spray of blooms lightly and inhales. It is wonderfully restorative and reminds her of something, just out of the reach of her memory. She can feel it filling her lungs as a blissful sensation spreads throughout her body. She has no idea how rare this moment is.

Isabella pats the trunk. "Thank you, tree."

Unbeknownst to her, the Yggdrasil tree has quietly grown a wide, comfortable seat for her and it rustles its leaves nearby so that she will notice. She smiles tiredly and slides onto the seat, sitting back to marvel at the view and search for the runners.

"Lovely tree." She murmurs and sighs contentedly.

When the trio eventually return from their warm-up run, the acolytes go to prepare the barriers in the training arena and Bryant climbs the stairs to the platform to find his wife. His hair is still tied back in a long ponytail and his arms are bare, contrasting with his simple black tunic over long breeks. The sigils etched into his white skin catch her eye again, as do his arm muscles as he hooks both hands over a branch above his head and stretches for a moment.

"Comfortable?"

Isabella grins. "I like this tree."

His gaze travels up the enormous trunk and high into the canopy. "It is indeed a special tree. It saved your life." She stares at him and his expression softens. "The Nightfevre poison should have killed you. The injection the Witch gave you contained the sap from this Yggdrasil tree. I confess, I did not know it possessed such power. But," he pats the trunk, "I am grateful to it."

Bryant drops a hand from the branch and holds it out to her. "Shall we see what the young Witches have in store for me in the training arena?"

She takes his hand and allows him to pull her up and into his snow-scent. As they stroll towards the steps, she suddenly halts and drops his hand. "Wait."

Turning, she moves back to the trunk and stretches out her arms, leaning against the tree. Again, every leaf stills. She holds the hug for some time then whispers, "Thank you, tree." She pushes herself back off and follows her husband down the steps.

As he helps her down, he has pause to wonder – what effect might the essence of an Yggdrasil have on alien physiology? However, as soon as they reach the arena, the acolytes call him in to spar and he leaves her standing with Foddi. The arena is an oval shape and only a single level. A waist-high wooden wall encircles the main sparring space, topped with a shimmering barrier of protective energy. The young acolyte explains that it is there to stop any stray pulses of energy from damaging the surrounding buildings.

The acolytes first engage Bryant separately, kicking and spinning, trying to get close enough to knock him off his feet. They are clearly skilled in combat but he is quicker. As Nari slams into the floor of the arena for the fifth time, Bryant steps forward and offers her a hand up. She takes it but once upright, she sighs dejectedly.

"I think I'm getting worse."

The Drw-ad regards her seriously. "You should be proud of yourself, acolyte. You are a quick study and you are intuitive." He turns to Mara, who approaches from the far side. "I am impressed by your skills, both of you."

They both look surprised then Mara nods a 'thank you' and prepares herself again. She narrows her eyes and both young women

353

attack him at once, ripples of power shimmering through the air. Bryant blocks each pulse but even Isabella can see that he is beginning to sweat. He halts the session and begins to teach them a new blocking move.

"They're impressive." Isabella grins at Foddi. "I wish I could fight like that. Maybe fewer people would try to kill me."

The young man shrugs. "Or maybe more." His tone turns more serious. "I'm surprised that your Drw is offering us such an advantage. One day we may have to face one another in battle."

When Isabella frowns at him, he smiles gently. "I suspect he is doing this for you, so that he can stay near you and prove that he can be trusted. He is a very unusual specimen, but you should always be mindful of the true nature of his people. One day, it might re-assert itself. You should be prepared for that."

They are interrupted by the appearance of a tall man in coveralls, with a pair of safety goggles perched upon his spikey salt-and-pepper hair. A small patch stitched onto the left-hand sleeve of the coverall proclaims it to be, "Neb's. Hands off." Alyss's husband slaps Foddi on the shoulder.

"How're they going?" He grins at Isabella.

"Nobody's killed anyone yet." Foddi shrugs. "It all seems weirdly civilized. Even Mara's behaving herself."

"Good to hear. But she's going to have to share, 'cos I want a word with him too. I'll just nip in through the back and then you can drop the shield." Neb turns and strides away.

A deep shuddering noise issues from inside the arena and both Isabella and Foddi turn to look.

"Mara, for the Goddess's sake!" Nari squawks. That nearly hit me!"

To Isabella's relief, Bryant still stands, although his normally perfectly smooth hair appears slightly dishevelled. She is so intent on him that she misses the stunned look on Foddi's face.

He stares down at her arm. The Anahera has leant forward and

354

placed her hand on top of the low wooden wall, straight through the energy barrier as if it were not even there. Touching the barrier should have flung her several feet backwards, but she appears fine. It is as if it does not exist at all.

"Uh, Isabella?" He realizes he will have to catch the moment quickly. "Remember I promised to help with your healing process?" She turns to him and nods, her hand still piercing the barrier. "Would you care to start that now? The healing tower is just over there. I have some new salves I'd like to try, to help that bruising disappear more quickly." He keeps his tone light, hoping she will agree.

Isabella raises an eyebrow. "You want to do some more tests, don't you?" His eyes widen and he stammers, but she smiles. "It's okay, it's a fair trade. Shall we?" She steps away from the barrier and as they move off, they hear the cheerful sound of Neb's voice.

"Lord Lathorne! I hear you've had some success with shield technology. Shall we take our second break of fast in my lab? I've got some questions…"

Isabella and Foddi spend a couple of hours ensconced in the medical suite. Foddi's tension eases and he and Isabella spend much of the time laughing and discussing ideas as he works. When she finally emerges, she smells like the entire contents of a high-end apothecary shop but she feels considerably better.

Alyss comes to meet her. "Come and have something to eat, you must be starving!"

She leads Isabella to the kitchen in her private quarters, a lovely warm space with a heavy wooden dining table in the centre. Herbs hang drying from racks above a large, powder-blue kitchen range. Alyss deposits a freshly baked fowl and leek pie and a bowl of salad on the table and loads a plate for Isabella. The Anahera dives in happily.

Once they are finished, the Witch sits back and looks at her. Her words take Isabella completely by surprise.

"You haven't had sex with him yet, have you." It is not a

355

question, rather a statement of obvious fact.

"Um…" This is a little more forward than Isabella is comfortable with, although she is slowly growing used to how forthright the Sisterhood Witch and her acolytes can be. Thankfully, her direct style is softened by a genuine warmth and concern for others, along with an earthy sense of humour.

Alyss's gaze is piercing. "It's not a criticism. I wanted to make sure." She taps her fingers on the wooden table for emphasis. "Yours is a unique situation. As far as anyone knows, this is the first Anahera/Drw-ad union ever. I have no idea if your systems will even complement each other at all."

Isabella swallows. There are many worries currently burrowing into her but this one is quite far back in the queue. She has vaguely wondered about what might happen, if anything at all.

The Witch continues. "But to be on the safe side, you'd probably do well to use this." She lifts a small leather parcel onto the table, pulls open the bindings and unrolls it to reveal a number of slender vials reminiscent of perfume samples, each containing an iridescent liquid.

Isabella's eyes widen.

Hjaltland contraceptives? How the hell are they deployed? Via syringe? No. Frikkin. Way.

Alyss slides a vial out of its loop and holds it up. "Tip one of these into your morning tisane, once every two weeks. Make sure you count the days carefully – the serum lasts a little longer than that but its efficacy differs between women from that point, so it's best not to take any chances."

"So…no babies?" Isabella guesses and Alyss smiles grimly.

"Definitely no babies." She slides the vial back into place. "And it deals with most sexually transmitted nasties too. Not," she grimaces, "that I can imagine that'll be a problem with him. I doubt anyone's touched him before you."

A little of the Sisterhood's ancient rancour has reared its head and

Isabella frowns, feeling a little disappointed in her. "Let's not be cruel." She feels increasingly protective of her odd husband.

Alyss rolls the parcel up and secures the bindings. She catches Isabella's expression. "Sorry. Old habits die hard, I guess." She rests both hands on the roll. "He's proving to be an unusual specimen. I have to admit, I'm starting to like him."

Isabella smirks wryly. "Did saying that cost you?"

Alyss laughs. "A little." Suddenly she is serious again. "You only know this one and it's true, he is very unusual. But I've fought many of them, killed them and seen good Sisters slaughtered in turn. The Drw-ad and the Sisterhood have been at war for thousands of years. It's hard for either of us to let that go."

"Yeah," Isabella nods, "I've got an oak tree table currently pumping out acorns to prove it."

Alyss laughs again, this time with genuine warmth. She pushes the wrap across to the Anahera. "Keep taking these and you won't be adding any little 'acorns' of your own to the Eyrie." She slaps her knees and stands up. "Right. Once more around the raised gardens. You've got to build up your strength. Off you go." She shoos Isabella from the kitchen.

Bryant does not return until late in the night and, not wanting to disturb her but increasingly needing to be near, slides in beside Isabella and settles himself. Having spent an enjoyable few hours discussing shield designs with Neb, he initially feels uncharacteristically content. As he has many times before over the last weeks, he reaches over and strokes back a curl from her cheek, but other than that he does not touch her. Instead, he sifts through a growing concern.

It is not just his lack of experience, nor the fear of rejection which needles him, it is the knowledge that First Mother will know of his actions by now. It is bad enough that he defied her to marry Isabella but if they consummate the marriage and the Goddess finds out, he has no idea what she will do. And what, if it were even possible, would she do if offspring resulted from their union? Now that he has grown closer to Isabella, he is beginning to understand the true peril of joining with another – the looming, gut-wrenching possibility of loss.

Once again, even without meaning to, his wife interrupts his spiralling despair. She turns in her sleep and curls into him, her head resting against his shoulder, her hand once again on his chest. For the first time, with no one prompting him, he wraps both arms around her and holds her fast.

Bryant wakes early and leaves to prepare for their departure. When he enters the kitchen, Alyss greets him warmly.

"You are welcome to stay longer, Drw. It has been a pleasure having you here."

Neb, seated at the table and enjoying a stack of nightberry pancakes with syrup, quickly stands and moves to grip his wrist. "Any time you want to work on a project, you know where I am. My forge is yours."

Bryant struggles to assimilate this. In the space of a couple of days he has gone from pariah and despised enemy to a trainer of Sisterhood acolytes and someone a powerful Sister Witch and her husband actually want to spend time with. There is a real warmth to this place and the people within which he never expected to find. That they would extend that warmth to him is even more shocking.

He bows. "I thank you for all you have done for us. Yet again, you have helped Isabella and for that I am in your debt."

The couple exchange a significant look. "It's our sacred duty. There is a need, so we help." Alyss lays a hand on his arm. "If you need us, just send a globe and we'll be with you. You're 'upswing' for this Haven Holm too." She winks.

Bryant takes his leave of them and heads towards the marron stable to secure two contracts back to the Citadel. As he walks, he ponders the Witch's words. He had no idea that the Sisterhood and the lift-helmers had such close ties.

The pounding of hooves jolts him from his thoughts and he steps back, leaning against the wall of the stables as a contingent of King's Own Uhlan thunder past, a slaver's cell wagon in their midst. He regards them for a moment and then slips in through the stable door.

Captain Eric Bannerman looks up and realizes where they are. The Mutinous Piglet is like a spiritual home to him and he can practically smell Alyss's famous pancakes from the wagon. He clutches the bars and looks longingly at the pub. It is a place of sanctuary and he wonders if he will ever get to sample Alyss's spicy food again. He curses, contemplating his list of possible fates; imprisonment, certainly demotion and the removal of his commission, shipped off to some far-flung border hole, public humiliation, perhaps even death. Another smell intrudes and he swivels to glare at the slaver, who reeks of stale sweat and grease. The man grins at him.

Eventually they reach the Citadel and although Lord Ethel demands that Captain Bannerman be dragged to the cells in chains, Delilah merely regards him sourly and helps Eric down from the wagon. His hands are shackled behind him and she throws a cloak around his back, attempting to grant him a little dignity. She leads him to the cells and ushers him into one, uncoupling the wrist cuffs and locking the door behind her. She is expected to attend the Commander's debriefing and once that unpleasant event has been endured, Captain Dae heads quickly up-terrace, searching for her father.

17. A FITTING PUNISHMENT

Commander Fallon leaves Bannerman to stew for two days. As he languishes in his cell, he realizes that it is just one along from where he last saw Isabella and he is plagued by that memory. His stomach twists as he recalls the look in her eyes when he left her, knowing that he didn't want to but that he did it anyway. He remembers the feeling of her hands over his on the bars, the scent of her and the way she made him feel, like a safe harbour at the edge of a dark sea. Try as he might, he cannot escape the guilt.

When the summons finally appears, he finds that Delilah and Sergeant Doric have volunteered to escort him to the Commander's office. They refuse to let any other Uhlan touch him. Captain Dae's face is tight and the Sergeant's scowl has deepened. Delilah opens the cell door and holds out the wrist cuffs.

Bannerman rises and growls. "I'm not gonna run, Del."

Captain Dae gives him a stern look. "It's expected, Eric. You'd do the same." She secures the cuffs around his wrists and leads him out.

As they make their way through the corridors and out across the main courtyard of the Huljun Terrace, they do not speak and even Doric is silent. There is a palpable tension between them and along the route to the Commander's office, other Uhlan pause and stare. They have all heard the rumours, the scuttlebutt moving fast through the Terrace upon the unit's return. A respected Captain assaulting a member of the Gentry is juicy news to chew over.

The black walls of the Commander's office are there before they know it and the three Uhlan come to a halt before the massive iron-studded door. Delilah removes Bannerman's wrist cuffs and she and Doric wait as he enters. The sergeant wanders to the end of the building and sparks a roll-up, leaning back against the wall and scowling.

The office is spacious, with large, oval shimmers attached to each wall, their screens shifting through a series of maps. A heavy desk sits in the centre and Bannerman halts in front of it, standing to attention and staring at the wall behind the Commander's head until the man grunts.

"At ease, Captain." He looks up from his paperwork and leans back in his chair. "Assaulting a commanding officer? Tell me why I shouldn't have you court-martialled and flogged?"

The Captain's eyes flick towards him for a moment, barely keeping himself in check. "Sir, he was about to..."

The Commander holds up a hand.

"I know what he was about to do. You are lucky the globe Captain Dae sent detailing the incident reached me just before Lord Ethel's did. Nevertheless, it is not my job to censure the Gentry, nor is it yours. Your actions now present me with a problem."

"Sir," Bannerman's words slip through gritted teeth, "he was about to rape a child after killing the mother who was trying to protect him. How can we not..."

"Captain! The remit of the King's Own Uhlan is to defend the realm, not to police those who rule us," the Commander snaps, leaning forward. "Just because you don't agree with their behavior does not mean you have any right to interfere with them." He watches the man in front of him grapple with his rage and is faintly impressed when he manages to contain it.

Bannerman places his hands behind his back and clenches his wrist tightly. He returns to glaring at the wall just behind the Commander's head.

"Lord Ethel comes from a powerful family and your actions must be answered for. If that were an end to it, I would have no compunction about punishing you to the fullest extent of our laws. However," the Commander picks up a message globe from his desk, "in the last two days I have received several messages of support for you."

Bannerman glances at him, frowning.

"Surprised? Considering your recent behavior, I can understand that. Apparently, you have some powerful connections. This," he waves the globe, "came from that Windpyre negotiator you told me about. Kahu Manaroa speaks very highly of you." He leans back in his chair once more. "Yesterday, Sallamon Dae himself came to request leniency for you. The Sabaton of the King's House Guard, no less! He reminded me of your previous service which, I have to admit, has been exemplary."

Captain Bannerman feels a burn of appreciation for Delilah and her quick actions in appealing to her father. They have relied on one another for years and he is glad to hear that she has his back even now.

The Commander narrows his eyes. "And then this morning, the damnedest thing happened." He shakes his head. "That bloody Tuatara ambassador appeared at my door with an appeal for you."

The Captain stares at him.

"Exactly. He...she...it...they..." Fallon struggles to identify the correct pronoun. "Informed me of your actions with the Anahera and how impressed they had been. Then they gave me a suggestion regarding your punishment." As the Captain's sharp eyes narrow, the Commander continues. "It's surprisingly simple and I know you're not going to like it. Lord Ethel however, seemed quite pleased."

"Sir?" Bannerman tenses.

"You've done good work over the years, so I'm going to give you a choice. Either accept the court-martial, a public flogging, jail time and dismissal, or..." He pauses, his gaze flicking over the Captain's

362

more visible scars. "Accept the position as Sabaton of Lord Lathorne's new House Guard."

Eric Bannerman stops breathing. For a moment the world seems to tilt and twist around him. The long years of slavery suddenly feel as if they are right behind him, just over his shoulder. He stares down at the floor, fighting the urge to throw up. Utter debasement and dishonour or…serve another Drw-ad.

"Sir…" He manages, but the Commander holds up a hand.

"Choose, Captain. I don't have all day."

Bannerman takes in a tight breath to steady himself. He opens his mouth and his mind snarls.

I choose dishonour, you cunt!

Instead, his mouth forms other words.

"The House Guard."

The Commander taps his ear. "What? I didn't quite catch that."

Bannerman manages to push the words through gritted teeth. "I will accept the commission."

The Commander nods. "Interesting choice. I wouldn't want to work for that bastard." He shrugs. "The order will be processed immediately. You are free to go." When Bannerman doesn't move, he waves a hand. "Dismissed, Sabaton."

The former Captain salutes and turns on his heel, striding from the office. He shoves open the door and stalks straight past Delilah and Sergeant Doric until he reaches the wall of the building opposite, where he halts and punches it, hard.

Delilah and Doric stare at each other then turn and approach him cautiously. He leans his forehead against the cool, stone wall and cradles his fist in the other hand. As they approach, he turns to face them, leaning back against the wall, his eyes closed. Sergeant Doric eyes the man's bleeding knuckles and holds out a hand.

"Let's have a look."

His eyes still closed, Bannerman holds out his fist for Doric to inspect. They have trained, fought and drunk together and he too has watched the Captain's changing behaviour with concern. He checks the battered hand carefully, flaring his magic to encourage the cells to regrow.

"Well?" Delilah places her hands on her hips. "What did he say?" She holds her tension close. Like Doric, Bannerman is one of the few people she trusts with her life.

He opens his eyes and tilts his head back, staring at the wintry sky. "He gave me a promotion."

"What?" Both soldiers react at the same time.

Doric snorts. "Maybe I should try it. There's many a Gentry I'd like to bounce off a wall."

Delilah crosses her arms. Something does not feel right and Bannerman is still staring at the sky, refusing to make eye contact. His silence is unusual and she doesn't like it.

"Eric." Her voice is stern. "What kind of promotion?" He finally looks at her and in his eyes, she sees a turmoil she has only ever glimpsed when he is deep in his cups, murmuring terrible words about his experience as a slave of the Drw-ad.

"You're looking at the new Sabaton of Lord Lathorne's House Guard."

He gives them a moment to take this in. Technically, it is a promotion. A House Guard is considered an honour to serve within and a significant step up from the King's Own. He knows that Delilah has had ambitions in that direction for years, hoping eventually to replace her father as Sabaton of the King Sarn's personal House Guard.

"I didn't think the Prissy White Bitch had a Guard." Doric spits on the cobbles.

"Apparently the King offered him one the other day, after his wife was abducted by slavers," Delilah explains, watching Bannerman's reaction carefully. He stares at her.

"She was abducted?" He feels like he has been punched. "Does she…live?" Darkness crowds around him and he forces himself to breathe.

The Captain nods her head. "Lathorne and the Prince went after them. She's been recuperating at the Piglet for several days." She looks sideways at him. "Eric, my father said that when Lathorne caught up with the slavers, he tore one of them apart. Literally into tiny pieces."

Doric has pulled a salve and a bandage from one of his numerous pockets and proceeds to tend to Bannerman's hand, but he pauses at this. "Fuck, that's a bit extreme." He looks at his patient. "Are you sure about this?"

Bannerman scowls. "I don't have much choice. Mind you, if the bastard can't even keep his own wife safe…"

"Eric," Delilah begins, but pulls herself back in. Perhaps this is the wrong time to bring up her suspicions about his feelings for the Anahera. She sighs. "Just…be careful. You're a fine Captain and you'll make an excellent Sabaton."

"If you don't fuck it up and end up in bits," Doric snorts, finishing his ministrations.

"You're a cheerful bastard, Sergeant." Bannerman shakes his head.

"But at least I'm pretty." The man smirks, in full violation of the truth. He winks at Delilah who rolls her eyes. "What d'ya say? A round of drinks before he has to bend over for the White Demon?" His smirk is contagious and even Bannerman catches it. He slaps Doric on the shoulder with his good hand.

"Excellent suggestion, Sergeant. And since I haven't been paid yet, the first round's on you." He exchanges a grin with Delilah as the man groans. "C'mon then."

The three veterans amble off, Delilah ruffling the Sergeant's hair and laughing at him, dodging away as he tries to grab her in return.

It is with great reluctance that Eric Bannerman arrives at the entrance to the Eyrie the next afternoon. He raises his hand to tap the bell pad

365

but stops midway, his hand curling into a fist. Hesitating, he struggles with himself then spins on his heel and takes three strides back down the wide corridor before halting again, his hand resting on the pommel of the sword at his hip. A growl of frustration crawls up his throat.

You are no coward. Suck it up.

With considerable resignation, he turns and strides back up to the towering doors, punching the bell pad sharply.

"Fuck."

Although it is mere seconds before the smaller panel set into the enormous doors opens, it feels like an eternity and he nearly turns again. He hears the locking mechanism whispering back into the wall and the door opens to reveal a maidservant. She plants her hands on her hips. She is no more than seventeen but her expression is confident and distinctly unimpressed.

"Sabaton Bannerman?"

He nods.

"You're late."

He opens his mouth to snap back a pithy reply but she has already turned away.

"C'mon." She flicks her hand for him to follow. "And close the door behind you." Her red curls bounce just above her shoulders as she strides into the atrium. The walls are covered in silk paintings of lush gardens and dotted with tiny bright birds.

"Wait here." She points to a spot on the flagstones in the middle of the room and waits until he has moved to stand exactly there. He does so, but makes his displeasure known by strolling forward with insolent slowness. She ignores his glower and disappears through the door to the inner sanctum. Soon after, the door opens and Bannerman wrinkles his nose at the sudden whiff of copper in the air, scenting the Drw-ad even before he enters the room. He has always hated that metallic smell.

He catches a brief glimpse of his new Lord, his black hair unbound and spilling down his back over a simple, fitted claret robe

366

which reaches to the floor.

Bannerman immediately drops his gaze to the Drw-ad's boots and he presses his fist to his chest in a salute.

"Sabaton Bannerman." Bryant's gaze flicks over the soldier, noting his tell-tale scars, the tension in his body and his resolute determination not to look up. He wonders if the Commander has sent this one to him as a way to get at him, something he has come to expect from the man.

"My Lord." The new Sabaton manages to make even this simple greeting sound like an insult.

"Welcome to the Eyrie." Bryant spreads his hands, ignoring the soldier's tone. "The King has decided that I am in need of a House Guard and Commander Fallon considers you the best man for the job of forming one."

Bannerman suppresses a bitter snort.

No, he thought it'd be a fitting punishment for both of us.

"I will do my duty, my Lord."

"There is a reason I agreed to this. After my wife was attacked in the marketplace, I realised that I cannot always be there to protect her." He pauses and his next words contain a mix of frustration and affection. "She will not countenance a minder of her own, so I will also require you to train her in martial skills so that she may at least be able to defend herself properly."

In shock, the Sabaton looks up and straight into Lathorne's dark eyes. He sees an appeal in them that he is not used to seeing from a Drw-ad.

"You want me to train her?"

The sound of bare footsteps on stone echoes from the entrance of the inner sanctum and Isabella appears.

"Bryant, were you going to…" She sees Bannerman and pulls up short. Her eyes snap into an almost feral glare.

"You!"

Unconsciously he falls into his customary stance when dealing with his former charge, hands on his hips and a sceptical posture, ready for anything she might throw at him. However, this time it is a way to hold himself together as bitter anger races through him, threatening to burst free as he watches her stand perilously near the Drw-ad.

"Isabella." Bryant is surprised by her rudeness. "Sabaton Bannerman is our guest. Please accord him the appropriate respect." He glances from one to the other and notes how the demeanour of the former Captain has changed. "You have met before?"

Bannerman sneers and Isabella, still fizzing with resentment, points at him.

"This is the soldier who 'rescued' me when I came through the Gate. He tied me up and dragged me over a mountain!"

Bryant's gaze turns to Bannerman and the entire atmosphere changes. His eyes deepen to a hard, jet black and tiny flames flare around each iris. The Sabaton's sneer fades as he registers the rising scent of copper in the room. The Drw-ad's voice is deceptively quiet.

"You hurt my wife?"

But Eric Bannerman has endured Drw-ad rage before and he merely shrugs. "In my defence, she kneed me in the balls and tried to run back in the direction of the slave traders."

To the Sabaton's surprise, the Drw-ad's eyes return to a semblance of normal and he looks back at his wife. "That is no way to treat a man who is trying to keep you from harm."

She gapes at him, something Bannerman finds strangely satisfying.

"You're on his side?! Honestly, bloody men." She jambs her hands onto her hips and snaps. "How was I supposed to know he was rescuing me? One violent bugger with a blood-spattered sword is pretty much like the next!"

Bryant looks to the Sabaton, who shrugs.

"I was just doing my job."

"Just!" Isabella snaps, struggling to suppress the desire to punch

368

him in the throat. Her chest aches with the pressure of betrayal.

You left me here! You let them auction me like a prize beast.

"My Lady, please." Bryant's calm, deep voice cuts through her rage and she takes a breath. "The King has granted us the honour of a House Guard and Captain Bannerman has been chosen to lead them as our new Sabaton."

Isabella watches Bannerman's eyes narrow at this and the tell-tale muscle in his stubbled cheek contracts. He is clearly not happy about it. Bryant's steady voice continues.

"You will have to find a way to work together." He reaches out and takes her hand. "Isabella, you are very valuable to me. I merely wish you to remain safe and this man has shown himself to be more than capable of achieving that aim." He. takes hold of her other hand. "Please, will you let the Sabaton do his job?"

She sighs. His dark eyes have taken on a decidedly Labrador-level of appeal, something she has always had trouble resisting, in either dogs or men. She squeezes his hands.

"Fine. I'll try to behave myself."

Bryant is a little cautious at her use of the word "try", but he realises that this may be the best he can expect from her at this point.

"Please ask Millie to show the Sabaton to his new quarters and acquaint him with the Eyrie layout." They both turn back to Bannerman who, feeling distinctly uncomfortable with even this small display of affection, is glaring pointedly up at the glittering chandelier above. Bryant inclines his head in a bow to his new Sabaton.

"I will require your presence in the solarium after supper to go over the logistics of your new post."

Despite his naturally insolent tendencies, Eric Bannerman is nonetheless a well-trained soldier and he pulls himself to attention smartly and salutes.

Bryant turns back to Isabella, raises her hand to his lips and kisses her knuckles.

369

"My Lady."

Please play nicely.

He leaves them and strides back into the inner sanctum and up to his solarium.

Isabella opens her mouth to speak but Bannerman surges forward in two strides and is suddenly snarling in her face. "Exactly which part of 'choose wisely' did you struggle with, you silly bitch?!"

She blinks in the face of this unexpected ferocity.

"Wh…what?"

"A fucking Drw?" He throws a hand in the air. "Of all the choices you had, of all the *species* in the whole of Hjaltland, you chose a Drw." He brings the hand down and unconsciously rubs the bolt scar embedded in it. "I warned you how dangerous they were, fuck, Emmeline warned you too! But no, true to form you had to go and throw yourself into the nearest fire pit just to prove you could survive!"

"That isn't why I…" She stammers.

He spins away and begins to pace back and forth across the room, gesticulating with every point.

"You can't tell me there weren't any other options but him. I know Sir Gellan made an offer. He was a damn fine soldier and he's a good man. You would've been *safe* with him!" He reaches the end of his arc and paces back again. "So what happened? Did he glamour you?"

He pauses for a moment and lurches toward her again. "He didn't use that foul blood magic on you, did he?" The scent of cardamom envelops her and she manages to pull herself together, her irritation returning.

"No, he did not! That's a ridiculous idea!"

He humphs and resumes his pacing orbit.

"I *knew* you would do something like this." He mutters. "I just knew it." He stops and looks back at her, the burning anger softening to something akin to concern.

370

"Girlie, they slaughter people for their blood. And that's after torturing them first, because they believe that pain makes the blood more potent." His grey eyes darken like clouds in a winter storm and Isabella realises that it is pain she can see, etched upon his face. "You can't trust 'em, ever. Not even him."

He points to the door of the inner sanctum. "They're not like us." His hand drops and he suddenly appears very tired.

Seeing such an unexpected change in the fierce Captain, Isabella's own anger dissolves. She moves closer to him, holding out both hands in a show of peace.

"Eric, *I'm* not like you, any of you. And mad as my choice seems to you, I chose him because he is different. He's treated me with real care and compassion and yes, I trust him. He has given me absolutely no reason not to." Bannerman's eyes flicker with cynicism, but she continues. "He's a good man and if you give him a chance, you'll see that."

The new Sabaton's cynical expression expands, the long scars running down his face appearing to deepen.

"When the slavers kidnapped me from the marketplace, he came after me. He pulled me from a cliff and he stayed with me while I healed."

Bannerman folds his arms across his chest and nods. "Aye, I heard what he did to that slaver. Was there anything left of him?"

Her reaction is not what he expects. Her hands drop to her sides and her chin lifts a little, a hard, imperious and oddly satisfied expression settling on her face.

"Nothing but a mist of blood. The scum-sucking leech bag was ripped apart."

The former Captain stares at her for a moment then shrugs, looking away.

"Fine. Whatever. This is my new commission and I have no choice. You can show me to my quarters now." His gravelly voice has entirely lost its fire.

"Eric..." She reaches for his arm but he moves towards the chamber door.

"I have work to do, my Lady."

She winces at his dismissal and sighs.

Why does this man have to make every interaction so damn complicated?

She gives in and moves through the door in front of him. "Millie!"

Bannerman follows her into the inner sanctum. It is large but surprisingly light and cosy. He spots what looks like a large dining table, carved in a simple style and ringed by high-backed chairs and he has the disconcerting impression it is covered in a thick mat of oak leaves.

Millie appears from an arched wooden doorway to the left and moves quickly to meet them.

"Please show Sabaton Bannerman to his quarters and explain the layout of the Eyrie to him. Lord Lathorne has requested a meeting with him this evening."

The maidservant bobs a quick curtsy and motions for him to follow. He leaves Isabella behind without a word.

Millie leads him along a pleasantly lit passageway which curves to the left. They come to a T-junction and she points to the right. "Take the stairs at the end of that passage and they will lead you to the solarium. This way," she indicates to the left, "will take you to the servants' service-lift entrance and eventually to the kitchens. Lady Kahn knows you've joined us so you can visit any time."

She stops beside a wooden door. "These are your quarters." She stands aside for him to enter first.

He steps through the doorway and into the main chamber. It is wide and spacious. A single bed, layered with yargswool blankets, sits against a long window. Bannerman's belongings have been delivered and are piled on the bed and the nearby desk. Carefully parcelled boxes filled with his books wait ready to be stacked onto the bookshelf above the desk. Across the room sits a wooden table and chairs beneath an oval shimmer attached to the wall. At the edge of the table is a samovar in polished mother-of-pearl, with a small stack of matching cups beside.

He turns to find Millie holding out a ring of keys.

"Ask, if you need to know anything." She bobs a curtsy and leaves.

The new Sabaton closes the door, turns and leans on it for a moment. The chamber is certainly bigger than he has ever had before. He moves to the bed, leaning over and peering out of the window. It also has a better view than he is used to, with no hint of the city on this side, only the wide valley, dotted with crofts and curving up to the mountains in the distance.

He sits heavily on the bed, and in the solitude of his new room, he suddenly feels very tired. Leaning his elbows on his knees, he runs his hands over his braid, pulling off the binding and teasing out the plait until his hair falls down over his shoulders. He rubs his face then drops his head into his rough hands.

A thick wave of loneliness washes over him and the gaping hole inside cracks open a little further. The bright anger and seeping humiliation of the last few days converge and threaten to drown him. His hands curl into fists and he presses the knuckles into the flesh of his forehead.

"Life never takes you where you expect it to go." Isabella had said to him on the Windpyre ship. Maybe not, but why did it have to take him so far into this wilderness, into the very heart of an enemy's home?

Isabella. Somehow, the sudden thought of that bloody mad woman halts the vicious tide, allowing him to breathe again for a moment. He unclenches his hands and runs them through his hair again. Isabella chose a Drw.

He shakes his head and the hint of a bitter smile tugs at his lips. This new commission promises to be a mad ride but at least now he can be on hand to stop her doing something completely ludicrous and

373

no doubt fatal. He slaps his knees, shaking off his moment of weakness and stands. What did he say to her on the side of that mountain?

You've got to keep going. If you stop, you die.

He moves to the desk and begins to unpack his books.

Sometime later, as the last flare of sunset illuminates the room, he hears a tap at the door. He closes the quire he has been using to identify potential new recruits for the fledgling House Guard and raises his voice.

"Enter."

Millie elbows the door open, balancing a tray. Bannerman moves aside at the desk and she slides the tray into the space. On it rests a covered platter, a plate piled with thick, newly baked bread and a jug of beer.

He lifts the lid of the platter and the smell of lush yarg stew envelops him. Succulent cubes of meat, simmered in a touch of sweet wine, with the heady scent of rosemary and garlic mixing with the aroma of the fresh bread. He perks up and Millie smiles at him.

"Welcome to the Eyrie. I'm glad you're here."

He glances up at her, surprised.

"Those two need someone else to look after them." She nods in the direction of the inner sanctum. "It's a full-time job and I'm bloody exhausted."

Millie moves to the door and freezes. She looks back at him. "It appears you already have a visitor, Sabaton." She steps into the corridor and curtseys. Into Bannerman's new quarters strolls the Tuatara.

Eric stands. "Ambassador?" He is suddenly deeply suspicious. He has no idea what the scaly bastard could possibly want with him.

Subtle Sands Shifting places a talonned hand on their chest and bows. They watch the dark expression resolve on the Sabaton's face and wonder for a moment if he is stable enough for the task they have in mind. But they have watched him for long enough and they are convinced he is the right one. They accept a seat in the chair that Bannerman offers. The Sabaton himself folds his arms and leans against the edge of his desk, his sharp eyes wary.

"Apologies for the interruption, but I thought to explain." The Tuatara crosses their legs and leans back. "You are very special, Eric Bannerman, which is why Sallamon Dae and Kahu Manaroa helped me work your Commander." Their lips peel back from their sharp white teeth. "We liked what you did to the Ethel-shit."

Bannerman's eyes narrow. "Thanks."

Subtle Sands Shifting waves a hand. "You wonder why I suggested this punishment? Sallamon argued, he said it was cruel." They tip their head and their eyelids flicker. "But I say you are strong enough. You still keep the rage...here." They pat their abdomen. "And you keep a moral heart."

The new Sabaton does not move. The Tuatara taps their thin lips. "You remember my promise on the pirate ship?"

Eric nods. He has had little time to wonder at it since but now he can see that the Tuatara is serious.

The lizard steeples their hands and looks over their talon tips at the scarred warrior. "We did not put you here to kill Lathorne. He is one of our oldest friends and fiercest allies."

Bannerman stares at them. "So, when you said you could help me with what I want, this wasn't it?" He struggles to keep the snarl from his voice.

They shake their head. "Nope. He's the one you have to keep *alive*. We need him. He's the weapon, the hammer. All we need to do is prime him...then unleash him. But that," they raise a talonned finger, "requires much planning." They tip their head sideways, the metal spikes at the end of their horns rattling as they take in the Sabaton's sceptical glower.

"Think, mighty [22]*toa*, think. Why kill one when you can destroy

---

[22] Warrior.

them all? Is that not more satisfying?" The Tuatara grins, sharp teeth glinting. "No more Drw-ad to make slaves of us and drain us dry."

Eric narrows his eyes. "He's your friend, but you want to sacrifice him for a bigger prize?"

The Tuatara sits up in shock. "No! Not sacrifice. Quickblade is dear to our heart. He just doesn't know his own power yet. We hope he will survive the cataclysm." They tap their talons sharply on the desk. "We both know how the Drw-ad behave. His goddess-bitch mama will not let him keep his wife. She will take her and when she is finished with her, he will *want* to kill his own."

They suddenly rise, tail flicking behind them. "Anyhoo, must dash." They wave a hand in the air. "You know how it is - deals to be made, prey to be caught. You have a good think now." They flick a mock salute and stride away.

Bannerman lets out a breath to steady himself. Having to work for an enemy is bad enough, but having to keep them alive for a greater purpose? It is an enormous ask. Another thought drifts in, causing his guts to twist; He realises the Tuatara is right. In choosing to marry the Drw-ad, Isabella has put herself in mortal danger, perhaps not from him but certainly from his mother.

Light flickers across the circle of the quire, reminding him that it is time for his first meeting with his new lord. He takes a moment to curse life in general then snatches up the quire, striding towards the solarium stairs.

Along the corridor, Subtle Sands Shifting stops by a large, arched window and opens it, climbing through and onto a service pipe running down the side. It is a route they had taken many times in years gone by in order to slip around the Citadel without others being able to track them. They decide to head for their favourite place in all the world, Lady Kahn's kitchen. They intend to keep her appraised of events. As they scuttle sideways across the stone, heading for the next pipe to shin down, the Tuatara muses on their first meeting with the

376

lone Drw-ad.

Belonging to the warrior-ambassador caste of the Tuatara, they visited the Citadel several times over the course of their childhood and adolescence, the first not long after Bryant had arrived there as a seven-turn old hostage. It was much colder in the Citadel than their southern homeland, so whilst waiting for their māngai kāwanatanga[23] to conduct business with the royal couple, the young Tuatara had sniffed out the warm palace kitchens with steaming pots and roasting ovens.

Lady Kahn welcomed them and brought them into the fold, allowing them to curl up in a seat near one of the ovens. She clearly knew that having a connection with a Tuatara from a young age would be beneficial in the long run for the Kahn clan. The youngling helped around the kitchens, scaling walls to unhook snarled pulleys, lifting heavy joints of meat easily from their spits and occasionally stirring batter with their tail wrapped around a wooden spoon whilst perched on the back of a chair, reading a book.

The first time they had seen Bryant come into the kitchens, Subtle Sands Shifting was up high, just under the vaulted ceiling and hanging from the pulleys that held up the drying racks. The Tuatara observed the strange black and white creature and Lady Kahn's surprisingly gentle actions towards him, feeding him and then giving him a bowl of apples to peel for a pie, for no one came into her kitchen who did not work for their food. They were surprised that the Drw-ad hadn't slaughtered everyone and blown a hole in the wall with their blood, as they expected him to do.

Intrigued, the young Tuatara curled back down the ropes like a circus acrobat and silently dropped behind Bryant. The Drw-ad was immediately aware of their presence and turned to stare coldly at them. Subtle Sands Shifting leaned back, truly surprised to see vicious red scrapes and bruises marring the white skin of the creature who

---

[23] Ambassador.

was meant to be their most powerful enemy.

"What happened to you?" They remember asking. For a moment, they could see pain, loss and a flare of anger welling up in the slender Drw-ad's dark eyes. However, it was quickly replaced by a dangerous glitter and he replied in a calm voice.

"I did not duck quickly enough."

Subtle Sands Shifting blinked their iridescent, scaled eyelids. "And you did not carve out your enemy's heart?"

The Drw-ad regarded them for a moment, running his gaze up and down the lithe individual in front of him. "You would have done this to an opponent?"

The Tuatara knew the Drw lad would have heard stories of their people's prowess in battle. They were fierce warriors, with vibrant blood more powerful than most, but no Drw-ad had seen one in years.

"Pfft!" Subtle Sands Shifting had tossed their head, battle scales rattling. "No. Shitty little Gentry brats not worth the hassle. I would have kicked them in the nuts – pop pop! Nice and juicy." The Tuatara grinned, displaying two rows of razor-sharp teeth. Even the normally stoic young Drw-ad had winced at the image.

"Perhaps I will try that next time they hunt me," he replied. "Apple?" He held up a Green Lush and the Tuatara cheerfully took it, their taloned hand curling around the fruit. At that stage, anyone who fed them had a friend for life. The next time the Black Drw-ad was hunted, the Gentry boys ran straight into the Tuatara and learned what happens when a lizard stops smiling.

High above the city, Subtle Sands Shifting pauses, perched for a moment on the Terrace wall and suddenly craving an apple. They have no desire to see one of their oldest friends hurt but they know that his time of trial will come, with or without their influence. And the Tuatara people know as well as any other in Hjaltland, that when the Drw-ad rise, others perish in the flames. Better to pay attention and step lively – this time the Tuatara will not fall. This time they will change the balance of power for good.

Playlist: Matrix & Futurebound - Control.

END OF BOOK ONE.

CPSIA information can be obtained
at www.ICGtesting.com
Printed in the USA
BVHW031157060622
639006BV00014B/637